www.Tameside.gov.uk

AS

KT-557-592

WITHDRAWN FROM
TAMESIDE LIBRARIES

The Enemy Within

TAMESIDE LIBRARIES

3801601930938 6

By Edward Marston

THE HOME FRONT DETECTIVE SERIES

A Bespoke Murder • Instrument of Slaughter • Five Dead Canaries
Deeds of Darkness • Dance of Death • The Enemy Within • Under Attack

THE RAILWAY DETECTIVE SERIES

The Railway Detective • The Excursion Train • The Railway Viaduct
The Iron Horse • Murder on the Brighton Express
The Silver Locomotive Mystery • Railway to the Grave • Blood on the Line
The Stationmaster's Farewell • Peril on the Royal Train
A Ticket to Oblivion • Timetable of Death
Signal for Vengeance • The Circus Train Conspiracy

Inspector Colbeck's Casebook

A Christmas Railway Mystery

THE RESTORATION SERIES

The King's Evil • The Amorous Nightingale • The Repentant Rake
The Frost Fair • The Parliament House • The Painted Lady

THE BRACEWELL MYSTERIES

The Queen's Head • The Merry Devils • The Trip to Jerusalem
The Nine Giants • The Mad Courtesan • The Silent Woman
The Roaring Boy • The Laughing Hangman
The Fair Maid of Bohemia • The Wanton Angel
The Devil's Apprentice • The Bawdy Basket
The Vagabond Clown • The Counterfeit Crank
The Malevolent Comedy • The Princess of Denmark

THE BOW STREET RIVALS SERIES

Shadow of the Hangman • Steps to the Gallows • Date with the Executioner

THE CAPTAIN RAWSON SERIES

Soldier of Fortune • Drums of War • Fire and Sword
Under Siege • A Very Murdering Battle

a&b

The Enemy Within

Edward Marston

Allison & Busby Limited
12 Fitzroy Mews
London W1T 6DW
allisonandbusby.com

First published in Great Britain by Allison & Busby in 2016.
This paperback edition published by Allison & Busby in 2017.

Copyright © 2016 by EDWARD MARSTON

The moral right of the author is hereby asserted in accordance with
the Copyright, Designs and Patents Act 1988.

All characters and events in this publication,
other than those clearly in the public domain,
are fictitious and any resemblance to actual persons,
living or dead, is purely coincidental.

All rights reserved. No part of this publication may be reproduced,
stored in a retrieval system, or transmitted, in any form or by
any means without the prior written permission of the publisher,
nor be otherwise circulated in any form of binding or cover
other than that in which it is published and without a similar
condition being imposed on the subsequent buyer.

A CIP catalogue record for this book is available from
the British Library.

10 9 8 7 6 5 4 3 2 1

ISBN 978-0-7490-2058-3

Typeset in 11/16 pt Adobe Garamond Pro by
Allison & Busby Ltd.

The paper used for this Allison & Busby publication
has been produced from trees that have been legally sourced
from well-managed and credibly certified forests.

Printed and bound by
CPI Group (UK) Ltd, Croydon, CR0 4YY

CHAPTER ONE

Kenneth Pearce knew the routine so well that he could perform his duties with his eyes shut – not that he'd dare to do that in a prison. It could prove fatal. After ten years as a warder at Pentonville, he was an established member of staff. Yet now he was actually thinking of leaving what he'd always considered a job for life. The pressure of events worried him. Since Germany had declared unrestricted submarine warfare, the noose had been tightened around Britain. Food shortages were causing serious problems and rationing was strict. Every time Pearce opened a newspaper, it seemed to contain bad news about the war.

He was a wiry man of medium height with a wispy moustache lending a touch of interest to an otherwise blank face. Pearce was preoccupied that evening. Wally Hubbard guessed what was on his mind.

'You decided yet, sir?' he asked, politely.

'Yes and no.'

'What does that mean?'

'*I* want to join up but my wife is begging me to stay where I'm safe.'

'If you didn't work here,' said Hubbard, 'you'd *have* to enlist.'

'That's what I keep telling her.'

'So what are you going to do?'

'I don't know,' said Pearce, removing his peaked cap to scratch his head. 'If I join the army, my wife will never forgive me; if I don't do my bit in France, I'll never forgive myself.' He replaced his hat. 'What would *you* do?'

Hubbard laughed grimly. 'I only wish I had the choice.'

Choices of any kind had disappeared from the life of Wally Hubbard. After being convicted of arson, he'd been given a long sentence and every decision was now made for him by someone else. He'd been deprived of his liberty, his personal possessions, his privacy and even his name. He was simply a number now. Many prisoners were seething with resentment when they first came to Pentonville and they caused endless trouble as a result. Hubbard was unusual in being ready to accept his punishment with a philosophical shrug. It had endeared him to Pearce. Most of the warders did nothing but bark orders at the prisoner but Pearce had conversations with him. While something close to a friendship had begun to develop, however, there was a dividing line between them that would never be crossed.

'Wasn't the missus upset about her brother-in-law?' asked Hubbard.

'Yes, of course, she was very upset. When we first heard the news of Leslie's death, she was heartbroken. But she doesn't want me to take his place. Because my brother was killed in the trenches, she thinks the same thing will happen to me.'

'Not before you've shot a few Krauts, I hope.'

'I've got this urge to join the fight. I feel so helpless, stuck here.'

'Me, too,' murmured the other.

'I've talked to the chaplain about it,' confided Pearce, 'and he told me to follow my conscience. But with a wife like mine, that's not so easy.'

'You got my sympathy, sir.'

They were on the landing outside Hubbard's cell. Pearce had just unlocked it to let the prisoner out before locking it again with one of the many keys that dangled from a large ring attached by a chain to his belt. He led the way along the landing, then descended the staircase. Hubbard followed him dutifully, their boots echoing on the steel steps. The warder then took his prisoner through a succession of doors, each one of which had to be unlocked and relocked. Since he was now a familiar figure in Pentonville, Hubbard collected nods of recognition from other warders. One of them even called him by his name. It was a moment to savour.

'I still think I should go,' said Pearce, solemnly. 'It's what Leslie would expect of me.'

'What would your brother have done in your position, sir?'

'Oh, there's no doubt about that. If *I'd* been killed in action, Leslie would join up in a flash. He wouldn't think twice about it. Mind you, there's one big difference.'

'Is there?'

'My brother wasn't married.'

'Ah, I see.'

'There was nobody to stop him enlisting. In my case, there is.'

'What about all those posters telling women to send their husbands off to war? Didn't your wife see those?'

Pearce sighed. 'My wife only sees what she wants to see.'

As they came out of the main door to the wing, he turned to lock it behind him and was momentarily off guard. It was a big mistake. Wally Hubbard suddenly came to life, producing a cosh from up his sleeve, knocking off the warder's hat and felling him with a vicious blow. After hitting him again for good measure, he dragged him off into the shadows. Their friendship was over.

CHAPTER TWO

Claude Chatfield would never be popular but even his enemies – and he had several of them – had to admire his commitment. Nobody at Scotland Yard worked harder or for longer hours than the superintendent. His stamina was almost legendary. Conscientious to a fault, he expected the same dedication from his officers. Any sign of laziness, fatigue or lack of concentration was pounced upon. He was delighted to be given an excuse to reprimand Harvey Marmion when the latter eventually came into his office.

'I sent for you fifteen minutes ago,' he complained.

'I was busy, Superintendent.'

'What were you doing – tidying your desk or counting your paperclips?'

'Neither, sir.'

'Then why didn't you respond instantly?'

'Your message came at an awkward moment,' explained Marmion. 'I didn't mean to keep you waiting.'

'It's not the first time, Inspector.'

'I'm sorry that I was detained, sir.'

'I don't want an apology. I just need you to obey orders for once.'

'The commissioner was with me.'

Chatfield had to bite back the tirade he was about to launch. If Sir Edward Henry was in the inspector's office, then Marmion had a legitimate reason for the delay. The Commissioner of the Metropolitan Police was a person who took precedence over everyone in the building. Nettled that he could not rebuke the inspector for his tardy arrival, Chatfield was also quivering with envy. Sir Edward, he believed, was far too indulgent towards Marmion. He had too high an opinion of the inspector and was always ready to defend him against criticism.

'What did the commissioner want?' asked Chatfield.

'It's a private matter, sir.'

'Does it concern a case in which you've been involved?'

'I'm not at liberty to say,' replied Marmion, enjoying the other man's patent exasperation. 'Do you have a new investigation for me, Superintendent?'

'Yes, I've been waiting for you to deign to answer my summons.'

'What does it concern?'

'It concerns a man named Walter Hubbard.'

'But he's cooling his heels in Pentonville. I put him there.'

'You may need to do the same thing again, Inspector.'

'Why?'

'He escaped yesterday evening.'

Marmion smiled. 'Wally Hubbard always was a slippery customer.'

'It's not a cause for amusement,' snapped Chatfield. 'Apart from anything else, a prison officer was badly injured.'

'I'm sorry to hear that, sir.'

'We've mounted a manhunt. I want you in charge of it.'

'Thank you,' said Marmion. 'What are the details?'

'All I know is that he overpowered the officer, used his keys to open a storeroom and hid the man there. Then, would you believe, he had the gall to change into the officer's uniform.'

'It sounds like just the kind of thing Hubbard would do.'

The superintendent glowered. 'There's an unwelcome note of approval in your voice, Inspector.'

'It was a daring escape, sir, and involved high risks. I'm just acknowledging the courage it must have taken.'

'That wasn't courage,' said Chatfield, rancorously. 'It was low cunning allied to brutality. The injured man was unconscious for hours.'

Marmion was genuinely upset by the news. He had great respect for prison staff, men who did an important job but got scant praise for doing so. Danger was an accepted part of their lot. Behind the high walls of Pentonville, assaults of warders were always a possibility.

The inspector was a chunky man in his forties who was the despair of tailors. Even in his best suit, he contrived to look dishevelled. Chatfield, by contrast, was impeccably dressed. He was a tall, stringy man with thinning hair who – when they were alone together – didn't bother to hide his dislike of Marmion.

'Well,' he said, rising to his feet, 'don't just stand there, man.'

'I'll round up Sergeant Keedy and get over there right away.'

'Don't tell the governor that you admire what Hubbard did or you may find it difficult to get out of Pentonville again. He hates an escape. It reflects badly on his regimen and it means he'll be pilloried in the newspapers.'

'That's never a pleasant experience,' said Marmion, ruefully. 'I've still got bruises from some of the treatment we've received from the gentlemen of the press.'

'Well, don't give them any more target practice. Find Hubbard and find him fast. After all, it's very much in your own interests.'

'Is it, sir?'

'You have a short memory,' said Chatfield, clicking his tongue. 'When your evidence helped to convict Hubbard, he had to be restrained in the dock. As they dragged him out, he swore that he'd kill you one day.'

Marmion was unperturbed. 'I'm used to empty threats, Superintendent.'

'In this case, the threat may not be quite so empty. An escaped convict is usually a desperate character. Take great care, Inspector,' he added, wagging a finger. 'Find this man quickly – before he finds you.'

Ellen Marmion had tried almost everything to bring her son out of his melancholy but all to no avail. Paul remained in a world of his own, silent, troubled and disengaged. He was a well-built young man with a surface resemblance to his father. Before the war, he'd been a lively, confident, happy-go-lucky lad but that person had now disappeared completely. Having enlisted in the army with the other members of his football team, Paul had had to watch as they'd been killed in action one by one. His best friend, Colin Fryatt, had been the last to die on the battlefield and Paul, close to him at the time, had been injured and blinded. Suffering from shell shock, he'd been discharged. While there had been a slow improvement in his eyesight, there'd been none at all in his attitude. None of the members of his family could reach him. Over a late breakfast, his mother made one more doomed attempt to do so.

'What are you going to do today?' she asked.

'I don't know.'

'Why don't you come to the shops with me?'

'No, thanks.'

'The fresh air will do you good, Paul.'

'I'd rather stay here.'

'It's not healthy, spending all your time in your room.'

'What else is there to do?' he said, gruffly.

'Well, you could get out and meet people of your own age.'

'I don't see the point.'

He'd said the same thing to his mother for months and it was lowering. Ellen took a deep breath. She was a plump woman of middle years with a homely face now distorted by age and lined with apprehension. When her son had first come home, he'd shuttled between extremes of gloom and exhilaration, frightened that he'd be blind for the rest of his life then seized by the hope that he'd make a miraculous recovery and be able to rejoin his regiment once more. That phase seemed to have ended. Paul now moved slowly around with an air of desolation.

'I'll need to change the sheets on your bed,' she warned.

'I can do that, Mummy.'

'It's no trouble.'

'Leave it to me.'

It was the only pleasing reminder of his army career. Paul had been taught to look after himself. He kept his room tidy and was always well groomed. Even when he could hardly see, he'd shaved himself carefully every day. He wore his hair short and polished his shoes relentlessly. There were moments when he looked like the proud young soldier on leave for the first time but they were only fleeting. There was no sense of pride about him now.

'Mrs Redwood is coming to tea this afternoon,' she said.

'Oh.'

'I suggested that she might bring her daughter along. You remember Sally Redwood, don't you? You were at school with her.'

'Was I?' he asked, uncertainly.

'She remembers you very well.'

'I can't place her.'

'You will when you see her, I'm sure.'

'Why?'

'It's because she's so pretty and full of life.'

'What I meant was why should I see her at all?'

'You have to be sociable, Paul.'

'Mrs Redwood is coming to see you, not me.'

'But she's bringing her daughter.'

14

'So what? *I* didn't invite her.'

'You'd have lots to talk about with Sally.'

'No, I won't.'

'Won't you at least *try* to be nice to her?'

He shook his head. 'I remember her now,' he said. 'She was a skinny girl with freckles. I didn't like her at school and I'm not going to start liking her now.' Getting up from the table, he headed for the door. 'I'll change the sheets.'

Ellen bit her lip. Yet another stratagem had failed.

On the drive to Pentonville, they sat side by side in the rear of the car. Harvey Marmion explained to Joe Keedy why they were going to the prison. The sergeant was a tall, lean man in his early thirties with the kind of features that earned him a lot of female attention. Highly conscious of his appearance, he made Marmion look shabby. In a relaxed setting, they dispensed with formalities. Keedy was engaged to Marmion's daughter, Alice, so the men were on first-name terms.

'We had quite a game catching Wally Hubbard,' recalled Keedy.

'We got him in the end, Joe.'

'My memory is that he put up a real fight.'

'Wouldn't you have done the same thing in his position?'

'Probably – he was facing a long sentence.'

'Arson is a heinous crime,' said Marmion, 'and it was also a case of attempted murder. It was just bad luck for Wally that the house he set fire to was empty.'

'Bad luck for him, maybe, but good luck for the man who lived there.'

'He'd have been burnt alive.'

'Hubbard is a nasty piece of work.'

'In some ways, yes, but I've got a sneaking regard for him.'

Keedy was surprised. 'Regard for that cruel bastard?' he said. 'You can't be serious, Harv.'

'You're forgetting *why* he torched that house.'

'He wanted someone to go up in flames.'

'But it wasn't any old someone, Joe. It was the man who seduced his daughter then dumped her when she became pregnant. It was a sad business. The child was stillborn and the mother died of complications that set in during her time in hospital.' His voice darkened. 'In those circumstances, I think that a lot of fathers might want to get vengeance on their daughter's behalf.'

'I get the message,' said Keedy, laughing. 'If I don't stand by Alice, you'll come after me with a box of matches.'

'I might be tempted.' As they turned into the Caledonian Road, he saw the prison looming up ahead of them. 'You've never been here before, have you?'

'No, I haven't.'

'It has a rich history. Some notorious villains have ended up in Pentonville. Dr Crippen was executed here and so was Frederick Seddon, the poisoner. Last year, of course, Sir Roger Casement, the Irish republican, was hanged here for treason. He went to Germany in search of assistance for the Easter Rising. I thought he was supposed to be a diplomat.'

'Seeking help from our mortal enemy was not very diplomatic.'

'He found that out the hard way.'

The car drew up outside the prison and the detectives got out. Keedy had his first close sight of Pentonville. The perimeter wall was long, high and daunting. He was struck by the awesome solidity of the place.

'I wouldn't want to be locked up in here,' he said with a shiver.

'You may have to be for a while, Joe.'

'Why is that?'

'I have a special job for you.'

'Oh?'

'While I talk to the governor, I'd like you to interview Wally Hubbard's cellmate.'

'How do you know that he *had* a cellmate?'

'This is not a hotel,' said Marmion with a grin. 'There are no single rooms with a bathroom attached. You have to share. As for the sanitary arrangements, all you get is a chamber pot that you're allowed to empty once a day. It's no wonder that Wally Hubbard decided to get out of here.'

In response to the bell, a small door was opened in one of the main gates and a prison officer glared inhospitably at them. When they identified themselves, the man stood back to admit them. They ducked their heads and entered the gatehouse. Another set of gates, barred this time, was facing them. The officer locked the first door then stepped into his office to make a phone call. He emerged a few moments later.

'You're to wait here,' he said, crisply. 'The governor is sending someone.'

17

The detectives looked through the bars. Built over seventy years earlier, Pentonville followed the standard Victorian design. It had a central hall with five radiating wings. It had originally held over five hundred inmates, each with a separate cell. Numbers had grown substantially since then and two-man cells were the norm. Although they had merely come through the main entrance, Keedy felt a keen sense of oppression. Marmion noted his unease.

'How would you like to be banged up in here for twenty years, Joe?'

'Twenty minutes is long enough for me,' replied Keedy. 'Look at the place, Harv. How on earth did Hubbard manage to escape?'

'That's not the question *I'm* asking,' said Marmion.

'Then what is?'

'Where the hell is he?'

Maisie Rogers was a short, buxom woman in her early forties with blonde hair trailing down to her shoulders and large blue eyes. Having slept until late, she awoke and dragged herself upright to test the temperature. When she realised how cold it was, she grabbed the dressing gown that was lying across the bed and put it on. After a protracted yawn, she got out of bed, stretched herself then reached for the curtains. When she pulled them back, she was startled to see a man crawling towards her on the roof of the shed below. Her first instinct was to scream but she then recognised him. Unlocking the sash window, she heaved it up and put her hands on her hips.

'What the devil are *you* doing here, Wally?' she asked in amazement.

'I'm freezing to death,' he replied, scrambling up to her. 'Get back into bed and warm me up a little. I'll explain everything afterwards.'

CHAPTER THREE

Geoffrey Wilson-Smith, the prison governor, was a big, broad-shouldered man in his fifties with a large paunch cunningly disguised by expensive tailoring. His bald head gleamed and his eyes blazed. Seated in a high-backed chair, he told his visitors what had happened, punctuating his tale by tapping on the desk with his knuckles as if using a secret Morse code. They listened patiently. When the recitation finally reached its conclusion, Marmion was ready with the first question.

'So you're not absolutely sure *how* Hubbard escaped, are you?'

'There are various possibilities, Inspector,' said the governor. 'The most likely one is that he mingled with the other officers when they came off duty and slipped out in the crowd.'

'Wouldn't he be recognised?'

'Not necessarily. He was wearing a uniform. At the end of a long day on duty, all that my officers wish to do is to get back home to a hot meal and to enjoy the luxury of putting their feet up. Also, of course, it was dark. Hubbard deliberately waited until evening.'

'Why was he out of his cell in the first place?'

'He was being moved to another wing.'

'There is another explanation,' suggested Keedy.

The governor turned to him. 'I'd be interested to hear it.'

'You mentioned a delivery van that brought in food supplies.'

'That's right. It comes every day at the same time. The diet here is not exactly enticing but we're duty-bound to feed the inmates.'

Keedy snapped his fingers. 'There's your answer then.'

'What is?'

'Hubbard could have concealed himself in the van and been driven out.'

'Give us some credit, Sergeant,' said the governor, loftily. 'We're not that stupid. Every vehicle is searched before it's allowed in or out of the prison.'

'I'm sure that they looked *inside* the van, sir, but did they go to the trouble of looking underneath?'

The other man began to bluster. Marmion jumped in quickly.

'I see what the sergeant is getting at, sir,' he said. 'We had a case last year where a prisoner on remand escaped by clinging to the underside of a lorry that had made a delivery. As soon as it stopped at a junction, he let go and made a run for it.'

Wilson-Smith lifted an eyebrow. 'Was he recaptured?'

'No, sir – he was knocked down by a car, but the point is

that he did actually enjoy a brief moment of freedom. Only a strong and determined man would dare to choose that means of escape. Hubbard, I can assure you, is both.'

'It's a possibility, I grant you,' said the governor, huffily, 'but I incline towards my earlier theory. He used his disguise to walk out of here. Hubbard was clever. When he picked on Pearce, he chose an officer with the same height and build as himself. The uniform fitted perfectly.'

'Right,' said Marmion, jotting something in his notebook, 'there are lots of other questions I have, sir, but I'd like to ask a favour before I do that.'

'What is it?'

'Could the sergeant please have permission to speak to Hubbard's cellmate?'

'Waste of time.'

'Why do you say that, sir?'

'I've already grilled the fellow myself and got nothing from him.'

'What's his name?'

'Barter – Vincent Barter. He's an incorrigible burglar. This is his fifth stay with us in Pentonville.'

'I'd still like to talk to him, sir,' said Keedy. 'What harm could it do?'

'You never know,' added Marmion. 'The sergeant might be able to elicit something from Barter. If he's a regular customer of yours, he'll have known the routine here inside out. That information would have been valuable to Hubbard.'

'Oh, I'm sure he was an accessory to some degree,' said the governor, 'but you'll never get him to admit it. Speak to him, if you must, Sergeant, but you'll come up against a brick wall.'

'Thank you, sir,' said Keedy, exchanging a glance with Marmion.

Picking up the telephone, the governor made a quick call. In less than a minute, an officer arrived to escort Keedy out of the office. Marmion was left alone with the governor.

'You've told us about his exemplary conduct here,' he said, 'and how he won the confidence of this particular officer. Have you considered the notion that he might have had an accomplice?'

The governor bristled with indignation. 'I hope you're not suggesting that one of my officers *helped* him? That's out of the question.'

'I was thinking of someone who could have thrown a rope ladder over the wall at a prearranged time. Hubbard knew the date when he'd be moved to another wing and seized his chance.'

'How could he get word to this phantom accomplice?'

'Quite easily, sir,' said Marmion. 'You allow visitors. Have you checked to see if anyone came here recently for Hubbard?' The governor looked embarrassed. 'Perhaps you'd do so, sir. Our starting point will be the friends and associates of the escaped man. The likelihood is that he'll have gone to ground with one of them.'

Getting up, the governor crossed to a filing cabinet and opened a drawer. He took out a thick ledger and put it on his desk, slapping it with a palm.

'I've got all the details you need in here, Inspector.'

'Thank you, sir.'

'You will find him, won't you?'

'Oh, I'm certain of it,' said Marmion, cheerfully. 'We caught him once before and we can do so again. I'm looking forward to renewing my acquaintance with Mr Hubbard. He led us a merry dance last time. We won't let him do that again.'

Maisie Rogers flopped back on the pillow and let out a full-throated laugh. Hubbard enjoyed watching the way that her breasts wobbled. She was the one person who'd have taken him in without a qualm. In the days when he'd run a pub in Brixton, Maisie had been one of his barmaids. She was loyal, efficient and straightforward. He liked that. Having told her in detail how he'd escaped from Pentonville, he warned her that he wouldn't be able to stay there long.

'Why ever not?' she asked, peevishly.

'I don't want to put you in danger, darling. Before too long, the coppers will be knocking on your door.'

'I'll get rid of them, don't you worry.'

'You're a close friend, Maisie. They'll guess that I might come here.'

'I'm surprised you didn't come earlier. Where did you spend the night?'

'I was on the move,' he told her. 'I couldn't stay in that uniform so I broke into a second-hand shop and helped myself to some old clothes and a big hat. In any case,' he went on, nudging her, 'it would have been rude to disturb a lady in the middle of the night. You might have had company.'

'Not me, Wally – I'm keeping myself pure for you.'

He cackled. 'What about that landlord who was making eyes at you?'

'Oh, he's harmless. Eric flirts with me but he does that with all the barmaids. The truth is that he prefers boys. He's never laid a finger on me.'

'Good – are you pleased to see me?'

'I was thrilled – once I got over the shock of spotting you on that roof.'

He pulled her close. 'This is what I missed most when I was locked up.'

'Why didn't you tell me you were planning to break out?' she asked. 'When I visited you in prison, you didn't even give me a hint.'

'I didn't dare, Maisie. Somebody's always listening.'

'What happens next?'

'This does,' he said, kissing her and fondling a breast.

She responded willingly and they were soon entwined but their pleasure was short-lived. There was a loud knock on the front door. Hubbard sat up.

'That sounds like the coppers.'

'Calm down, Wally. There's no need for alarm.'

'Yes, there is. I've heard that knock before.'

'Leave them to me,' she said, hopping out of bed and putting on her dressing gown. 'I'll send them on their way.'

After stepping into her slippers, she opened the door and went quickly downstairs, running a hand through her hair. As she went along the passageway, the frail voice of her landlady came from the front room.

'Will *you* see who that is, Maisie?'

'Yes, Mrs Donovan. I'm on my way.'

'Thank you.'

Maisie pulled back the bolt and opened the door. Bracing herself for the sight of a policeman on the doorstep, she was instead looking at a small, bird-like woman in her sixties who peered at her through wire-framed spectacles. She was clutching a pot in both hands.

'Good morning, Miss Rogers,' she said, sweetly.

'And the same to you, Mrs Abberley.'

'I've brought some more broth.'

'That's so kind of you,' said Maisie, standing back to let her in. 'Mrs Donovan will be very grateful. Why don't you come in and give it to her?'

'I'll heat it up when she's ready for it.'

'You know where the kitchen is.'

'I should do.'

'Yes, indeed.'

'How is she this morning?'

'You'll be able to ask her.'

After closing the door, Maisie showed the visitor into the front room. Her landlady was virtually bedridden and relied on neighbours like Mrs Abberley for companionship and for occasional treats such as hot broth. Maisie was relieved that it had not been the police and pleased that she would not have to spend any time doing chores for her landlady. Since she'd been taken ill, Mrs Donovan needed more and more help and her lodger had become an unpaid carer as well. Maisie was now off duty. The visitor would take care of everything now. The two old ladies would talk happily for hours. Running back up the stairs, Maisie went to her room to pass on the good news to Hubbard and to climb back into bed with him.

There was, however, a problem. He was no longer there.

* * *

The room was bare and featureless, with a naked light bulb and a barred window high up in the wall. A table and two chairs comprised the only furniture. It was like every other interview room that Keedy had been in when visiting a prison. It was resolutely depressing. He had a lengthy wait before a warder arrived with Vincent Barter in tow. The prisoner was told to sit on one side of the table. Keedy took the chair opposite him. Having locked the door, the warder stood in front of it.

Barter was a short, skinny man in his fifties with close-cropped grey hair and a rat-like face. His ingratiating grin annoyed Keedy. For his part, the other man was weighing up the detective, wondering if he could wrest some small favour from him or gain some slight advantage. When Keedy introduced himself, Barter winked at him slyly.

'Haven't got a spare fag, have you, sir?'

'No, I haven't.'

'Pity – I'm gasping.'

'You know why I'm here,' said Keedy, brusquely. 'Tell me about Hubbard.'

'I already spoke to the governor.'

'Well, I want to hear you now.'

Barter shrugged. 'There's not much to tell.'

'When you share a cell with someone for months, you must get to know them pretty well. Do you agree?'

'Yes,' said Barter, sniggering. 'You soon discover if they fart in their sleep.'

'What was Hubbard like?'

'He kept himself to himself.'

'I don't believe that.'

'I was there, Sergeant. You weren't.'

'We arrested Wally Hubbard,' said Keedy, 'and he never stopped talking. He worked in the pub trade most of his life. There's no such thing as a quiet landlord. So don't try to fob me off by telling me he'd taken a vow of silence.'

'He was an angry man,' conceded Barter. 'Deep down, that is. On the surface, he was all smiles but that didn't fool me.'

'Did he ever talk to you about escape?'

'No, he didn't.'

'Did he ever ask you about the geography of the prison?'

'No, he didn't.'

'Did you ever describe the routine here to him?'

'Never,' said the other, feigning innocence. 'All he ever talked about was missing a woman and missing the smell of beer.'

'Did you see any signs that he might be hoping to get out of here?'

'None at all, Sergeant – and that's the honest truth.'

He smirked at Keedy as if he'd just scored a debating point. Having withstood an interrogation by the governor, Barter was confident to the point of being downright cocky. His manner irritated Keedy.

'When did you start to go blind, Mr Barter?' he asked.

'There's nothing wrong with my sight,' protested the other.

'When did deafness begin to set in?'

'What are you on about?'

'I'm talking about your unfortunate deficiencies,' said Keedy, looking around the room. 'You spend the majority of each day in a cell no bigger than this and yet you neither see nor hear anything that arouses your suspicion. Criminals – even hopeless ones like you – usually have heightened senses. They read people for signs of danger or hints of weakness. You did that to Wally Hubbard.'

'We never talked about escape,' insisted the other.

'Then what did you think he was going to do with that cosh?'

'What cosh?'

'The one used to knock Mr Pearce unconscious. It was discarded in the storeroom where the victim was left. According to the governor, Pearce was trussed up like a Christmas turkey. That means Hubbard had a gag and some rope hidden about him when he left here yesterday evening.' Keedy leant across the table and fixed him with a stare. 'Where did he get them?'

'Search me.'

'You must have seen them.'

'I didn't, I swear it.'

'My guess is that you even told him how to get hold of them.'

'That's slander!' howled Barter.

'I've met dozens of people like you,' said Keedy with disgust. 'They know how to survive in prison. As soon as they're jailed, they quickly get to know everyone and everything in there. They learn who to befriend and who to avoid. They lap up information like sponges because it could come in useful. That's what happened with Wally Hubbard, isn't it? You had information that he needed.'

'I never told him a thing.'

'How much did he pay you, Barter?'

'I don't know what you're talking about,' said the other, defensively.

'You'd have to be blind, deaf and half-witted not to realise

30

what he was up to. And Hubbard obviously trusted you enough to turn to you.'

'I was kept in the dark. I'd take my Bible oath on that.'

'Come on,' said Keedy, 'I've seen the way it works. You can get almost anything in prison if you have money and Hubbard was more than smart enough to bring some in with him. You wouldn't have helped him out of the kindness of your heart, would you? So you had to be bought. He had to pay you to get hold of the things he needed to escape.'

Barter laughed wildly. 'You're making this up.'

'You were his accomplice, weren't you?'

'That's ridiculous.'

'You helped him work out every detail of his plan.'

'It's a rotten lie.'

'It was you who told him to work on Pearce.'

'I wasn't involved in any way.'

'Then why didn't you warn the staff what Hubbard had in mind?' asked Keedy, raising his voice. 'You must have realised that it would be bad for you if he escaped. Everyone would assume that you were in league with him and add a few more years to your sentence. Do you actually *like* being caged in here?'

'No,' snarled Barter, 'I hate every bleeding day. That's why I did my best to talk Wally out of it. I knew I'd suffer as a result.'

Keedy sat back in his chair and smiled. He'd got the confession he was after. Barter could no longer pretend that he had no intimation of what his cellmate had had in mind. The prisoner's head had drooped. It was time to press home the advantage.

'*Why* did he want to get out of here?'

'We *all* want to get out of this hellhole.'

'But what was the reason Wally Hubbard gave?'

'He had a score to settle.'

'Go on.'

'Wally said that he had to get out of here to kill someone.'

'And who was that someone – Inspector Marmion?'

'No,' replied Barter.

'Then who was it?'

'It was a man he hated – Ben Croft.'

CHAPTER FOUR

It had never been Alice Marmion's intention to join the police force. She'd been perfectly happy in her job as a teacher, enjoying the work and being adored by her pupils. War had rearranged her priorities. After a testing spell with the Women's Emergency Corps, she'd followed her father and her fiancé into law enforcement. Unlike them, she had limited powers and was not involved in dealing with serious crime of any kind but she nevertheless felt that she was performing a useful duty. When she was out on patrol that morning, her partner was Iris Goodliffe, a chubby young woman whose only previous job had been in a family pharmacy business. On a chilly day, they kept up a steady, unvarying pace.

'You ought to be promoted, Alice,' said Iris.

'Don't be silly!'

'I'm being serious. You're too intelligent to walk the beat.'

'Everyone has to do that at the start.'

'Yes, but you've served your apprenticeship now. Inspector Gale must see how much brighter you are than the rest of us. Police work is in your blood. Your father is a famous detective.'

'That's the very reason I'll never be considered for promotion,' said Alice, resignedly. 'Gale Force will never forgive me for being the daughter of a detective inspector and engaged to a detective sergeant. She can't cope with it somehow.'

'Don't underestimate her. She has her virtues and she knows a good policewoman when she sees one.'

'I agree – unless she happens to be looking at me.'

Alice gave a brittle laugh. After all this time, she was still having problems with Inspector Gale, a woman who seemed to divide people into friends and enemies. While Alice was kept very firmly in the enemy section, Iris was treated as a friend. It was deliberate and it irked Alice. She was always pleased to be on patrol with Iris because the latter was such pleasant company. Committed to her job, Iris was vigilant and quite fearless when having to confront someone. Though her uniform was still too tight for her, she now looked and sounded like a real policewoman.

'There are some good films on at the moment,' she said, fishing gently.

'I wish I had the time to see one of them.'

'Try to *make* time, Alice.'

'I've got too much to do.'

'All work and no play . . .'

'I'm not *that* dull, am I?'

34

'No, of course not,' said Iris with a laugh. 'You should pamper yourself a little more, that's all. If you want to see a film, I'll always go with you.'

'Thanks, Iris, I'll bear that in mind.'

'It's ages since we went to the cinema.'

Alice remembered the occasion only too well. It had been months ago. They saw and enjoyed a film together before going on to a bar. Having only seen Iris when she was sober, Alice was not prepared for what happened when her friend had had a couple of drinks. Iris had become loud, brash and very embarrassing. In the end, Iris had had to be hustled out of the bar by Alice. It was an experience that was never repeated. Happy to work alongside her, Alice kept her at an arm's length when off duty.

'I'm going to the hairdresser on my day off,' said Iris.

'You deserve a treat.'

'I'm going to change the style completely and have it much more like yours.'

Alice was wary. 'Is that wise?'

'What do you mean?'

'Well, it may not suit you.'

Iris grinned. 'What you mean is that it's perfect for a lovely face like yours but it would be wrong for someone like me with a big head and bulging cheeks.'

'You have a very nice face.'

'It's too fat.'

'Mummy says that mine is starting to look too thin.'

'Then I wish I knew how you managed it,' said Iris, wistfully. 'I'm eating less and getting more exercise but my weight keeps going up.'

'We can't all be the same.'

'I'd just like to be *attractive*.'

'You *are*,' promised Alice. 'Men are not blind. Sooner or later, one of them will notice. In fact, one of them already has. Joe said how good-looking you were.'

Iris rallied. 'Did he?'

'Yes, he did and he meant it.'

Though Alice was glad to put a broad smile back on her colleague's face, the latest news worried her. Iris already wore her hat at the same angle as her and had picked up all of Alice's favourite phrases. Having started using the same cosmetics as her when off duty, she was now planning to have a similar hairstyle. Iris was aping her in every way. There was an even more disturbing development to come.

'How is your brother?' asked Iris.

'Oh, he's . . . very much the same.'

'Does he still spend all his time alone?'

'Yes, he does.'

'Then he needs a girlfriend, someone who could bring a spark into his life. What happened to him at the Somme was terrible. He needs help to get over it.' Iris turned to her. 'I'd love to meet him one day.'

Alice felt quietly horrified.

With the governor as his guide, Marmion followed the route that Wally Hubbard had taken. When they started outside the main door to one of the wings, the inspector noticed the bloodstains on the ground. That was the point where Pearce had been clubbed into unconsciousness. The storeroom to which he'd been carried or dragged was only a short distance away. It would have taken seconds to get there. In the gloom, nobody would have seen a thing. When they inspected the storeroom, Marmion saw some more blood spatters. Evidently, the warder had been hit very hard.

'I'd like to question him, if I may, sir,' said Marmion.

'He's still a bit groggy.'

'Has he been able to tell you anything?'

'Not really,' said the governor. 'He keeps mumbling apologies.'

'The poor man must feel very guilty at what happened.'

'Pearce must take some blame, Inspector. It was a bad mistake and a great pity. Until now, he had a spotless record.'

'Is he a married man?'

'Yes, his wife has been informed that we had a . . . spot of bother. We're not letting her see her husband until he's in slightly better shape.' He extended a hand. 'This way, Inspector . . .'

It was a fair walk to the hospital area but it gave Marmion the chance to see parts of Pentonville he'd never visited before. In the wake of the escape, security had been tightened. More officers were on duty and all prisoners had been kept locked in their cells. When they entered the room where the wounded man was being tended, they saw that he had dozed off. Pearce was in a sorry state. His head was encircled with thick bandaging and he'd acquired ugly bruises on his face as he'd struck the ground. One lip was badly swollen. The governor offered to rouse him but Marmion raised a hand, indicating that he was ready to wait until the warder woke up in his own time. He sat down beside the bed. Wilson-Smith left him alone with the patient and the nurse.

In the event, Pearce seemed to know that someone wanted to speak to him. His eyelids fluttered, his head moved and he slowly stirred. The nurse moved in to help him sit a little more upright.

'Hello, Mr Pearce,' said Marmion, gently. 'I hate to bother you like this but you may be able to help us. I'm Inspector Marmion from Scotland Yard and my job is to catch the man who escaped.'

It was an effort for Pearce to speak. The words dribbled out slowly.

'Wally Hubbard tricked me.'

'So it seems.'

'If it hadn't been for my brother, it would never have happened.'

'I don't follow.'

'Leslie was killed in combat in France, Inspector.'

'I'm sorry to hear that, Mr Pearce.'

'Have you any idea what it feels like to lose a member of your family?'

'As a matter of fact, I have,' explained Marmion, softly. 'My father was murdered when he was on duty as a policeman. As for the war, my own son was injured at the Battle of the Somme and invalided back home. I know all about grief, believe me,' he said, soulfully, 'but that's not to minimise what *you've* suffered. The news must have come as a shattering blow. Tell me about your brother.'

'Leslie was a policeman before he joined up,' said Pearce, fondly. 'He always wanted a job with plenty of action. As soon as the war broke out, he enlisted like a shot. He thought we'd give the Germans a good hiding and that it would all be over by Christmas.'

'A lot of people made the mistake of thinking that.'

'The war dragged on and on and our lads died in their thousands. But Leslie was somehow untouched. He seemed to have a charmed life and walked away from every battle.' His eyes moistened. 'Then his luck ran out.'

'How did you hear?'

'We had a telegram. That's what started it off, see.'

'I don't understand.'

'I mentioned it to Hubbard. I told him about Leslie.'

'And he pretended to be sympathetic, I daresay.'

'Yes, he did,' said Pearce, bitterly. 'I know he committed a dreadful crime but he's not rotten to the core like some of them. I'd never turn my back on most of the people in here, Inspector. It would be too risky. Wally Hubbard was different. He showed an interest. That's why I told him about my plan. Because of what happened to my brother, I was thinking of joining up. To be honest, I could think of nothing else.'

'So you were distracted when you let him out of his cell.'

'I was – and *this* is the result.'

He touched the bandage and winced in pain. Marmion felt sorry for the man. Nursing a private sorrow, he'd made himself vulnerable and the prisoner had struck.

'I could lose my job over this,' said Pearce, sadly.

'That's very unlikely. The governor knows you have a good record here.'

'I'd have expected it of Barter – but not Hubbard.'

'What is his cellmate like?'

Pearce wrinkled his nose. 'He's the scum of the earth, Inspector,' he said. 'As soon as he's released, he'll go back to his old ways.'

'How did Hubbard get on with him?'

Marmion probed him for details of anyone who seemed to have befriended Hubbard and who might conceivably have aided his escape. Pearce could think of nobody. Hubbard, he explained, had taken care to isolate himself.

'He kept his head down, Inspector.'

'Did anyone bother him?'

'They wouldn't dare. He was convicted of trying to burn someone to death. That gave him status. Respect is important in here. Compare him to Barter, who used to burgle houses in Stepney and snatch bags off old ladies. Nobody respected him.'

Pearce talked at length about life in Pentonville and how Hubbard had appeared to fit into it so easily. But he was not simply reviewing what had happened. He was slowly working his way towards an important decision.

'My wife will just have to put up with it,' he said at length.

'Put up with what?'

'I don't care if I *do* get the sack.'

'There's no chance of that, I'm sure.'

'I've finished with prison life for a while,' said the warder, firmly. 'If they don't boot me out, I'll resign. My place is in the trenches. Leslie can't fight for this country any more but *I* certainly can.'

Marmion thought about his son's situation and he quailed inwardly.

'Whatever you decide,' he said, quietly, 'I wish you the best of luck.'

- * * *

40

The visitors came earlier than expected but Ellen Marmion had everything ready. She'd got the best china tea set out and baked a cake for the occasion. Patricia Redwood belonged to the same sewing group as Ellen, meeting on a regular basis to exchange gossip about the war and to knit gloves and other items they deemed useful in the trenches. She was a fleshy woman with a habit of talking too loudly and laughing inappropriately. Her daughter, by contrast, was thin, flat-chested and desperately shy. Because of her ginger hair, she'd been known as Sally Redhead at school and Paul Marmion had been one of the boys who routinely used the irritating nickname. She was not looking forward to meeting him again and was clearly there under duress.

'Sally was so keen to meet Paul after all this time,' said her mother, clearly unaware of her daughter's real feelings. 'She hasn't seen him for years.'

'He's changed a lot,' warned Ellen.

'Yes, he's a war hero now, isn't he?'

'I don't think that Paul would call himself that.'

'Where is he?'

'He's upstairs in his room at the moment, Pat. I'm hoping that he'll pop down in due course. Let's have a cup of tea while we're waiting, shall we?'

While Ellen made, then later poured, the tea, her friend delivered a non-stop monologue about the effects of wartime privations, letting out an incongruous laugh from time to time. Even when she was offered a slice of cake, she didn't stop. She simply popped it into her mouth and carried on speaking.

'If you ask me,' she said, 'these submarines are out to starve us all to death. You can't fight a war on an empty stomach, that's what I say. Everything will be rationed before long, mark my words. I've seen it coming.'

'And what about you, Sally?' asked Ellen, determined to bring her into the conversation. 'What are you doing with yourself?'

'Sally has a new job,' said her mother, proudly.

'Is that right?'

'Yes,' replied the girl, nervously. 'I start on Monday. It's in Newsome's, the jewellery shop in Queen Street.'

'It shows how much they trust her,' Patricia argued, 'and it's a big step up from Woolworth's. Sally will meet a better class of customer.'

'Are you looking forward to it?' asked Ellen, deliberately aiming the question at the girl. Sally nodded. 'What did they ask you at the interview?'

'They just wanted to know what experience I'd had.'

'They'll train her,' said the mother, pausing long enough to gulp down some tea. 'Sally will learn about watches and jewellery, won't you, dear?'

'Yes, Mummy.'

'That was lovely cake, Ellen.'

'Thank you,' said Ellen, 'would you like another slice?'

'I think I can force another one down.'

Patricia Redwood rocked with laughter and her daughter gave an obliging titter. Ellen was already regretting the invitation she'd given them. Trying to reunite Paul and his old school friend had not been a good idea. He was hiding upstairs and Sally was shaking with trepidation at the prospect of meeting him again.

'How is his eyesight now?' asked Patricia.

'It's steadily improving,' said Ellen.

'Is he able to get around on his own?'

'Oh, yes. Paul is very independent.'

'Sally could always take him for a walk.'

The suggestion made Ellen squirm in her seat. It sounded as if Paul was a dog that needed to be taken out on a lead. She was grateful that he was not there to hear the suggestion. When she least expected it, however, she heard his bedroom door open and footsteps descending the stairs. Paul stuck his head into the living room.

'I'm going out,' he said.

'But we have visitors,' Ellen pointed out.

'Yes, Sally and I came especially in the hope of seeing you,' said Patricia with a girlish giggle. 'You're much bigger than I remember. What do you think, Sally?'

'He looks much the same to me,' the girl piped up. 'Hello, Paul.'

'Hello, Sally Redhead,' he replied with a derisive sneer.

He disappeared at once, leaving the visitors shocked and his mother mortified.

'You'll have to forgive my son,' she said, awkwardly. 'He has moods . . .'

After some hours spent in Pentonville, the detectives had adjourned to a nearby cafe so that they could have a lunchtime snack and compare notes. Apart from his lawyer, only two people had visited Wally Hubbard in prison. The first had been an old friend of his, Felix Browne, who had owned a few pubs with Hubbard. They'd had great difficulty tracking him down because he always seemed to be one step ahead of them. It was late afternoon when they eventually cornered him in a small, terraced house that he'd just bought. Browne was supervising renovations to the property. He was a lanky individual with a flashy suit and long dark hair slicked down with brilliantine. At a glance, he knew that they were detectives. Marmion performed the introductions.

'Wally told me about you two,' he said.

Keedy smiled. 'It's always good to be mentioned in dispatches.'

'You wouldn't have said that if you'd heard what he called the pair of you.' Browne exposed a row of tobacco-stained teeth. 'How did you find me, anyway?'

'Your wife said you'd be driving around your properties.'

'You seem to have quite a lot of them,' said Marmion.

'That's what I do,' explained Browne. 'I buy, sell and rent out property. Not looking for a place, are you, gents? I got this wonderful three-bedroomed house to rent in Camden Town. Used to belong to a friend of mine, Wally Hubbard, but he won't be needing it for a while.'

'I see that you don't read the newspapers, Mr Browne.'

'Why – have I missed something?'

'Hubbard escaped from Pentonville yesterday evening.'

Browne chuckled. 'The wily old devil!' he exclaimed. 'How ever did he manage that?'

'We thought he might have told you,' said Keedy, levelly. 'When someone breaks out, they usually make for a trusted friend.'

'Not in this case, Sergeant. Last time I saw Wally was when I visited him in prison weeks and weeks ago. He told me to go ahead and put his house on the market, then he gave me a list of things he wanted kept in store for him. Nothing illegal in that, is there?' he asked, spreading his arms. 'I'm not aiding and abetting a criminal, am I? I'm just doing a favour for a friend.'

They both had the feeling that Browne knew about the escape but they didn't press him on the subject. Instead they asked him where the fugitive was likely to go. After some persuasion, Browne gave them a few names and addresses. The first person mentioned was already in Marmion's notebook.

'Yes, we know Maisie Rogers,' he said.

Browne grinned. 'Once seen, never forgotten.'

'He was in the Dun Cow with her when we arrested him.'

'She still pulls pints there, Inspector. Maisie is a game girl. She and Wally have known each other for donkey's years. But she's like me. The law is the law. We obey it. We'd never harbour an escaped convict – even if he was a friend.'

'But you might tell him where he *could* lie low.'

'I might,' said the other, chirpily, 'but I didn't.'

'Well, if he does turn up, be sure to get in touch with us.'

Browne put a hand to his heart. 'You got my solemn promise, gents.'

'There are severe penalties for aiding a prisoner on the run,' cautioned Marmion. 'I don't think you'd fare well in Pentonville somehow, sir.'

'You're right there. The place stinks. When I paid my visit, I couldn't wait to get out again. I like my home comforts.

But don't be too hard on Wally,' he added, airily. 'He's a good man at heart.'

'Good men don't put a prison warder in hospital.'

'Is that what he did?'

'I visited the fellow,' said Marmion. 'Hubbard cracked his skull open.'

'I'm sure that he regretted doing that.'

'Try telling that to the warder in question.'

'Wally's not a violent man.'

'He was violent enough when we arrested him,' said Keedy. 'We had a real struggle to get the handcuffs on him.'

'Look,' said Browne, seriously, 'I don't condone what he did, whether it was setting fire to a house or bashing someone over the head. That's wrong in my book. What I can tell you is this, and I speak as someone who's known him for ages.'

'Go on,' said Marmion.

'Wally Hubbard is one of the most kind, gentle, law-abiding people I've ever met. Yes, he has a dark side, maybe – we all have. But, as a rule, he's as decent and honest a man as you could wish to meet. You can quote me on that.'

The pounding in his head made it hard for him to sleep. Though Pearce dozed off time and again, he always awoke soon after. No matter how many times he adjusted his position in the bed, he could not get rid of the pain. Having drifted off once more, he dreamt that something heavy was pressing down on him. When he came awake again, he realised that it was no dream. A brown paper parcel had been put on his chest. He recognised the colleague standing beside the bed.

'What's this, Arthur?' he asked.

'Open it up and find out.'

'You do it for me.'

'Right,' said the other, starting to undo the string. 'It was delivered to the main gate by some scrawny kid. He said a man paid him sixpence to hand it over.' Putting the string aside, he opened the brown paper. 'It looks like someone sent your uniform back, Ken. And there's a note inside.'

'What does it say?'

'See for yourself.'

He held the scrap of paper in front of Pearce. The message was in capitals.

I'M SORRY

CHAPTER FIVE

A continuing theme of Superintendent Chatfield's criticism was that Marmion did not keep in touch with him enough in the course of an investigation. After the meeting with Felix Browne, therefore, the inspector made a point of returning to Scotland Yard to deliver an interim report. Chatfield listened intently from start to finish.

'You seem to have asked all the right questions,' he said, grudgingly.

'We did our best, sir.'

'This fellow, Browne, interests me.'

'We'll be keeping a close eye on him.'

'There are a lot of crooks in the property business.'

'Felix Browne doesn't have a criminal record, sir. I checked. On the other hand,' said Marmion, 'I got the distinct impression that he sails close to the wind.'

'How involved are he and Hubbard?'

'They're old friends and business partners.'

'And they're both reasonably successful, by the sound of it.'

'They've had joint ownership of more than one pub.'

'In other words,' said Chatfield, 'neither of them is short of money. Your report mentioned Sergeant Keedy's belief that Hubbard bought certain items in readiness for the escape. Is that right?'

'It's more than likely, sir.'

'But how did he get the money into prison in the first place? Surely, everyone is thoroughly searched before he's put in a cell.'

'There are ways of getting around that, Superintendent.'

'Tell me more.'

'I don't think you really want to know.'

Chatfield sniffed. 'I don't shock easily.'

'Five-pound notes are so flimsy that they can be twisted into a very tight roll. It's then inserted into a bodily orifice and goes unnoticed during the search.' He saw the pained look on the other man's face. 'Do you want me to go on, sir?'

'No,' said Chatfield in disgust. 'I think I can guess the rest.'

'It's not always easy to retrieve. Sometimes they need a spoon to—'

'That's enough, thank you!'

'You did ask, sir.'

'Let's move on to this woman, Maisie Rogers.'

'I intend to interview her as soon as I leave here.'

'What about Sergeant Keedy?'

'He's tackling the problem from the other end, so to

speak,' said Marmion. 'Hubbard escaped for the sole purpose of wreaking his revenge on Ben Croft. He needs to be found before Hubbard gets anywhere near him. We don't have a last known address for Croft, of course, because his house was burnt to the ground, but the sergeant is very resourceful. He'll soon pick up a trail.'

'I hope you're right.'

Marmion rose to his feet. 'I'll be on my way, then.'

'Wait a moment,' said Chatfield, glancing down at the notepad in front of him. 'I have some news for you. Not long before you returned, I had a phone call from the Governor of Pentonville.'

'What did he say?'

'Well, he was complimentary about you and Keedy. You obviously contrived to create a good impression during your visit, but that wasn't the reason for the call.'

'Then what was?'

'A package was delivered to the prison by a small boy who'd been paid by someone to hand it over. You'll never guess what was in it.'

'I think that I would, sir.'

'Well?'

'It was the uniform stolen from Mr Pearce.'

Chatfield was crestfallen. 'How on earth did you know that?'

Remembering what Felix Browne had said about his friend, it had come to Marmion in a flash. He seized a rare opportunity to impress the superintendent.

'I've met Hubbard, sir. It's typical of him.'

* * *

Maisie Rogers had always enjoyed working in a pub. The bar was her natural habitat. She liked the noise, the bustle and the invigorating banter. Since the war had started, however, there was progressively less of each. Opening hours were curtailed, beer was eventually watered and the convivial atmosphere was somewhat diminished. Many customers had vanished altogether into the army, never to reappear or, if they did so, were limping on crutches or bearing hideous wounds. The most striking change was one that Maisie applauded. More women were coming into the pubs without the need of a man to accompany them. War had melted some of the boundaries between the sexes. Because women now did many of the jobs traditionally reserved for men, they'd gained confidence and suddenly had money to spend. Female munition workers or motor mechanics were now a familiar sight to Maisie.

She got to the Dun Cow well ahead of opening time in order to do her chores. One of them was to clear away the empty beer bottles left by customers that morning. They'd been stacked in wooden crates under the bar. Heaving the first one up, Maisie took it into the back room then rested it on a table while she unlocked the door to the yard. Stepping out, she put the crate on top of an existing stack of empties to await collection. Before she could turn around, she felt an arm around her waist and a hand over her mouth.

'Boo!' whispered Hubbard.

Releasing her, he turned her around and tried to give her a kiss.

'You must stop popping up like that, Wally,' she complained, holding him off. 'It's not good for my nerves.'

'I knew I'd find you out here at this time. I wanted to hear what the coppers said when they called.'

'It wasn't them. It was old Mrs Abberley with a pot of broth. She looks after my landlady when I'm not there.' She punched him. 'Why did you disappear?'

'I wasn't taking any chances, Maisie.'

'Where did you go?'

'It's better if you don't know.'

'When will I see you again?'

'When I need some more of this,' he said, kissing her on the lips and provoking a warm response. 'That was well worth the risk.'

'What do you want me to do?'

'Get in touch with Felix. Tell him I need some money.'

'Why can't you do that yourself?'

'Just do as I ask – please.'

'How much do you want?'

'Felix will know.'

'And how do I get it to you?'

'I'll be in touch.' He snatched another kiss. 'Must be off, darling,' he went on, 'Inspector Marmion arrested me here once. He's not going to do it again.'

'You fought like a demon.'

'I'd have got away if it hadn't been for that sergeant. Keedy's got a punch like the kick of a mule. I'm going to keep well clear of that bastard.'

Finding him was going to be a problem. Joe Keedy accepted that. Ben Croft was a man who left few footprints. As a seasoned philanderer, he always kept two or three women in tow so that he had different places to stay in London. If they became pregnant – like Lisa Hubbard – he'd drop them like a stone and go in search of a replacement. He'd fathered a couple of children but, to her chagrin, his wife had remained childless. It was one of the reasons she was estranged from him. There were several others. Veronica Croft was a slender, sharp-featured woman whose good looks were masked by a permanent scowl. When Keedy called on her, she'd just come home from work at a nearby factory and was still wearing dungarees. Her tone was unfriendly. Instead of inviting him in, she'd kept him on the doorstep.

'What do *you* want, Sergeant?'

'I need to locate your husband, Mrs Croft.'

'Well, don't expect me to help you. I haven't a clue where he is and, frankly, I don't give a damn.'

'Mr Croft is in serious danger.'

'Who cares?'

'We do, as it happens,' said Keedy. 'Did you know that Wally Hubbard has escaped from prison?' She looked startled. 'Good – at least I've got your attention now. You can guess who he's looking for.'

'I'm not surprised. Ben treated Hubbard's daughter dreadfully. He can be so callous when he wants to be. It happened to the others as well. The wonder is that nobody went after Ben until now.'

'Mr Hubbard is not intending simply to slap his wrist.'

She snorted. 'He can hack his lying head off for all I care!'

'Isn't that rather harsh, Mrs Croft?'

'You don't know what he did to me.'

Keedy could see the obvious effects of it. Ben Croft had betrayed his wife time and again, turning a once attractive woman into a sour and resentful harridan. Instead of raising the family she'd hoped for, Veronica had been forced out of the comfortable home she'd shared with her husband and was now living with her mother again in a drab terraced house in a dismal backstreet. Keedy remembered how embittered she'd been when he met her in the wake of the fire.

'I still feel the same,' she asserted. 'I was glad when that place was burnt to a cinder. It held so many painful memories for me. My only disappointment was that Ben was not inside when it was set alight.'

'Has Mr Croft been in touch with you recently?'

'He wouldn't dare.'

'Doesn't he provide you with any money?' She laughed scornfully. 'I thought he'd inherited a sizeable amount when his parents died.'

'He did, Sergeant, but I didn't see a penny of it. He used it to lavish on his latest conquest. Ben's legacy was big enough to make him give up his job as an insurance agent. He leads a life of luxury – until someone catches up with him.'

Keedy was momentarily surprised. When she tilted her head and struck a pose, he noticed something that he hadn't seen when he'd met her for the first time. She looked uncannily like Alice. It took his breath away.

'Are you all right?' she asked, peering at him.

'Yes,' he said, recovering quickly, 'my mind wandered for a second. I'm sorry about that. Where was I?'

'You were asking about money. Ben keeps it for himself.'

'What about his former colleagues at the office? Is he still in touch?'

'Ask them.'

'Somebody must know where he is, Mrs Croft. He can't just have vanished into thin air. What about his latest—'

'The word is "victim", Sergeant.'

'Do you happen to know her name?'

'I don't keep a scorecard of my husband's sordid little triumphs,' she said with withering contempt. 'I've had a long day at the factory, Sergeant. I need a good wash and a hot meal. Was there anything else?'

He met her challenging stare. 'You know where to find me, Mrs Croft.'

'Goodbye.'

She turned on her heel, went into the house and shut the door firmly behind her. Keedy was saddened. Her future was bleak. She must once have loved Croft enough to marry him, he reasoned, and had been eager to bear his children. What poison had entered the marriage and how corrosive had it been? He thought of Alice and vowed that he'd never treat her as heartlessly as Veronica Croft had been treated. It went beyond cruelty. The fleeting resemblance between the two women had unnerved him. It had also reminded him how long it had been since he'd seen Alice. He missed her badly.

It was weeks since Alice Marmion had visited her mother so, the moment her shift finished and she'd fielded the usual unflattering comments from Inspector Gale, she bade Iris Goodliffe farewell and hastened to the appropriate bus stop. Thirty minutes later, she was ringing the doorbell at her home. Opening the door almost immediately, Ellen was so delighted to see her daughter that she flung herself into Alice's arms and burst into tears.

'Whatever's the matter, Mummy?'

'Oh, it's such a relief to see you!'

'Why – what's happened?'

'Come in and I'll tell you,' said Ellen, producing a handkerchief to dab at her eyes. 'What a terrible welcome to give you! Please forgive me.'

'There's nothing to forgive, Mummy.'

They went into the living room and sat side by side on the sofa. Ellen told her about the visit from Patricia Redwood and her daughter and how badly Paul had behaved towards them. Alice couldn't believe that her brother could be so rude to a girl he once knew at school. It bordered on malice.

'He'll have to apologise,' she said, determinedly.

'I wouldn't dare to ask him, Alice.'

'Then I'll speak to him.'

'It would have to be your father,' said Ellen. 'Paul does actually listen to him. I don't believe that he hears half of what I say to him. It's very hurtful. The trouble is that your father is so rarely here. Paul is always in bed by the time he gets back.'

'Daddy is not late *every* night, is he?'

'He is when it's a murder investigation. After the last one was finally over, I'd hoped I'd see a little more of him but something else has come up.'

'Another murder?'

'No,' said her mother, 'it's that prisoner who escaped from Pentonville. Since your father caught him the first time, he's been asked to do it again. He rang me from Scotland Yard earlier on. He's not supposed to use the telephone for personal use but he wanted to warn me that he'd be late back.'

'Oh, dear! That means Joe is going to be working all hours as well.'

'It's that man who set a house on fire.'

'I remember the case, Mummy. Joe told me all about it. He also showed me the bruises he picked up during the arrest.'

'It was my turn to pick up a few bruises today,' said Ellen, wearily. 'Just because they're not the kind that show, it doesn't mean they don't hurt.'

'You can't let it go on like this. After what happened today, you'll be afraid to invite anyone here in case Paul insults *them*. How did Mrs Redwood react?'

'She was wounded – and so was Sally. They left almost at once.'

'It must have been awful for you!'

'It was far worse for Pat and her daughter. They weren't expecting it.'

'Is Paul here now?'

'No, he's still out somewhere.'

Alice gritted her teeth. 'Then I'll wait until he gets back.'

'I don't want the pair of you fighting.'

'Someone has to put him in his place, Mummy. It's long overdue.'

'We have to remember what he's been through.'

'There you go again,' said Alice, 'making excuses for him.

You can't excuse bad behaviour like that. Paul is not a child. He should know better. I'll make sure that he understands that. We offer him the love and support he needs and all he does is throw it back in our faces.'

'It's not that bad . . .'

'We've put up with more than enough. Since you're here with him most of the time, you get the worst of it. It's got to stop, Mummy,' said Alice, hotly, 'and if that means hauling Paul over the coals, that's what I'm going to do.' She looked towards the window. 'Where exactly is he?'

Ellen shrugged. 'I don't know. He never tells me.'

Hands in his pockets, Paul Marmion ignored the chill wind and stared at the building conjured out of the gathering gloom. He hadn't thought about his junior school since he'd come back to England. It belonged to a past that had been more or less obliterated by more vivid memories of action on the battlefield. The visit of Sally Redwood – unwelcome as it had been – somehow revived his interest. The school was virtually unchanged, a Victorian structure of brick and stone with a slate roof on which he'd once climbed to prove how brave he was. Generations of young children had passed through the school. As he got closer, he could almost hear children laughing in the playground as they chased each other in circles or had mock fights. The school bell rang and the pandemonium slowly subsided until it became an uneasy silence. It was soon shattered. From somewhere in the middle of the playground came the anguished cry of a girl with ginger hair. A boy was pulling her pigtails as hard as he could. Having enjoyed hurting Sally Redwood at the time, he did so in his mind all over again. Paul put back his head and laughed.

As the man who'd founded the company, Hallam Beavis occupied the largest of the offices in the suite. Now in his fifties, he was a short, stout, middle-aged man with a firm handshake and a professional smile. The smile disappeared the moment that Keedy explained why he was there.

'I'm beginning to wish that I'd never known Ben Croft,' he confessed.

'Was he any good at his job?'

'He was extremely good, Sergeant. He was a born salesman – plausible, persuasive, effortlessly charming and, in the best sense of the word, ruthless.'

'Unfortunately, those same qualities could be brought into play when he was selling himself instead of an insurance policy. Lisa Hubbard discovered that. According to her father, he mesmerised her by sheer force of personality.'

'His private life was nothing to do with me.'

'Even when it had an adverse impact on your firm?' asked Keedy. 'I can't believe that, sir. How did you feel when Croft's house was burnt down and he was described in the newspapers as a former employee of Beavis Insurance Ltd?'

Beavis frowned. 'We could have done without the publicity.'

'Have you any idea where he is?'

'No, I haven't. Ben and I rather lost touch when he resigned.'

'Given the time he worked here, I'd have thought a bond must have developed between the pair of you and that you continued to see each other socially.'

'Ben had too many social commitments elsewhere,' said Beavis with a meaningful stare. 'I've seen neither hide nor hair of him.'

'What about your colleagues?'

'I can't speak for them, Sergeant.'

'In that case, I'd be grateful if you could give me their names and addresses.'

'I'll be happy to do so, though it may be a pointless exercise.'

Keedy smiled. 'Unfortunately, that's an essential ingredient of police work.'

'Why are you so keen to trace Ben?'

'I'm not the only person eager to find him, sir. I daresay that you read about Hubbard's escape. He'll assume that you know where Croft is.'

'Well, if he turns up here, I'll get in touch with the police immediately.'

'Oh, he's unlikely to do anything as rash as that, sir. Hubbard will bide his time until he can catch you on your own. He'll pop up like a jack-in-the-box when you least expect him. Be warned. He's dangerous.'

'He won't hurt me, surely?'

'He'll hurt anyone he believes is holding back information from him. We're talking about a man in the grip of an obsession, Mr Beavis. He'll do *anything* to get his hands on Mr Croft. Nobody is as much aware of that as Croft himself.'

'Then he'll have gone into hiding somewhere.'

'I need to get to him first.'

'Isn't Hubbard deterred by the fact that he'll be hanged if he murders Ben?'

'He never thinks of his own fate, sir – only that of his daughter.'

Beavis was fearful. 'What shall I do if he corners me?'

'Tell him the truth. He'll know if you're being honest or not.'

'I haven't the slightest idea where Ben could be.'

'Do you know anyone who might?'

Beavis became thoughtful. 'There's one person,' he said at length, 'but it's only a guess. I know that he had one dalliance after another but he usually went back to Veronica in the end. You might try his wife, Sergeant.'

'I've already done that, sir. She won't hide him. I'm afraid that the iron has entered her soul. She's washed her hands of Mr Croft.'

'There'll be another woman, then. There always is.'

'Do you have a name you could give me?'

'No, I don't,' said the other, sharply. 'I didn't want to know about Ben's romantic escapades.'

'I'm not sure that there was much romance involved.'

'There was for the women. He beguiled them into thinking he'd marry them.'

'That's a fair point,' conceded Keedy.

'What happened must have shaken him badly. He'd never imagined that somebody would seek revenge on a daughter's behalf.'

'When he picked on Lisa Hubbard, he thought he could just take his pleasure then walk away scot-free. But there were consequences – dire consequences.'

'Yes, Ben was never the bravest man. He'd have been absolutely terrified when he saw his house go up in flames.'

'There was a consolation, sir.'

'Was there?'

'Yes,' said Keedy, unable to stop himself. 'In view of his profession, I daresay that the property was insured to the hilt.'

CHAPTER SIX

Ellen Marmion was at once pleased and alarmed, glad that she had her daughter's support but worried at what might happen if Alice challenged her brother about his behaviour. As the evening wore on, she became progressively more uneasy.

'Perhaps it's not such a good idea, after all,' she said.

'You have to make a stand, Mummy.'

'I can't help remembering what happened to him in France.'

'Try remembering what happened when Mrs Redwood came here for tea with her daughter. Paul was disgraceful. You admitted that yourself.'

'It's true. The worst of it is that Pat will tell everyone else in the group. I'm not looking forward to going back there, Alice. They've all been very sympathetic in the past. They'll take a different tone from now on.'

'Not if I can force an apology out of him.'

'He won't apologise for something he doesn't believe is wrong.'

'He must do.'

'His mind is very confused since he came back. You never know what he's going to do or say. It's frightening. He can't seem to tell the difference between what's right and what's wrong any more.'

'Then I'll have to remind him.'

'I can't see him taking orders from you, Alice.'

'I'll reason with him first.'

Ellen was about to point out that her son had resisted all her attempts to reason with him when she heard the sound of a key being inserted in the front door. She tensed immediately. Alice got to her feet at once. Moments later, Paul looked into the room and saw his sister.

'Hello,' he said, dully. 'What are you doing here?'

She drew herself up. 'I'd like a word with you, Paul.'

'Are you going to arrest me or something? Is that why you're in uniform?'

'Don't be ridiculous!'

'Alice came here straight from work,' explained Ellen.

'I don't care two hoots where she's been,' he said with vehemence, 'I hate being talked down to by people in uniform. I had years of that in the army. And it was the same with Uncle Raymond. I used to like him when I was younger, but every time I see him in that Salvation Army uniform, I just want to run away.'

'Uncle Raymond does a wonderful job,' said Alice.

'He does a wonderful job for waifs and strays – but I'm not one of them.'

'Nevertheless, you do need help, Paul.'

'Who says so?'

'We all do.'

'Then you can all mind your own bleeding business!'

'Paul!' exclaimed his mother, getting up. 'I'm not having that language here.'

He had the grace to look shamefaced and even shrugged an apology but he was not going to let his sister dictate to him. Hands on hips, he confronted her.

'Whatever you've got to say, I don't want to hear it.'

'Well, you're going to *have* to,' she said, taking a step forward. 'Mummy told me what happened when Mrs Redwood came here with her daughter.'

'Nothing happened. I said "hello" then went out.'

'You insulted them, Paul.'

'How do you know? You weren't here.'

'They were very upset when they left here.'

'Good.'

'Do you have to be so uncaring?'

'I never liked Sally Redhead.'

'Redwood,' corrected his mother. 'Her name is Sally Redwood.'

'And it doesn't cost anything to be polite,' said Alice. 'Don't you realise how embarrassing this is going to be for Mummy? She'll have to see Mrs Redwood in her sewing group. Everybody there will have heard how you behaved today.'

'So?' he asked, shoulders hunched. 'What am I supposed to do?'

'Well, you might begin with an apology.'

'But I don't feel sorry.'

'You ought to feel thoroughly ashamed, Paul.'

'Since when have *you* had the right to tell me what to do?'

'I'm only trying to bring you to your senses.'

'No, you're not. You're trying to boss me and I'm not going to put up with it. Just because you put on that stupid uniform, it doesn't mean that you can lay down the law in here. I wore a *real* uniform, Alice,' he went on, voice rising in volume and intensity. 'I joined the army and put my life in danger. Do you know what it's like to be under fire day after day? Do you know what's it's like to be told that you must kill or be killed? No, of course you don't. Well, *I* do. That's why I've got no time for people like Sally Redhead and that mother of hers with the big gob. I live in the *real* world. You haven't a clue what that is, Alice, so why don't you just shut up?'

'Paul!' cried Ellen.

'Don't walk away,' ordered Alice.

But he ignored both of them and strode quickly out of the room before hurrying upstairs. Ellen turned a mournful face to her daughter.

'You see what I'm up against?'

'I'm not letting him walk away like that,' said Alice, resolutely.

When she tried to go after him, however, she was held back by her mother.

'Leave him be, Alice,' she said. 'It's the best way.'

* * *

68

Maisie knew that he'd turn up sooner or later. She'd only met Marmion once and it had been in distressing circumstances when she'd witnessed the violent arrest of her close friend. Once he and Keedy had overpowered Wally Hubbard, however, Marmion had been very apologetic towards her and to the landlord for the fracas. Though she was sorry to see Hubbard being hauled off, she was struck by the inspector's pleasant manner and by the way he'd helped to pick up fallen chairs and an overturned table. When she saw him coming into the pub again, Maisie knew that the furniture would be safe this time. She gave him a guarded welcome. There were not many patrons there as yet, so the landlord made no objection when Marmion took her aside for a quiet chat.

'I'm sure you know why I'm here, Miss Rogers,' he began.

'I do, Inspector, and the answer is no.'

'You've neither seen nor heard from Wally Hubbard?'

'Our last meeting was on visiting day in Pentonville.'

'Yes, I saw your name in the prison records. What sort of a state was he in at the time?'

'Nobody is happy to be locked up in there,' she said.

'But was he quietly excited in any way?'

She grinned. 'I'd certainly like to think so. He's always been fond of me.'

He smiled at her forwardness. 'What I'm asking,' he said, 'is whether or not you had any inkling of an impending escape attempt? Did he ask you to do anything for him?'

'Such as?'

'Provide him with certain items.'

'He didn't ask me to dig a tunnel under the prison wall, if

that's what you're getting at. Wally was . . . well, he was just Wally, making the most of a situation. He was no different from how he'd been the other times I'd visited him.'

'Where do you think he'd go when he broke out?'

'That's anybody's guess, Inspector.'

'Mine would be 24 Richards Terrace.'

'That's *my* address,' she protested.

'I know. I've just been there. Your landlady let me in,' he said. 'Actually, it was a neighbour who opened the door but Mrs Donovan was happy for me to be there. She described you as an absolute treasure, Miss Rogers.'

'I like to help the poor dear, that's all.'

'There aren't many lodgers who'd do what you do. Anyway, I did what I went there to do and established that Hubbard was not hiding under your bed.'

She was outraged. 'Did you go into my room?'

'Mrs Donovan allowed me to look around the whole house.'

'You had no right to be there without a search warrant.'

'I was invited in,' said Marmion, calmly, 'and given free rein. I even had a nice cup of tea made for me. When you get that kind of cooperation from the public, you don't need a search warrant.'

'Wally has not been anywhere near the house.'

'Would you swear to that in a court of law?'

'I'll swear it in the Houses of Parliament, if you like,' she said, angrily. 'Why would Wally come anywhere near me when he knows you're aware that we're good friends? He won't take any chances.'

Stroking his chin, he studied her. 'What about Felix Browne?'

'What about him?'

'I take it that you know him.'

'Oh, yes, he was part-owner of a pub I once worked in. Felix is a clever man. He's got the Midas touch.'

'How close were he and Mr Hubbard?'

'They were partners in certain ventures.'

'Do you like Browne?'

'I'm not answering that question.'

'Why not?'

'Because I may work in one of his pubs again. If you have any sense, you have to keep on the right side of Felix.'

'Is he a man who could be trusted?'

'He's always played fair with me, Inspector. If you want to find out about Felix Browne, I suggest you go and meet him.'

'We've already done that, Miss Rogers.'

'I see.'

'And you're right. He's clever. He's a master of the art of talking to you without giving a single thing away.'

'Yes, that's Felix.'

'When did you last see him?'

'I haven't set eyes on him for ages.'

'But you know where he lives, I daresay.'

'I know his address in London,' she admitted. 'It's a posh house in Bishop's Avenue. But he also has a property in Devon where he and his wife spend weekends. Until the war broke out, he had his eye on a villa in the south of France.'

'We had the feeling that he was quite prosperous.'

'People like Felix never starve.'

'Let's go back to Maisie Rogers, shall we?'

'You'll have to be quick,' she warned as a group of six people came through the door of the pub in a convivial mood. 'The place will start to fill up from now on. I don't get paid for talking to Scotland Yard detectives.'

'I only have one last question,' said Marmion, watching her carefully.

'What is it?'

'Suppose – for the sake of argument – that Wally Hubbard *did* make contact with you, what would you do?'

She gave an enigmatic smile. 'The honest answer is that I don't know.'

'Why do I get the feeling that you're being *dishonest* with me?'

'You have a suspicious mind, Inspector. You always think the worst of people. Why not try trusting someone for once?'

Before he could reply, she went swiftly behind the bar and started serving drinks to the newcomers. Marmion was content. Though he'd found no evidence at her flat to support his theory, he was certain that she'd seen Hubbard since his escape. Maisie Rogers merited being put under surveillance. There was, however, a problem. Making the decision was easy enough. Persuading the superintendent to ratify it would be considerably more difficult.

Keedy was increasingly frustrated. He seemed to be going down a series of blind alleys. Working through a list of names given to him by Hallam Beavis, he made no headway whatsoever. Former colleagues of Ben Croft had no idea where he might be. Each and every one of them had entertaining anecdotes to tell about Croft but none of them had the address to which he'd

moved after his house had been burnt down. Keedy did not
have to knock on all of the doors himself. He and Marmion had
a small team of detectives at their disposal and some of them
were deployed in the search for the former insurance agent.
When they reported back to Keedy, they told the same story.
Ben Croft had not been seen by anyone for several weeks. It was
almost as if he'd disappeared off the face of the earth.

As the evening wore on, Keedy became less and less
interested in Croft and more and more desperate to see Alice.
She'd provide a refreshing distraction from the escape of a
prisoner and the disappearance of the man he'd once tried to
kill by setting fire to his house. When he got back to Scotland
Yard, Keedy first shut the door of the office then he courted a
stern reprimand by using the telephone to make a personal call.
After a short wait, he heard Ellen Marmion's voice at the other
end of the line.

'Is that you, Harvey?' she asked.

'No,' said Keedy. 'It's me, Ellen. How are you?'

'I'm fine, thanks.'

'Look, this is a long shot. I just wondered if you had any
idea where Alice was this evening.'

'Yes, Joe. As a matter of fact, she's right here.'

'Wonderful!' he cried. 'At last, I've got something to show
for all my efforts today. Put her on, please.'

Seconds later, Alice spoke to him. She was pleased and
excited.

'Where are you, Joe?'

'I'm breaking a golden rule because I love you,' he said. 'This
telephone is strictly for police business.'

'We're both in the police force, aren't we? This *is* police business.'

'I need to see you, Alice.'

'That would be marvellous – when and where?'

'It will have to be rather late.'

'I don't care if it's the other side of midnight,' she said, laughing. 'Name a time and place and I'll be there. As it happens, I need your advice, Joe.'

'What about?'

'It's Paul – he's getting worse.'

Alone in his bedroom, Paul Marmion sat on a chair with a notepad perched on his knee. Using a pencil, he drew a portrait slowly and carefully, occasionally pausing to examine it critically and, if it didn't meet his standards, using a rubber to erase a particular feature. He was far too engrossed in his work to hear his sister's shouted farewell or to catch the sound of the front door opening and shutting. After shading in the area behind the head, he held the portrait up to the light. Since he had no real skill as an artist, it was a crude piece of work but he flattered himself that he'd caught the essence of his subject. The pigtails, in particular, were a masterpiece.

Crossing the room, he used a drawing pin to fix the paper to his dartboard, then he retreated a few yards. He picked up the darts on the bedside table and sized up his target. With a malevolent smile, he hurled the first dart and was delighted when it landed exactly on the spot he'd aimed at.

Sally Redwood looked woefully back at him, a dart embedded in her forehead.

He took aim again.

* * *

74

'I don't think it's necessary at this stage, Inspector.'

'I urge you to think again, sir.'

'You've heard my decision and that's final.'

'But it's our best way of finding Hubbard,' argued Marmion. 'Miss Rogers is a close friend. Instinct tells me that she's the first person he'd turn to.'

'I need rather more than your instinct to authorise additional expenditure,' said Chatfield, introducing a peremptory note. 'As you well know, we have to work within a budget and our manpower is already stretched.'

'We need to put a pair of eyes on Maisie Rogers, sir.'

'It would cost too much money.'

'So what do we do – just sit back and wait for Hubbard to commit murder? That's what will happen, Superintendent. Ben Croft will end up on a slab and you'll be grilled by the press for letting it happen.'

'Don't tell me my job, Marmion.'

'I wouldn't dream of doing so.'

'You seem to have forgotten that you applied for this post as well,' said Chatfield with a thin smile. 'I was chosen over you because I was deemed to have all the appropriate skills and experience.'

'Nobody disputes that, sir.'

'Then have due respect for my superior rank.'

Marmion smarted under the rebuke. It was true that they'd been rivals for the position of superintendent and Marmion had, in fact, been the slight favourite. As time passed, however, he'd come to realise how much he enjoyed the job he already had, heading a murder investigation and getting out in the field. As a superintendent, he'd have more power and a larger income but most of his time would be spent either behind a desk or at a series of interminable meetings. Thriving on action, Marmion decided that he didn't actually want the promotion and he deliberately bungled the interview. Unaware of the fact, Claude Chatfield believed that he'd been selected because of his superior ability and he loved to hold the whip over Marmion. It meant that there was always an unresolved tension between them.

'Hubbard has two problems,' said Chatfield. 'The first one is that he has to stay out of sight. We're not the only ones involved in the manhunt. We've appealed for the help of the public as well. Hubbard's photograph is on the front page of every newspaper. That will force him to be very cautious.'

'Wally Hubbard is a man who's prepared to take chances.'

'My bet is that he'll lie low for a while.'

'I'd never put money on him doing that, sir.'

'His second problem is the bigger one. He has to find Ben Croft. All we have to do is to locate Croft before he does and the game is up.'

'Does that mean you're offering Croft police protection, sir?' asked Marmion with a mischievous glint in his eye. 'He'll need at least two officers guarding him twenty-four hours a day, so you'd have to work out a rota. That could be expensive.'

'You're being very irksome today,' said Chatfield with a sigh. 'We simply take Croft away from London altogether and put him somewhere safe.'

'But nowhere *is* safe,' insisted Marmion. 'That's the point

76

about Hubbard. If he's clever enough to plot an escape from Pentonville, he'll be able to sniff his way to his victim in time. It's rather more than *we've* managed to do so far,' he admitted. 'I spoke to Sergeant Keedy before I came in here and the search for Mr Croft has been fruitless. If we're to get to him first, we need more officers at our disposal.'

'You already have an adequate number.'

'That's a matter of opinion.'

'Correctly deployed,' said Chatfield, airily, 'your detectives should have tracked him down by now.'

'Mr Croft has read about the escape, sir. What would you do in his position?'

'I'd turn to the police, of course.'

'He doesn't trust us,' Marmion reminded him. 'The arson attack did not come entirely out of the blue. Ben Croft had already reported that he'd received a death threat from Hubbard. We took no action to verify that threat.'

'We would have done so in due course.'

'That was too late, sir. Wally Hubbard struck before we could intervene. Croft learnt his lesson. He has to ensure his own safety.'

'We did that when we arrested Hubbard,' said Chatfield, refusing to concede that the police had been in any way at fault. 'We can't be blamed for his escape. That responsibility falls on the staff at Pentonville.'

'The long and the short of it, sir, is that Croft has no faith in us.'

'Then we'll have to give him a reason to do so.'

'The best possible reason is the prompt recapture of Wally

Hubbard. That, in my view, will be more easily achieved if we put Miss Rogers under surveillance.'

Chatfield slapped the desk. 'It's out of the question.'

'I've spoken to the woman, sir. She's the key figure here.'

'You heard my decision.'

'That doesn't mean I have to agree with it, Superintendent.'

'If you wish to make a formal complaint against me,' warned the other, 'I'll take you off the case and hand it over to someone with a clearer understanding of the structure of power within the Metropolitan Police. Is that what you want?'

'I want to catch Hubbard and save Croft's life,' said Marmion, seriously. 'I have a stake in this investigation and I'll not yield control of it to anybody. I'd just like to put on record that we will need additional manpower at some time in the future. This case will not be resolved quickly unless I can have Miss Rogers shadowed wherever she goes.'

'I'm not convinced that she's involved in any way, Inspector.'

'I am, sir.'

'Has it ever occurred to you that you may be wrong for once?'

'I'm often wrong,' confessed Marmion, 'but not in this case. I'd put my pension on the fact that Wally Hubbard is being helped by Maisie Rogers.'

'This should be enough,' said Felix Browne, handing over an envelope with a wad of banknotes inside it. He held up a key. 'And you'd better give him this as well.'

'What is it?'

'It will get him into an empty property of mine in Islington. Wally will know where it is. Nobody will find him there.'

'Thank you, Mr Browne. Is there any message for him?'

'Just wish him good luck.'

'I will,' said Maisie.

She walked briskly off into the night.

CHAPTER SEVEN

The owner of the cafe was just about to close it for the night when they got there. Recognising Keedy, he let them in, pulled down the blinds then served them light refreshments. Left to themselves, they sat either side of a little table covered by a check cloth with tea stains on it. The cafe had few refinements but they were warm and they were together at last. Alice rubbed her knees against Keedy's.

'What's all this about Paul?' he asked.

'Mummy is at her wits' end.'

'Is he really getting worse?'

'You can judge for yourself.'

Measuring her words, Alice gave him a shortened account of her clash with her brother, then described some of the incidents she'd heard about from her mother. Keedy could hear the mingled anger and anxiety in her voice.

'As his sister,' she said, 'I should love Paul, but he makes it very difficult sometimes. Mummy admitted to me that there are moments when she hates him and that must be a horrible feeling for any mother.'

'It's almost as if he has a destructive streak in him.'

'He's so wilful. You just can't reason with Paul.'

'I'd be more likely to give him a clip around the ear,' said Keedy. 'You were in a terrible state when I picked you up. I'm not letting anyone upset you like that, Alice, even if he is your brother.'

'Mummy is the one who suffers the most.'

'I know. Your father's always complaining that he isn't at home enough. And whenever he does get back, he has to listen to the latest litany of woes.'

'Talking to Paul is like walking through a minefield.'

'You'd have expected the army to have done more to sort him out.'

'He's still under the supervision of a doctor for his eyesight.'

'It's not his eyes that are the problem,' he suggested. 'It's his mind. It's been warped by what happened to him. Paul is so wrapped up with himself that he can't be bothered to be civil to anyone – even the members of his own family.'

'I don't know how much longer it can go on like this.'

They paused to sip their tea and nibble at a biscuit. Alice made an effort to cheer up. She reached across the table and squeezed his arm.

'It's wonderful to see you, Joe,' she said. 'I'm sorry to dump our problems on you like that. Let's forget about Paul, shall we?

Mummy told me that you're trying to recapture that escaped prisoner. Have you made any progress?'

'No, Alice. To be honest, we haven't. Hubbard is very elusive.'

'Isn't he the one who gave you that black eye?'

'Yes,' he replied with a chuckle, 'but he got a few cracked ribs in return, so I felt that I came off best. While your father is trying to catch Hubbard, I've got the job of finding the man he's sworn to kill – Ben Croft. So far I've got nowhere.'

'Why is that?'

'Heaven knows!'

'Somebody must know where he is.'

'Well, they're not ready to tell me, Alice. You've no idea how many false trails we've followed. It's maddening. We're on his side, after all. We're trying to keep the man alive but Croft has covered his tracks far too well.'

'Why should he want to do that?'

'You tell me.'

'He had no cause to disappear,' said Alice, thinking it through. 'The man who wanted to kill him had been convicted and imprisoned. His intended victim was no longer in danger because Hubbard was serving a very long sentence.'

'He chose to shorten it dramatically.'

'Yes, but Mr Croft didn't know that was going to happen. He can't just have disappeared in the wake of the escape.'

'He didn't, Alice. There have been no sightings of him for weeks. He's not just hiding from Wally Hubbard. He seems to be hiding from *everybody*.'

'I wish that Paul would do that. Oh,' she exclaimed, putting a hand to her lips, 'that's a dreadful thing to say about my own brother and I take it back. I should be trying to help him, not wishing that the problem would just go away of its own accord. He's our responsibility.'

'At the moment, he's a ton weight around your neck.'

'It certainly feels like it sometimes, Joe. Do you know what upsets me most?'

'What?'

'Paul has no respect for any of us. His manner is so contemptuous. And it's not only us. There was a time when he looked up to Uncle Raymond. As a boy, he almost idolised him. Paul admired what he was trying to do in the Salvation Army.'

'I've seen Raymond's work at first-hand, Alice. He does an amazing job.'

'And he's the nicest man in the world.'

'Are you saying he's even nicer than *me*?' asked Keedy with mock indignation.

'Nobody can compare with you, Joe,' she said, stroking his arm, 'but there is something special about Uncle Raymond. He's the nearest I'll ever get to meeting a saint.'

Raymond Marmion had the same solid frame and the same pleasant, open face as his brother. Younger than Harvey Marmion by a few years, he had far less hair and it seemed to be receding visibly. At that moment, his head was covered in a peaked cap that matched his uniform. He was out on one of his usual night-time patrols in the East End, looking for people sleeping rough. One of the men with him carried a large pot of hot soup. On a cold night, it would be especially welcome. Raymond's wife, Lily, was at his side, fiercely proud of her husband's commitment to helping others and doing her best to emulate him. She was a tall, full-bodied woman in her forties who seemed to have been born in a Salvation Army uniform.

As they walked along the street, they glanced in every shop doorway to see if it had an occupant or two. When they reached the end of the row, they found someone curled up under a piece of rotting cardboard. He was wearing filthy clothes, a moth-eaten woolly hat and a tattered scarf. Raymond bent down to touch his shoulder. When there was no reaction, he shook the man.

'Are you all right?' he asked.

'Who are you?' replied the other, curling up protectively. 'Police?'

'We're from the Salvation Army.'

'We've brought you some hot soup,' said Lily, bending over him. 'Would you like some?'

The man sat up and tried to rub the sleep out of his eyes. Some of the group held lanterns. In the flickering light, the man looked at them. Sensing kindness, he was about to accept the offer of the soup when he began to cough uncontrollably. Raymond tried to pat him on the back but that had no effect at all. He was a slight individual in his thirties with tousled hair and a straggly beard. Lily could see that he'd been a handsome man at one time but was now stricken with ill health. After a couple of minutes, he finally stopped coughing.

'He needs more than a bowl of soup, Raymond,' she said.

'I think you're right.'

'Let's take him back to the hostel.'

'You're coming with us, my friend,' said her husband, bending over the man before scooping him up and standing him on his feet. 'Don't worry. You'll have something to drink.'

'Thank you,' croaked the man.

When the bowl of soup was poured and given to him, he held it in both hands and sipped noisily. They gathered round him to shield him from the wind. He took his time to finish the soup then handed back the bowl with a smile of thanks.

'We're taking you to somewhere warm,' said Lily.

'I see. Thank you.'

'You'll have a good night's sleep for once,' added Raymond. 'You look as if you need it. What's your name?'

The man didn't seem to have heard him. Instead of replying, he bent down to pick up a battered briefcase from under the cardboard and held it to his chest.

'We need to call you something,' said Lily, gently. 'What will it be?'

There was a long pause as the man looked around the ring of faces.

'It's David,' he said at length. 'My name is David.'

Breakfast was eaten in almost total silence. Ellen knew better than to expect a conversation with her son and, in some ways, she was grateful. Since he hardly ever spoke without managing to upset her, she found that it was preferable if he said nothing at all. If he'd been more amenable to a chat, she'd have asked him why he spent so much time playing darts in his room the previous night. She heard the darts thudding into the board time and again. When she'd first met his father, she recalled, Marmion played in a darts team at the local pub. The first great test of his affection for her came when she'd asked him to resign from the team in order to spend more time with her. After wrestling with his decision, Marmion had agreed.

The sad thing was that such a memory – important to her – would be utterly meaningless to Paul. If she told him about the incident, he'd only sneer. Details of his parents' courtship had no interest for him. Ellen wondered sometimes if he was starting to despise them. He'd certainly shown no love towards his sister the previous night. None of his family seemed to matter to him any more.

After finishing his breakfast, Paul did rise to a mumbled word of thanks then went out of the kitchen. Ellen cleared everything off the table and did the washing-up. She then took the bucket from under the sink and went out to empty it in the bin. Lifting the lid, she was about to tip the rubbish in when she caught sight of a piece of paper with a drawing on it. She picked it up and realised that it was a rough portrait of Sally Redwood. Her whole face was covered in freckles. What made Ellen gasp in horror was that the freckles were tiny holes, put there by the darts Paul had thrown.

Folding up the paper, she slipped it into the pocket of her apron.

At the end of another long and unrewarding day, they met in a pub to exchange complaints and to adjust their plans. Over a restorative pint apiece, Marmion and Keedy bemoaned the amount of time they'd spent on their respective searches. Neither of them had anything substantive to show for their efforts.

'It's dispiriting,' said Marmion.

'I can think of another word for it, Harv, but I don't want to swear.'

'I must have done so a dozen times today, Joe. I've been to every known haunt of Wally Hubbard and the cupboard was bare.' Keedy groaned. 'Sorry – I couldn't resist that.'

'I got the same result with Croft. Nobody knows where he is.'

'He'll be with a woman somewhere.'

'Lucky devil!'

'Watch it, Joe,' said Marmion, jocularly. 'You're spoken for.'

'I know and I'm glad of it. I managed to snatch an hour with Alice when I came off duty last night. It was a real tonic.'

'Did she tell you about Paul?'

'Yes, but I expect you got the fuller version at home.'

'Ellen was torn between annoyance and despair. It just goes on and on. There was a time when Paul had good days and bad days. He only has bad days now.'

'I'm surprised that he hasn't linked up with some of the other lads who've been injured and sent home.'

'He tried that but hated the way they went on about the war all the time.'

'It's an experience that changed their lives,' said Keedy. 'There's no getting away from that. It certainly changed Paul's life. He's reminded of that every time he looks in the shaving mirror.'

'That's true.'

They fell silent and reviewed their respective days. Each one of them had covered a fair amount of London as the hunt continued. A day that had started with hope ended in a searing disappointment. Marmion eventually spoke again.

'There are three of them, Joe.'

'What are you talking about?'

'There are three missing persons.'

'I've only counted two. Who's the third?'

'Paul,' replied the other. 'I'm after Wally Hubbard, you're after Ben Croft and we're all looking for the real Paul Marmion who was lost at the Battle of the Somme. He's the one we may *never* find.'

'Have we lost him altogether?'

'It's beginning to look that way.'

'What about Wally Hubbard?'

'Oh, we'll find him in the end, Joe. He won't stay out of sight for long. As soon as he gets a whiff of where Croft has gone, he'll be after him with whatever weapon he's decided to use.'

'Hubbard is a tough man. He could commit murder with his bare hands.'

'It may well come to that.'

Keedy was puzzled. 'Why did he wait?'

'What do you mean?'

'Why did Hubbard wait until his daughter had lost the baby and died in hospital before he turned on Croft? Having met him, I would've thought that Hubbard was the sort who'd hold a shotgun on Croft the moment he dumped the girl.'

'Maybe she didn't tell him who the father was.'

'Oh, I think he'd have demanded to know. What father wouldn't?'

He shot Keedy a glance that contained a warning. Before he and Alice had got together, the sergeant was known as a ladies' man with a string of dalliances behind him. In his younger days, he'd been the envy of the other constables in the station house. Marmion belonged to a generation that expected to keep a firm control of any romantic developments among their children. Ellen had been watched like a hawk by her father and Marmion's access to his future wife had been severely restricted. As a result, they'd had to wait until their honeymoon to make discoveries that other couples had made earlier in a relationship. Though he tried hard to fend off such speculation, he did occasionally wonder what Keedy and Alice had been up to. It would be highly embarrassing for all of them if a baby appeared before the marriage.

'Have you and Alice finally set a date yet?' he asked.

'Yes,' replied Keedy, sourly. 'It's the day after I find Ben Croft, so it may be several years away yet.'

Marmion laughed. 'We'll get him soon. And if *we* don't . . .'

'Wally Hubbard will find him for us.'

Instead of going straight home to her flat that night, Maisie Rogers caught a bus to Islington to see her friend. She'd already met Hubbard once that day. When she'd left the house, he appeared magically out of an alleyway to relieve her of the money she was carrying and to be given the key that Felix Browne had entrusted to her. The encounter had lasted less than a minute. Their second meeting of the day, she hoped, would be much longer. In the event, it went on for a couple of hours, starting in the main bedroom then moving to the kitchen. With the money from Browne, he'd bought food, milk and alcohol. He'd also acquired some new, smart clothing. They toasted their reunion with a cup of tea.

'Here's to Felix!' he said, raising his cup.

'I'll drink to that.'

'I knew he wouldn't let me down. I've now got a fully furnished house in a lovely part of the city and a gorgeous woman to keep me company.'

'Are you sure it's safe here?' she asked, nervously.

'Yes, nobody saw me moving in and, even if they did, they wouldn't recognise me from that photo in the newspapers. It's amazing what a bowler, a pair of glasses and a turned-up collar can do for you. My own mother wouldn't know me.'

'You gave me a real scare this morning when you pounced on me. You've changed completely, Wally.'

'I've had to, darling. Every copper in London is on the lookout for me.'

'I meant to tell you about that,' she said, 'but you whipped me upstairs before I could get a word out.'

'Are you complaining?' he asked with a wicked grin.

'No, I'm not. That bed is so much better than the one I have to sleep in.'

'And you had me as a hot-water bottle!' They shared a laugh. 'Right, you were going to tell me something. It's about Inspector Marmion, isn't it?'

'He came to see me at the pub.'

'That's a good sign.'

'Is it?'

'Yes, Maisie,' he told her. 'If he had cause to believe that we'd been in touch, he'd have hauled you off to the nick. You'd have been under real pressure there. If he came to the pub, he just wanted an informal chat.'

'There was more to it than that, Wally.'

'Oh?'

'He'd not only been to my flat, he persuaded Mrs Donovan to let him search it. He obviously came up with some clever excuse because she was as nice as pie to me when I got back. The old dear had no idea that I was under suspicion.' She gave a quiet smile. 'Mrs Donovan told him that I was a treasure.'

'I'd go along with that!'

Her face clouded. 'I'm worried, Wally.'

'There's no need.'

'I didn't like the way the inspector looked at me. It was as if he *knows*.'

'You're imagining things,' he assured her. 'He went to your flat and found nothing. You're in the clear, Maisie. If he really suspected you of helping me, he'd have had you tailed and we'd both have been arrested by now.'

'That's true.'

'Have you had any sense that someone's been following you?'

'None at all,' she said.

'There you are, then.'

Maisie relaxed slightly. While she was well aware of the risk she was taking, she saw that there were compensations. She'd not only shared some intimate moments with Hubbard, she liked the frisson of excitement she got from breaking the law by helping a friend. However, her reunion with him could only be temporary. She was realistic about that. Hubbard could never stay at liberty indefinitely.

'Do you *have* to kill Croft?' she asked, worriedly.

'Yes, I do,' he replied, jaw tightening.

'But you know what will happen then, Wally.'

'I don't worry about that. Once I've settled a score with that slimy bastard, they can put a noose around my neck with pleasure.' Maisie winced. 'You met my daughter,' he said. 'You saw the state she was in because of him. Lisa was almost gibbering. He made all those promises to her then kicked Lisa out of his life without a second thought.'

'He told her that he was getting a divorce from his wife.'

'Well, he wasn't – and he still isn't.'

'How do you know?'

'I spoke to her earlier today.'

She was astonished. 'You talked to Mrs Croft?'

'Yes,' he said, 'we got on very well. Veronica and I have got a common cause. We both hate her husband.'

'What if she reports you to the police?'

'She won't do that, Maisie. She doesn't want anything to do with the coppers. As it turns out, Sergeant Keedy has already been in touch with her. Veronica told him what she told me. She's happy to have Ben Croft out of her life for good.'

'That may be so,' she said, 'but she didn't tell the sergeant that she wanted her husband murdered, did she? And she didn't tell you that either.'

'No, Veronica didn't say that in so many words.'

'Then I think she lied to you. She'll speak to the police.'

'Not a chance.'

'How can you be so certain?'

'Because she was ready to help me.'

'In what way?'

'She gave me the name of a woman Croft had been seeing,' he explained. 'It was someone he met a couple of months ago. Veronica thinks he might still be calling on her from time to time, telling her the same pack of lies he told Lisa. That's where I spent most of the evening. I was keeping watch on her house in case Croft turned up to get his money's worth. Unfortunately, he didn't. If he doesn't show up tomorrow, I'll have to put the squeeze on her.'

Maisie said nothing but her heart had suddenly started beating like a drum.

He looked very different now. As he ate his meal with the other men at the hostel, David felt so much better. He'd been given a bath, a warm bed and regular food. On the two nights he'd spent with the Salvation Army, he'd been shown kindness and concern. He was not really like the others. Raymond Marmion and his wife could see that. The other men who'd been rescued from the streets were long-term outcasts, drifters who'd lived rough for years and, in some cases, had stolen food and drink to keep themselves alive. Most of them were known to the police. What set David apart from the others was the fact that he was educated. Though he said very little, he was articulate and well mannered.

Raymond and Lily watched him with a mixture of satisfaction and curiosity.

'I wonder why he won't talk about himself,' she said.

'A lot of them are like that, Lily. They want to bury their past.'

'I wish he'd shave that beard off. It doesn't suit him.'

'I don't think he's very concerned about his appearance. At least we've got him into clean clothing and given him decent meals.'

'I just wish we knew more about him,' said Lily. Turning away, she picked up a copy of the morning paper. 'Did you see that your brother is in the news again?'

'Yes, Harvey is trying to recapture an escaped prisoner.'

'Well, he's not doing very well at it so far, according to this article. It's very critical of him.'

'He's used to being unfairly chastised in the press,' said Raymond with brotherly affection. 'Don't worry about Harvey. He'll make them eat their words. He always gets his man in the end.'

Marmion and Keedy stood side by side in front of the superintendent's desk awaiting his strictures. For a couple of minutes, he pretended to be reading some paperwork. By the time he looked up at them, he'd rehearsed what he was going to say.

'Your report was deplorable,' said Chatfield.

'We're as disappointed as you are, sir,' admitted Marmion.

'You've made no progress whatsoever.'

'That's not true,' said Keedy, going on the attack. 'We've eliminated a number of possibilities, Superintendent. As you know, that takes time and effort. We've explored every avenue thoroughly. In my view, that deserves approval rather than reproach.'

'Be quiet, Sergeant.'

'I'm only making a fair point, sir.'

'Well, now you've made it, please shut up.'

'The sergeant is correct,' said Marmion, coming to his defence. 'He's been as diligent as usual and so have I. We are searching for two men who have no wish to be found. We expected Hubbard to be slippery but we had no idea that Croft had also gone into hiding – or so it appears.'

'What am I to say at the press conference?'

'You don't need to say anything at all, sir. Since you obviously don't enjoy being under fire, then I'll be more than happy to take your place. Apart from anything else, I can tell them in detail what we've been doing since the investigation began. All that you can do is to paraphrase my reports.'

'The inspector is right, sir,' said Keedy. 'Let him take over. He has a way of handling the press that – with all your virtues – you can't really match.'

It was a home truth that Chatfield would never accept. Stung into action, he leapt to his feet and ordered Keedy to hold his tongue. Turning his ire on Marmion, he didn't mince his words.

'Responsibility for the press conference will remain with me,' he said, acidly. 'Thank you for your kind offer, Inspector, but I reject it outright. You're altogether too abrasive with the press. That antagonises them. I know how to get their help.'

'There's not much help in today's editions,' Marmion pointed out. 'I get fifty lashes for what they perceive as a lack of effort and you come in for some harsher words for your performance in front of them yesterday.'

'The *Daily Mail* described you as mealy-mouthed,' Keedy interjected.

'I told you to shut up,' snarled Chatfield.

'They never say that sort of thing about the inspector.'

'Why are we arguing about the press?' said Marmion, jumping in. 'Facts are facts. We haven't made the headway we hoped for. The only way to appease hostile journalists is to get results. In other words, sir, we should be out on the streets again as soon as possible. Do we have your permission to leave?'

'No, you don't,' said Chatfield. 'I haven't finished with you yet.'

They stood there calmly while he rid himself of some biting comments about what he claimed was their lack of imagination. Having withstood many similar bursts of invective from the superintendent, they'd learnt how to close their ears to it. When the diatribe was over, Marmion had a question.

'Have you reconsidered my request for more detectives?'

'No, I haven't. You already have enough.'

'When do you *intend* to reconsider it?' pressed Marmion.

'I don't.' Chatfield snapped his fingers. 'That will be all.'

'Thank you, sir.' He winked at Keedy. 'Time to go, Sergeant.'

They left the office and closed the door behind them. Unpleasant as the attack on them had been, there was some justification for it. They had so far achieved very little. Marmion was annoyed.

'Chat is refusing to give us the proper resources,' he said.

'It's always the same.'

'If *he* was in charge of this case, he'd be screaming for

a dozen more men. Because I'm at the helm, he's cut our manpower to the bone.'

'It's almost as if he doesn't want us to succeed,' said Keedy.

'Oh, he does, Joe. He wants to have his moment of triumph when he can unveil the recapture of Wally Hubbard to the press. Chat will get all the praise while we languish in the shadows.'

'It makes my blood boil, Harv.'

'Let's forget him and try a new strategy.'

'What is it?'

'If we can't have someone on surveillance duty, one of us will have to do it himself. Since you're younger and fitter than me, it will be your job.'

'That suits me.'

'You can start this morning, Joe.'

'I know where Maisie Rogers works but I'll need her home address.'

'You won't be keeping tabs on her.'

'But you felt certain she'd been in touch with Hubbard.'

'I'm equally certain she'll watch her back as a result,' said Marmion. 'For that reason, I'm assigning you to someone else.'

'Who's that?'

'Felix Browne.'

Having worked at home in his office for most of the morning, Browne looked up when his wife brought in a cup of tea.

'Thank you, sweetheart,' he said.

'This just came through the letter box,' she told him, handing over an envelope with nothing but his name on it.

He was mystified. 'I wonder who sent this.'

Using a paperknife to slit it open, Browne extracted a sheet of paper. Wally Hubbard's message was in bold capitals.

THANKS, FELIX. YOU'LL GET YOUR REWARD IN HEAVEN.

CHAPTER EIGHT

Ellen Marmion decided that she could not simply stay away any longer from the sewing circle. Even if she got a frosty reception there, she felt that she had to go. She'd been postponing far too many things. When she found the portrait of Sally Redwood, her first impulse was to confront Paul but she was afraid to do that in case it sparked another row. On the previous night, Marmion had come home very late, looking jaded and weary. Since he already had far too much on his plate, she chose to say nothing to him about her son's worrying venture into art. It showed a cruelty that she'd never associated with him before and she wondered why he had taken against such a harmless girl. The portrait stayed in her handbag. The last thing her husband needed was yet another source of anxiety.

On the walk to the sewing circle, she thought about Paul's girlfriends. Though he'd never been short of one at school, they rarely lasted very long. At the time he volunteered, however, he'd finally found a steady girlfriend and Ellen was beginning to think that Sylvia Dyce might one day change her maiden name to Marmion. On his first leave, Paul could not wait to see her again and the couple had been drawn closer. Afterwards, the girl's mother had confided breathlessly to Ellen that they'd talked about an engagement. It was not to be. On his second return home, Paul had lost all his buoyancy and readiness to please. He was rude, distant and uncaring towards Sylvia. In the hope that he was only going through a phase, she stood by him but the relationship was foundering. After an acrimonious row, they split up.

There had been nobody else until he had a letter out of the blue from Mavis Tandy, the former girlfriend of Colin Fryatt. Since Paul and he had been so close, she wanted to hear everything he could tell her about him, especially the way that he'd died on the battlefield. Ellen never knew what went on between them but she'd noticed a new intensity in her son's interest. All of a sudden, it had disappeared. Something had happened and he'd never gone off to see her again. Unable to make friends of either sex, Paul had become a disgruntled loner. His response to an old school friend like Sally Redwood was to throw darts at her portrait.

When she got to the place, she had to stand outside for a few minutes to screw up her courage to go in. At length, she took a deep breath and opened the door. There were a dozen women there, sewing or knitting. Each one of them looked up, giving her a smile or a word of welcome. There was no hostile atmosphere at all.

'Where's Pat?' asked Ellen, looking around.

'We haven't seen her for days,' replied someone.

'Oh, I see.'

'We missed you yesterday, Ellen.'

'Something came up,' she said, the lie slipping easily from her lips.

'There's still some tea in the pot.'

'Thank you.'

'How's that son of yours getting on?'

'Oh, he's getting better . . . much better, in fact.'

This time a lie left a burning sensation in her throat.

Her name was Helen Graydon and she was older than the others. Lisa Hubbard had been barely nineteen when Ben Croft took an interest in her and he'd told her he preferred the company of younger women because they were still open to new experience. Helen Graydon was at least thirty and she was married. Watching the house from a concealed position, Wally Hubbard surmised that Croft had made a deliberate switch from vulnerable teenagers who might have vengeful fathers. In choosing Helen, he had an insurance policy. She would not expect to marry him. While her husband was away in the army, she was enjoying herself with Croft because he provided some excitement. It would end when her husband returned. From Croft's point of view, there was a decided bonus. As a mature woman, she had ample sexual experience. He didn't have to waste time breaking down her inhibitions.

103

After making a few discreet and casual enquiries, Hubbard had built up a picture of Helen's life. She was an attractive, intelligent woman who lived alone in a neat villa and craved more than a life of lonely evenings at home. During the day, she worked as a secretary to the managing director of a paint factory. On the previous day, Hubbard had followed her there and back without arousing any suspicion. He only wished that he'd followed his daughter with the same manic interest. Had he done so, he might have prevented the disastrous friendship with Croft into which she'd been cleverly lured. Guilt at his negligence was another of the impulses that drove him on. He was atoning for his mistakes as a father.

When she'd emerged from her house that morning, Helen had walked right past Hubbard, blithely unaware of the fact that he'd follow her again. There'd been no sign of Croft so far but he didn't believe the man could stay away from such a striking woman for long. Helen Graydon was his bait. All that Hubbard had to do, he thought, was to bide his time and his victim would, hopefully, soon make an appearance.

'You're very quiet today, Alice.'

'Am I?'

'You've hardly said a word since we set off on our beat.'

'I'm sorry,' said Alice, suppressing a yawn. 'I had a very late night and I'm paying for it. I'll make an effort to stay awake.'

'Did you see Joe?'

'Yes, I did.'

'I wish I had a gorgeous man like that who'd walk with me in the moonlight.'

'There was no moon last night, Iris. The sky was black and we got caught in a shower. We had to dive into a bus shelter.'

They came to a junction, waited for the traffic to go past, then crossed the road. Alice Marmion and Iris Goodliffe matched each other stride for stride. During their months together, they'd blended into a real partnership.

'I thought you were going to visit your mother,' said Iris.

'I did visit her. I was just lucky that Joe rang the house while I was there.'

'Did you see your brother?'

'I had a brief chat with him.'

'How is he?'

'Paul is . . . more or less the same, really.'

'That means he's terribly lonely.'

'That's his choice, Iris. He's sort of withdrawn from the world.'

'He's a bit young to turn into a monk,' she said. 'When most army lads come back home, all they want is beer and excitement. We've seen them turning out of a pub late at night. They say the cheekiest things.'

'I try not to hear them.'

'They don't mean any harm, Alice. I feel sorry for them. It may be the last chance of a bit of fun they get. They'll soon be back on the boat to France. If they're not killed by the Germans, they may end up in the same pickle as Paul.'

'He's not in any pickle,' argued Alice, hurt by the choice of phrase. 'He's getting better each day. Paul can read a newspaper without any trouble now and Mummy doesn't have to worry any more about him getting run over if he goes out alone. To all intents and purposes, he looks as healthy as you and me.'

'But he's *not* as healthy, is he, Alice? I can tell.'

'He will be one day.'

'I read an article about shell shock. It's so unpredictable.'

'Lots of people make a complete recovery.'

'And just as many are subject to fits and tantrums and gruesome nightmares that wake them in the middle of the night. It can last for years, apparently. That's what the article said.'

'Yes, we've read everything there is to read about the subject,' said Alice, hoping to terminate the discussion. 'And my parents had a long talk with the army doctor. They know what to expect.'

'Why doesn't he have a girlfriend?'

'Paul doesn't have any kind of friend at the moment.'

'That's unnatural.'

'It's his choice, Iris. We accept that that's what he wants at the moment.'

'But it will only hinder his recovery. In the article—'

'I don't care about the article,' said Alice, interrupting her. 'Every case is different. Paul is dealing with his problems his way and we support him in that.'

'Have you ever told him about me?'

'He's not very interested in *my* work, I'm afraid.'

'But you're his sister. He ought to be proud of what you do.'

'Is your sister proud of what *you* do, Iris?'

'Not really,' said the other with a giggle. 'She'd much rather have me working back in one of our pharmacies. To be honest, I think she's a bit jealous of me.'

'Why?'

'It's because I do a dangerous job and work alongside Inspector Marmion's daughter. Even my sister has heard of your father. He's a sort of legend at Scotland Yard. He never seems to fail.'

Harvey Marmion was all too conscious of his failures. Though they'd toiled for two whole days, they still had no idea where the escaped prisoner was and even less idea where his intended victim could be. Hubbard had good reason to stay out of sight but Croft's disappearance was inexplicable. Marmion had toyed with the notion of putting an appeal in the newspapers, urging him to make contact with the police as soon as he could. What stopped him from doing so was the realisation that if Croft had felt the need of police protection he'd have already come forward of his own volition. That thought had dictated his change of tactics. He moved Keedy from the hunt for Croft to the surveillance of Felix Browne, friend and erstwhile business associate of Hubbard. If the police could not locate Ben Croft, reasoned Marmion, then Hubbard would have even more difficulty because he had far less resources. It was a point he put to Maisie Rogers.

'How can he hope to find Ben Croft?' he asked.

'You're asking the wrong question, Inspector.'

'Am I?'

'Yes,' she said. 'You should be asking how Wally could possibly escape from Pentonville. And yet he did somehow. Never put anything past him.'

'Is that what he told you?'

'No, it isn't, because I haven't been in touch with him.'

'Doesn't that make you feel neglected?'

'It makes me grateful that Wally is so considerate,' she replied. 'If he comes anywhere near me, he'd be putting me in danger and he doesn't want to do that.'

'So Hubbard is considerate, is he? That's not a word that Kenneth Pearce would ever apply to him. He's the warder who was knocked unconscious during the escape. Hubbard was very inconsiderate towards him.'

'He's always been very gentle with me,' she said, loyally.

'Was that *before* his imprisonment or since?'

'It was *during*, Inspector. I used to pop into Pentonville on visiting days to cheer him up. We had some good times together.'

Marmion laughed. They were standing outside the house where she had a flat. Maisie had been on the point of going to work when she saw the police car draw up outside. She left the house immediately so that Marmion didn't come inside again. Maisie didn't want her landlady to realise what was actually going on. It might lead to a search for new digs.

'Why are you bothering me again?' she asked.

'I just wondered if you'd changed your mind.'

'About what?'

'Being sentenced to a long spell in prison.'

'I've done nothing wrong.'

'That's because – or so you claim – Hubbard hasn't been in contact with you. If he does so, he's putting you in a very awkward position. You'd not only be helping an escaped convict, you would, in effect, be condoning murder.'

'No, I wouldn't,' she protested.

'Do you *want* to see him kill Ben Croft?'

'Of course I don't!'

'Then help us to catch Hubbard.'

'How can I when I don't know where he is?'

'You're close to him,' he said, 'and I daresay you know who his other kindred spirits are, don't you?'

'Yes,' she said, 'but it would be a very long list. Everyone who ever worked for Wally Hubbard liked him. He had that effect on people. You sort of became part of his family. He was just very . . .'

'Loveable?' suggested Marmion.

'Let's settle for "friendly", shall we? That way you won't get the wrong idea about how close Wally and I really were.'

'What about his daughter? You knew her, presumably.'

'Yes, I met Lisa a couple of times.'

'Did she live with Hubbard?'

'No,' said Maisie, 'that was part of the problem. He never saw much of her. She shared a flat in Highgate with a girl called Daisy Drew. Wally reckoned that she was no daisy. She was as ugly as sin, he said. That's why I remember her name.'

'And Lisa?'

'She was very, very pretty but a bit unworldly, if you ask me.'

'So she'd be an easy target for someone like Croft?'

'I'm afraid so. She never even mentioned his name to Wally and, of course, her mother had died years ago so she couldn't confide in her either. Lisa was spotted by Croft and, in no time at all, she was hooked.'

'When did Hubbard first become aware that she was in trouble?'

'It was months after she'd been dumped. The stupid girl blamed herself for what had happened and refused to tell Wally the name of the father. It was only when she'd lost the baby and was dying in hospital that he got the truth out of her. All he could think about then,' she went on, 'was making Ben Croft pay.'

'I know the rest of the story.'

'Does that mean I can catch my bus, Inspector?'

'No, it doesn't.'

'I have to be at the Dun Cow in half an hour.'

'We'll get you there sooner than that,' he said, indicating the car at the kerb. 'You've been very helpful, Maisie. The least I can do is offer you a lift.'

She stood her ground. 'I'd rather take the bus, if you don't mind.'

Raymond and Lily Marmion worked tirelessly to help others. They made sure that anyone staying at the hostels had regular meals even though they were unable to enjoy that luxury themselves. Having seized a spare moment to have a cup of tea and a sandwich, the couple were in the kitchen.

'He doesn't mix with the others at all,' she observed.

'It's his first time, Lily. He doesn't know the ropes yet. David will be fine when he settles in.'

'But he won't be staying.'

'Who told you that?'

'David told me himself. It was the longest conversation I've ever had with him. He actually managed three whole sentences. He said that he doesn't fit in here.'

'Would he rather sleep in a doorway under a piece of cardboard?'

'David needs to keep on the move.'

'Why?'

'He wouldn't tell me that.'

'What a strange fellow he is!' said Raymond, shaking his head. 'If we hadn't rescued him, he'd have ended up in hospital or coughed himself to death. Here at the hostel, he's been warm, well fed and properly looked after – yet he plans to leave.'

'He doesn't feel safe here – you can see it in his eyes.'

'Nowhere is safer than a Salvation Army hostel, Lily.'

'David doesn't agree.'

'Has he taken against us or something?'

'No, Raymond, it's nothing like that.'

'Then what is it?'

She glanced towards the day room. 'He's frightened of something.'

Joe Keedy was becoming increasingly impatient. When he'd been given the job of tailing someone, he was very pleased, especially as he had a car and a driver at his disposal. He'd nursed high hopes that Felix Browne would come furtively out of his house, get into his car and drive off to a secret rendezvous with Wally Hubbard. The sergeant could then arrest them together. In reality, however, all that happened was that Browne left his home, drove to his main office and went inside. Keedy spent a long time outside, idling away his time by walking up and down. He did make the mistake at one point of looking in the shop window at the extensive display of houses for sale and rental. Some of the prices quoted made his eyes water. He and Alice could never afford to buy any of the houses, yet they had to live somewhere. He began to speculate on which area they'd choose and how much they could afford.

Browne eventually emerged from the building and went to an expensive restaurant for a late lunch. Keedy was condemned to watch outside from a safe distance and listen to the rumbling of his stomach. Browne's next move was to the side street where he'd parked his car. Keedy's interest was ignited at once. He got into his own vehicle and ordered the driver to follow Browne's car. After weaving through a labyrinth of streets for a couple of miles, the estate agent pulled up outside one of his branch offices and went inside. Keedy was left cooling his heels. When he risked walking past the shop window, he saw a very different selection of houses on display. They were invariably small terraced properties in deprived areas of the city, slum dwellings renovated by Browne so that he could put up the asking price. Most were offered for rental rather than sale. While they were very much within the range of the notional budget of Keedy and Alice, he didn't feel able to ask her to consider a single one of them. They were universally unappealing.

Felix Browne clearly operated at both ends of the market. He sold large and desirable houses to middle-class clients and acted as a slum landlord to those of more slender means. Keedy returned to the car and watched through the window. It was another long and unproductive wait.

Wally Hubbard was undergoing the same experience. He'd spent the whole day following Helen Graydon to work, loitering near the factory, trailing her back to her house then lurking in a doorway nearby. It was now Saturday evening, the obvious time for Croft to call on his mistress yet there was no sign of him. After waiting for a couple of hours, he elected to take a more direct approach. He pulled his hat down even more and knocked on the front door of the house. Helen soon opened it.

'Can I help you?' she asked.

'Are you Mrs Graydon?'

'Yes, I am.'

'Hello,' he said, venturing a smile and speaking softly, 'I'm sorry to disturb you. My name is Inspector Marmion from Scotland Yard. We're trying to find a gentleman by the name of Ben Croft. We were given this address.'

Helen became flustered. 'I've never heard of anyone called Croft.'

'That's odd. Our information is that – when his own house burnt down – he spent occasional evenings here. Are you quite *sure* you don't know him?' He flashed another reassuring smile. 'He's not in any trouble, Mrs Graydon, but it's very much in his interests that we make contact with him.'

Helen had been thrown into confusion. The very fact that anyone knew about her clandestine relationship was worrying enough. To have a detective inspector knocking on her door in search of Croft was terrifying. Her lover had sworn to her that he was extremely discreet. The prospect of her husband discovering the truth about her infidelity made her quiver all over.

'I don't know where he is, Inspector,' she gabbled.

'Ah, so you remember him now, do you?'

'The truth is that I haven't seen him for a month or so.'

'You can't expect me to believe that, Mrs Graydon. You're a very lovely woman. Any man lucky enough to win your friendship would never stay away from you for long. The temptation would be too strong.'

'Well, that's exactly what happened,' she said with evident sincerity. 'I didn't know Mr Croft well. He was just someone I happened to meet. Then, without warning, he suddenly disappeared. I haven't heard a word from him since.'

'Have you any idea where he went?'

'No, I don't.'

Her eyes moistened and he could see how hurt she'd been by what she viewed as rejection by her lover. Helen's claim to be only a casual acquaintance was palpably a lie. She and Croft had been very close at one time.

'Thank you, Mrs Graydon,' he said, touching the brim of his hat. 'I won't mention this conversation to anyone else. Our interest is in Mr Croft, not in you.'

'I see.'

Retreating into the house, she closed the door and burst into tears.

They met at a pub not far from Scotland Yard. It was frequented by off-duty policemen and they recognised many familiar faces. Over a pint of beer at a quiet table, Keedy poured out his woes.

'It's not fair, Harv,' he moaned. 'Some people have all the luck. We work around the clock in this job for meagre rewards while someone like Felix Browne drives around in that big car of his and earns a fortune.'

'Yes, Joe,' said Marmion, putting a hand to his breast, 'but we enjoy heart-warming rewards.'

'It's more likely to be cardiac arrest. I'd forgotten how boring surveillance work can be. It wears you down. As for Browne's house, have you ever been down the Bishop's Avenue?'

'Yes – many times. There's nothing there that *we* can afford.'

'Felix Browne's place is sitting in the middle of a couple of acres.'

'It makes you green with envy.'

'Oh, I'd love to find that he's been helping Wally Hubbard,' said Keedy with relish. 'Just think of knocking on that door in the Bishop's Avenue with a pair of handcuffs ready.'

'Do we have evidence to justify such a visit?'

'No, we don't.'

Fretting at his lack of progress, the sergeant addressed himself to his beer.

Marmion took over. 'Well, at least I've had a more interesting day than you, Joe. It started with another chat with Maisie Rogers.'

He described their meeting outside her flat and repeated his conviction that she was in touch with Hubbard. There were, however, limits to what she could provide, which was why Felix Browne had to be watched. Marmion had paid a number of visits throughout the day but the one that yielded a dividend had been a call on a friend of Lisa Hubbard.

'Her name was Daisy Drew,' he said.

'It sounds like someone out of a children's storybook.'

'Nobody would put this young lady in a book, Joe. She's far too dull.'

'Who is she?'

'It was Maisie Rogers who put me on to her. During the time that Lisa was involved with Croft, she used to share a flat with Daisy. The girl still lives there, luckily. That's how I found her. Daisy is a nice girl and keen to help. Lisa was the pretty one, apparently, and her friend was the Plain Jane.'

'I can see why Croft chose Hubbard's daughter.'

'Oh, I don't think his charm would have worked on Daisy. She didn't like him at all. She thought he was smarmy and she told Lisa to have nothing to do with him.'

'Maybe she was just jealous.'

'No,' said Marmion, 'I think she saw Ben Croft for what he was. But it was too late. Lisa was already enthralled by him. Daisy told me about the way that he'd ignore her for a week or two then treat her as if she was the most important person in his life. Daisy was certain he was seeing someone else as well but Lisa wouldn't hear a word against him.'

'Then she became pregnant and he fled the scene.'

'Lisa clung to the belief that he'd turn up one day but he never did.'

'You have to feel sorry for her.'

'She wasn't the only victim, according to Daisy. More recently, there was someone else who got pounced on by Croft then dropped completely when he tired of her. Daisy knew her – or, at least, she used to.'

'What do you mean?'

'She committed suicide, Joe.'

'That's dreadful!' exclaimed Keedy.

'It may explain something,' said Marmion. 'What would

you do if your daughter had killed herself after being cruelly exploited then cast aside by Croft?'

'For a start, I'd geld the bastard.'

'Some fathers would want to do more than that.'

'I see what you're driving at.'

'That's the reason Ben Croft has disappeared,' said Marmion. 'Wally Hubbard has got competition. Another furious father may well be after Croft's blood. He's been forced to go into hiding.'

Sunday began early at the Salvation Army hostel. After a short service was held there, the band would form and they would march through the streets to proclaim the Word by means of rousing hymn tunes. Before that, however, was the important matter of breakfast. Those staying at the hostel never had to be awakened in the morning. The smell of cooking was an infallible alarm clock. The men were sitting around the table long before the meal was ready to be doled out. Raymond Marmion noticed that there was someone missing.

'Where's David?' he asked his wife.

'I haven't seen him this morning.'

'I do hope he hasn't sneaked off somewhere.'

Raymond asked the others if they'd seen the missing man but none of them had even glanced towards his bed. Getting their breakfast was something that focused the mind intently. Raymond was disturbed. He went into the men's dormitory and looked along the lines of beds. They were all empty. David's bed had obviously been slept in and the battered briefcase was on the pillow. Raymond surmised that he must still be on the premises because he'd never leave without it. He began to search the other rooms, calling out David's name as he did so. There was no response. When he checked the bathrooms, the mystery was eventually solved. As he opened the door of the first one, Raymond saw him stretched out fully clothed in an empty bath. David was motionless. He was staring up at the ceiling in disbelief. Rushing across to him, Raymond took him by the shoulder to help him sit upright. It was then that he noticed the blood from a scalp wound and the ugly red weal around the man's neck. Their guest would never require breakfast again. He was dead.

CHAPTER NINE

Sunday morning found Harvey Marmion seated at his desk in Scotland Yard as he collated all the reports that had come in from his detectives. It was slow, repetitious work but it was an essential part of any investigation. As well as being a record of the search for Wally Hubbard, it was proof of how thorough he and his team had been and could therefore be used to keep Claude Chatfield at bay. When his telephone rang, he was certain that it would be the superintendent so he picked up the receiver with an air of resignation.

'Inspector Marmion . . .'

'Ah, I'm glad I caught you, Harvey,' said his brother. 'I've got a nasty shock for you, I'm afraid.'

'Why is that, Raymond? Has something happened to Lily and the boys?'

'Something has happened to *all* of us.'

'What is it?'

'We've got a murder on our hands.'

Marmion was startled. 'Who's the victim?'

'It's a man we rescued from a shop doorway the other night.'

'Well, I'm not really the person you ought to be speaking to,' said his brother. 'I'm already tied up with another case. A murder investigation will be handled by someone else. If you've got a pencil, I can give you a number to ring.'

'I've already got the right number, believe me.'

'I don't understand.'

'We read the newspapers, Harvey, and we know that you're looking for an escaped prisoner. He was convicted of arson when he burnt down the house of a man named Ben Croft.'

'So what?'

'We only knew the murder victim by the name of David.'

'Look, I'm sorry, Raymond. This is nothing to do with me.'

'I think you'll find that it is,' insisted his brother. 'He had an old briefcase with him and I've just looked into it. His papers are in there. His full name is Benjamin David Croft – are you interested now?'

'Yes,' said Marmion, his mind racing.

Reaching for a pencil, he asked for the details and jotted them down on a pad. When he'd heard the full story, he thanked his brother and promised that he'd come over to the hostel as soon as he'd reported to the superintendent. He put down the receiver and ran down the corridor to Chatfield's office, bursting straight in.

'You're supposed to knock first,' said Chatfield.

'I've just spoken to my brother, sir.'

'Please spare me any family tittle-tattle.'

'There's been a murder at the Salvation Army hostel.'

'Then you must give me the details so that I can assign detectives to the case.'

'You've already done that, sir,' said Marmion. 'The name of the victim is Ben Croft. It seems that he's been garrotted.'

'In that case you must take some of the blame, Inspector.'

'Why?'

'You allowed Hubbard to get to him before you did.'

'How could I possibly know that Croft would be in a hostel?'

'Your brother runs the place, doesn't he?'

'Yes, but when they first picked him up, Croft wouldn't tell them who he really was. He said that they could call him David, which turns out to be his middle name. And with respect, sir,' added Marmion, 'it's unwise to jump to the conclusion that he was murdered by Hubbard.'

'Nobody else had a motive to kill Croft.'

'That's where you're wrong, Superintendent. I heard only yesterday of a young woman who was so distraught at being discarded by Croft that she committed suicide. Imagine how her father must feel. You have daughters of your own. Wouldn't you have murderous impulses in that situation?'

'Certainly not,' retorted Chatfield. 'To begin with, neither of my daughters would *ever* be in that situation. They've been brought up properly. Secondly, I'd never take the law into my own hands. This is Hubbard's revenge,' he asserted. 'It's as plain as the nose on your face. Get over there as quickly as you can. I'll alert the Home Office pathologist to meet you at the hostel. It's in Stepney, isn't it?'

'Yes, sir, it is.'

'Well don't waste time, man – off with you. And once you've finished over there, you can do something that you should have done already.'

'What's that, sir?'

'Recapture Hubbard before he decides to murder someone else.'

Ellen Marmion was looking in the hall mirror to adjust her hat when Paul came downstairs in his dressing gown. She glanced towards him.

'You'll have to make your own breakfast,' she said. 'I'm off to church.'

His reply was an indecipherable grunt.

'I suppose there's no point in asking you to come with me?'

'No – I've finished with all that nonsense.'

'Paul!'

'I don't believe God exists,' he said with a sneer. 'If you'd seen some of the things I've seen, you'd feel the same.'

'No, I wouldn't. In your position, the first thing I'd be doing was thanking God for keeping me alive.'

'I don't want to be kept alive. I'd rather have died beside Colin.'

'That's an awful thing to say.'

'I was *there* – you weren't. The gunfire was deafening and the mortars were even worse. Men were dying horrible deaths all round me. It was hell.'

'And who was one of the first people to visit you in the field hospital?' she asked. 'It was the chaplain, wasn't it? You said how kind he'd been to you. You had time for religion then. What's happened to change your mind?'

'Everything,' he said with a gesture of disgust.

'People are only trying to help you.'

'I hate chaplains talking down to me and telling me how to live.'

'They're not giving orders, Paul. They're just offering guidance.'

'Well, I don't need it.'

'I'd say that you do.'

'Why don't you just go off to church and leave me be?' he said, dismissively.

'It's because I want to ask you something first,' she replied, feeling a sudden rush of courage. She took a piece of paper from her handbag. 'I found this in the bin. It's a picture of Sally Redwood, isn't it?'

'Yes,' he replied with a snigger, 'I put all her freckles in.'

'That was cruel of you, Paul. I heard you throwing those darts.'

'It did no harm.'

'I think it did and I'm sure that your father would agree. As it happens, I haven't shown it to him yet. I'd rather keep him out of it altogether, to be honest. This is something between me and you. I was the one who invited Mrs Redwood and her daughter here.'

He laughed. 'I was just having a bit of fun, that's all.'

'You were doing it at Sally's expense. That was unkind, Paul. What has she ever done to deserve this?' she went on, holding up the portrait. 'And what got into you to make you behave so rudely towards her?'

'Forget Sally Redhead.'

'She's a nice girl and she's just got herself a new job. On

123

Monday morning, she starts work at Newsome's, the jewellers.' He cackled. 'What's so funny?'

'It's the idea of Sally selling jewellery she'll never be able to afford herself and wedding rings she'll never wear. Let's face it, who'd want a wife like her?'

'Don't be so wicked.'

'She's gone now and, thanks to me, she won't be back.'

'You used to treat girls properly at one time,' she reminded him. 'When you first met Sylvia, you couldn't be nicer.'

'That's all in the past,' he muttered.

'And what about that other girl, the one who used to be Colin Fryatt's girlfriend? When she first wrote to you about Colin, you couldn't wait to see her, could you? For a time, you seemed really fond of her.'

Unpleasant memories came back to haunt him and he chewed his lip. Ellen could see that she'd caught him on the raw and wondered why. Before she could question him further, Paul turned on his heel and headed for the kitchen.

'Go to church,' he said over his shoulder. 'I'm hungry.'

On the drive to Stepney, Joe Keedy tried to absorb the news he was being given.

'What the hell was Ben Croft doing in a Salvation Army hostel?' he asked in amazement. 'From what I've heard about him, I wouldn't say he was the type who wanted to play the bass drum in the band.'

'Raymond said there was something peculiar about him.'

'Sleeping rough is what you do when the money runs out completely. That wasn't Croft's case. He could afford to stay in

124

a decent hotel or – if he was trying to hide – why not catch a train to Scotland or somewhere?'

'Unfortunately, it's too late to ask him.'

'Now for the big question, Harv . . .'

'Go on – I know what's coming.'

'How on earth did Wally Hubbard track him down and kill him?'

'I'm not sure that he did.'

'You told me that Chat was absolutely certain.'

'He should have more sense, Joe.'

'You think it could have been someone else?'

'I'm keeping my options open,' said Marmion. 'Croft must have thought he'd be safe if he disappeared from sight and I don't believe it would occur to Wally to trawl the East End for tramps and misfits. Whoever looks in shop doorways after dark except the police and nightwatchmen?'

'Don't forget your brother.'

'Good reminder – Raymond and his team do a regular sweep of the area on a cold night.'

'How did he sound when he reported the crime?'

'He was as calm and collected as usual, Joe. You can't shock someone who lives the kind of life my brother does. He sees desperate people every day. It's part of his mission.' The car turned a corner and began to slow down. 'Here we are,' said Marmion. 'It's obvious that word has got out.'

There was a sizeable crowd outside the hostel and they were pleased to see a uniformed policeman there, holding them back. Summoned by Raymond, an ambulance was waiting nearby to remove the body once it had been examined by the pathologist.

When the car stopped, the detectives got out. They didn't need to show their warrant cards to the policeman because he recognised them at once and let them through.

'That's the virtue of having our photographs in the newspapers,' said Keedy.

'I'm never entirely happy about that, Joe. I prefer anonymity.'

'I'd rather let the villains know who we are.'

As the detectives entered the building, Raymond and Lily Marmion came over to them and there was an exchange of greetings. After kissing his sister-in-law, Marmion shook his brother's hand warmly.

'I'm sorry that this is not a social call.'

'So am I,' said Raymond.

'Where is everybody?'

'Staff and visitors are all in the dining room. Nobody who was in the building at the time I discovered the body has been allowed to leave.'

'Excellent,' said Marmion. 'Sergeant . . .'

'Yes, sir?'

'Start taking statements, please.'

'I'll show you where the dining room is,' said Lily, leading him down a corridor. 'As you can imagine, everybody is badly shaken up.'

'Lily is right,' said her husband. 'The staff can cope with any emergency but the people we save from the streets are usually frail and vulnerable. In addition, some of them have mental problems. They've been devastated by what happened.'

'I'd like to see the body.'

'It's in the bathroom.'

'Has anything been touched or moved?'

'Nothing at all,' said Raymond with a smile. 'When your brother is a detective inspector, you do tend to pick up a few tips.'

'I'm glad I actually have some use.'

They went along one corridor then turned into another on the right. At the end were the men's bathrooms. To stop anyone entering the one where he'd made the grim discovery, Raymond had put a couple of large chairs in the way. A sign pinned to the door was unequivocal – KEEP OUT.

'I never thought we'd meet because of a murder,' said Raymond.

'Neither did I – it's rather convenient.'

'Convenient?'

'You'll save us so much time,' said Marmion. 'You've already done that by reporting the crime as soon as you stumbled on it. Also, you're highly articulate. That's an enormous help. Many of the people we deal with aren't. If they find a corpse, they lose their nerve completely and simply jabber at you.' He waited while Raymond moved the chairs out of the way. 'Right,' he continued, 'let's take a look at him, shall we?'

Marmion went into the bathroom while his brother lingered in the open doorway. The body had been left in the bath with the head lolling against the enamel. Marmion bent over to inspect the wounds without touching them. He then felt in the man's jacket and trouser pockets but all he found was a dirty handkerchief.

'Did he have any money when you found him, Raymond?'

'There was a wallet in his coat but I've no idea what was in it.'

'The chances are that it was taken by the killer.'

'Is that the motive, then – easy pickings?'

'Hardly!' said Marmion with a wry smile. 'Only a very stupid thief who rob a man who was unlikely to have anything valuable about him. No, my guess is that he was murdered for a very different reason.'

'We wondered if it was an act of vengeance. That escaped prisoner we read about had vowed to kill Ben Croft. What was his name . . . Hubbard?'

'Wally Hubbard – but I can tell you now that he was definitely not the killer.'

Raymond was amazed. 'Are you certain of that?'

'I'd put my life savings on it. He'd have no cause whatsoever to kill this man.'

'But isn't that why he broke out of prison? He hates Ben Croft.'

'There's one small problem, Raymond.'

'Is there?'

'The murder victim is not Croft. We interviewed him at the time his house was burnt down. There are similarities, I grant you,' he went on, looking down at the body, 'but they're only superficial. What I can state categorically is that this man is not Ben Croft. So Wally Hubbard would have no motive to murder him.'

Hallam Beavis had been upset by the warning about Hubbard but, as time went by, he became less and less worried that he might get a surprise visit from the man. Though he'd been Croft's boss at one time, he'd not been in touch with him for several weeks and, in view of what happened subsequently, had been very grateful. Beavis stopped taking the elementary precautions he'd adopted in the wake of Keedy's visit. He ventured out alone and felt no sense of threat. It encouraged him to believe that he was perfectly safe. Part of his Sunday morning ritual was to take his dog for a walk in the park. The animal, a frisky cocker spaniel, loved to race to and fro across the grass. Beavis had taken an old tennis ball with him and threw it for the dog to retrieve. The two of them enjoyed the game for some while until Beavis felt the need of a rest. Leaving the dog to scamper off into the trees, he lowered himself onto a park bench.

Within seconds, he had company. Someone came out of the bushes to sit very close beside him and put a restraining hand on his knee. Wally Hubbard's voice was low but filled with menace.

'We need to talk about Ben Croft,' he said.

The sensational development meant that a press conference was quickly arranged. Marmion and Keedy briefed the superintendent beforehand. The inspector passed on the pathologist's immediate response when he first examined the body while the sergeant gave a summary of all the statements he'd taken.

'The folly of a snap judgement was shown once more, sir,' said Marmion. 'You were too hasty in assuming that Croft was the victim and Hubbard the killer.'

'And you were wrong on both counts,' added Keedy.

'Anybody could have made the same mistake,' said Chatfield, spikily.

'*We* didn't, sir.'

'According to the identity papers you found, the victim *was* Croft so, to some degree, I'm exonerated.'

'There was something worth noting about that, sir,' said Marmion. 'When my brother found the briefcase, its flap was open. The only things inside were the papers, yet when they first found the man in a shop doorway the briefcase was obviously full and he was clutching it as if it contained all his worldly goods. Raymond, my brother, said that he even took it into the bathroom with him.'

'But not on this occasion, it seems,' said Chatfield.

'We can't be certain of that.'

'It was found on his bed, man.'

'That doesn't mean he left it there, sir.'

'I agree,' said Keedy. 'It could have gone into the bathroom with him and been emptied by the killer after he'd garrotted his victim. Having taken out what he came after, he could have left it on the bed and slipped out of the building.'

'You're making too many wild guesses, Sergeant,' said Chatfield.

'It's a theory I share with the inspector.'

'What I need are answers to the questions that will inevitably be fired at me. Who is the man? Why was he murdered? Why was he carrying papers that gave his name as Ben Croft? And how did the killer get into the building so easily?'

'There's another question to add,' said Marmion.

'Go on.'

'How did he know that his target was staying at the hostel?'

'None of this is a great help to your brother,' said Chatfield.

'The one thing that attracts people to a Salvation Army hostel is that it's a clean, decent and safe environment. Murder is a bad advertisement for them.'

'That's the least of Raymond's concerns. He's preoccupied with calming the other people staying there and making sure that nothing like this happens again. Would you like me to sit beside you at the conference, sir?'

Chatfield was curt. 'No, I wouldn't.'

'But my brother is a key person in this enquiry. How often does that happen?'

'We've never had a case like it before,' said Keedy. 'It's unique. The press will make a great deal of the fact that two brothers are involved.'

'It's purely accidental, Sergeant.'

'They'll want to hear from the inspector directly.'

'What they'll want even more is some indication of progress, so the two of you can now get back out there to find the evidence we need.'

'Before we can do that,' said Marmion, 'we'll need additional detectives.'

'There are none available.'

'Take them off less urgent investigations.'

'We're already at full stretch.'

'Then you might as well tell the press that we have very little chance of a successful resolution because we are under-resourced. We're still hunting for Wally Hubbard, remember. The murder is a parallel investigation. It remains to be seen if the two of them are actually linked in some way. To do that, we need more men.'

Chatfield was adamant. 'I'm unable to spare them.'

'Then I must ask your permission to speak to the commissioner.'

'Keep him out of this.'

'It's way beyond my capability to do that,' said Marmion. 'You know how sensitive he is about the way we're portrayed in the press. What happened at the hostel will be front-page news. He'll want an explanation.'

'Then he'll get it from me,' insisted Chatfield.

'I'd like to have a word with him myself, Superintendent.'

'No – permission is refused. You are *not* to go over my head.'

'Then we're hampered from the start,' Keedy pointed out.

'You have a team of excellent detectives, Sergeant. Deploy them wisely and you are bound to reap the benefit in terms of evidence. Assign fewer men to the search for Hubbard and divert the others to the murder enquiry. It's as simple as that.'

Keedy was about to answer back but a glance from Marmion silenced him. They were on the point of leaving the superintendent's office when there was a tap on the door. It was opened immediately and Sir Edward Henry swept into the room.

'Excuse me for interrupting,' he said, 'but I'd like to know more about this appalling business at a Salvation Army hostel. It demands a robust response from us. I'm sure that you appreciate that, Superintendent. Additional detectives must be brought into action at once.'

'Yes, Sir Edward,' said Chatfield, deferentially, 'I was saying the very same thing myself only a moment ago. I'll draft in more men immediately.'

Marmion was impassive. 'Thank you for responding to our plea, sir.'

'This is an emergency, Inspector. You'll get all the help you need.'

Keedy had to control the urge to laugh.

The atmosphere at the hostel had undergone a complete change. Calm had been replaced by naked fear. Certainty had become doubt. Men who'd slept in the same dormitory as the victim were badly shaken by the realisation that a stranger could enter the building without apparent difficulty and commit murder. It made them restive. Loud arguments broke out. One grizzled old man rounded on the person who'd slept in the bed next to David.

'It could have been you,' he said, accusingly.

'Shut yer gob!'

'You were the last in here for breakfast.'

'So what?' demanded the other, a thickset man with a mottled pate.

'You were alone in there with David.'

'No, I wasn't.'

'I bet it was *you* who killed him.'

'That's a bleeding lie.'

'I saw you eyeing that briefcase of his.'

'I never touched it.'

'Well, I say you did. You strangled David to get it.'

'You're asking for it!'

Smarting at the accusation, he threw himself at the old man and there was a violent scuffle. They had to be dragged apart but

133

they continued to snarl at each other across the room. When the incident was reported to Raymond Marmion, he went into the dining room at once and spoke to all of them, stressing the importance of remaining calm and helping the police in every way. The shouting stopped but the undercurrent of anxiety was still palpable. It would never be entirely removed until the crime was finally solved.

Raymond adjourned to his office and his wife joined him to ask what had caused all the commotion. He told her about the brawl.

'That's very worrying,' she said. 'They've got on so well until now.'

'They're starting to suspect each other, Lily. I'll have to make sure they're never left alone.'

'I thought things would improve when the body was taken away.'

'The opposite has happened – they've become tetchy and aggressive.'

'I still feel jangled myself,' she admitted.

'We need to brace ourselves. Harvey said that the press would soon be here like a swarm of angry bees. Let me do the talking when they come.'

'I'm so glad that your brother is in charge of the case, Raymond.'

'Yes, we see so little of him as a rule. It's a pity it takes a murder on the premises to get him here.'

'I haven't had time to ask him about Ellen and the children.'

'He's not paying us a social call, Lily.'

'I wonder if Paul is still causing trouble.'

'We have enough trouble of our own at the moment,' he said with a grimace. 'Let's forget about Paul until we've sorted everything out here.' A noise from the street made him go to the window. 'The band is forming up. They'll be off fairly soon. Even when we have a crisis, we have to make our presence felt on a Sunday.'

He was about to turn away when he saw a car drawing up outside. He heaved a sigh of relief when his brother emerged from the rear of the vehicle and stood to admire the band. Raymond went quickly out of the building to greet him.

'I'm so glad to see you again, Harvey,' he said as they shook hands.

'How is everything going?'

'Not very well – we had a fight earlier on.'

'Have they started accusing each other?' Raymond nodded. 'Joe Keedy has ruled them out as suspects. When he took individual statements, he said that it was clear that none of them could possibly have been involved.'

'It hasn't stopped arguments breaking out.'

'What steps have you taken to control them?'

'I gave them a stern warning. If anybody starts a fight again, they'll be back out on the streets. That brought them to heel.'

The band was now in marching order and their leader took up his position. After giving them instructions, he started them off with their favoured processional, 'Onward Christian Soldiers'. Brass instruments predominating and bass drum booming, they set off confidently. Marmion watched them until they turned a corner and were out of sight. He and his brother then went into the building and headed for Raymond's office. Lily was still there. After giving her a kiss and embrace, Marmion explained what was happening.

'We've deployed our men to knock on doors in the vicinity,' he said. 'It may just be that, earlier this morning, someone saw suspicious activity outside here.'

'This is the East End,' said his brother with a wry smile. 'There's *always* suspicious activity here.'

'Somebody must have come in by the back door,' said Lily.

'But it was locked, my love.'

'It was unlocked when you discovered the body. You went and checked.'

'That's how the killer made his escape.'

'But how did he get in here in the first place?'

'I think I know the answer to that,' said Marmion, thoughtfully. 'He didn't need to sneak in at the back because he walked in through the front door.'

'Somebody would have seen him,' she pointed out.

'They might have *seen* him, Lily, but they wouldn't have challenged him.'

'Why not?'

'The answer came to me when I was watching the band. No disrespect to either of you but, when you put on that uniform, you do tend to look the same.'

'That's intentional,' said Raymond. 'We're instantly recognisable as Salvationists and we wear our uniform with a sense of honour.'

'I fancy that somebody wore it as a disguise,' said Marmion. 'That would explain how he could walk in here almost unnoticed. When the man you knew as David was alone in the dormitory, he wouldn't have looked twice at someone in uniform. He'd have been off guard.'

Lily was aghast. 'Are you saying that the killer is one of *us*?'

'Not at all – he only pretended to join the Army for a short while. Instead of bringing salvation, however, he was here to squeeze the life out of his victim and steal something from his briefcase. I'm glad I arrived when the band was outside,' he continued. 'They helped me to guess what must have happened.'

CHAPTER TEN

After serving breakfast to her landlady on a tray, Maisie Rogers felt that she'd done her good deed for the day. Neighbours soon arrived to keep Mrs Donovan company and to take care of her so Maisie was able to go for a stroll in the morning sunshine with a clear conscience. She did not get far. When she reached the end of the street, a car drew up alongside her. Felix Browne opened the passenger door and beckoned her in. When she climbed in beside him, he drove off.

'Good morning, Mr Browne.'

'Good morning, Maisie. I needed to see you.'

'Why didn't you knock on the front door?'

'I didn't wish to hang about,' he explained. 'I was followed yesterday. The police obviously think I'm going to lead them to Wally. Another car trailed me today but I managed to shake it off.'

'I'm glad they didn't follow *me* yesterday evening. They'd have caught the pair of us together.'

'That's what I wanted to speak to you about. Keep away from Wally.'

'Why?'

'It's too dangerous, Maisie.'

'I like to see him.'

'I know – and Wally's desperate to see *you*. I don't blame him.'

'Without you and me, he'd be struggling.'

'I'm only helping from a distance,' said Browne, 'so that nobody ever sees us together. If he makes a mistake and gets caught on one of my properties, I'll say that he must have broken in.'

'He's very grateful for the key and for the money.'

'Wally's a friend. I couldn't let him down. That said, he's not going to get *me* into trouble. Friendship only goes so far.'

'He appreciates that, Mr Browne.'

'When have you arranged to see him again?'

'Tonight.'

'Tell him it's the last time.'

Maisie hesitated. 'That would be difficult . . .'

'You've got to put yourself first,' he urged. 'Let's be realistic. We both know where this is going to end. Wally is too clever to be recaptured so he'll beaver away until he eventually finds Ben Croft. What happens then?'

'Wally will kill him.'

'And Maisie Rogers will be an accessory to murder. Do you really want to end your life with a rope around your neck and a black bag over your head?'

'No,' she said, nervously fingering her throat.

'Then don't let Wally drag you down with him.'

'It may not come to that, Mr Browne.'

'What do you mean?'

'Well, you seem to think that he'll get his revenge on Croft then be captured by the police. It's not what Wally is planning. He told me that, whatever happens, he's not going back to prison again. They'll be waiting for him in Pentonville.'

'Oh, I'm sure they will, Maisie. They hate someone escaping. Wally will get a very hostile reception.'

'Once he's done what he needs to do, he's talking about leaving London altogether and changing his identity. He wants to start afresh somewhere else.' She swallowed hard. 'He asked me to go with him.'

'You'd be a fool to agree,' said Browne, sharply.

'I haven't committed myself either way.'

'Do you *want* to spend the rest of your life on the run?'

'No, I don't.'

'Then do some serious thinking.'

'I will.'

'I know you feel obliged to Wally.'

'It's true, Mr Browne, I do.'

'But you must feel even *more* obliged to Maisie Rogers. She has a real future ahead of her. Wally Hubbard doesn't.'

Though she hadn't noticed, he'd been driving in a wide circle so that he eventually came back to the exact place where he'd picked her up. Browne waited until she got out and closed the door behind her. He gave her a farewell wave and drove off.

Able to begin her walk at last, Maisie had a lot to think about. She was beginning to regret that Wally had escaped from prison in the first place. If he'd stayed behind bars, her life would have been far less complicated. On the other hand, it would also have been bereft of the thrill and excitement he'd given her.

Sunday was the one day of the week when she usually managed to spend time with Joe Keedy but she was out of luck on this occasion. Since she was deprived of one pleasure, Alice Marmion sought another by catching a bus and going to call on her mother. Delighted to see her, Ellen told her daughter the news.

'I've just spoken to your Aunt Lily,' she said. 'There's been a murder at their hostel. A man they rescued from the streets was killed there this morning.'

'Do they know who did it?'

'Your father has only just started his investigation.'

'But Daddy is already involved in another case.'

'He thinks it may be related to the murder somehow,' said Ellen. 'According to his identity papers, the victim's name was Ben Croft.'

'Isn't that the man whose house was burnt down?'

'That's what your father thought, Alice. When he actually saw him, however, he said that it wasn't Croft at all.'

'So who was he?'

'They're still trying to find out.'

'I suppose it could be a coincidence,' said Alice. 'Ben Croft is not an unusual name. There could be two of them. In fact, there are probably several more.'

'According to Lily, the victim had papers with the name of the man whose house was burnt to the ground. That was the address given.'

'How bizarre!'

'Your father is going to be busier than ever now.'

Alice pulled a face. 'And so is Joe.'

'That's one of the penalties of marrying a policeman.'

'I can live with it.'

'You still haven't set a date, have you?' said Ellen, probing gently.

'We never seem to be together long enough to do so.'

'The church will have to be booked well ahead, Alice, and the banns will need to be read. In fact, when I was in church this morning, the vicar was asking me if you were starting to make plans for the wedding.'

'We've made the decision that matters, Mummy – there will *be* a wedding.'

Ellen made a pot of tea and they settled down in the kitchen. Inevitably, the talk turned to Paul and the drawing of Sally Redwood was produced. Alice was shocked at what her brother had done.

'He was throwing *darts* at her?'

'That's why he drew the portrait in the first place, Alice.'

'It's a terrible thing to do.'

'I told him that.'

'What was Daddy's reaction?'

'I haven't shown it to him and I don't know that I will.'

'You ought to, Mummy. He deserves to know what Paul gets up to. This is more than a case of making fun of the girl. It's vicious.'

'When I first found it in the bin, my blood ran cold.'

'Let me speak to Paul.'

'What good would that do?'

'We can't just let him carry on like this, Mummy. His mind is twisted. What he really needs to do is to talk to an army psychologist.'

'When I suggested that, Paul flew off the handle.'

'It's all the more reason to report him. He's getting out of control, Mummy.'

'Most of the time I don't even see him, so in that sense, he's no trouble and he keeps his bedroom clean and tidy. There is that. His behaviour scares me sometimes but then I look at some of the other lads invalided out of the army. Mrs Harris's son, who lost a leg, was arrested for throwing stones through people's windows and Ian Cotter, who went to school with Paul, became so violent that they've put him in a mental hospital.'

'That's where Paul is heading if he goes on like this.'

'Perhaps we should stand back, Alice, and give him more breathing space.'

'And what's he going to do with it?' asked her daughter. 'Draw pictures of somebody else and throw darts at it? He's *got* to be challenged.'

It was a paradox. A man who specialised in being an amiable host was now being forced to frighten people. Wally Hubbard had been a popular pub landlord with a gift for spreading goodwill among his patrons. Even when he'd gone on to own some hostelries, he'd enjoyed popping into them from time to time and helping behind the bar. Mine host was now taking on a different role. Unable to find Ben Croft, he'd ambushed the man's former employer in a park and bullied a list of names and addresses out of him. He'd now begun a systematic search among Croft's former colleagues, demanding information from them and threatening dire consequences if they dared to tell the police that he'd been in contact with them. Moving from one to the other, he left a trail of terror behind him.

Yet there was still no hint of where Croft might have gone. Hubbard went back to the one person who might be able to help him. He called on Veronica Croft again and was reluctantly admitted to the house. Alone with him in the front room, she was very uneasy.

'You promised not to come here again,' she said.

'I had no choice, Mrs Croft.'

'There's nothing else I can tell you.'

'I believe that there is. You gave me useful information last time.'

'Did you find that woman?'

'Yes,' said Hubbard, 'I found her, watched her and eventually spoke to her. Mrs Graydon was naturally upset that anybody knew about her friendship with your husband but she struck me as an honest woman who'd been bewitched.'

'What did she tell you?'

'She claimed that she hadn't seen him for a month or so and she said it with a bit of steel in her voice. Mrs Graydon obviously thinks that she was cast aside without any explanation. It's left her bitter.'

'I know the feeling,' said Veronica, pursing her lips.

'He's either gone on to a new woman or he's back with one of his old flames.'

'I can't help you with a new name. The last person I knew about was Helen Graydon because he boasted that he'd finally found someone he could really love. Ben let her name slip out and I remembered it.'

'She's an attractive woman, Mrs Croft,' he told her, 'but she's not a patch on you. I promise you that.'

The compliment drew a rare smile out of her and he had a glimpse of the woman she must have been before resentment had set in. Being forced to return to the family home had been a severe blow to her pride. Having to take a mundane job in a factory had inflicted further damage.

'I need some names from you, Mrs Croft.'

She shook her head. 'I don't have any.'

'Yes, you do. I know you told me you didn't keep a record of his old flames but, if a husband is going astray, most wives would want to know who the woman was. I'm sure that you're no different.'

'I'm sorry,' she said, firmly, 'I can't help you.'

'Don't you *want* me to catch up with him?'

'That's not the point, Mr Hubbard.'

'Then what is?'

'It was wrong of me to talk to you the first time,' she said, earnestly. 'You're a wanted man. If the police knew I'd helped you, they'd arrest me at once.'

'But they *don't* know, do they?'

'Frankly, I'm panic-stricken.'

'There's no need to be,' he said, gently. 'People may have seen me knocking on your door but none of them recognised me. What I'm wearing is a pretty good disguise. I put it to the test yesterday by asking a policeman the way to Bond Street. He gave me very good directions,' he went on with a chuckle. 'You're in no danger, Mrs Croft, I promise you. Now tell me some names.'

She folded her arms. 'I can't.'

'It's important to me.'

'I don't want Ben's murder on my conscience.'

'You didn't *have* a conscience the last time we met.'

'Well, I do now and it's troubling me. That doesn't mean I'm going to report you to the police. I just don't want anything to do with you again.'

His eyelids narrowed. 'It's a bit late to decide that.'

'No, it isn't. I've had sleepless nights thinking about it.'

'Then let me give you something else to think about, Mrs Croft. If you don't give me what I want, I'll be reporting *you* to the police as my accomplice. How much sleep will you get then?'

'You wouldn't do that!' she gasped.

'I'll do whatever's necessary.'

'That's cruel!'

'No,' he growled. 'What your husband did to my daughter was cruel. That's why I'll move mountains to get to him. If you won't help me, you can have the pleasure of explaining to the police why you talked to an escaped prisoner and failed to mention it to them.' He put his face close to hers. 'What are you going to do, Mrs Croft? Make a decision *now*.'

* * *

Claude Chatfield examined the briefcase at some length. After looking at the papers found inside, he turned the object over and ran a finger along its edge. Joe Keedy watched him. He'd been sent back to Scotland Yard with the murder victim's briefcase so that he could bring the superintendent up-to-date with the investigation.

'This has seen better times,' decided Chatfield, putting it down on his desk. 'It's high-quality leather. When it was new, it would have cost a pretty penny. What was it doing in the hands of a down-and-out?'

'That's not what he was, sir. He didn't belong with the others.'

'So why was he sleeping on the streets?'

'That's still a matter of speculation,' said Keedy. 'Might I ask what you said at the press conference?'

'Why?'

'You obviously stirred up the reporters. They descended on the hostel like a pack of ravening wolves. The inspector is still fending them off.'

'I told them enough to give them a story but held back certain details. It's important that we always know that little bit more than the press in any investigation. The utmost discretion is called for when dealing with them.'

'Did they ask why Inspector Marmion was not there?'

'I explained that.'

'What did you say about the search for Wally Hubbard?'

'I told them it would continue with renewed vigour. Now,' he said, settling back in his chair, 'there's something I must ask you. Has the inspector – or his brother, for that matter – established how someone could enter a Salvation Army hostel and commit a murder without being seen by anyone?'

'He *was* seen, Superintendent.'

'Really?'

'That's what the inspector believes, anyway, and I agree. He feels that the killer put on a Salvationist's uniform and became, in effect, invisible. It's the same with the police, sir. People look at our uniform rather than at our faces.'

Chatfield was dubious. 'That could be the answer, I suppose.'

'The inspector's guesses are uncannily accurate.'

'I dispute that.'

'I work alongside him, sir. I've seen it happen so many times.'

'Can he explain *where* the Salvationist's uniform came from?' asked Chatfield, 'or is he assuming that the killer is in fact a member of the Army – the Salvation Army, that is?' Light sarcasm came into his voice. 'Murder is in direct contravention to everything it stands for.'

'The uniform could have been stolen from the place that supplies them.'

'It would surely be closed on a Sunday?'

'Yes, I suppose that it would,' admitted Keedy.

'Then we can eliminate that possibility.'

'Inspector Marmion favours another theory, sir.'

'I'd be interested to hear it, Sergeant.'

'He thinks that it was taken – by force, probably – from a Salvationist with the same build as the killer.'

'That's a rather fanciful notion, if you ask me.'

'There is some evidence to support it.'

'Is there?'

'Yes,' said Keedy. 'When they assembled this morning, a member of the band was missing. It's one of their cornet players.'

Bound and gagged, the man lay on the floor and winced as cramp set in again. He was lying on the straw in an empty stable, wondering how he'd been stupid enough to be tricked into looking into it by a stranger. His head was still pounding from the blow he'd received. His cornet lay in the straw beside him.

No matter how late he was going to be, Ellen was determined to wait up for her husband. She sat on the sofa with her latest library book and was soon deep into a story of whirling romance. She managed to fight off fatigue for hour after hour but it eventually got the better of her. When he finally got back, she was fast asleep with the book open in her lap. Marmion picked it up gently, folded it before putting it aside, then bent over to give his wife a kiss on her forehead. Ellen blinked.

'Oh, it's you, Harvey!'

'Who were you expecting?' he asked with a grin.

'What time is it?'

'It's well past midnight.'

She sat up. 'Lily rang me earlier.'

'That was my suggestion.'

'She said that the whole place was in turmoil.'

'It was, Ellen. It was hours before everything settled down again.'

'I see.'

'What have you been doing all day?'

'Well,' she replied, 'first of all, I went to church then I had the call from Lily and, soon afterwards, I had a lovely surprise.'

'Paul behaved like a human being for a change?'

'If only he had,' she said with a hollow laugh.

Marmion sighed. 'Has he been upsetting you again?'

'I don't want to go into that now, Harvey. It's very late and you're exhausted.'

'It's never too late to talk about our son.'

'Leave it until the morning.'

'I'll be rushing off to work then,' he said. 'Tell me now and explain what you meant by a lovely surprise.'

He sat beside her and held her hand. Ellen took a moment to gather her thoughts. When she was ready, she told him everything and even got Paul's drawing of Sally Redwood from her handbag to show him. Marmion was dismayed that their son had been so unpleasant towards visitors.

'Pat Redwood won't ever forgive him,' said Ellen. 'I saw her in church this morning with Sally. They avoided catching my eyes and I was very grateful.'

'Paul must make amends somehow.'

'That was Alice's idea. She insisted on tackling him again.'

'What happened?'

'Tempers flared up and they hurled abuse at each other.'

'Alice should have known better than to get drawn into a dogfight,' he said. 'It's part of police training that you don't let an argument get out of control by joining in. You try to pacify.

You take the heat out of a row. Alice should have known that.'

'She told him that it was time he behaved like an adult and Paul started to tease her about being engaged to a man who was much older and had had a lot of other girlfriends before her.'

'Yes,' said Marmion, 'in fairness to Paul, I had those reservations as well.'

'But you never used them to goad Alice.'

'No, I held my peace and hoped that I was wrong about the match.'

'You were, Harvey. They're ideal for each other.'

'I know, love, and I couldn't be happier.'

'So what are we going to do about Paul?'

'The best thing I could do is to find him an alternative father, one who's actually here to set him right when he kicks over the traces. Seriously,' he went on, raising a palm to cover a yawn, 'we ought to get some medical advice. It's not normal for a young man to throw darts at a picture he's drawn of someone whose only crime was to come here for tea. On top of everything else, it makes things so uncomfortable for you.'

'Yes, it was an ordeal in church this morning.'

'Have you spoken to Mrs Redwood about what happened?'

'No, I've deliberately kept out of her way and, as it happens, she's avoided the sewing group. There's a message in that for me.'

Marmion felt the usual surge of guilt and he blamed himself for being an absentee father. The demands of his job gave him no chance of a proper family life. He couldn't remember the last time that he, his wife and the two children sat down for a meal together. Because he'd been on duty so much, he'd never managed to forge a real bond with Paul and that made him sad. He put an arm around Ellen.

'Do you forgive me?'

'It's not your fault, Harvey.'

'I feel that it is somehow.'

'You can't take the blame for what happened to Paul,' she said. 'It was the war that turned him into the person he is. It's made him coarse and horribly selfish. And he thinks it's funny to hurt people's feelings.'

'That's got to stop.'

'Let's go to bed.' She got up from the sofa. 'We're both dropping.'

He rose to his feet. 'I may not have the strength to climb the stairs.'

'I haven't even asked how the investigation is going.'

'There are two investigations now, Ellen,' he said, wearily, 'and we've got absolutely nowhere with either of them. That's the truth. If it goes on like this, they'll be bringing me home on a stretcher.'

Putting an arm around her, he took her slowly off to bed.

The stable was down an alleyway that few people used. Ordinarily, policemen on night duty would walk past it without giving it a second glance. It was different that night. As two of them approached the alleyway on their beat, they heard a strange sound. It was as if someone was trying to blow into a mouthpiece without quite managing it. Interest aroused, they used torches to guide their footsteps through the gloom.

The noises were coming from inside the stable. One of them unlocked it and opened the door wide. Their torches illumined a startling sight: arms and legs bound tight, a man in his shirt and underwear was squirming in the sawdust. Having managed to bite through the gag, he'd tried to raise the alarm by shouting till he was hoarse, then blowing the cornet that lay beside him. His face lit up with relief.

'Thank God you've come!' he said. 'This place stinks of manure.'

'I'll have to go,' she said.

'Why not stay the night?'

'Mrs Donovan will miss me.'

'Are you saying you prefer that old duck over me?'

'Of course, I don't.'

'That's not very flattering, Maisie.'

'She relies on me.'

'And so do I,' said Hubbard, nestling against her. 'She hasn't got the whole of the Metropolitan Police on her tail.'

He rolled over and kissed her but made no objection when she got out of bed. As she began to put on her clothes, he enjoyed looking at the contours of her body. For her part, Maisie Rogers was doing her best to find the courage to give him an ultimatum. There'd been no chance to do so when she'd first arrived because he'd lifted her bodily and carried her upstairs.

'Thanks for coming, darling,' he said. 'I needed you.'

'You made no bones about that.'

'I've had a depressing day. When I got some names out of

Croft's missus, I thought I was on the right trail at last. One by one, they let me down. Croft hadn't been anywhere near them for six months or more and they were angry with him.'

'Why don't you accept that you'll never find him, Wally?'

'Oh, yes I will!' he vowed, sitting up in bed.

'Everyone has said the same thing. Croft has disappeared.'

'Why is that?'

'He was afraid you'd come after him.'

'I had to get out of prison first and that took some doing. Croft had no idea if and when I'd break out. Mrs Graydon said that he vanished a month ago and she took it personally.'

'You might never find him.'

'That won't stop me looking.'

She stepped into her skirt and zipped it up. 'There's something I've been meaning to say, Wally.'

'Then why not say it?'

'You don't make it very easy for me.' He put both hands over his mouth and made her laugh. 'I can't do this again.'

The hands came down. 'Have you gone off me or something?'

'No, it's not like that.'

'Then what is it like?'

'I'm frightened, Wally. Every time I see you, I risk being arrested.'

'But you haven't been, have you? We're in the clear.'

'Our luck is bound to run out in time.'

'Well, I mean to find and kill Ben Croft before it does.'

'If you do that, you'll be putting a noose around my neck.'

'What is this?' he asked, getting out of bed and crossing to her. 'I never thought you'd get cold feet, Maisie. In the old days, you were game for anything.'

'The stakes weren't quite so high then.'

'We talked about going off together afterwards.'

'No,' she asserted, 'that's what *you* talked about. I didn't say yes or no. It was sort of left in the air.'

'So tell me what you've decided.'

'That's what I'm trying to do.'

He looked at her shrewdly. 'Someone's been getting at you, hasn't he?'

'No, this is my decision.'

'But it was prompted by Felix. I can hear his voice in what you're saying.' He grabbed her by the shoulders. 'He spoke to you, didn't he?'

'You're hurting me,' she bleated.

'Tell me the truth!'

'Yes, he did.'

She wrested herself free and took a cautionary pace backwards. Putting on her blouse, she began to do up the buttons. He regarded her for a few moments.

'I didn't mean to hurt you, Maisie,' he said, softly.

'You'll be claiming next that you didn't mean to burn down Ben Croft's house,' she said, 'but you did. You mean everything you do, Wally. That's your nature. Your needs *always* come first. It's not fair.'

When she turned away, he got between her and the door.

'Look, please don't go like this. All right, I know I make demands, very big demands, but there are rewards. When I asked you to run off with me, it was no joke. It's what I want.

I need to become someone else, Maisie, someone who's a bit kinder and more considerate. Come with me,' he implored. 'The police will never find us in a hundred years. Come with me and we'll start a new life together.' He produced a disarming smile. 'What do you say?'

CHAPTER ELEVEN

For a period of several weeks, Helen Graydon's life had veered between exhilaration and shame. Ben Croft had been a revelation. Until she met him, she hadn't realised what a clumsy lover her husband had been. He'd groped, fumbled and, as he took his pleasure, paid little attention to hers. Croft was very different – gentle, considerate and inventive. Even though they were followed by a sense of apprehension, the times they'd spent together were magical. Hoping that they'd continue, Helen had been cut to the quick when he'd apparently just walked away from her without warning or explanation. As she ate her breakfast that morning, she looked back on their relationship and realised just how clever he'd been. After picking her out, Croft had contrived a meeting with her and started the slow, patient process of seducing her. He'd told her that they were, to some extent, in the same position. She had a husband fighting abroad and he, allegedly, had a sick wife who slept alone. He persuaded her that they should give each other comfort.

Croft never made excessive demands and kept well away from her house during daylight hours. Her reputation was never in danger. Helen had been grateful for that. To the neighbours, she was an attractive, lonely woman pining for the return of her soldier-hero. In reality, however, it was Croft's return for which she pined. Helen did her best to despise him but warm memories of his touch and his purring voice kept breaking in. He'd given her an experience she'd never get elsewhere. In any case, his disappearance might be nothing to do with a rejection of her. If the police were searching for him, then he might have had a legitimate reason to go somewhere and had not had the time to forewarn her. Helen came round to the view that Ben Croft should be given the benefit of the doubt.

On the way to work, she recalled some of the special moments they'd shared together. While she'd never dare to wear the ring he'd given her, she kept it unseen around her neck on a chain. It was a keepsake she would treasure for that morning at least. On other days, it had been hurled contemptuously aside as she reviled her faithless lover. Today, he was back in favour.

Work as a secretary in a paint factory had its disadvantages. There was always a strong whiff in the air and intrusive noise from the factory floor. But the job was not irksome and she liked her colleagues. As she arrived that morning, she went through the usual routine, walking into the reception area and collecting her boss's mail and his newspapers. When she got to his office, she discovered he'd not yet arrived so she took the things through and set them down on the desk. It was only when she put the newspapers there that she glanced at the front page of the one on top. There was a headline about a murder at a Salvation Army hostel. The investigation was being led by Inspector Marmion and a stock photograph of him was on display. Helen was about to walk away when she took a second look at the inspector.

It made her shudder.

'The most popular items are in the window,' said the manager, a short, fussy man in a dark suit and sober tie. 'We keep our more expensive stock in the safe.'

'I see, Mr Lycett.'

'You won't be handling any of that, of course.'

'I understand.'

'What you'll probably be selling are watches and clocks. There's always a demand for them. You'll be taught how best to present them to a customer.'

Sally Redwood was enjoying her first morning at work. Her colleagues were very welcoming and she felt that it was a feather in her cap to secure a position in such a well-known jeweller's shop. She lapped up everything that Lycett told her. Following instructions, she'd put on a smart black dress and borrowed a gold brooch from her mother. It had been bought from the shop for Patricia Redwood's wedding anniversary and Lycett recalled serving her husband. Sally was glad to wear it. The new job was a far cry from working in Woolworth's and facing the daily tumult. At Newsome's, there was a more refined atmosphere altogether.

'Needless to say,' said Lycett, 'we've had a surge in the sales of wedding rings. It's a product of the war. Soldiers and sailors have been desperate to get married before they go back into battle again. That's understandable, I suppose. Some of them know that they'll never come back again. It's tragic.' He adjusted his tie in a mirror. 'Enough of that – we've a business to run. Well, Miss Redwood, I hope that you'll soon settle in. We don't bite and we're always ready to lend you a hand. Now, then, what would you like to ask me first?'

When he went into the superintendent's office that morning, Marmion had some news to pass on to him. Though his face was motionless, he was smiling inwardly.

'My brother has been in touch to say that the missing bandsman has been found. Discovered during the night, he'd been stripped of his uniform and was trussed up in a stable.'

'Oh,' said Chatfield, discomfited, 'that's interesting.'

'I was right, after all, sir.'

'Yes, yes, I suppose you were.'

'The sergeant said that you described my theory as fanciful but I couldn't see how else the killer could get inside the hostel. The bandsman in question is a cornet player, by the way. As he passed an alleyway, he was struck over the head. Too dazed to resist, he was dragged along to the stable, divested of his uniform, then tied up. By the time his mind cleared, his attacker was putting on the uniform.'

'Did he get a good look at the man?'

'Not really, sir.'

'Does he have any idea of his age, height, build?'

'All he could say was that he was not young and of average height.'

'What about the attacker's own clothing? Did he leave any of that behind?'

'No, sir.'

'What's your brother's view?'

'Raymond is just grateful that the bandsman survived the ordeal. He thinks that the killer must have tracked his victim to the hostel then bided his time. Everyone knows that the band goes marching on a Sunday morning. It would be the best opportunity to acquire a Salvationist's uniform.'

'But how did the killer know where his target was?'

'I've no answer to that, sir.'

'And who, in the name of all that's holy, *is* the deceased?'

'He was someone posing as Ben Croft.'

'Then where is the *real* Ben Croft?' asked Chatfield with vexation. 'The bandsman only lost a uniform. Croft lost his whole identity.'

'Did he lose it,' asked Marmion, 'or did he *exchange* it?'

'That's absurd.'

'You're probably right, Superintendent. It's absurd and . . . fanciful.'

Chatfield glowered then took a moment to mull over what he'd just heard.

'Do you see a connection here, Inspector?' he asked.

'A connection, sir?'

'Yes – between the escape and the murder, of course. Both involve someone being knocked out, deprived of his uniform, then tied up and gagged. The only difference is that the bandsman didn't end up in hospital.'

'Are you suggesting that the ambush is the work of Wally Hubbard?'

'The similarities are unmistakable.'

'Only at first glance,' said Marmion, warily.

'According to the bandsman, his attacker was of average height and not young. That description fits Hubbard like a glove.'

'I think you'll find that it fits a vast number of men, sir.'

'You have doubts, obviously.'

'I do, Superintendent.'

'Yet you must concede that it's a possibility worth considering.'

'In a case as baffling as this one,' said Marmion, 'I'm ready to consider *any* possibility. This one, however, does not hold water.'

'Why not?'

'It assumes that Hubbard mistook the man at the hostel for the real Ben Croft. Is that conceivable? I don't think so, sir. Hubbard has spent months thinking about how he'd kill Croft. He's *seen* the man and would recognise him anywhere. He'd never mistake the murder victim as Croft – and, having met Croft, neither would I.'

'Oh, I see,' said Chatfield, grumpily.

'To begin with, the victim is somewhat younger.'

'Then why wasn't he in the army?'

'I don't know, sir.'

'And what was his relationship with Croft?'

'We can't be certain that there was one.'

'Of course, there was – he had Croft's papers.'

'He had documents purporting to belong to Ben Croft,' said Marmion, 'but we don't know if they are genuine. I'm having them checked to see if they're forgeries. And even if they're not,' he continued, 'they may not have been handed over. They could have been stolen from Croft. Since the war broke out, there've been a lot of mislaid identities. The first thing army deserters do is to change their name.'

'We *must* find out who the victim is,' declared Chatfield, 'and we must recapture Hubbard soon. At the press conference yesterday, they tried to give me a roasting because he was still at large. Fortunately, I had the experience to cope with aggressive questioning. You might not have been so adept.'

Marmion pretended to agree. 'You may be right, sir.'

'Have there been *no* sightings of Hubbard?'

'None whatsoever.'

'What about that friend of his?'

'I'm still having Felix Browne watched, sir, but it's something of a challenge. He has a fast car and an excellent knowledge of London backstreets. My fear is that he may realise he's being followed. The surveillance vehicle lost him yesterday.'

'That's worrying.'

'I've asked Sergeant Keedy to have another word with Mr Browne.'

'He needs to be leant on hard.'

'The sergeant knows how to do that, sir.'

'What about that woman friend of Hubbard's?'

'She's only a barmaid,' replied Marmion. 'She has no means of hiding him or providing him with money. Felix Browne can do both. He's a fly customer, sir, a man from a modest background who's made a name for himself selling and renting out properties. Sergeant Keedy will need to have his wits about him.'

Felix Browne was at the head office of his little empire, seated behind a desk as he flicked through the morning's correspondence. When his secretary told him that he had a visitor, he was unperturbed to hear that it was Keedy and asked for him to be sent in. He stood up to give the sergeant a warm smile and a handshake, then waved him to a chair. Browne spoke as if they were old friends.

'What would you like – tea, coffee, something stronger?'

'I'd like some information about Wally Hubbard, please.'

Browne laughed. 'I've told you before. That's in short supply.'

'I don't accept that, sir.'

'Suit yourself. Oh, by the way, can I ask you a favour?'

'What sort of favour?'

'One of your cars followed me on Saturday,' said Browne, 'and it tried to do the same thing yesterday. I did my very best to help by staying in sight of it but I'm afraid it got hopelessly lost. Never let it be said that I don't cooperate with the police,' he added, complacently. 'Before you leave, why not ask my secretary for a list of my appointments for this week? That way, your detectives will know exactly where I am and they won't go astray again.'

Keedy bristled. Having disliked Browne on their first encounter, he began to loathe him now. The man was hideously overconfident. More to the point, he was wearing a suit that must have cost at least four times the one that the sergeant had on. While Browne could afford the best bespoke tailor in

London, Keedy – punctilious about being smartly dressed – had to scrimp and save to buy a well-cut suit. He was keen to wipe the oily grin from the other man's face.

'I believe that you know where Mr Hubbard is,' he began.

'I wish I did, Sergeant, because I could then get in touch with you at once.'

'You're pulling my leg, sir.'

'No, I'm serious. Much as I hate putting him there, I want Wally safely back in custody. I'd much rather have him serving a sentence for arson than being hanged for murder. I'd prefer to save his life.'

'Do you know the kind of life he'll have in prison?'

'It's not ideal, maybe, but it's preferable to execution.'

'Mr Hubbard may not agree with you.'

'I wouldn't know. We've had no opportunity to discuss the subject.'

'He can't survive without money.'

'I agree.'

'So where would he get it from?'

'Not from me – I wouldn't give him a penny.'

'Why not?'

'I value my freedom too much.'

'It may be in danger if you're lying to me, Mr Browne.'

'I wouldn't *dare*.' He glanced at the newspaper on his desk. 'Anyway, why are you so concerned about finding Wally? You and Inspector Marmion are mentioned in today's paper. You're leading a murder investigation. Isn't it more important to catch someone who has already *killed* than someone who is simply thinking about it?'

167

'We intend to arrest both of them in due course, Mr Browne.'

'But the search for Wally will be less intense now, surely.'

'Not at all,' said Keedy. 'In fact, more detectives have joined the manhunt.' He was pleased to see that he'd finally jolted Browne. 'It means that we have the resources to track down all his friends and associates. You have pride of place among them, sir.'

'I feel honoured.'

'I shouldn't preen too much, if I were you.'

Browne indicated the newspaper. 'It says here that the murder victim was a Ben Croft.'

'That was just a name he was using, sir. We don't know his real identity.'

'Why did he choose that particular name?'

'That will become clear in time.'

'It's a weird coincidence, isn't it?'

'We're not entirely sure that it *is* a coincidence, sir,' said Keedy, evenly, 'but perhaps you can assist me. How will Hubbard react when he reads the news?'

'I haven't a clue, Sergeant.'

'Will he think that someone has already killed Croft and stolen his identity?'

'Ask him when you catch him.'

'Or might he suspect that the man he's after has been party to an exchange so that he can hide under a false name? In short, will he give up the chase?'

'No, he won't.'

'Is that what he told you?'

'I know Wally Hubbard. He *never* gives up.'

'Croft may already be dead.'

'He won't believe that until he's able to dance on the grave before pissing all over it.' He put the newspaper aside and smirked. 'Who's been appointed to keep an eye on me today?'

'You won't be under surveillance, sir,' said Keedy.

'Does that mean you've finally decided to believe me?'

'It means that detectives can be better deployed elsewhere.'

'Ask for a list of my appointments, nevertheless,' suggested Browne. 'You'll be able to see how hard I work then.'

Keedy stood up. 'We're not strangers to hard work ourselves, sir.'

'But it isn't very productive, is it? At the end of each day, I can retire to bed in the knowledge that I've actually achieved something. You can't do that. You've been after Wally for days without getting a sniff of him and you're now dealing with the murder of a man whose real name you haven't been able to find out. You and the inspector were struggling the first time I met you,' he went on. 'The pair of you are really floundering now.'

'Good day to you, Mr Browne.'

'Give my regards to Inspector Marmion.'

Keedy let himself out of the room and came into the outer office. Browne's secretary was behind her desk but he didn't ask for the list of her employer's appointments. The receptionist was in the window, putting some new photos on display. When he went outside, he took the trouble to see which properties were now on the market. Each one of them was worthy of interest, even though all were way beyond his price range. Though he and Alice had talked about buying a house, they might be forced to rent one temporarily until they'd saved up enough money. His eye therefore went enviously to the rental properties. A minute later, an idea struck him and he took out his notebook. He recorded the details of a number of houses and took particular care to get the right addresses before walking to the car on the other side of the road. As Keedy got in, the driver looked over his shoulder.

'Am I going to follow him again today, sir?'

'There's no point,' said Keedy. 'In any case, I've got another job for you.'

Even though it meant a long bus ride, Ellen Marmion was glad of an excuse to visit her brother-in-law and his wife. She saw far too little of Raymond and Lily Marmion. Only at Christmas or on special anniversaries was she certain of meeting them and their children. When she got to the hostel, she was greeted by Lily who took her into the office and offered refreshment. Over tea and biscuits, they were able to talk at leisure for the first time in months.

'I'm sorry we're in such chaos, Ellen,' said Lily.

'That's not your fault. You didn't commit the murder.'

'It was our responsibility to prevent one and we failed. We should have been more vigilant. Raymond keeps chiding himself about that.'

'You can't watch everyone twenty-four hours a day.'

'They wouldn't stand for it,' said Lily. 'They come here for peace, rest and regular food. If we stood over them all day and all night, there'd be complaints and we've had enough upheaval as it is.'

She told Ellen about the fight between the two men and how a pervasive atmosphere of unease still lingered. They had to win back the confidence of the people who routinely used the hostel, she said. The crime had left a stigma.

'I suppose they think it could have been any one of them,' said Ellen.

'They do, but they're wrong.'

'How do you know?'

'You must talk to Harvey. He said that David – or whatever his real name happens to be – was singled out. None of the others had anything worth taking but there was something in David's briefcase that the killer wanted.'

'Have you ever had anybody else in here with a briefcase?'

'No, we haven't. Most only have the clothes they're wearing.'

'Is that what made this man unusual?'

'There were other things as well, Ellen.'

Lily went on to talk at length about the murder victim, explaining what set him apart from the others and how he always had his briefcase beside him. She was just about to offer her visitor a second cup of tea when Raymond came in.

'Ellen!' he cried, embracing her warmly. 'Why didn't you tell me you were here?'

'Lily said you were busy.'

'I've been rushed off my feet but I'd still have found time to speak to you. If you'd come earlier, you'd have found Harvey here.'

'That might not have been such a good idea, Raymond. Your brother likes to keep his work and his home life separate. He rarely tells me very much about the latest case he's working on. It was Lily who explained what had happened.'

'I'm glad it brought you to our door, anyway,' said Lily.

'How is Paul getting on?' asked Raymond, producing a grimace from his sister-in-law. 'Is it that bad?'

'He's getting worse,' she said.

'Why – what's happened?'

She told them about recent incidents and they responded with an amalgam of sympathy and disapproval. Lily was outspoken in her view of her nephew.

'Some straight talking is needed,' she said. 'He needs to be reminded just how much effort you've all put in on his behalf. I wouldn't have tolerated such behaviour from our children. Hasn't his father tackled him?'

'He's done so on the rare occasions when they're actually under the same roof. Harvey has even got an apology out of Paul from time to time. His sister has never managed that,' Ellen went on. 'They always end up yelling at each other.'

'It's difficult to get through to him,' said Raymond. 'When I tried, he was very rude to me. At a time when he most needs help, he spurns it.'

'The latest incident has put me in an embarrassing situation.'

'Why?' asked Lily.

'It's cost me the friendship of a woman at the sewing circle. As for the way Paul treated her daughter . . . well, I still can't believe he was so spiteful.'

Sally Redwood's first day in her new job had been highly satisfactory. She'd learnt her way around the shop, been taught how to handle certain items and, at the end of the day, even been allowed to sell an alarm clock to a customer. Having been at her elbow throughout, the manager was complimentary. Sally was not yet allowed to use the till so Lycett had taken care of the money. There had been a slight distraction that morning. Proud of her daughter's promotion, Patricia Redwood had deliberately gone past the shop to wave to Sally through the window. Sally had blushed. Fortunately, none of the other members of staff had seen her mother.

As a final chore, she began to put away some of the items that had been taken from the window to show to potential customers. It was a delicate operation. If her hand or arm jerked, she was in danger of knocking over a whole display or, worse, causing damage to some of the stock. Sally therefore unlocked the door at the rear of the display cabinet cautiously and inserted the items one by one. It took all of her concentration. When she'd finished, she glanced up and realised that somebody was staring back at her. With his nose pressed against the glass, Paul Marmion looked grotesque. He made an obscene gesture and grinned.

Closing the door, she retreated in fear to the back of the shop.

Marmion seemed to have spent most of the day in perpetual motion, going from one place to another, asking questions, making notes, moving on. He was glad, therefore, to be back at the end of the day in the relative serenity of his office at Scotland Yard. As he prepared a report for the superintendent, he was interrupted by the news that someone wished to speak to him urgently. Her name meant nothing to him but he agreed to see the woman. An agitated Helen Graydon was shown in. Her voice trembled as she introduced herself.

'Do sit down, Mrs Graydon,' said Marmion. 'I can see

that coming here has put something of a strain on you.'

'It has,' she confessed.

'Why did you wish to see me?'

'You *are* Inspector Marmion, aren't you?'

He smiled. 'I like to think so.'

'And are you the *only* person of that name here?'

'I don't think the Metropolitan Police could put up with two of us, Mrs Graydon. Yes, I am the only person of that name. Why do you wish to know?' She lowered her head. 'You can speak freely. Anything you say will be confidential.' With an effort, she raised her eyes to meet his. 'Well?'

'I've been very gullible, Inspector.'

'Have you?'

'When a man called at my house and claimed to be Inspector Marmion, I took him at his word. Then I saw your photograph in the morning paper.'

'Did this man show you a warrant card?'

'No, he didn't.'

'Can you please describe him for me?'

'He was a very personable man in his forties, I suppose,' she said, 'and there was a craggy look to him. But he was extremely polite.'

'And what did he ask you?' She hesitated. 'He asked you where he might find Ben Croft, didn't he?' She nodded her head. 'Mrs Graydon, I'm not the slightest bit interested in how you come to know Mr Croft but I have to tell you that we are eager to find him. If you can give us any indication of where he might be, we'd be more than thankful to you. Believe me, I'm not overstating the situation when I say that it's a matter of life and death.'

She was alarmed. 'Does someone want to *kill* Ben?'

'I'm afraid so.'

'Who would do such a thing?'

'I fancy that you've met the man, masquerading as Inspector Marmion.'

'I *knew* there was something not quite right about him.'

'His name is Wally Hubbard. He's on the run from prison.'

'Dear God!' she exclaimed. 'And I let him into my house.'

'What did you tell him?'

'There was nothing to tell. I had no idea where Ben—where Mr Croft was. I haven't been in touch with him for over a month.'

'What did Inspector Marmion say to that?'

'He was obviously disappointed. Then he thanked me and left.'

Marmion could read the woman's face clearly. In coming to him, she was admitting that she'd been an intimate friend of Ben Croft and the confession had been a painful one. Fearing that he'd be disapproving and intrusive, she was reassured by his pleasant manner. He was not blaming her in any way.

He reached for his notebook. 'I want you to tell me when he came to your house and what he actually said. Take your time, Mrs Graydon. Every detail, however slight, may be of use to us. Now,' he went on, pencil poised, 'start by telling me what he was wearing . . .'

'I will, Inspector. What did you say his real name was?'

'Hubbard . . . It's Wally Hubbard.'

Wally Hubbard was mystified. He'd bought four separate newspapers to read the story. The murder had even shunted the latest news of events in France to an inside page. Marmion's face appeared on two of the front pages and he was mentioned in the other two newspapers. All of them stressed that the murder victim had been carrying papers that identified him as Ben Croft. The first time he'd read that, Hubbard had the sinking feeling that somebody had killed Croft before he could get at him. He felt cheated and was enraged. It was only when he read the details that he realised the dead man was not his target. The police had no idea who he really was and were appealing to the public if they knew of a missing person who matched the description given. Hubbard was relieved. Croft was alive. He could still be stalked.

The problem was that he was no nearer finding the man than he'd been on the day he broke out of Pentonville. At that point, he'd had clear lines of enquiry planned in his mind. Each and every one had ended in a cul-de-sac. Though he'd questioned a number of people, none of them knew where Croft was or where he'd been for the last four of five weeks. The trail was cold.

Relaxing on the bed in the front bedroom, he had the newspapers scattered all round him. The waters had been well and truly muddied. Not only had his intended target disappeared, someone bearing his name had been murdered at a Salvation Army hostel. The streets of London would now be flooded with policemen, making his task all the harder. For the first time, Hubbard began to have doubts. Having relied on help from Maisie Rogers, he was not sure that he'd ever see her again. Having depended on money from Felix Browne, he'd felt betrayed when he'd learnt that his friend had urged Maisie to break away before she was dragged down by Hubbard. All the certainties in his plan had melted away.

He was still bemoaning his fate when he heard a car drawing up outside the house. Crossing to the window, he peeped out in time to see Joe Keedy getting out of the vehicle. Hubbard remembered him only too well. They'd fought each other until the sergeant had overpowered him. He didn't wish for another encounter like that. His cracked ribs had given him great discomfort. Letting go of the curtain, Hubbard took to his heels, racing down the stairs and out through the back door of the house. As he climbed over the fence into the adjoining garden, he wondered which of his friends had contacted the police and how he should make them pay for their treachery.

CHAPTER TWELVE

Joe Keedy had sharp eyes. When the curtain in the front bedroom twitched, he had a fleeting glimpse of a face he'd seen before. It was Wally Hubbard. Hurrying to the front door, he banged on it with his fist. Nobody came to open it. As he peered through the front room window, he heard a door at the rear of the house open and slam shut. Keedy identified the sound at once. Hubbard had bolted. Sprinting back to the car, he told the driver what had happened and ordered him to go slowly round to the opposite side of the block. As the car set off in one direction, he trotted in the other, then swung right, down the first turning. Between them, he hoped, they could cut off the fugitive's escape down one of the side entries to the houses. By the time he reached the car again, Keedy had run well over eighty yards and was puffing slightly. Braced for action, the driver was standing beside the vehicle.

'Any sign of him?' asked Keedy.

'No, sir,' replied the man. 'I kept my eyes peeled in case he popped up from one of the houses but he didn't.'

'It was the same with me. I didn't spot him either.'

'Do you think he's hiding somewhere?'

'He must be,' said Keedy. 'We'll have to start banging on a few doors.'

'Yes, sir.'

'Ask people if they've seen someone climbing into their garden.'

'Right, sir.'

'Let's split up and get busy. Work your way back to the house where we first started – and be ready for a fight if you bump into him.'

'Why is that?'

'Hubbard is the kind of man who will always resist arrest.'

'Thanks for the warning.'

They began the laborious work of questioning residents. Since the block comprised eighty houses, it was going to take time and Keedy held out little hope of success. At the rear of the properties was a veritable rabbit warren of gardens, most with garden sheds or other convenient hiding places. Their quarry could have gone to ground anywhere. In fact, he was already three streets away, walking briskly along, then catching a providential bus that came around the corner. Hubbard didn't care where it was headed. He just needed to put distance between himself and the police. He laughed at the thought of their futile efforts. Keedy and the driver were searching for someone who was no longer there.

* * *

It was a curious experience for Marmion. Once he'd won the confidence of Helen Graydon, the conversation changed completely. She'd come to report the fact that she'd been deceived by someone claiming to be Inspector Marmion. Alone with the real inspector, she warmed to him quickly. He was kind, attentive and sympathetic. Moreover, he seemed to understand the suffering she'd been through. Instead of simply passing on information, therefore, Helen took the opportunity to talk honestly about her situation. The room was turned into a kind of confessional box.

'You must think very badly of me, Inspector,' she said.

'Not at all, Mrs Graydon.'

'In your eyes, I'm a scarlet woman.'

'You're someone who had the misfortune to be led astray. Having spoken to you, I'm quite sure that nothing like this has ever happened before.'

'No, no, I swear it.'

'The person who should bear most of the blame is Mr Croft.'

'Don't let me off the hook that easily,' she said, eyes moistening. 'What I did was wrong – very wrong – and I know it. Every time I look at myself in the mirror, I wonder how I could be so wicked.'

'I'd say you were naïve rather than wicked, Mrs Graydon.'

'If it had not been for the war, this would never have happened.'

'We all have situations like that,' he said, thinking of his son. 'That's not to excuse what's happened. As you freely admit, it was very wrong of you. Only you will know if you can rebuild your marriage when your husband finally returns.'

'Do you think I should *tell* Trevor?'

'I can't give advice on that score.'

'But you must have an opinion.'

'I'm a policeman, Mrs Graydon, not a parish priest.'

'It's so confusing,' she said, face puckering. 'Most of the time, I tell myself that what I did was unforgivable, but every so often' – tears started to stream down her face – 'every so often,' she repeated, 'I feel that, if I had my time over again, I'd do exactly the same thing. He made me feel so *wanted*, Inspector.'

Marmion was careful to avoid passing any moral judgements. In spite of her infidelity, he felt sorry for her. She was still partly in love with Croft. That being the case, he didn't destroy her illusions by telling her that Croft had had a long string of dalliances before meeting her and that his wife was not ill at all. The important thing to remember, he felt, was that Croft had made her feel special. He'd transformed her humdrum life into something with a core of excitement. Rocked as she'd been by his disappearance, she nevertheless wanted him back.

'You can imagine the shock I had this morning,' she said.

'Yes, seeing my photograph in the paper must have shaken you badly.'

'It was not only that, Inspector. The murder victim's name was given as Ben Croft. I thought at first that it was my . . . the man who'd been my friend. Thankfully, it was not. He's still alive, isn't he?'

'We believe so, Mrs Graydon.'

'Then where is he?'

'I wish we knew.'

'And does the person who claimed to be you really want to kill him?'

'I'm afraid so.'

'Then that must be the explanation,' she said, almost cheerily. 'Ben didn't run away from *me*. He simply went into hiding from Mr Hubbard.'

'That could be the explanation,' said Marmion with a non-committal smile. He was touched by the way she'd confided in him but he was also a trifle embarrassed by her frankness. 'When you and Mr Croft were . . . friends, did he take you anywhere?'

'We had an occasional meal together at a quiet restaurant.'

'What I meant was . . . did he take you away for the night?'

'It was only that once.'

'And where did you go?'

'We stayed in Weston-super-Mare. He loved the sea. In fact . . .' A memory surfaced to switch on a light in her eyes.

'Go on,' he encouraged.

'No, no,' she said, 'it was probably only a passing remark.'

'I'd be interested to know what it was, Mrs Graydon.'

'Well, it was something he said the last time we were together. I paid no attention at the time, which is why I'd forgotten it until now. He told me that he'd have to sail somewhere fairly soon.'

'But he didn't tell you where he was going?'

'No, he didn't. I wonder if he was warning me that he had to go away.'

'That may well be the case,' said Marmion, pensively.

'It must be.' She became anxious. 'Will that terrible man visit me again?'

'The false Inspector Marmion? Oh, I very much doubt it.'

'What if he does turn up?'

'Pretend that you take him at his word, Mrs Graydon. It's safer that way. And as soon as he's gone, get in touch with me instantly.'

Keedy did not stand on ceremony. As soon as he got back there, he marched across the outer office, banged on the door of Felix Browne's sanctum and went straight into the room. Browne looked up angrily from the document he was studying.

'You need to learn some manners, Sergeant,' he said, frostily.

'And you need to obey the law, sir. I have to ask you to accompany me to Scotland Yard for questioning.'

Browne was relaxed. 'On what possible grounds, may I ask?'

'There are so many to choose from.'

Keedy explained that, acting on instinct, he'd made a list of empty properties owned by Browne. Thinking that Hubbard might be hiding in one of them, he went from one house to the other. At the last property, he'd seen the escaped prisoner.

Browne was unruffled. 'Where exactly was it?' he asked.

'Number 43 West Terrace.'

'Come with me, Sergeant.'

He took Keedy back into the outer office and unlocked a cupboard. On a series of hooks were the keys to all the properties he owned. Browne searched for the one in West Terrace and, when he found it, lifted three sets of keys off the hook. He dangled them in front of the sergeant.

'They're all here,' he said, shaking them. 'No set is missing.'

'Then how did Hubbard get into the place?'

Browne sniggered. 'What a stupid question!' he exclaimed. 'It's unworthy of you, Sergeant. A man escapes from one of the most secure prisons in Britain and you ask me how he got into a house. He *broke* in, that's how. It would have been child's play for someone like Wally.'

'Yes, but why did he choose that particular house?'

'He liked the look of it, I suppose, and I don't blame him. It's a fine house. I daresay that he did exactly the same as you. He looked at our window display.'

'Then he popped in here to pick up the keys.'

'No, he didn't – on my honour.'

'Let's not use words that have no meaning,' said Keedy, cynically. 'Honour and you are complete strangers. Just look at the facts. Hubbard needs a place to hide and you provided it.'

'I did, but it was unwittingly.'

'Do you expect me to believe that, Mr Browne?'

The other man put the keys back on the hook and locked the cupboard door. He then led Keedy back into the privacy of his office and squared up to him.

'If you don't mind,' he said, 'I'd rather you didn't hurl baseless accusations at me in front of my staff. I'll be happy to accompany you anywhere you wish to answer your questions. But if you're foolish enough to apply for an arrest warrant, then I must warn you I have an excellent lawyer.'

Keedy was checked. He was certain that Browne had provided a place of shelter for his friend but the evidence could be contested. Unless he could prove that the man had handed over the key to the property, he could not secure a warrant.

'I know you don't believe me,' said Browne, solemnly, 'but

185

I give you my word that I have not set eyes on Wally Hubbard since he broke out of Pentonville. I don't *want* to see the mad fool until he's safely back in prison where he belongs.'

'That's very public-spirited of you, sir.'

'I revere the law.'

'Only because you're cunning enough to circumvent it,' said Keedy, looking him up and down. 'Be so good as to give Hubbard a message from me. I found him once and I'll damn well find him again.'

'I hope you do, Sergeant. Look,' he went on, feigning amiability, 'I can't say that I enjoyed seeing you charge into my office like an enraged bull but, since you are here, would you care for something to wet your whistle?'

Keedy left at once.

While it had been an enjoyable reunion with Raymond and Lily Marmion, Ellen did not stay long because they were obviously under great pressure. They'd had some petty crime at the hostel in the past but nothing as serious as a murder, especially one that was shrouded in mystery. Because his family was involved, Marmion was at last in charge of a case that he could discuss in detail with his wife. Ellen looked forward to his return that evening. She'd been in the house less than ten minutes when there was a loud knock on the door. Opening it, she was confronted by the angry figure of Patricia Redwood.

'Oh, hello, Pat,' she said, standing aside. 'Come in.'

'No, thank you,' said the other. 'I'm not staying. I just want to say my piece.'

'Why – what's happened?'

'You son has behaved atrociously.'

'Yes, I know and I've apologised for that. It was bad of him to be so rude to you and Sally when you came here for tea.'

'I'm not talking about that, Ellen.'

'Then what's upset you so much?'

'You obviously don't know, do you?'

'I've been out all afternoon. I've only just got back home.'

'Sally started her new job today,' said Patricia, tight-lipped.

'Oh, yes – how did she get on?'

'She got on extremely well until the end of the day. Sally was putting things back in the window when Paul pressed his nose against the glass and made a filthy gesture at her. I think it's high time you learnt to control your son, Ellen.'

'Are you *sure* that's what he did?'

'Sally doesn't tell lies. She was in tears when she got home. Sally was terrified that your son would follow her. Newsome's is her place of work. What's the manager going to say if Paul keeps turning up to mock our daughter?'

'It won't happen again,' promised Ellen.

'It should never have happened at all.'

'I agree, Patricia. I'll tackle him straight away.'

'If you don't, my husband will do so. He'll be as disgusted as I was when he hears what Paul did. Please control your son.'

'I can't tell you how sorry I am, Patricia.'

'I don't want empty apologies. I want your son to stop frightening Sally.'

'He will,' said Ellen, grimly. 'I give you my word.'

'As for the sewing circle,' said the other, curtly, 'you may as well tell them that I won't be able to come any more. If they ask why, say that I'm no longer happy with the company I keep there.'

The snub was like a punch in the stomach for Ellen. Though she tried to reason with Patricia, it was pointless. The visitor turned abruptly and walked away. Ellen was furious that she'd been put in such an awkward position. Closing the door, she went straight upstairs to Paul's room and called his name aloud. When there was no reply, she opened the door and went in. The room was empty but there was a disturbing new development. Another drawing of Sally Redwood had been pinned to the dartboard for target practice. The earlier one had simply shown her face. This one was a full-length portrait. What made Ellen turn her head away in revulsion was the fact that the girl was stark naked.

When he got back to Scotland Yard, Keedy went immediately to Marmion's office to tell him about the sighting of Wally Hubbard. He described his interview with Felix Browne and was patently annoyed that he didn't have enough evidence to arrest him.

'It *had* to be Browne who gave him access to that house,' he argued.

'I agree, Joe.'

'He's too clever by half. He taunted me about having him followed.'

'At least we know where Hubbard was holed up. That's the second report about him today.'

'Second?'

'Yes, Joe. He's gone back into the acting profession.'

'Eh?'

'After impersonating a prison officer so well, he pretended to be a detective and passed himself off as Inspector Marmion.'

Keedy was incredulous. 'You're joking, Harv.'

'I'm not, honestly. Wally has the cheek of the devil. He rolled up on the doorstep of one of Croft's mistresses and told her that he was me.'

'Did she believe him?'

'Mrs Graydon had no reason *not* to believe him. It was only when she saw my photo in the newspaper today that she realised she'd been misled. Side by side, Wally and I look nothing like each other.'

'Thank goodness this woman had the sense to report the incident.'

'Given her relationship to Croft,' said Marmion, 'it was very brave of her to come forward. She's a married woman, after all. To admit to adultery was a big decision for her.'

He gave Keedy an edited account of his conversation with Helen Graydon, carefully omitting the fact that she'd used him as a sort of father-confessor. The sergeant was inquisitive. 'How did Wally know that she had any connection with Croft?'

'He didn't tell her that.'

'Didn't she ask him?'

'I think she was too humiliated to be found out,' said Marmion. 'In the wrong hands, that information could be dangerous. Someone could blackmail her. Luckily, all that Wally was after were details of Croft's whereabouts. She couldn't help him. As for how he knew about her little secret, I think I know the answer to that.'

'So do I,' said Keedy. 'He went to see Veronica Croft.'

'We're going to do the very same thing.'

'We can ask her why she didn't report Wally's visit to us. That amounts to withholding crucial information from us about an escaped prisoner.'

'Oh, that's not the only thing we have to tax her with, Joe.'

'What else?'

'Well, it turns out that the papers found in the briefcase are not fakes at all. They appear to be genuine. We can show them to Mrs Croft and ask her if she's seen that briefcase before.'

'Were any fingerprints found on it?'

'Quite a few,' replied Marmion, 'but most of them would have belonged to the murder victim. His killer must have handled it but we can't separate his fingerprints from others on there. Chat seemed to think that we'd find Wally Hubbard's dabs on it because of the way disguise was used. I disagreed. Wally might dress up as a prison officer and claim to be Inspector Marmion without turning a hair, but he was not inside that stolen Salvationist's uniform.'

'You're right.'

'He had no motive to kill a stranger.'

'The briefcase is still with Chat,' said Keedy. 'We can tell him about the two sightings of Wally Hubbard when we reclaim it from him. We know what he'll ask, of course.'

'Yes,' said Marmion. 'Where is Hubbard *now*?'

Maisie Rogers was a creature of habit. She always caught the same bus for her evening stint at the Dun Cow. The woman beside her tried to engage her in conversation but Maisie's mind was elsewhere. She nodded as if she'd heard every word and even contributed the odd comment but she was preoccupied with memories of her time with Hubbard the previous night. She was in a cleft stick. If she deserted him, she might ensure her own safety but she'd lose the friendship of someone who'd been very close to her. Yet if she stayed with him, she risked being dragged into a murder as an accessory. Whatever choice she made, it involved pain and remorse. Maisie was still trying to come to a decision when she got off the bus.

It was dusk and the gas lamps shed only a very patchy light. As she walked along the pavement, she saw an old man in a pair of dark glasses coming towards her, tapping away with a white stick. His head and face were virtually invisible under his hat. Maisie was about to walk past him when his hand shot out and gripped her wrist. Before she could protest, she was dragged into a doorway.

'Hello, Maisie,' said Hubbard.

She blinked in amazement. 'Is that you, Wally?'

'Why did you do it?'

'Do what?'

'Set the coppers on to me.'

'I did nothing of the kind,' she protested.

'Then how did they know where I was? I heard a car draw up outside the house. When I peeped out, there was Sergeant Keedy.'

'Well, I didn't tell him where you were. I'm shocked that you even thought that it could be me. Have you forgotten what happened last night and the one before?'

'No,' he said, releasing her wrist. 'I haven't. It meant everything to me.'

'I was going to come back again tonight,' she said, making her decision there and then. 'Why should I warn the coppers?'

He embraced her. 'In my heart of hearts, I knew it wasn't you, Maisie.'

'What happened?'

'I scarpered.'

Embellishing the story, he told her how he'd gone from garden to garden before going down the side entry of a house and waiting until Keedy ran past. Having been shocked at his accusation, she was now laughing. When he removed the dark glasses, she saw the question in his eyes.

'It must have been Felix,' she concluded.

'I trusted that bastard.'

'So did I, Wally, but only so far. He always puts himself first. He told me that he'd only help you from a distance. Felix didn't want to see you himself.'

'What sort of a friend is that?'

'Don't rely on him too much.'

He nodded. 'From now on, I won't rely on him at all.'

Veronica Croft was surprised and troubled when the detectives arrived at the house. She hustled them into the front room, then told her mother that two friends had just popped in for a moment. After a day at the factory, she'd changed into a dress and wore a thick cardigan. She was palpably anxious to make their visit a short one. They had other ideas. Marmion led the questioning.

'Have you had any unexpected visitors lately?' he asked.

'Nobody – apart from Sergeant Keedy, that is.'

'Think again, Mrs Croft.'

'Why?'

'You've overlooked the visit of Wally Hubbard.' She blanched. 'It's no good denying it. Thanks to help given by you, Hubbard went to see a Mrs Graydon and asked if she knew where your husband might be. I've spoken to her. She wondered how he could possibly have got hold of her name.'

'You gave it to him, didn't you?' asked Keedy.

'No, no . . . I didn't,' she said, weakly.

'Don't waste our time, Mrs Croft,' said Marmion, quietly, 'or you'll be charged with aiding and abetting an escaped prisoner.'

Looking from one to the other, she saw that further evasion was unwise. Only complete honesty would satisfy them. She blurted the truth out.

'I had no choice, Inspector. He scared me.'

'How did he do that?'

'It was the way he looked at me. He was so determined.'

'We are equally determined,' said Marmion. 'Now why don't you tell us when he came, how long he was here and what he actually said to you. Oh,' he added, 'and you might care to explain why you didn't alert us immediately.'

'I was going to,' she whispered, 'but he . . . threatened me and my mother.'

'I can imagine him doing that,' said Keedy.

'Mr Hubbard said that he'd *know* if I turned to you.'

Veronica was unnerved. She was in deep trouble. In giving Hubbard the name of Helen Graydon, she'd not only been helping a wanted man, she'd tacitly supported someone bent on the murder of her husband. Only now that she was being called to account for her actions did she realise their serious implications. Hitherto, she'd blocked all thought of consequences from her mind. Now she had to face up to them. She remembered the exact time when Hubbard had called on her and reported most of what he'd said verbatim. Hubbard's visit had clearly made a big impression on her. Veronica had been desperate to get him out of the house. As it was, she'd had to tell a pack of lies to her mother about the stranger. When she recalled what he'd been wearing, Keedy took down the details in his notebook. Hubbard's appearance and attire matched exactly the description given to Marmion by Helen Graydon.

When she finished what had been a searing confession for her, Marmion took the briefcase from the larger bag in which he'd carried it. He offered it to her.

'Have you ever seen this before, Mrs Croft?'

'No, I haven't,' she replied.

'Have a closer look.'

She took the briefcase and examined it briefly before shaking her head.

'No, Inspector, I'm sorry. It's not Ben's. He had a briefcase but it was in much better condition than this.'

'Open it,' said Marmion.

'Why?'

'There's something inside.'

She did as she was told and took out the contents of the briefcase. Her eyes widened in recognition.

'You've obviously seen *those* before,' he observed.

'They belong to my husband.'

'So they are genuine?'

'I think so. Where did you get them?'

'The briefcase belonged to a man who was murdered at a Salvation Army hostel in Stepney.'

Her face creased in dismay. 'How on earth did they get there?'

'We thought that the briefcase might have been stolen from Mr Croft,' said Keedy. 'Apparently, it contained other items when it was first brought into the hostel but they disappeared when the crime took place. All that was left behind is what you can see.'

'I don't understand,' she said, plainly confused. 'Ben took great care of his things. He'd never let anything as important as this go astray. I'm starting to get very worried about him.'

'We can do without any hypocrisy, Mrs Croft,' said Marmion, levelly. 'The fact remains that you gave help to a man whose sole aim in life is to murder your husband. A show of sympathy for Mr Croft comes a little late in the day.'

'What's going on?' she bleated, handing the papers and briefcase back to Marmion. 'Who had these things?'

'It was a man who called himself David.'

'What was his surname?'

'He refused to tell them.'

'But we did notice a coincidence,' said Keedy. 'We saw that your husband's middle name was David – Benjamin David Croft.'

'That wasn't the name he was christened, Sergeant.'

'Wasn't it?'

'David was Ben's own choice. He hated his middle name so he changed it before we were married. The other children used to poke fun at him in school because he had an unusual name. You know how cruel children can be.'

'Oh, yes,' agreed Marmion, 'they can be merciless. So what was Mr Croft's name before he changed it to David?'

'Dieter.'

'That *is* unusual.'

'Why was he called Dieter?' asked Keedy.

'He was named after his grandfather,' she replied. 'They were a German family from Freiburg. My husband used to stay with them when he was much younger. Things have changed since then, of course. Given the way things have turned out, Ben was very glad that he *didn't* have a German name any more.'

Ellen had to wait for hours before she could confront her son. In the interim, her anger and sense of humiliation simmered away. It was bad enough for Paul to sneer at Sally Redwood in the privacy of his bedroom. To do so in public was disgraceful. The temptation to ring her husband was very powerful but Ellen fought it off. Since he was in charge of two major investigations, it would be quite wrong to pester him at Scotland Yard with a domestic matter. If she did so – and the superintendent got to hear of it – there would be unpleasant repercussions for Marmion. Ellen had to handle the situation on her own.

Pacing up and down the living room, she recalled the bruising meeting with Patricia Redwood. She'd been defenceless. Ellen could neither deny nor excuse her son's behaviour. It had cost her the friendship of a woman with whom she had worked happily at the sewing circles since the start of the war. If Paul went unchecked, it could cost his mother a lot more.

When he eventually returned, he let himself into the house and shut the door behind him. Ellen shot out of the living room to bar his way.

'Mrs Redwood called here earlier,' she said with asperity.

'Then I'm glad I wasn't at home.'

'She told me what you did, Paul.'

He shrugged. 'What *did* I do?'

'You turned up at Newsome's and pulled faces at Sally.'

'I wanted to make her laugh, that's all.'

'You went there on purpose to upset her,' she said, 'because you've decided to persecute the girl for some reason. What got into you? Mrs Redwood was breathing fire when she came here. The next time anything like this happens, her husband will come looking for you.'

'Let him,' said Paul, casually.

'Is that all you can say?'

'What do you want me to say?'

'Well, you might start with an apology.'

'Why? I've got nothing to say sorry for.'

'On her first day in a new job,' she said, 'you caused Sally a lot of anxiety and embarrassment. Why didn't you leave her alone?'

'I just happened to be passing the shop and saw her in the window.'

'Don't lie to me, Paul. You watched and waited for the right moment.'

'How do you know?'

'Because I'm beginning to see the way your mind works,' she went on. 'It wasn't enough for you to draw a picture of Sally

197

and throw darts at it. You had to spoil a very special day for her. I'm *ashamed* of you, Paul, thoroughly ashamed. And on top of all that, I find that dreadful portrait of Sally in your bedroom. I was so revolted that I tore it to shreds.'

'You shouldn't have been in my room,' he said, angrily.

'This is our house, Paul,' she yelled at him. 'We're entitled to know what goes on under this roof. Your father will be outraged when I tell him the kind of monster you're turning into. Are you proud of hurting an innocent girl?'

The sheer force of her fury stunned him for a moment. Paul stood there without quite knowing what to do or say. Ellen continued to berate him, pointing out that he used to be so much more considerate towards other people. She demanded to know what it was about Sally Redwood that prompted him to hound her.

'Why have you decided to pick on *her*?'

'I don't know,' he said with a sly grin. 'I just enjoy doing it.'

CHAPTER THIRTEEN

Felix Browne knew the importance of maintaining contacts in the business world. To that end, he dined at his club at least twice a week so that he could mix with friends and associates and pick up the current gossip. Since there were also rivals of his there, he could enjoy boasting to them about the success of his company. After an excellent meal with some cronies, he left with the feeling of being an important figure in the local business community. Though he'd drunk heavily, he felt well able to drive properly. He walked unsteadily around the corner to the side street in which his vehicle was parked.

As he got into the car, someone hopped nimbly into the passenger seat.

'Get out!' snapped Browne.

'Don't you recognise an old friend, Felix?'

'Get out of my car or I'll call the police.'

'That's why I'm here.'

Browne peered at him. 'It can't be . . .'

'Yes, it is,' said Hubbard.

'Where did you come from?'

'I got evicted from that house of yours because you put the coppers on to me.'

'I did nothing of the kind,' said Browne. 'I *helped* you, Wally.'

'That's what it felt like at first. You gave me some money and a place to lay my head. Next minute, I look out of the bedroom window and see Sergeant Keedy coming to get me.'

'Yes, I know about that.'

'Of course, you do. You're the two-faced bastard who ratted on me.'

Hubbard grabbed him by the tie and pulled him close. Browne spluttered.

'I counted on you, Felix.'

'I know . . . and I did my best.'

'That's not how it looks to me, I can tell you.'

'You're strangling me,' gasped Browne. 'Let me go and I'll explain.'

Hubbard released him. 'If you dare to lie to me,' he warned, 'I'll kick seven barrels of shit out of your lousy carcass.'

'And you'd be right to do so, Wally. I'd *never* betray you like that.' He straightened his tie. 'The first I heard about it was when Keedy stormed into my office and accused me of providing you with a hiding place. He's a clever so-and-so. When he suspected that I might have helped you, he made a note of all the empty properties I own and went around them in turn. *That's* how he turned up at West Terrace.'

Hubbard curled a lip. 'Expect me to believe that nonsense?'

'How many coppers showed up?'

'Well . . .'

'It was just Keedy and his driver, wasn't it?'

'Yes,' said Hubbard, recalling the event, 'I suppose it was.'

'There's your answer, then. If I'd told them where you were, they'd have rolled up in numbers and surrounded the whole block. You'd never have got away.'

'That's true.'

'The coppers have been following me by car. When I shook them off easily, Keedy came to the office to lean on me but I gave nothing away. How was I to know he'd look at the window display and make a list of available properties?'

'You weren't,' conceded Hubbard. 'Sorry if I gave you a fright.'

'You're the one who had the fright, Wally. Your eyes must have popped out of your head when you saw Keedy bearing down on the house.'

'I've never run so fast in my life.'

'I'm glad you gave him the slip,' said Browne. 'Keedy tried to arrest me but I swore that you must have broken into the property.' He offered a hand. 'Are we still friends?'

'Yes,' replied Hubbard, shaking hands with him. 'I need somewhere else where I can lie low now.'

'I know just the place. I'll drive you there.'

'Thanks.'

'How is the search going?'

'I've got no leads at all, so far.'

'What about his girlfriends? One of them should know.'

'I tried the last one but she was no help at all. She's looking for Croft herself. He just walked out of her life without a word.'

'So where is he?'

'I don't know but I'll find him eventually.'

'What if he's dead?'

'I'll dig up his corpse and hang it from the nearest lamp post,' said Hubbard, harshly. 'Even in his grave, Ben Croft is not safe from me.'

Between them, they had a great deal to report and, to his credit, Claude Chatfield listened to it all without interruption. Marmion went first, describing the visit from an unnamed woman – he didn't identify Helen Graydon – who'd revealed that she'd been approached by Hubbard. It was Keedy's turn next and he elicited a smile of approval from the superintendent when he explained how he'd made a note of empty properties belonging to Felix Browne and visited each one. Ultimately, he'd found Hubbard. What really excited Chatfield, however, was the information they'd picked up from Veronica Croft.

'So Ben Croft is of German extraction, is he?'

'His mother was from Freiburg, sir,' said Marmion. 'She came to England to stay with relatives who owned a shop here. That was how she met Croft's father. They settled down in London and had one child – Ben Croft.'

'What did the father do?'

'He worked in the Civil Service. His daughter-in-law told us that he had quite an important job. Anyway,' said Marmion,

'Croft was brought up speaking English to his father and German to his mother. Both parents died last year.'

'Did you arrest Croft's wife?'

'No, sir.'

'We thought it was best to wait,' explained Keedy.

Chatfield was puzzled. 'But the woman helped an escaped prisoner, then failed to report the fact that he'd been to see her. Those are criminal acts, Sergeant.'

'They're not ones wilfully committed, sir. She gave information to Hubbard under duress. That doesn't absolve her entirely of blame, of course. However, we felt we should leave her alone for a while.'

'Why is that?'

'Hubbard may come back,' said Marmion. 'He got no help from one of Croft's mistresses so he may well pay another visit to the man's wife. This time, she told us, we'll be informed straight away.'

'I hope she honours that promise.'

'She will, sir. There's no question about that.'

'What about this . . . other woman?'

'She'll report any contact made by Hubbard.'

'This is such a tawdry business, Inspector,' said Chatfield with distaste. 'I hate the notion of having to rely on an estranged wife and an adulteress for information. Neither of them seems to realise that marriage is a lifetime commitment. Their behaviour is deplorable. It's an affront to the vows they took before the altar.'

Marmion and Keedy rarely contradicted the superintendent when he drifted into homiletic mode. As a strict Roman

Catholic, he followed the church's teaching in every detail. He viewed any departure from that as an act of gross debauchery. They were grateful that neither Veronica Croft nor Helen Graydon had been exposed in person to Chatfield's censure. Faced with his finger-wagging scorn, they'd have been far less inclined to cooperate with the police.

'Has there been any response to the press appeal?' asked Marmion.

'Not as yet,' said Chatfield, 'but these are early days. It's a pity we had no photograph of the murder victim to display. A fairly basic description of him is not as eye-catching, even though I asked the press to give it prominence in their respective newspapers. Unfortunately, the description doesn't match any of the missing persons already reported to us.'

'Someone may turn up one day and give us his full name.'

'What was he doing with Ben Croft's papers?' wondered Keedy.

'I've been thinking about that,' said Marmion, reflectively, 'and it may be that he didn't have those papers, after all.'

'But they were found in the briefcase,' said Chatfield.

'That doesn't mean they belonged to him, sir.'

'Stop talking in riddles, Inspector.'

'What if something was taken *out* of the briefcase and the papers were put in?'

Chatfield laughed. 'Can you think of a reason why anyone would do that?'

'Oh yes, sir – it was done to cause confusion.'

'It's done that very effectively,' said Keedy. 'But how did the killer come to possess those papers in the first place?'

'Perhaps they belonged to him, Sergeant.'

'Are you saying that . . . ?'

'It merits consideration,' suggested Marmion. 'It's evident that Ben Croft wanted to disappear. One way of doing that is to become someone else entirely. He could have killed the man known as David, stolen his papers from that briefcase and left his own in their place.'

'That's too far-fetched an idea,' said Chatfield, peremptorily. He thought about it for a moment. 'On the other hand . . .'

There was nobody else to whom she could turn. Ellen Marmion was incensed. Her son's behaviour had been inexcusable yet he refused to apologise for it. Nothing his mother had said to Paul could make him accept that what he'd done to Sally Redwood was truly appalling. He revelled in his dislike of the girl. When she heard the darts thudding into the board again, Ellen knew that he'd drawn another picture of her. As she sat on a bus that took her across the city, she wondered what they could do to make Paul treat people with more respect. If he started to behave towards her other friends as he had towards Sally Redwood, she'd become a social outcast.

Ellen was so eager to see her daughter that she was halfway there before it occurred to her that Alice might not be at her flat that evening. It meant that the remainder of the journey was spent in a state of doubt and anxiety. Alighting in due course from the bus, she more or less ran to the house. To her relief, it was Alice who answered the doorbell and she fell into her daughter's arms.

'Whatever's happened, Mummy?'

'Can't you guess?'

'It's not Paul again, is it?'

'I'm afraid so.'

'Come inside and tell me all about it.'

Alice took her mother into the lounge that was shared by all four of the young women who rented a flat there. Nobody was allowed to entertain guests in their own rooms and male guests were forbidden after a certain time. The landlady's attitude towards the opposite sex was clearly reflected in her choice of furniture. There was no sofa and the individual armchairs were set far apart. Ellen was more than ready to put up with her uncomfortable chair. Alice was there. That was all that mattered.

'I went over to Stepney,' said Ellen. 'Your uncle and aunt send their love.'

'Thank you. How are they?'

'To be honest, they're at sixes and sevens.'

'I read about it in today's paper,' said Alice. 'Uncle Raymond spends all his life coping with crises but this has to be the worst one so far.'

'He and your aunt feel so guilty. They have a responsibility for those staying under their roof. Your Aunt Lily said that they'd let the man down.'

'They mustn't blame themselves.'

'That's what your father told them, apparently.'

'Do they have *any* idea who the victim is?'

'I don't think so, Alice.'

'Well, let's leave them to get on with it, shall we? You didn't come all this way to talk about the murder. Something else is preying on your mind.'

'It is. Paul did something disgusting.'

206

She went on to describe the incident at the jeweller's shop and how shocked she was when she found the naked picture of Sally Redwood in her son's room. Ellen was grateful that neither Sally nor her mother knew about the dartboard. Unable to sit still, Alice leapt up when her mother finally stopped speaking.

'Come on,' she said. 'We'll both go back and take him on right now.'

'No, Alice, that's not the answer.'

'Then what is?'

'I really don't know. I just needed to *tell* someone to get it off my chest.'

'I've said it before, Mummy. The fact is that Paul needs professional help that we can't give him.'

'He refuses to go to the doctor.'

'Then we must get the doctor to come to him. Otherwise, he'll go on losing your friends for you and making your life a misery.'

'He enjoyed it,' said Ellen, helplessly. 'When I asked him why he persecuted Sally, he grinned at me and said that he enjoyed it.'

'That's perverse.'

'It's something far worse than that, Alice. He just has no sympathy for other people and that includes the family. Uncle Raymond and Auntie Lily have a murder to contend with but he shows no real interest in them. For all he cares, they could be complete strangers. Whenever I try to talk to him,' Ellen bewailed, 'he seems to look straight through me. It's a most cruel twist of fate. I've got the most wonderful daughter in

207

the world and a son that I loathe more and more each day.'

She got up to embrace Alice impulsively. Both of them were crying this time.

'It wasn't him.'

'How do you know?'

'Felix wouldn't lie to me. He knew I'd have broken his neck.'

'Where did you see him?'

'I caught him in his car,' said Hubbard, 'which was very handy. He was able to drive me to his office, get the key to this place, then bring me here. I'd put the fear of death in him so he'd do anything to oblige. That's why I got him to drop off this address for you at the Dun Cow.'

'Someone shoved an envelope across the counter to me.'

'Felix would have paid a stranger to do that.'

'Aren't you afraid?'

'No, Maisie.'

'The same thing might happen again,' she said. 'If Sergeant Keedy has a list of all the available properties, he might go around each of them again.'

'This house isn't on the market yet, so nobody knows where it is. The other one was bigger and better,' he said, kissing her, 'but anywhere is special when I've got you beside me.'

They were in a small, furnished house at the end of a terrace. Neither of them was impressed by the taste of the previous occupants but they were ready to endure the hideous patterned wallpaper and the garish curtains. Because it was a temporary stay, they would even put up with the ugly mock-leather furniture and the fading carpet. Maisie had been summoned from the pub for the night. Hubbard was pleased to see that she'd decided to support rather than desert him. For her part, she had lingering doubts about Felix Browne. The first thing she did on arrival was to check all possible exits.

'Relax, Maisie,' he said, pouring her a glass of whisky. 'We're safe.'

'How long will that last?'

'It'll last as long as I need it to.'

'But that could be ages, Wally.'

'We don't know that.'

'You haven't a clue where Croft is.'

'Neither have the coppers, from what I can gather,' he said, handing her the drink and pouring one for himself. 'If *they* can't find him, they can't protect him, can they?'

'Where will you start the search?'

'I'll have another crack at his wife. She needs to be squeezed a little harder.'

'Won't she get in touch with Inspector Marmion?'

'I frightened her too much.'

'What about that tart of Croft's?'

'Which one?' he asked with a laugh. 'There's a lot to choose from.'

'You got her name from his wife.'

'Forget her. She told me all she knew, which was next to nothing. Croft had his money's worth then got rid of Helen Graydon. He's found someone else. It's what he does. He's probably bouncing up and down on top of her right now.'

She sipped her drink and studied him for a moment. He blew her a kiss.

'I'm worried, Wally.'

He chuckled. 'Tell me something new.'

'I feel that they're closing in on you.'

'No, they'd never think of looking here.'

'What if they start following Felix?'

'They've already tried that. He led them in circles then shook them off.'

She held his arm. 'Did you mean what you said?'

'It depends what it was, darling.'

'You told me that . . . well, we could make a go of it.'

'Yes, Maisie, and we will one day.'

'Why not make a start tomorrow? No, listen to me,' she went on quickly, silencing his attempted interruption with a hand. 'You've got money and I've got my savings. We could disappear from London tomorrow without telling a soul – not even Felix. I can find work as a barmaid somewhere and you can stay out of sight until they get fed up with hunting you. I know Birmingham well. Years ago, I used to stay with an aunt there. Manchester's even better, farther away from here. What do you think?'

'Ben Croft comes first.'

'Let's at least go away for a few weeks,' she urged. 'Then you can come back and start afresh.'

'I'm not leaving London until I've got him, Maisie.' He drained his glass in one long gulp. 'That's it. No more argument.'

She choked back a reply. He was in charge.

It was late evening but they were still at work, going over existing evidence and trying to decide where to look for more.

Both were showing early signs of fatigue. Marmion could feel a yawn threatening and Keedy was troubled by an aching back, made all the more painful by the fact that he realised there was no hope at all of seeing Alice for some while.

'You were in the Civil Service at one point, weren't you?' said Keedy.

'I often wish that I still was, Joe.'

'Do you miss it that much?'

'Oh, no,' said Marmion, 'it was dull and repetitive. I was only on the lowest grade. But I always knew when I'd start and when I'd finish. Even though the pay was poor, there was a reassuring safety in being a civil servant. Why do you ask?'

'I was thinking of Croft's father,' said Keedy. 'What grade was he?'

'I've no idea.'

'Don't you think it might be worth finding out?'

'Why?' He saw the expression on the sergeant's face. 'Thank heavens that one of us is awake. You're right, Joe. I should find out. Mrs Croft told us her father-in-law's name, didn't she? What was it?'

'Edwin – Edwin Croft.'

'It was the mention of a German wife that interested me. If I'd married a German girl, the first thing I'd do would be to learn her language.'

'I'd make sure that I *didn't* learn it,' said Keedy, grinning. 'That way, I wouldn't understand a single word when she started swearing at me.'

'A civil servant fluent in German could be very useful during a war, Joe.'

'I was thinking the same thing.'

'Not that we were fighting the Kaiser when Edwin Croft was still employed. But language skills of any kind are important in the defence of the realm. You never know which country is going to fall out with us next.'

'Do you think that something of his father rubbed off on Ben Croft?'

'I'm certain that something of his mother did. According to his wife, he spoke faultless German. At a time like this, that could be a real asset.'

'It would account for the fact that Croft has somehow vanished. How can we find out, do you think?'

'I'm sure that Chat is already making enquiries along those lines,' said Marmion. 'He pounced on the fact that Croft had German connections like a dog spotting a juicy bone. I could see his mind clanking away.'

'Will he get anywhere, Harv?'

'If he doesn't, it won't be for lack of effort. I know we laugh at Chat but he sticks at something when he gets his teeth into it. Meanwhile, I'll start looking into Edwin Croft's career in the Civil Service.'

'It might just be the answer,' said Keedy, shaking off his weariness. 'If Ben Croft is working as a spy, we might find out what's really happening.' He was dubious. 'I don't know, though. Would a seasoned lady-killer like him be employed as a secret agent?'

'I don't see why not, Joe. I have a different problem.'

'What is it?'

'Croft could well be a spy,' said Marmion, thoughtfully, 'but . . .'

'Well?'

'Which side is he on?'

At the end of a long and taxing day, Raymond and Lily Marmion were finally able to relax and speak to each other properly for the first time.

'It's ridiculous,' he complained. 'We've been under the same roof yet I've hardly seen you.'

'We both had other things to do, Raymond. You spent all that time with your brother while I had other duties. Oh, and there was Ellen's visit, of course.'

'I wish I'd had more time to talk to her.'

'She really came to pour her heart out about Paul.'

'I know. We only exchanged a few words but I could see how agitated she was. The problem seems to be escalating.'

'Paul used to be such a nice, friendly boy.'

'That was before they put a rifle in his hands and taught him how to kill,' said Raymond, darkly. 'The war has transformed people like Paul. They've come back with a burning resentment and lash out when you least expect it. You'd think he'd calm down as time went on but the opposite has happened.'

'Yes, Ellen told me everything. She fears the worst.'

'You mean that . . . ?'

'I do, Raymond. She's afraid that he might have to be locked up in a mental hospital eventually. That's how bad he is.'

'I do hope it never comes to that.'

After discussing Ellen's worries, they turned to their own. Raymond had news.

'Less than half an hour ago, I had a call from the local

police station,' he told her. 'They found the uniform that was "borrowed" from our bandsman.'

'Where was it?'

'It had been stuffed in a garden shed a few hundred yards from here. The killer had used it as his changing room, apparently. I'm glad we've got it back. Replacing it would have been expensive.'

'Will the bandsman still want to wear it?' asked Lily.

'What do you mean?'

'It was used as a disguise by the killer.'

'That wouldn't worry him, Lily. In cold weather like this, the bandsman will just be delighted to get it back again. '

'It's a shame he didn't get a good look at his attacker.'

'He was able to give Harvey some useful information. For instance, he was only hit hard enough to make him lose consciousness briefly. Then he was put carefully on a thick pile of straw. It was almost as if his attacker was trying to make him comfortable.'

'The man was a *killer*, Raymond.'

'A killer with a conscience, it seems.'

'There's no such thing.'

'I disagree.'

'If he'd had a conscience, he couldn't possibly have committed a murder.'

'Harvey told me, privately, that it might be something else.'

'What did he mean?'

'Well, he was struck by how quick and professional the man had been. He was in and out of here in a matter of minutes and none of us was ever aware of him. It was no random killing. David was carefully targeted.'

'A murder is a murder, Raymond.'

'Harvey mentioned another word to me.'

'What was it?'

'Assassination.'

Marmion was driven home from Scotland Yard through a blanket of darkness. No street lamps were alight and blinds were drawn in every house. Zeppelin raids were still a constant threat so all kinds of cautionary measures had been enforced. It was almost midnight when Marmion was dropped off outside his house. Hoping that his wife would be fast asleep in bed, he let himself in as quietly as possible but Ellen nevertheless heard him. She hurried out of the living room in her dressing gown and slippers and threw her arms around him.

'What a lovely welcome!' he said. 'But you should be in bed, Ellen.' When she pulled her head back, he saw the distress in her face. 'Oh, no,' he sighed, 'not again, surely.'

'I'm afraid so.'

'What's he done this time?'

'It's late,' she said, 'and we're both tired. I'll tell you in the morning.'

'No, no, I want to hear it now.'

'But you've had such a hard day, Harvey. It's unfair on you.'

'This is important.'

He took her into the living room and they sat down side by side on the sofa. Fighting off fatigue, she told him about the way that Paul had frightened Sally Redwood at the jeweller's shop and how the girl's mother had come to the house in a temper and abruptly severed her friendship with Ellen.

'That must have been horrible for you,' he said, sympathetically.

'It was awful. What's going to happen if Patricia tells other people about it? Thanks to Paul, I'll lose even more friends.'

'Did you point that out to him?'

'I tried to, Harvey, but he doesn't listen.'

'I'll *make* him listen.'

'Wait,' she said as he tried to get up, 'there's something else you need to know.'

When she told him about the second drawing of Sally Redwood, she was quivering with embarrassment. The news shocked and disgusted him. Ellen had to grab him to stop him charging off upstairs.

'Don't go, Harvey,' she pleaded. 'It's too late.'

'I don't care about that.'

'I don't want you to get involved in a row with Paul.'

'Somebody has to, Ellen, and it's not right to leave it to you. He's got to show some respect for that girl. We can't let him stalk her the way he did. It will terrify her. Paul has got to have the facts spelt out to him. He can't go on like this or he'll have to be put away somewhere.'

'That's what I said to Alice – and to Lily.'

'Then it's time it was said to Paul himself.'

'Don't be too harsh on him.'

'How can you say that after the way he's treated you?' he asked. 'He's ignored you, insulted you and landed you in humiliating situations. That's it, as far as I'm concerned, Ellen. I don't care two hoots if it's late and he's asleep. I'm going to roust him out of bed and give him a good talking to.'

'I don't think he'll listen, Harvey.'

'We'll see about that!'

With Ellen at his heels, he marched out of the room and up the stairs. Determined to confront their son, they went along to his room and pounded on Paul's door. When there was no response from within, he knocked even harder then flung the door open and switched on the light. What they saw made them gasp. The room was empty. The bed had been made and everything had been tidied away. Most disturbing of all was the fact that the window had been left open and a stiff breeze was making the curtains swing to and fro. The window had clearly been his means of escape. Marmion tugged the curtains back and gazed down at the garden.

'Where the hell has he gone?' he exclaimed.

CHAPTER FOURTEEN

It was early when the telephone rang but Raymond Marmion was already up and about. When he heard his brother's voice on the line, he anticipated good news.

'Hello, Harvey,' he said, hopefully. 'Have you found out his name yet?'

'Whose?'

'The murder victim, of course.'

'No, we haven't.'

'Do you know who the killer is, then?'

'I'm afraid not.'

'Oh.'

Marmion's voice was strained. 'That's not why I rang.'

'I'm sorry. I assumed that it was.'

'Paul's disappeared.'

Raymond was stunned. 'What do you mean?'

'Exactly that,' said Marmion. 'When we went to his room last night, there was no sign of him. He'd put some clothing in a bag and climbed out through the window.'

'That's dreadful!'

'I've been walking the streets all night. Ellen is distraught. That's why I rang. I don't suppose that Lily could find a moment to pop over here? I don't like leaving Ellen alone. She needs company.'

'Lily will be only too glad to help.'

'They talked about Paul only yesterday. Lily was very supportive.'

'Have you any idea where he might have gone?'

'None at all,' admitted Marmion. 'That's what's so upsetting, Raymond. He just left without a single word.'

'Didn't he leave a note of some kind?'

'No, he didn't.'

'Are there any friends he might go to?'

'We can't think of any. As you know, he joined up with the rest of the football team. Over half of them were killed in action. One of them, Colin Fryatt, was Paul's best friend and that made a deep impression on him. The survivors from the team are still in a trench somewhere in France.'

'So what are you going to do?'

'I've raised the alarm so the Metropolitan Police will be looking for him but he may not even be in London any more. He could be a hundred miles away. The worst of it is,' said Marmion with concern, 'that we don't know *why* he went.'

'Did you have a row with him?'

'I was about to when we went to his room. But he wasn't there.'

'What a time for this to happen!' said Raymond. 'You're already heading a murder enquiry and trying to recapture a prisoner on the run. How can you do either properly when Paul has vanished?'

'That's something I'll have to discuss with the superintendent.'

'Do that. As for Lily, I'll send her over this morning.'

'I can't thank you enough.'

'What about Alice?'

'She needs to be told. I'll leave a message at work for her.'

'It must have been a terrible night for you, Harvey. I can hear the strain in your voice. You and Ellen have our sympathy.'

'We just want to know where he is,' said Marmion, trying to collect himself. 'If he's that unhappy at home, we can find somewhere else for him. We simply want reassurance, Raymond. You read frightening things about lads who've been injured in battle and sent home. Some of them are in despair over their disabilities and feel they have no future. There have been suicides.'

'That's not what's happened in this case,' said Raymond, firmly, 'so you can put it out of your mind. Paul wouldn't have gone to the trouble of packing some clothes if he'd decided to take his own life. We deal with despair all the time, so I know the signs. I didn't recognise any of them in Paul.'

'Thanks, Raymond. That helps.'

'Ring me again if you need to.'

'You've already given me the sensible advice I needed,' said

Marmion, gratefully. 'We must stop thinking the worst and try to be more positive.'

Raymond was about to bid his brother farewell when an idea nudged him.

'I've just had a stray thought, Harvey.'

'What is it?'

'No, no,' said the other, having doubts, 'I'm probably very wide of the mark.'

'I'd like to hear what you're thinking, nonetheless.'

'Well, this may sound strange but . . . is there any chance that Paul might have gone off to join the army again?'

Wally Hubbard was out of luck. Having learnt from Veronica Croft where she worked, he was outside the factory as people streamed towards it for their shift. He hoped to intercept her and get some more information out of her but the chance never came. When Veronica finally appeared, she was in the middle of a gaggle of women. They swept past without giving him so much as a glance. Hubbard waited until he saw a square-jawed, middle-aged man walking on his own.

'Half a mo,' he said, stepping in front of him. 'You work here?'

'Yes, why do you want to know?'

'What's it like?'

'It's not bad. Money's gone up since the war.'

'What about all these women?'

The man grinned. 'They brighten the place up.'

'Do they work the same hours as you?'

'Same hours but less pay, thank goodness.'

'That's as it should be,' said Hubbard with an ingratiating

smile. 'We can't let them take over from us, can we? So what time will their shift finish?'

'Six o'clock on the dot.'

'Thanks.'

After patting him on the arm, Hubbard began to pick his way through the oncoming crowd, resolving to be back when Veronica came out of the factory.

Ordinarily, Alice Marmion took care to keep out of the inspector's way as much as possible. Thelma Gale was a martinet. She set high standards for the women under her and was renowned for the severity of her reprimands. Alice had suffered at her hands a number of times. When she was summoned by the inspector again, therefore, she went in trepidation. Her fears were groundless. The woman actually smiled at her for once and handed her an envelope.

'Your father left this for you,' she said.

Alice took it from her. 'Oh, thank you, Inspector.'

'Aren't you going to open it?'

Alice hesitated, having intended to do so in private. Thelma Gale stood up.

'Your father did indicate the gist of his message,' she said, softly.

'Did he?'

'He wouldn't have taken the trouble to come here unless it was important.'

'No, no,' said Alice, 'he wouldn't.'

When she opened the letter, the first line was enough to make her blench.

'I may have to ask for time off, Inspector,' she said, close to panic.

'Calm down, Constable.'

'My brother has disappeared. I'm needed elsewhere.'

'And where is that supposed to be?'

'I don't know but—'

'Why don't you read the rest of the letter before you start asking for leave?'

Heart pounding, Alice did as she was told and saw that her father was actually advising her to get on with her patrol as usual then to go home to see her mother afterwards. He just wanted her to be aware of the emergency. Alice's mind was in turmoil as she wondered why her brother had left and where he could possibly be. The inspector interrupted her febrile speculation.

'There's nothing you can do,' she said with uncharacteristic sympathy. 'The word has gone out and everyone is looking for your brother. Listen to your father's counsel. Get on with your job and try to remain calm.'

'How can I do that?' asked Alice, worriedly.

'You've been trained to cope in an emergency.'

'But this is my *brother*, Inspector.'

'He'll be found in due course. Meanwhile, you'll be doing a valuable job in the Women's Police Service. That will be all. Goodbye.'

Alice left the office in a daze.

Marmion was having a similar experience in Claude Chatfield's office. He was finding reserves of kindness and compassion in his superior that he never suspected were there. On hearing the news about Paul, the other man had been quick to help.

'Take as much leave as you require, Inspector,' he said.

'I don't need any at all, sir.'

'Of course you do. I'll draft in someone to replace you.'

'I've no wish to be replaced.'

'But your son is missing.'

'Yes, Superintendent,' said Marmion, lips tightening for a moment. 'I have a light bulb in my brain constantly flashing that message. It's one of the reasons I must stay at the helm of the two investigations. They'll give me something else on which I can concentrate. That's important to me.'

What he didn't say was that he was not going to yield up control to anyone else. Marmion was sufficiently vain to be stung by the threat of being replaced by a colleague. Having worked so intensely on the two investigations, he was eager to see both through to their resolution. He also knew how unhappy Joe Keedy would be if forced to work under a new inspector and having to explain everything to him painstakingly. Though Chatfield was showing genuine sympathy to someone in distress, Marmion refused the offer of time off.

'How is your wife coping?' asked the superintendent.

'My sister-in-law is with her. She'll be a great help.'

'What about your daughter?'

'She's aware of what's happened, sir.'

'I can't imagine how you and your wife felt at the moment of discovery.'

'It's not something I'd care to go through again, sir. However,' said Marmion, straightening his back, 'I'd prefer to forget about it for the moment and address myself to the problems in hand.'

'You have my utmost admiration.'

It was such an unlikely compliment that Marmion was tempted to ask for a written version of it, if only to astound his colleagues. None of them would believe that the peppery and self-regarding superintendent could be so considerate.

'Did you do what I suggested?' asked Marmion.

'Of course,' replied Chatfield. 'I've arranged for you to interview the head of the Civil Service this very morning. He's expecting you.'

'Thank you, sir.'

'He's a crusty old fellow so don't expect too much from him.'

'What about my other advice?'

'That's more difficult to follow, Inspector.'

'There must be some way of making contact, sir.'

'Not at our level, alas,' said Chatfield. 'British Intelligence is, by its very nature, notoriously secretive. I certainly have no authority to secure a meeting. The only person who can do that is the commissioner.'

'I'd be happy to go with Sir Edward,' volunteered Marmion.

'He's better off on his own. He speaks their language.'

The sight of two well-dressed, well-groomed elderly gentleman seated in high-backed armchairs as they drank tea would have made most observers assume that they were old friends discussing their retirement plans. In fact, each of them was still highly active in his respective post. Sir Edward Henry was the Commissioner of the Metropolitan Police and his companion, Patrick Fielden, was, in addition to being a deputy commissioner, the Head of Special Branch. Well known to each other, they were in the latter's office. Fielden was a fleshy man in his sixties who'd cultivated a luxuriant moustache to replace his thinning hair. He had a gift for talking at great length yet giving nothing whatsoever away. The commissioner had spoken on the telephone to him the previous day and explained what he wanted.

'I'm not sure that we can help you, Sir Edward,' said Fielden.

'That's disappointing.'

'I understand your problem. When you have a murder of a man with a fake identity by an unknown assailant, it's tempting to think – among other possibilities – that you may be dealing with a crime that involves an enemy within.'

'It's a theory put forward by Inspector Marmion and I hold his instincts in high regard. His report noted how swift and professional the killer had been.'

'That doesn't mean he's a German spy,' warned Fielden. 'He could equally well be an Irish Republican. Since the Easter Rising, they've been causing us major headaches. Some of them are trained assassins.'

'We feel that there's a German element somehow.'

'That's only supposition.'

'This fellow, Croft, had a mother who was born in Freiburg.'

'Yet his father, you say, is a true-born Englishman and therefore more likely to have had the major influence over the son. When the war broke out,' said Fielden, as if addressing a larger audience than one man, 'we had some 50,000 or so Germans living in these islands. That's the largest immigrant group after the Irish and Jewish communities. We acted promptly and introduced the Aliens Restriction Act. Within a month of the start of hostilities, we interned over a third of German residents and many more have been added since.'

'What are you telling me, Patrick?' asked the commissioner.

'Don't give way to overexcitement.'

The commissioner smiled. 'I've never been accused of that before.'

'Spy fever is something that was foolishly whipped up by the press and there are sensational novels to make it worse.'

'You don't need to lecture me on that subject. In the autumn of 1914, my officers arrested 9,000 people suspected of being German agents. We were left with red faces when not a single one was convicted.'

'There *are* German spies at work here but we've been able to catch or neutralise most of them. What they seek is intelligence about secret government decisions. I doubt if any of them believe that they can find it in a Salvation Army hostel.'

'That depends on what was in the murder victim's briefcase.'

'Have you ever considered that it might simply have been money?'

'Yes, of course we have.'

'Murder for gain is an obvious motive.'

'My detectives are too experienced to plump for obvious motives,' said the other, tartly. 'They like to look beneath the surface of a crime. In this case, they've identified a possible connection with a German agent.'

'Which one is he?' said Fielden, quizzically. 'Is he victim or killer?'

'We have no idea, Patrick. I trust you to assist us on that score.'

'That's impossible.'

'Why?'

'You have insufficient evidence.'

'I gave you the name of Ben Croft. Have you found him in your records?'

'No, we haven't.'

'May we have access to them?'

'You wouldn't know where to look. They comprise 250,000 report cards and some 27,000 personal files on potential dissidents. Besides, they're strictly confidential.'

'We expect cooperation.'

'Then you must bring more compelling evidence.'

'I didn't expect you to be quite so obstructive, Patrick.'

'We have our job to do, Sir Edward, and you have yours.'

'Part of my job is to assist Special Branch. I'm shocked that you are unable to reciprocate so willingly. It's a matter I'll take up with the Home Secretary.'

'He's a busy man. You may have a long wait for an answer.'

The commissioner gave him a long, hard look. 'Why do I get the feeling that you're concealing something from me?'

'I've told you the truth. We have no interest in Ben Croft.'

Fielden talked at length about his remit and his support from the highest reaches of government. The commissioner knew that the other man was creating a deliberate smokescreen. When he rose to go, he asked a final question.

'If Croft *was* retained by you as a British agent, would you admit that?'

Fielden's moustache twitched. 'I'll look into the matter, Sir Edward,' he said, non-committally. 'That's all I can promise.'

* * *

Alice Marmion found it hard to keep her mind on her job. As she and Iris Goodliffe walked their beat, they talked about Paul incessantly. Iris was full of sympathy and kept suggesting places where he might have gone. Alice ruled them out immediately. She had her own theory.

'Paul isn't going anywhere in particular, Iris.'

'He must be.'

'I don't think he has a destination. He's not going *to* someone or somewhere. He's simply going away from us. We've driven him to it.'

'You mustn't blame yourself, Alice.'

'It's the truth. We made it impossible for him to stay.'

'I don't believe that,' said Iris with sudden passion. 'You all loved him and cared for him. Yes, you had rows with him. That happens in families. But you did nothing at all to make him feel unwanted.'

Alice was touched by her colleague's uncritical backing. It meant a lot to her. Before she could thank Iris, her attention was diverted. A car pulled up at the kerb beside them and Keedy jumped out. Alice flung herself instantly into his arms. Iris walked quietly away to leave them alone.

'I can't stop,' said Keedy. 'I just had to see you.'

'Where are you going?'

'I've got to interview a potential witness. Knowing your beat, I asked the driver to make a detour in the hope of finding you.'

'It's so wonderful to see you, Joe.'

'Your father told me that he'd sent you a letter. You know the worst.'

'I still have trouble believing it.'

'Paul will be all right,' he said, soothingly. 'He knows how to look after himself. Three or four months ago, it would have been different. His eyesight was still very poor then.'

'What did we do *wrong*?' she cried.

'Nothing at all.'

'Then why did he run away from us?'

'It looks as if he just wanted some freedom.'

'He already had that, Joe. He could have gone anywhere he wanted.'

'Paul saw things differently.'

'Why did he leave no word of explanation?'

'It could be that he went on the spur of the moment.'

'Or it could be that he wanted to hurt us.'

'Don't think that, Alice. Have more faith in your brother.'

'You're right,' she said. 'I should give Paul the benefit of the doubt.'

He squeezed her by the shoulders. 'I must go,' he said, apologetically. 'I'll find a moment to see you again very soon. Go on – catch Iris up and tell her what a gorgeous man I am.' He kissed her on the cheek. 'Goodbye.'

Keedy got back into the car and waved through the window as it shot off. Alice felt somehow better. It was the briefest of meetings but it had lifted her spirits. As she hurried to catch Iris up, she was smiling through her tears.

Marmion was grateful. During his time as a humble member of His Majesty's Civil Service, he thought he'd led a fairly contented existence. It was only when he resigned in order to join the police force that he realised what he'd been missing.

He'd never for a moment regretted his decision. As he entered the building where he had once worked as a clerk, he felt a surge of gratitude that he was no longer employed there. He now found the whole atmosphere oppressive. Marmion had to wait until the head of the civil service, Brian Pitter, was ready to see him. Eventually, he was shown into an office that was three times the size of the one he had at Scotland Yard and far tidier. Pitter gave him a cordial welcome. He was a thin, almost ascetic man in his sixties with white hair like a sprinkling of snow and false teeth that were slightly too large for his mouth.

When they settled down on their chairs, Pitter eyed him shrewdly.

'You're not at all how you look in the newspapers, Inspector.'

'Is that good or bad?'

'Oh, it's very good. Press photos make you look slightly sinister.'

Marmion laughed. 'You're the first person who's ever said that, sir.'

'I must say this is quite exciting,' said Pitter. 'I've never been involved – even marginally – in a murder investigation.'

'All we need from you is some background information.'

'Might it help to unmask the killer?'

'It might point us in his direction, sir,' said Marmion.

'Then let's get down to business, shall we?'

The older man reached for a thick file on his desk and flicked it open. He then took the pince-nez that dangled from a ribbon around his neck and fitted them on his nose with extreme care. The dentures came into sight.

'Superintendent Chatfield explained what you are after,' he

said. 'When we talked on the telephone, I got the impression that he is a highly competent man.'

'That's what he is, sir,' conceded Marmion.

'Razor-sharp mind, clear diction, sense of authority – I like all that.'

'What have you found for us?'

'Well, you'll be able to examine the file for yourself as long as it doesn't leave the building. It's a record of the career of Edwin John Croft. In essence,' Pitter went on, 'it's the story of an archetypal civil servant, of an intelligent and deeply loyal man who worked hard and secured a series of well-deserved promotions. I wish that everyone we employ had the same dedication to our values.'

'Is there any mention of his wife, sir?'

'Yes, he was married to an Eva Lindenmeir and they had one child.'

'Ben Croft.'

'Benjamin Dieter Croft, to be exact.'

'He later changed his middle name, sir.'

'Really? We've no record of that.'

'What sort of work did his father do?'

'It was the usual routine of a senior civil servant,' said Pitter. 'That's to say it was largely administrative and well within his capacities. As you'll see, there were times when he was seconded abroad because of his linguistic skills.'

Marmion was curious. 'Where did he go?'

'Well, the first place was South Africa during the Boer War. We were fighting the Afrikaners but everyone knew that they were getting support from Germany. Who better to send than a man who spoke both German and Dutch like a native?'

'And was Mr Croft of any real use when he was there?'

'Oh, yes,' said Pitter. 'He won a medal for his work.'

Ellen was thrilled to see her again. The moment that Lily stepped into the house in her Salvationist's uniform, Ellen stopped weeping. After dabbing at her eyes, she put the handkerchief away in the pocket of her apron and fell on her visitor.

'It's so silly, isn't it?' she said. 'We don't see each other for months then we meet two days in a row.'

'Yes,' agreed Lily. 'Emergencies have a habit of bringing families together.'

'I've been sick with worry.'

'I can imagine.'

'Paul didn't even leave us a note.'

'Is that so surprising? You told me how uncommunicative he was. You said that he seemed to live in a world of his own.'

'That's true, Lily.'

'Raymond and I just wonder what it was that prompted him.'

'Prompted him?'

'Well, if he was going to walk out of here, why didn't he do it during the daytime? He wouldn't have needed to climb through his bedroom window then. Why go when he did?'

'That was my fault,' said Ellen, guiltily. 'I had another argument with him about Sally Redwood.'

'Yes, you told me yesterday how rude he'd been to her.'

'He did something far worse than that, Lily.'

She explained what had happened at the jeweller's shop and how Patricia Redwood had come to the house to complain. Lily listened with growing unease. When Ellen told her about the way she'd confronted Paul, she said she believed that it was the trigger for his disappearance.

'In other words,' she wailed, 'it was *my* fault.'

'That's not true at all, Ellen.'

'I yelled at him, so he ran away.'

'You were right to yell at him. What he did was . . . beyond belief. From now on, Sally Redwood will be afraid to look out of the window of that shop in case she sees Paul pulling faces at her. It's the kind of thing a *child* would do,' said Lily. 'You don't expect it of someone in his twenties.'

Ellen shook her head. 'We've learnt to expect anything of Paul.'

Taking charge, Lily brewed a pot of tea and, while she was doing it, talked about the problems they were having at the hostel. In talking about the murder and its aftermath, she made Ellen see her family crisis in a different perspective. It was only when they moved to the living room that they talked about Paul again.

'Did you hear what Raymond thinks?' asked Lily.

'Yes, Harvey told me. He thinks that Paul might try to enlist.'

'Do you agree?'

'No, I don't. Technically, he's still unfit for service.'

'That hasn't held other young men back. As soon as they're on their feet again, they want to return to the front. If they're turned down, some of them change their names, go to another recruiting station and tell a pack of lies to get accepted.'

'Paul wouldn't do that, Lily. When he first came home, he

talked about wanting to go back to France but his eyesight was bad and all those shrapnel wounds hadn't healed. Over the last couple of months,' said Ellen, 'he's turned against the army and the way it's treated him.'

'So where do *you* think he might be?'

Ellen was dejected. 'I think he's a long way away from his family. That's what all this is about, Lily. Paul *hates* us.'

Claude Chatfield was fizzing with fury. Expecting the commissioner to return with vital information, he'd been told that Sir Edward had been stonewalled at the Secret Service Bureau. Marmion and Keedy watched the superintendent pace up and down his office with his hands behind his back, occasionally bringing them into play to gesticulate. Chatfield said that they must find a way to demand cooperation. It was only when his superior finally ran out of steam that Marmion was able to speak.

'I had a more rewarding visit,' he declared.

'What did you find out?' asked Chatfield, perching on his desk.

'Before I tell you that, sir, let me make a comment on what you've just told us. The Secret Service Bureau operates by its own rules. We can never penetrate it completely. If, as it seems, Mr Fielden was deliberately unhelpful, it may be that he doesn't *wish* the murder to be solved.'

'Why not?' asked Keedy.

'What if the victim was a British agent? He'd want to cover that up.'

'That would be perverting the course of justice,' said

Chatfield, rapping his knuckles on the desk. 'Nobody is above the law.'

'During a war, I'm afraid that they are. They control information, sir. That gives them immense power.'

'Well, they'll have a fight on their hands. Sir Edward is going to tackle the Home Secretary in person.'

'I could be wrong, of course,' admitted Marmion, 'but I remain suspicious. However, let me speak on a happier note . . .'

He described his interview with the head of the civil service and the man's readiness to let him see confidential files. Like him, they were interested to hear that Edwin Croft had been sent to South Africa and subsequently deployed elsewhere abroad for short periods.

'What are you telling us, Inspector?' asked Chatfield. 'Croft was a *spy*?'

'Mr Pitter went out of his way to explain that he was not gathering intelligence in any of his deployments. His role as a translator was strictly functional.'

'*Our* job is strictly functional,' said Keedy, 'but we don't expect to get a medal for it. There must have been danger involved.'

'I saw no mention of it in the file.'

'What *did* you see?'

'It was a record of an exemplary civil servant,' said Marmion. 'It's a shame that his son didn't follow in his footsteps. Had he done so, a lot of young women would have been spared the pain of a broken heart.'

'This case gets more frustrating by the hour,' said Chatfield, irritably. 'What about you, Sergeant? Do you have anything of interest to report about our escaped prisoner?'

'I believe so, sir. There's been another sighting of him.'

'Where and when?'

'It was close to the Dun Cow, sir. It's where Maisie Rogers works.'

'And who was your witness?'

'Jack Ryde,' said Keedy. 'He's an old man who plays the accordion at the pub on certain nights. When he went there yesterday evening, he caught a glimpse of Maisie Rogers talking to someone in the gloom. Ryde admits that the light was poor but he swears that the man was Hubbard because of the way he walked.'

'It's true,' said Marmion. 'Wally does have a distinctive gait.' He turned to Keedy. 'How does Ryde come to know him?'

'He worked in one of Hubbard's pubs for years until he was sacked – unfairly, he says.'

'So he has an axe to grind.'

'Did he challenge Maisie Rogers about talking to Hubbard?' asked Chatfield.

'No, sir, he had more sense than to do that. She'd have been bound to deny it then run off to warn Hubbard afterwards.'

'Is Ryde a credible witness?'

'He is when he's sober, sir. Last night, he was tottering. It was only when he woke up this morning that he remembered he had something useful to tell us.'

'That settles it,' said Chatfield, moving away from the desk. 'Arrest the woman and I'll get the truth out of her.'

'That would be a mistake, sir,' contended Marmion. 'This man has only told us what we already knew. Maisie Rogers *has* been helping Hubbard. If we arrest her, however, we simply alert him. We tried having Felix Browne tailed and that misfired. I think it's time to switch surveillance to her. What's your opinion, Sergeant?'

Keedy nodded. 'I agree. She'll be easier to follow than Felix Browne.'

'Yes, Maisie will be on foot.'

'What if she *doesn't* make contact with Hubbard?' asked Chatfield.

'There's no chance of that happening, sir,' Marmion said, confidently.

'Why not?'

'He was in Pentonville for a fair amount of time.'

'That's right,' said Keedy, cheerfully. 'Hubbard has had enough of celibacy. He's ready to enjoy life to the full again now. *That's* why Maisie will go to him.'

CHAPTER FIFTEEN

Staying well behind her, Hubbard bided his time. When she came off work, Veronica Croft was part of a crowd that hurried past him. She was involved in an animated conversation with a group of workmates. One by one, they broke away. Eventually, it was Veronica's turn to bid farewell and strike out on her own. When she walked off down a side street, Hubbard quickened his step to catch her up. Making sure that nobody could see them, he suddenly pounced on her with a hand over her mouth.

'I'm not going to hurt you,' he said, gently. 'I just need your promise that you won't be stupid enough to call for help if I let you go. Is it a deal, Veronica?' She nodded eagerly and he released her. 'Good girl.'

'There's nothing more I can tell you.'

'I believe there is.'

'The police have been after me,' she said, nervously. 'Because I didn't report that I'd seen you, they said I'd committed a crime.'

'Yes, you did but you were forced into it. That makes a difference.'

She looked around. 'What if someone sees us together now?'

'What if they do? All they'll see is a handsome man talking to an attractive woman. There's nothing suspicious in that.'

'Inspector Marmion warned me that I had to tell them if you approached me again. He said I could be arrested.'

'Then you must tell them the truth. I stopped you for a chat.'

When he put his face close to hers, she took an involuntary step backwards.

'You frighten me, Mr Hubbard.'

'But we're *friends*.'

'No, we're not,' she said. 'You want to kill my husband.'

'So did you at one time,' he recalled. 'When we first met, you admitted that there were several moments when you'd like to have murdered him. I daresay you'd have cut his balls off afterwards but you were too much of a lady to confess that. He treated you deplorably, Veronica, then he tossed you aside like a rag doll.'

'It's true,' she said, sourly, 'but that doesn't mean I want him dead.'

'Is he any use to you *alive*?'

'Well, no . . . I suppose not.'

'Let's walk on, shall we?'

'Where are we going?'

'We're just having a friendly natter,' he said. 'I'd rather do it on the move.'

Veronica set off and he fell in beside her. Seeing the chevron of concern between her eyebrows, he slipped an arm around her to give a comforting hug.

'I'm worried about the police,' she said.

'They haven't put a tail on you, if that's what you mean. I made sure of that before I spoke to you the first time.'

'I don't want to go to prison, Mr Hubbard.'

'Why don't you call me Wally?'

'It's cruel of you to put me in this position.'

'All I'm after is information.'

'You've already had it.'

'There are lots of things you *didn't* tell me, Veronica.'

'Such as?'

'I've got a list up here,' he said, tapping his forehead. 'We'll work through it as we stroll along.'

'Then what?'

'I disappear and you'll never see me again.'

'Yes, but what about me, Mr Hubbard?'

'Wally,' he corrected.

'What do *I* do afterwards?'

'You do as you're told and report this meeting to the police. Tell them the truth. Inspector Marmion doesn't worry me,' he said with a flick of his wrist. 'He and Sergeant Keedy couldn't find me in a month of Sundays. I'm Mr Invisible.'

Lily Marmion was a calming presence. During the hours she spent at the house, she made Ellen feel less depressed and more optimistic. When Lily left, however, doubt and grief crept up on Ellen. She tried to fight them off by throwing herself into frantic activity, searching every nook and cranny in the house for clues that might lead her to her son or at least explain why he'd gone. Ellen was shaken to realise how much he'd taken from his wardrobe. It was as if he was expecting to stay away for a long time. His favourite photographs and ornaments had also gone. Of the items he'd left behind in his room, the dartboard dominated. She tried to imagine what had driven him to draw some rough portraits of a young woman and hurl darts at her out of spite. What perverse pleasure did he get?

When she finally ran out of rooms to search, she flopped wearily on to the sofa. The house felt cold and empty. It was ironic. When Paul was there, locked away in his room, his presence was like a weight that pressed down on her and she'd many times wished that he'd go out and give her a temporary breathing space. Now that he'd done just that, she was bereft, wishing she could hear a sound that told her he was still there, even if it was only the rhythmical thudding of darts into a board. It was at that point she became conscious of somewhere she'd missed. Ellen had only looked *inside* the house. Pulling herself up, she hurried to the back door and let herself out. She then lifted the lid of the bin cautiously as if half expecting her son to pop up. When she took a tentative look inside, her eyes widened in surprise.

'I suppose it will be my turn next,' said Keedy.

'Your turn?'

'Yes, Wally Hubbard obviously likes dressing up as someone

else. He started off as a prison warder, then he promoted himself to the rank of inspector and, when he was seen outside the Dun Cow, he was pretending to be a blind man. I'm starting to feel left out, Harv. When is he going to pretend to be *me*?'

'He doesn't have the looks for it, Joe.'

They shared a laugh. After going in separate directions for most of the day, they'd met up at a cafe near Scotland Yard for some refreshment and for a discussion that couldn't be interrupted by Claude Chatfield. They felt that they worked best without the interference of the superintendent. Keedy swallowed a last piece of cake and washed it down with a mouthful of tea.

'How reliable is Jack Ryde?' asked Marmion.

'I trust him.'

'But he only saw them for a few seconds.'

'That was enough, he told me. Maisie was chatting to a blind man with a stick. Except that, when he walked away, he wasn't using the stick at all. That's when Ryde recognised him as Wally Hubbard.'

'I still think it's strange he didn't mention it to Maisie.'

'He was afraid that, if he did, she'd set Hubbard on him. Wally knocked him about a bit once before and he didn't want a second helping. Also, he was late for his stint with the accordion. Ryde earns his beer money by playing songs from the front.'

'Some of those can tug at the heartstrings.'

Keedy chuckled. 'And others are quite filthy.'

'Paul used to play "It's a Long Way to Tipperary" over and over on his mouth organ. Ellen said that it almost drove her insane. Actually, it was Colin Fryatt's mouth organ, now I come to think of it. He really *could* play it. Paul kept it with him all the time. It was more than just a souvenir.'

'What happened to it?'

'I don't know, Joe. It just disappeared one day.'

'But it meant so much to him.'

'We used to think *we* meant a lot to him as well,' said Marmion, morosely. 'No,' he went on, making an effort to shake off his sadness, 'I'm not going to brood. I'm on duty now. Let's take Hubbard first. What have we got so far?'

'We've had sightings of him,' said Keedy. 'One of them was by me. We know that Felix Browne is acting in collusion with him but we can't actually prove it. We do have a witness who saw Hubbard with Maisie Rogers, so it's time to have her followed.'

'It will have to be discreetly.'

'There's also Veronica Croft, of course.'

'Yes, Hubbard hasn't finished with her yet.'

'It will be interesting to see if she comes to us when he does turn up again.'

'Oh, I think she'll report him next time, Joe.'

'That leaves Helen Graydon,' said Keedy. 'I fancy that it's highly unlikely he'll go back to her. Your face has been all over the papers. Hubbard will know that she realises she was duped.'

Marmion was concerned. 'Do you think I look sinister?'

'Why do you ask?'

'Mr Pitter, the Head of the Civil Service, told me that I looked so much better in the flesh. Press photos made me look sinister, he said.'

'That's rubbish.'

'Thanks, Joe. That's reassuring.'

'I think they make you look like an undertaker – and I come from a family of them, remember.'

Marmion was hurt. 'An *undertaker*?'

'You have that air of solemnity about you. Right,' he went on, 'we've dealt with Hubbard. What about the murder?'

'There are still too many unknowns, Joe.'

'Who is the victim?' asked Keedy.

'That's one of them.'

'Why was he hiding in a Salvation Army hostel?'

'Keep going, Joe.'

'Who killed him?'

'That may be more difficult to find out.'

'What was in that briefcase?'

'There were some papers belonging to Ben Croft.'

'What was taken out of it by the killer?'

'I've no idea.'

'Did he come primarily to steal something?'

'One last question.'

'Where is Croft and what's his connection to the murder?'

'The only lead we have there comes from Mrs Graydon,' said Marmion, 'and it's a very skimpy one. When he told her he was going away for a while, Croft said that he'd be sailing somewhere. Where to, I wonder?'

Details of the murder victim's age and appearance had appeared in all of the national newspapers. Some people had come forward suggesting his identity but all of the names they gave were soon discounted. The man known only as David retained his mystery. Inevitably, there were a few members of the public who simply craved attention and who turned up with spurious claims about the dead man. Easily exposed, they were either sent away with a stern warning or arrested for deliberately wasting police time. Chatfield was in his office when he was told of the latest person to respond to the appeal. A detective constable came to his office.

'We have a gentleman who wishes to see you, sir,' he said.

'What does he want?'

'He thinks he knows who the murder victim was.'

'They all claim that,' said Chatfield, irritably. 'You don't need to bother me with this. Check the details he gives you and send him on his way.'

'He insists on seeing the corpse, sir.'

'Why?'

'It may well be his son.'

Nobody else had made such a claim or had asked to see the body. Chatfield was therefore curious and asked for the visitor to be brought in. In a couple of minutes, he was exchanging names with Reuben Ackley, an elderly man with rounded shoulders, a greying beard and the look of an academic about him. The newcomer went straight to the point.

'I must view the body,' he said. 'I believe it to be my son.'

'What gives you that idea?'

'We had a feeling that he'd end up on the streets one day.' He thrust a hand into his inside pocket. 'I have a photograph of him here. You, presumably, have seen the cadaver?'

'Yes, I have.'

'Is this the person you were looking at?'

He showed a fading sepia photograph to Chatfield. The

superintendent studied it and noticed a faint resemblance to the victim but it was far from decisive. Ackley could see that he was doubtful.

'This was taken six or seven years ago when we were on better terms.'

'Better terms?'

'I'm ashamed to say that David and I were estranged.'

Chatfield clicked his tongue. 'I can't be certain,' he said. 'In some ways, it looks like him but in other ways, it doesn't.'

'There must be police photographs of the victim.'

'It's standard practice in all murder cases, sir.'

'Why weren't they published in the newspapers?'

'It's because they were taken *after* the man was dead,' explained Chatfield, 'and, as a consequence, they're rather gruesome. They can never be made public. We're very fastidious regarding any photographic material we release to the press.'

'Quite right, if I may say so. I'd like to see those photographs.'

'I'd have to know a lot more about you and your son before I can do that, sir. We never pander to the morbid interests of certain individuals. They always turn up in the wake of a murder – the more horrific, the better for them – and ask to see photographs of the deceased in order to get a macabre thrill. Now,' he went on quickly, 'I'm sure that *your* interest is a sincere one and not tainted in any way. But I'd like to know with whom I'm dealing. Tell me more about yourself, please.'

'I'll be happy to do so.'

Sitting in the chair indicated by Chatfield, the visitor spoke slowly and movingly about his life as Professor of Jurisprudence at Oxford. His work absorbed him and he freely admitted that he never spent enough time with his son, an only child, when he was growing up. As a result, a gap gradually opened between them until it reached a point where it couldn't be bridged.

'Politics, Superintendent,' he said. 'That's what did the damage.'

'Was your son a dissident?'

'Indeed, he was. He came under the spell of Communism during his time at university and got involved in all sorts of . . . questionable activities.'

'Was he ever in trouble with the police?'

'I don't think so.'

'Did he ever take part in protests?'

'He seemed to do little else.'

'When did he leave home?'

'It was when I pointed out that it was time he earned a living instead of sponging off his parents and foisting his disagreeable political opinions on them. David walked out there and then,' said Ackley with an anger tempered by regret. 'To be candid, I was glad to see him go.'

'Did he have an income of any sort?'

'Not from us – my wife and I were agreed on that.'

'How did he live?'

'I imagine that he slept on sofas in flats belonging to friends, but you can't do that indefinitely. Even the best friends tire of being exploited. It grieves me to admit it,' he continued, 'but my son was destined for the streets.'

Ackley spoke so honestly about himself and his family that Chatfield was convinced that he had good reason to suspect that the murder victim might be his son.

'I hesitate to show you the photographs,' he said, 'because they are brutally explicit. No parent should see a child in that condition.'

'I'd like to see them, nevertheless. I have a strong stomach, Superintendent.'

'You'll need it, sir. As a first step, however, I'd like to show you something that was in his possession.' Opening a drawer, he took out an evidence bag and pulled the battered briefcase out of it. Ackley's jaw dropped open. 'It's your son's, isn't it?'

'No,' said the other. 'It's mine – David stole it from me.'

The moment she came off duty, Alice Marmion took to her heels and ran to the bus stop. She knew how her mother must be feeling and was desperate to offer support while getting it from Ellen in return. The day had been an extended torture for her, following her normal routine and dealing with the petty squabbles she and Iris encountered when all she wanted to do was to be at home. The one bright moment in the day had been provided by Joe Keedy, but its lustre was not strong enough to sustain her. She was tense, fearful and bewildered.

When she finally got to the house, Ellen was strangely quiet and listless. She gave her daughter a token kiss then held both her hands.

'Thank you so much for coming, Alice.'

'It was Daddy's suggestion but I want to be here, anyway. You shouldn't be alone at a time like this, Mummy.'

'Lily came over earlier.'

'That was thoughtful of her. Aunt Lily is a rock.'

'I keep longing for someone to ring with some good news about Paul but I know that it will never happen.'

'He'll be found, Mummy.' Ellen shook her head. 'It's only a matter of time.'

'No, it isn't.'

'Paul may even come back of his own accord.'

'There's no hope of that, Alice. Do you know what I did when Lily went?'

'Tell me.'

'I searched the house. I went through everything in Paul's room in the hope of finding some hint – however tiny – of where and why he'd gone. I went through the whole house. It was only when I sat down from exhaustion in the living room that I remembered something. I hadn't looked *outside*.'

'The bin,' said Alice, pointing a finger. 'That's where you found that drawing of Sally Redwood, isn't it?'

'I found something far more upsetting this time.'

'What was it?'

'I'll show you.'

Still holding her hands, Ellen led her into the kitchen then let go of her. On the table was a sheet of paper with a message scrawled on it by Paul.

THIS IS WHERE I BELONG

Alice was staggered. 'What does he mean?'

'It means what it says. Paul believes that he belongs in the bin with the rest of the rubbish. He thinks he's worthless, Alice. That's what scares me. When he's in that sort of mood, he could do *anything*.'

They got back to Scotland Yard to find Veronica Croft waiting for them. Marmion invited her into his office. Both detectives noticed how anxious she was.

'He came to see me again,' she said.

'We had a feeling that he might,' said Marmion. 'What did he want?'

'He had lots more questions about Ben.'

She told them about her unwelcome meeting with Hubbard and how he'd pestered her for details of Croft's favourite places in London. He was particularly keen to get a list of pubs and restaurants frequented by him. He also demanded the names of Croft's relatives outside the city, people with whom he stayed on occasion. When she'd finished, Marmion thanked her for reporting the incident.

'Will I get into trouble?' she asked, eyes darting.

'I don't think so, Mrs Croft.'

'I'm sorry I didn't tell you about the first time he came.'

'That's water under the bridge now.'

'Thank you,' she said with relief.

'Talking of water,' Keedy interjected, 'we understand that your husband was fond of the sea. Is that true?'

'We always spent our holidays on the coast, Sergeant. Ben liked to wake up to the sound of seagulls.'

'Did he go sailing at all?'

'We went on a short pleasure cruise now and then.'

'He didn't have his own boat, then?'

'No, no, he just enjoyed being afloat. Ben was no sailor.' About to leave, she paused in the doorway. 'Do you know where he is?'

'I'm afraid not,' said Marmion, 'but we will in due course.'

'I see.'

'We'll also recapture Mr Hubbard so he won't be able to bother you again.'

'He doesn't bother me, Inspector – he terrifies me.'

As soon as she'd gone, they reviewed what she'd told them, then Marmion went along to see the superintendent. Chatfield was still talking to Reuben Ackley. For the first time since the murder, he was in a buoyant mood.

'We've made a significant advance, Inspector.'

'That's very gratifying, sir.'

'This gentleman is Mr Ackley. The murder victim was his son.'

He introduced the visitor to Marmion and they exchanged a handshake.

'Are you quite certain that it was your son, sir?' asked Marmion.

'Oh, yes,' replied Ackley. 'I recognised the briefcase he had with him and, when the superintendent showed me the photographs, there was no mistaking him. It was David. We haven't seen him for years, alas. He left home after we . . . fell out and, eventually, ended up on the streets, sleeping rough. And now he's finished up on a slab in the morgue. It's a sobering thought for any father.'

Marmion thought of Paul. 'Yes,' he said, 'it is.'

* * *

254

Maisie Rogers soon picked him out. He came into the Dun Cow and ordered a pint of beer, studiously ignoring her as she pulled it for him. He then chose a table in the corner and put his tankard and his newspaper on it. The man was in his thirties and wore a nondescript raincoat and a trilby, removing both before he settled down. Maisie carried on as if she hadn't realised who the stranger must be. At one point, when she was collecting glasses from the tables, she peered through the window and saw a shadowy figure loitering in a doorway opposite.

There were two of them. Hubbard had warned her that she was bound to be followed at some stage and she obeyed his instructions. At the end of her shift, she put on her coat and hat before leaving. Instead of making for the hiding place, she caught the bus home. The man in the doorway took over surveillance now, sitting well behind her in the bus then letting her get off before he did. Maisie walked through the dark to her house and, as she took the key from her pocket, she managed to resist the temptation to wave farewell to the detective behind her. It began to rain. She laughed. He was going to have a wet night standing outside her flat.

When they needed someone to escort Reuben Ackley to the morgue, Joe Keedy was pressed into service. Because of his experience with the family undertaking business, he was accustomed to the sight and smell of death. Chatfield felt that the task was beneath him and, since his press photograph had been described as making him look like a funeral director, Marmion was keen to keep well away. The murder victim's father was therefore conducted by Keedy to the room where

David Ackley was stretched out under a shroud. It was an ordeal for his father and, as he felt a strong upsurge of conflicting emotions, he needed a couple of minutes to prepare himself. When he was ready, he nodded to Keedy who, in turn, gave a signal to the pathologist's assistant. The shroud was drawn back to expose the face and upper body. Though he'd seen the police photographs, Ackley was overwhelmed by the reality. The sight of his son's ghastly white face and of the vivid memento around his neck was too much for him. He closed his eyes, rocked and began to retch.

Keedy caught him as he fell.

'Where are they?' said Alice, impatiently.

'They'll come when they can.'

'Daddy will certainly come. I just hope that he brings Joe.'

'Joe Keedy is a good detective,' said Ellen. 'It won't take him long to realise that you'll spend the night here at a time like this.'

'You're right, Mummy.'

'Get used to it, Alice. This is what marriage to a policeman means – late nights and lots of anxiety.'

'Don't forget that Joe will be married to someone in the police force as well.'

'That's true.'

After drinking endless cups of tea and speculating on where Paul could possibly be, they'd ended up in the living room. Since her mother was close to despair, Alice had to take on the role of the comforter.

'There's no point in fearing the worst, Mummy.'

'It's that note he left.'

'I wish you'd never found it.'

'Paul *intended* me to find it,' said Ellen. 'He knew that I'd lift that lid before too long. That's how we'd discover the truth.'

'It's only *part* of the truth. We don't know the full story.'

'We know enough, Alice. He's walked out of here for good. There's no escaping that. And the reason he did it is that he sets no value on his life. We failed him. More especially, *I* failed him,' she went on, wringing her hands. 'I should have seen that Paul was in such pain.'

'It wasn't pain, Mummy, it was confusion. He doesn't know what he wants.'

'Yes, he does. He wants to get away from here and it's my fault.'

'You did everything humanly possible.'

'Yet I simply couldn't get through to my own son.'

Ellen was about to start crying again when they heard the sound of a car approaching then slowing down. Both of them got up and hurried to the front door. When it was opened, they saw Marmion and Keedy getting out and waving the driver off. Before they could enter the house, the men were each locked in a warm embrace. Marmion eased his wife indoors and Keedy did the same with Alice. All four of them went into the kitchen and the men saw the message left by Paul.

'Where did that come from?' asked Marmion.

'It was in the rubbish bin,' replied Ellen in dismay. 'Our son walks out of our lives and all we have to remember him by is that.'

'It's horribly final,' said Keedy.

'He scribbled it on impulse,' argued Alice.

'I'm not so sure. Paul must have planned his disappearance in advance. It's not the kind of thing you do on a whim, Alice.'

'He's been very unsettled lately, Joe. He doesn't know what he's doing.'

'I wonder.'

'What do you think, Daddy?'

Alice turned to her father who'd been looking at the blunt message as if trying to decipher it. Averting his gaze, he became practical.

'Joe and I have had a long and difficult day,' he said, abruptly. 'We'd love a cup of tea and something to eat.'

The women responded at once. While Alice made the tea, Ellen produced some bread, cheese and pickled onions. Having moved the scrap of paper with Paul's message on it off the table, they sat around it in a brooding silence. It was Alice who remembered there were crises other than the disappearance of her brother.

'Have you made any progress?' she asked.

'We've made very little with regard to Wally Hubbard,' said Keedy, 'but there's been real progress in the murder investigation. We know who the victim was now.'

'How did you find that out?'

'His father turned up and asked to view the body,' explained Marmion. 'When the superintendent showed him the briefcase belonging to the victim, Mr Ackley said that his son had stolen it from him.'

He went on to describe Ackley and what the man had said about his son. As he talked about David Ackley's plight, they were painfully aware of the parallels with Paul who – having turned his back on his family – had gone off alone. Keedy took over to tell them what had happened to Reuben Ackley at the morgue.

'I think he was overcome by guilt as much as by anything else,' he said. 'Because he detested his son's political activities, he drove him away. We may have been right all along. We had the feeling that the murder might be connected to a foreign spy. Instead of involving a German agent, however, this case may be about someone who got entangled with Russian intelligence.'

'That's pure guesswork at this stage, Joe,' said Marmion.

'Mr Ackley did say that his son taught himself Russian at university.'

'That doesn't necessarily make him a spy.'

'When the war started,' recalled Alice, 'the newspapers were telling us that spies were hiding around every corner. They kept on and on about the "enemy within".'

'In a sense,' said Keedy, bluntly, 'that's what Paul was.'

'Joe!' she exclaimed in horror.

'How can you say that?' demanded Ellen.

'I don't mean that he's a foreign agent or anything like that,' said Keedy. 'He was just unable to fit back into the family. Whatever he did was designed to hurt other people. It wasn't just that girl, Sally Somebody. He treated all of us with a kind of veiled contempt. Look at the vile things he said about me, for instance.'

Ellen was deeply upset. 'You're the one saying vile things now.'

'I think that you should apologise, Joe,' said Alice.

'I'm only telling you how it looked to me,' he said.

'You didn't know Paul.'

'I knew that he was causing upheaval in the whole family. That makes him an enemy, surely? He was doing it deliberately. You offered him love and friendship and he threw it back in your faces. Your brother was certainly *your* enemy, Alice.'

'No, he wasn't!'

'*We're* the ones at fault,' insisted Ellen. 'We let him down.'

There was a long, resentful silence. Marmion eventually broke it.

'There's an element of truth in what Joe says,' he acknowledged.

'Thank you, Harv,' said Keedy. 'I'm glad that someone recognises that.'

'I just think you could have expressed yourself more diplomatically.'

Alice was roused. 'I wish that he hadn't said anything at all.'

'So do I,' added Ellen.

'What on earth got into you, Joe?'

'I'm entitled to my opinion,' he said, reasonably.

'Not when it's so hurtful.'

'All I want,' said Ellen, mournfully, 'is to know where Paul is.'

'He doesn't know himself, love,' Marmion told her. 'In my view, that's what's happening. Paul doesn't fit in any more. He can't work out who he is and what he's supposed to do with his life. Look at that message he left. He's telling us that there's no place for him here now.' He put an arm around his wife's shoulders. 'He's gone to find himself. Paul went off to discover who he really is.'

* * *

Huddled in the corner of a bus shelter, Paul Marmion cursed when the wind shifted and the rain was blown into his temporary refuge. On the first night of a new life, he was cold, wet and alone.

CHAPTER SIXTEEN

The day got off to a bad start for Claude Chatfield. He'd hardly sat down behind his desk when he got a telephone call from Geoffrey Wilson-Smith. The Governor of Pentonville prison dispensed with pleasantries and issued a demand.

'We want Hubbard back behind bars and we want him *now*.'

'That's something we all want, Governor.'

'Then why is he still at liberty?'

'It's not for want of effort on our part, I promise you.'

'I've rather lost faith in your promises, Superintendent. Hubbard has been on the loose for a week now. You promised he'd be recaptured very soon.'

'We'd not expected him to be so elusive.'

'Do you have *any* hopes of doing your job and actually finding him?'

'Yes, of course,' said Chatfield, insulted by his tone.

'Then why have you made no progress?'

'It's unfair to say that, Governor. We've deployed a large team of detectives. We've had two of Hubbard's close friends under surveillance and there have been sightings of him.'

'There was no mention of that in the newspapers.'

'We don't tell the press everything. It's not always politic to do so.'

'What's this about sightings of him?' asked Wilson-Smith, suspiciously.

'Hubbard approached two women for information about Ben Croft, the man he's sworn to kill. One was Croft's wife and the other was a close friend of his. My officers have interviewed both women.'

'Did either of them know where he's hiding?'

'They didn't, alas. A third sighting took place outside a public house. A witness reported seeing Hubbard talking to one of the barmaids there.'

The governor was tetchy. 'Why didn't he summon the police immediately?'

'Hubbard was walking away at the time,' said Chatfield, defensively. 'That's how he was recognised. Hubbard was disguised as a blind man, it seems. The witness noticed his familiar gait.'

'This is absurd. In spite of your efforts to catch him, Hubbard is able to wander at will around London, talking to women whenever he wishes and having no fear of discovery. It seems to me,' said Wilson-Smith, over-enunciating his words, 'that the Metropolitan Police are behaving like blind men as well. You haven't so much as caught a glimpse of him yourselves.'

Chatfield smouldered. 'I take exception to that remark, Governor.'

'It was justified.'

'As it happens, one of my detectives did more than just *see* Hubbard.'

'Oh?'

'Sergeant Keedy knew that his closest associate was an estate agent and reasoned that Hubbard might be hiding in one of the man's empty properties. He not only tracked him down,' stressed Chatfield, 'he chased him out of the house and almost caught him. So I'll ask you to stop casting aspersions on our efficiency. If your safety procedures had been good enough,' he said, acidly, 'then Hubbard wouldn't have escaped in the first place. There's enough crime for us to solve in London without having to waste time wiping up a mess that you and your staff made. Good day to you, Governor. When we have more news, I'll be in touch.'

Before the other man could speak, he slammed the receiver back down.

Chatfield was still pulsing with fury when Marmion knocked and entered.

'Good morning, sir,' he said.

'You're late.'

'Are you all right, sir? You look flushed.'

'The surprise is that I'm not foaming at the mouth,' said Chatfield. 'I've just had the Governor of Pentonville harassing me on the phone because we haven't delivered Hubbard to him in a big box with a red ribbon around it. Is there any word from the men watching Maisie Rogers?'

'They saw nothing untoward, sir,' reported Marmion. 'She finished her shift at the Dun Cow and was followed home to her flat. The detective who stayed outside all night was soaked to the skin.'

'That's irrelevant.'

'He didn't think so.'

'Is there any chance that Hubbard was actually *inside* her flat?'

'I know he's as bold as brass, sir, but even he wouldn't be that daring. He must know that we'd keep an eye on Miss Rogers at some point and wouldn't want to incriminate her by moving into her flat.'

'We already have enough to arrest her.'

'What use is that? Left free, she might lead us to him. Locked up, she's no use at all.' He glanced at the newspapers on the desk. 'I thought you did a masterly job at the press conference yesterday, sir. Now that you've named the murder victim, we should have people coming forward.'

'I'm not sanguine about that.'

'Why not, sir?'

'You heard what the father said. David Ackley was very secretive by nature. He belonged to some sort of Communist cell.'

'We've come across hotheads like that before,' said Marmion. 'They believe in Revolution by Friday though they never tell you *which* Friday it is. And yes, they do like to hide in the woodwork for the most part but Ackley's death might bring one or two of them out.'

'Don't hold your breath, Inspector.' Remembering something, he adopted a quieter tone. 'Has there been any . . . ?'

'No, sir, we've had no contact from our son.'

'It must be a frightful ordeal for your wife.'

'It's put the whole family under intense pressure,' admitted Marmion, 'but, when I stepped into this building, I left that problem at the door. I'm giving the murder investigation my full attention.'

'What about Sergeant Keedy?'

'He's following up some leads about Hubbard, sir. When she came to see us yesterday evening, Mrs Croft told us that he'd cornered her again and demanded a list of his favourite haunts along with details of relatives with whom Croft might be staying. Armed with the same list, the sergeant is checking to see if Hubbard has been paying any visits we should know about.'

'If he has, people will report it, surely.'

'I'd like to think so,' said Marmion, 'but they'll no doubt be warned by Hubbard to keep their mouths shut. He can be very intimidating. When a self-appointed killer issues a threat, people take it seriously. Also, of course, there's another reason why so many of them hold back.'

'Yes,' said Chatfield, peevishly. 'They don't want to be involved.'

'It's the bane of our profession, sir.'

'So what will you be doing, Inspector?'

'My first task is to call on my brother and tell him what we learnt from Mr Ackley yesterday. I'd also like to question the people who were in the same dormitory as his son. When they gave their initial statements to Sergeant Keedy, they were upset and confused. Now that they've had time for reflection, they may recall something else.'

'See if any of them know what was in that briefcase of his.'

'I think we know the answer to that, sir,' joked Marmion.

'Do we?'

'It was a signed copy of *Das Kapital*.'

Impervious to humour, Chatfield just glared.

Alice Marmion was unusually subdued that morning, allowing Iris Goodliffe to fill the void with one of her rambling narratives. As they walked along, her companion heard very little of what she said. All that Alice could think about was Keedy's suggestion that her brother was the 'enemy within' the family. His comment had rocked her at the time and she still felt shaken. Was that how Paul appeared to the person she was going to marry? Had her brother set out to undermine the family on purpose? Or was Paul just flailing around in desperation because they didn't understand his needs?

'You're very quiet today,' said Iris as if noticing at last.

'Am I?'

'Did you sleep at home last night?'

'Yes, I did.'

'How was your mother?'

'She's as shocked and mystified as the rest of us.'

'What about Joe? Have you seen him at all?'

'Yes,' said Alice, voice hardening a little. 'He came back with Daddy.'

'What did he feel about your brother?'

'Oh, he was . . . Joe simply offered support.'

'I thought it was so considerate of him, snatching a moment to see you yesterday when we were on duty. Not many men would do that sort of thing. He obviously loves you.'

Alice was about to say that she didn't feel very loved when Keedy had made unkind remarks about Paul but she held her tongue. Once again, she was unwilling to let Iris get any closer to her and her private life. Her friend continued to pepper her with questions that were politely deflected. Ahead of them was a minor crisis. A horse was being driven around a corner so fast that the heavily laden cart it was pulling slid out of control, struck the kerb and lost most of the wooden crates it was carrying. The pavement was covered with the debris. Alice was delighted by the interruption.

'Come on,' she said, 'it's time for our first good deed of the day.'

Joe Keedy had the thankless task of going to a series of pubs and restaurants favoured at one time by Ben Croft. Wherever he went, he discovered that Wally Hubbard had been there before him, asking if anyone had seen Croft recently or if they had any idea where he might be. Most people didn't realise that they'd been talking to an escaped prisoner with murder on his mind. The few that did were simply glad when he moved on. Having exhausted London venues, he had to look further afield. He also had to take time and money into consideration. Marmion wouldn't thank him for disappearing to distant places like Scarborough or Carlisle and being out of action for a lengthy time, even though Croft had relatives in both places. Chatfield would howl at him for putting a strain on the budget by making excessive car journeys. In the end, Keedy opted for a compromise and asked his driver to head for Brighton.

Miss Janet Latimer was an elderly maiden aunt of Ben Croft's and she lived alone in a small, quaint, whitewashed cottage near the seafront. She had nothing but praise for him. Age had shrunk her size and bent her back but her memory was unimpaired. She talked fondly of the many holidays Croft spent with her as a boy and how she'd always been pleased to see him and his wife.

'They're such a lovely couple, Sergeant,' she said. 'Don't you agree?'

'I haven't seen them together, I'm afraid.'

'They're still so very much in love. It's so touching.'

She was clearly unaware of the estrangement between them and Keedy did nothing to disillusion her. On the principle that the more he learnt about Croft, the better, he listened to her meanderings without interruption.

'When did you last see them, Miss Latimer?' he asked when opportunity arose.

'Oh, it must be four or five weeks ago – perhaps less.'

'Did he stay here?'

'It was just for one night. It was lovely to see him again.'

'He came alone, I take it.'

'Yes, he did.'

'Have you any idea where he was going afterwards?'

'He said something about sailing,' she replied, sweetly. 'In his heart, he'd have loved to have joined the navy, you know, but his parents wouldn't let him. As a boy, he spent all his time on the pier, watching ships and boats through an old telescope.'

'Did he tell you *where* he was sailing?' pressed Keedy.

'No.'

'Did he say anything at all about his plans?'

'No, Sergeant, he didn't say a word.' She screwed up one eye and studied him carefully through the other. 'Why have you come all the way from London to ask these questions?'

'I'm anxious to trace Mr Croft.'

'That's what the other man told me.'

'What other man is that?'

'The other detective,' she replied. 'He drove all the way down from London in search of Ben, though he wouldn't say why. But he did tell me that he was from Scotland Yard, just like you. Why did you *both* have to come?' she asked. 'One was enough, surely. The superintendent could have told you what I said.'

Keedy gaped. 'Did you call him "the superintendent"?'

'That was his name – Superintendent Claude Chatfield. He was charming to me. It was a pleasure to meet him.'

Wally Hubbard had the feeling that he was slowly getting somewhere, picking up bits of information about his target and getting a clearer definition of him. He'd enjoyed his time with Janet Latimer, all the more so because she was the person who'd seen him last. She'd also saved him the trouble of going to Scarborough or Blackpool by telling him which members of the extended family lived there and why it was highly unlikely that Croft would be staying with them. Having shed his incarnation as a detective superintendent, Hubbard took the train back to London and wondered what his next step should be.

Maisie Rogers was being followed. That much was certain. Nothing else could explain the fact that she hadn't turned up the previous night. Her occupation meant that she'd spent many years walking home alone in the dark and was therefore attuned to danger. She would not be in touch with him until she felt it was absolutely safe. He accepted that. For the time being, he was on his own. Hubbard tried to while away some of the time by reading the newspaper he'd bought at the railway station in Brighton. It told him the name of the murder victim.

'David Ackley, eh?' he said to himself. 'So how did you come to have Ben Croft's papers in your briefcase?'

Though he was keen to focus on the case in hand, Marmion spent the first five minutes of his visit to the hostel fielding questions from his brother and his sister-in-law. They wanted to know if there was any news about Paul and how everyone was coping with his unheralded departure. Raymond seized on a phrase.

'Joe called him the "enemy within"?'

'Yes,' said Marmion.

'That's very harsh,' said Lily.

'Yet there's a grain of truth in it,' said Raymond. 'He was lying low and pretending to be one of the family until he was ready to show his true colours.'

'And what are they?'

'He wants to be independent, Lily. Paul wants to be his own man.'

'If that's really the case,' said Marmion, 'we can all stop worrying so much.'

He spoke to a number of residents there and heard the same description of David Ackley each time. The man was shy, uneasy and avoided everyone. There was, however, an exception to the rule. When Howie Vernon spoke to the inspector, he talked about a different person altogether. Vernon was a hirsute old man with a patch over one eye and an almost total lack of teeth.

'I didn't like the sod,' he declared.

'Everybody else seemed to get on with him,' said Marmion.

'They didn't know him like I did.'

'How would you describe him, Mr Vernon?'

'He was sly and nasty.'

'What makes you say that?'

'I was the one who had the fight with him, wasn't I?'

'But I was told how meek and mild he was.'

'He wasn't very meek the time I caught him in the bathroom,' said the old man. 'I didn't mean to go in but the lock doesn't work properly. If you shove hard enough, the door will open.'

'What happened?'

'I went in there for a piss and he snarled at me like an animal. Anyone would think I'd gone in there to bugger him. Meek and mild, is it? The language that came out of him was foul. If I hadn't got out quickly, he'd have attacked me.'

'Was he in the bath when you went in there?'

'No, he was fully clothed.'

'What was he doing?'

'He was sitting on the lavatory with that briefcase across his knees,' said Vernon, bitterly. 'And he was writing something in this thick notebook. Sly and nasty are the words for him, Inspector. He'd sneaked off on his own and, when I went in there by mistake, he bared his teeth at me as if he was a mad dog. Whatever was in that notebook of his, he was ready to defend with his bleeding life.'

* * *

Keedy decided that it was time to rattle Felix Browne's cage again. When he was asked to wait a few minutes, he didn't burst into the man's office as he'd done on his last visit. Browne's secretary eventually came out and ushered him in. Browne was on his feet with his hands on his hips.

'I see that you've mastered the art of waiting,' he teased.

'Every visit here is a learning process of sorts.'

The other man laughed. 'And what lesson will you take away from today?'

'That depends on how honest you are.'

'I'm *known* for my honesty, Sergeant.'

'Well, *I'm* known for my lack of trust in people,' said Keedy.

'That's a failing.'

'I've learnt to live with my disability.'

Laughing again, Browne indicated a seat. Both of them sat down and regarded each other warily. Keedy saw the photographs of properties on the desk.

'Where have you put Hubbard this time?' he asked.

'I haven't put him anywhere because I haven't set eyes on him. Given the choice, I'd put him straight back in prison so that you could have a good night's sleep at last. You look tired, Sergeant.'

'I'm certainly tired of your lies, Mr Browne.'

'It's nice to find you so ready with your compliments.'

'When did you last see Maisie Rogers?'

Browne sniggered. 'Why should I want to bother with a barmaid?'

'She'd save you the trouble of seeing Hubbard in person,' said Keedy. 'Maisie could act as an intermediary – a go-between.'

'I know what an intermediary is.'

'Has Maisie been here?'

'She can't afford my prices, Sergeant.'

'That's no disgrace. Neither can I.'

'Is that why you're here – to negotiate a discount?'

'I'm here to tell you that your friend, Wally Hubbard, is starting to take chances. He was seen talking to Maisie outside the Dun Cow, where she works. He's also been breathing down the neck of Veronica Croft again. She gave him a list of her husband's relatives.'

'Why should I wish to know all this?'

'You might care to warn him that we're getting ever closer.'

'Wally can look after himself.'

'Unbelievably, he made a favourable impression on Miss Janet Latimer.'

'Who, in God's name, is she?'

'She's Croft's dear old aunt in Brighton. I arrived at her house half an hour after Hubbard had left. Do you see what I mean about taking chances?'

'I've no control over him, I'm afraid.'

'But you're still his friend.'

'Of course I am. That will never change.'

'Then you're liable to offer him help, aren't you?'

'Oddly enough,' said Browne, easily, 'he's never asked for any.'

'Then how did he end up in West Terrace?'

'Like me, he knows a good house when he sees one.'

'When he ran away,' said Keedy, 'we retraced our steps to the property. There was no sign of the break-in you suggested. Are you sure you didn't *let* him in?'

'I'm certain,' replied Browne, impassively.

'It's the kind of thing a good friend would do.'

'A good friend wouldn't be so stupid. Self-interest would get in the way.'

'That might be your motto, Mr Browne.'

'Yes, it might. Self-interest is my guiding star. It's the reason I've done so well in a dog-eat-dog world.'

Keedy got up. 'Pass on a message to Hubbard for me.'

'I've no means of doing so.'

'There have been too many sightings of him. That's carelessness on his part. Tell him that he's making it too easy for us.'

'What would you advise?'

'He should give himself up.'

'You've spent all this time chasing after Wally and you still don't understand him, do you? He's on a mission,' said Browne, seriously. 'He thinks about Ben Croft night and day. There's no stopping missionary zeal, Sergeant, and I can tell you now that it flows through Wally Hubbard's veins like hot lava.'

Ellen did anything and everything to take her mind off Paul's disappearance. She went out shopping, joined the sewing circle for an hour and returned to the house to clean every room with manic intensity. The one bedroom left untouched belonged to her son. She simply opened the window to its full extent and let the cold air blow in for a while. Like Alice, she'd been badly jarred by Keedy's reference to Paul as an enemy, yet to some extent, she had to concede, it was an accurate description. Her son neither took part nor showed any interest in the family. He lived apart from them.

The key to his strange behaviour, she believed, lay in his volatile attitude towards the opposite sex. As a tall, good-looking, amiable youth, Paul was never short of female attention at school. He'd had a series of girlfriends before settling on one in particular. Everything had been going well until war interrupted the romance. It survived his first leave but, on his second visit home, he was so coarse and uncaring that the girl was forced to break off the relationship. Nobody had taken her place until Paul had been approached by Mavis Tandy. Though he'd been remarkably secretive about her, he'd shown a keen interest in her, arranging three meetings in quick succession. After the first two, he came home with a sense of quiet elation. On the third occasion, however, he returned with his head down and ignored his mother's greeting. Paul seemed to retreat from everyone. The treasured mouth organ belonging to his friend, Colin Fryatt, was never seen or heard again. Music of any kind vanished from his life.

From that moment on, he'd never sought female company. When his mother invited Sally Redwood into the house, she did so in the hope that it would revive pleasant memories of their schooldays together. All that it did was to bring out the worst in Paul, turning him into a complete lout. He insulted the girl, tormented her in the shop where she'd just started work and, worst of all, made an obscene drawing of her for the sole purpose of throwing darts at it. Ellen winced at the memory of what she discovered in his bedroom.

How could someone capable of love and tenderness stoop to such malicious treatment of a girl like Sally? Was he simply reverting to an old hatred of her or did she represent all young women and have to be punished on their behalf? Ellen didn't have the answer but she felt that someone might provide it. With luck, she might even be able to say where Paul had actually gone.

Mavis Tandy had to be found.

Hubbard missed Maisie Rogers. She was much more than a compliant woman. At a time when he needed one most, she was a true friend. Now that she was being followed, he'd have to do without her for a while. Pacing up and down the living room, he kept one eye on the net curtains in the bay window. In case the police came unexpectedly, he'd be ready. Hubbard had already planned his escape route. He slept with his clothes on so that he could flee instantly.

He was in the window when the shape of a car glided by. Immediately on the alert, he drew the curtain back an inch and peered out. Hubbard laughed. The car belonged to Felix Browne. His friend was getting a box out of the car. It contained provisions for his guest. Hubbard opened the door before Browne could press the bell. He took the box, checked its contents then put it on the kitchen table. The estate agent was at his elbow.

'I had a visit from Sergeant Keedy,' he said.

'I hope that you gave him my regards.'

'He came with a warning for you, Wally. You're getting slack.'

Hubbard tensed. 'Who says so?'

'Half an hour after you left someone's house in Brighton, he turned up there.'

'I was on the train by then.'

'What if he'd come half an hour earlier?'

'I'd have pulled rank on him,' said Hubbard, chortling, 'because I was acting as Superintendent Claude Chatfield at the time.'

'It's not funny, Wally.'

'I enjoy being someone else.'

'I know,' said Browne. 'You turned up outside the Dun Cow as a blind man but the trick backfired. You were recognised.'

'Was I – who by?'

'Does it matter? The fact is that you can't go on like this.'

'What else am I supposed to do?'

'Leave London and go to ground somewhere else.'

'How can I possibly find Croft if I do that?'

'We don't know that he's here, Wally.'

'He is. I feel it in my water.'

'The longer you stay in London, the more chance there is of getting nabbed. And if you're arrested in one of *my* properties, the coppers will come after me.'

Hubbard grabbed his lapels. 'Are you losing your nerve, Felix?'

'I'd never do that.'

'It's beginning to sound like it.'

'Let go of me,' said Browne, brushing away his hand.

'I'm starting to get somewhere,' insisted Hubbard. 'Croft's aunt told me he'd sailed off somewhere but that was well over a month ago. He must be back by now. He can't have gone far. Where the hell can you sail when there are German subs all round us? Croft is somewhere in this city. I can *smell* him, Felix.'

'Right, so you smell him, you find him, you kill him. What happens next?'

'I disappear from your life for ever.'

'Where will you go?'

'I'll go where the wind blows me.'

'Will you be alone?'

'Oh, no,' said Hubbard, 'I'll be taking Maisie with me. After what she's done for me since I escaped, she deserves it. Her days of pulling pints for drunken lechers are numbered. It's her turn to escape now.'

Though Maisie couldn't actually see the man, she sensed that he was there. He'd been waiting outside her flat and followed her to the bus stop. When she'd reached the pub, she could feel his eyes still on her. During her afternoon break, she walked to the park and had a late lunch, eating the sandwiches she'd made earlier and tossing some of the bread to the birds. If the detective was expecting Hubbard to turn up, he was bitterly disappointed. The only person to speak to her was the park keeper and he was far too old, short and stout to be the fugitive. Being continuously watched was both irritating and inhibiting but Maisie bore it well, carrying on as if totally unaware that she was being shadowed.

'What was he writing, do you think?'

'I wish I knew, Joe.'

'It must have been something important if he lost his temper like that.'

'Maybe I was right, after all,' said Marmion, smiling. 'It was a case of many a true word spoken in jest.'

'You've lost me,' said Keedy.

'Chat and I were wondering what was in that briefcase of his. For a joke, I suggested that it might be a copy of Karl Marx's *Das Kapital*.'

'Did he laugh?'

'Need you ask? Chat wouldn't recognise a joke if it jumped up in front of him and sang the national anthem. As for the briefcase, I still reckon that David Ackley was hiding something of political significance in there. The trouble is,' he continued, 'that we may never know what it is.'

They were in Marmion's office in Scotland Yard, comparing what they'd learnt in the course of the day. Keedy was interested to hear about another side to David Ackley's character. Evidently, he was not the shrinking violet he was reported to be.

'If Chat hates jokes, he won't like Hubbard's latest prank.'

'Why, what's he been up to this time, Joe?'

Keedy told him about the visit to Miss Latimer and how Hubbard had called on her earlier, posing as the superintendent. Marmion guffawed. The two of them were still shaking with mirth when Chatfield walked in.

'I'm glad the both of you can find something to laugh at,' he said, making them react guiltily. 'We have a vicious murder to solve and a prisoner who escaped custody by using excessive violence. Then, Inspector, we have the small matter of your son's disappearance. I fail to see any excuse for amusement in all that.'

'I'm sorry, sir,' said Marmion.

'So am I,' murmured Keedy.

'May I know what struck you both as so funny?'

'In hindsight, it wasn't funny at all, sir.'

Marmion picked up some sheets of paper. 'My report is ready for you, sir.'

'Thank you,' said Chatfield, taking it from him. 'I'll read it while the pair of you are doing something useful. I've just had a phone call about the murder victim and discovered something that I suspected from the start.'

'What's that, sir?'

'You'll find out when you meet Donald Breen.'

'I don't think I know that name,' said Marmion.

'He works for Special Branch.'

CHAPTER SEVENTEEN

'Hello, Mrs Fryatt,' said Ellen.

'What do you want?'

'I'm hoping that you may be able to help me.'

'Why should I do that?'

'Colin was Paul's best friend.'

'I don't need reminding of that,' said Barbara Fryatt, resentfully. 'My son died while yours lived. *Why?* It's not fair. What's so special about Paul Marmion?'

'Nothing,' said Ellen, trying to placate her. 'He was lucky, that's all.'

'He always was.'

Folding her arms, Barbara stood there and glowered. She had changed. When her son had been killed in action, she'd been immensely grateful for the consolation that Ellen had offered. Her attitude was different now. It was clear that her visitor would get no further than the doorstep. Ellen had been looking forward to meeting the woman again and expected cooperation. It was not forthcoming. Tall, big-boned and running to fat, Barbara Fryatt exuded anger and bitterness in equal degrees.

'Why are you bothering me?' she asked.

'I'm anxious to track down Colin's girlfriend, Mavis Tandy.'

'Whatever for?'

'I need to speak to her, Mrs Fryatt.'

'Why?'

'She may be able to help me. Do you know where she lives?'

'I might do.'

'Then I'd be very grateful if you could tell me.'

'I'll need to know why first.'

Ellen had been hoping to get the information without having to disclose a reason for needing it but that was clearly impossible. Barbara had the advantage over her. Only the truth would encourage her to help.

'Paul has disappeared,' she admitted.

'What do you mean?'

'Just that – he's run away and we're trying to find him.'

'Why did he do that?'

'We don't know, Mrs Fryatt. I wish that we did.'

'How does Mavis come into this? Paul doesn't even know her.'

'Yes, he does – or, at least, he did.'

Ellen explained that Mavis had written to her son, asking him to meet her so that she could hear the details of her former boyfriend's death on the battlefield. Paul had got in touch with her. Though a friendship seemed to be developing between the two of them, it came to a sudden end. Ellen wanted to know why.

'So he was trying to *steal* Colin's girlfriend, was he?' challenged the other woman. 'That's a terrible thing to do.'

'It wasn't like that.'

'I think it was. It would be typical of Paul.'

'That's unkind!'

'Don't talk to me about kindness, Mrs Marmion. Your son didn't know the meaning of the word. He always had to be first in everything and pushed Colin into the shade. He made my son trot after him like a pet dog. I'll never forgive him for that.'

Ellen had to hold back a biting retort. There was no point in alienating the woman completely or the front door would be shut in her face.

Barbara's grim face was lit by a smile but there was no kindness in it.

'So he's run away from you, has he?' she said, relishing the news.

'Paul has been under a lot of strain lately.'

'You know what it's like to lose a son now.'

'It's . . . very painful,' confessed Ellen.

'What if he doesn't want to come back?'

'We'll respect his decision, Mrs Fryatt. We just need to know where he is and why he left without a word.'

'And you think he might be with Mavis?'

'No, no, I'm certain that he isn't.'

'Then why bother her?'

'When he met her, Paul liked her. I could see that. They

were both very fond of Colin. That gave them a bond. It's just that . . . well,' said Ellen, face crumpling, 'he might have confided things to Mavis that will help us to track him down.'

'Why can't your husband do that? He's a detective.'

'He's a very *busy* detective, Mrs Fryatt. That's why I've taken over.'

Barbara regarded her with a sense of pleasure fringed with sympathy. Glad that Ellen was patently suffering, she could nonetheless see a way to alleviate her distress.

'I don't have Mavis Tandy's address,' she said.

'Oh, I see.'

'But I do know that she lived in Gillingham.'

'Yes, I knew it was somewhere in Kent. Paul was seen getting on to a bus.'

'Then you should be able to find Mavis.'

'Why?'

'Her father's a vicar there.'

Relations between the Metropolitan Police and Special Branch were never entirely free from friction. Since each of them felt that it had the more important role, there were bound to be occasional clashes. The police force consisted of almost 20,000 officers, supported by a separate force of 1,100 men in the City of London itself. While it was tiny by comparison, Special Branch nevertheless felt that it had a senior role, dealing, as it did, with military intelligence vital to the security of the whole country. Detectives like Marmion and Keedy solved major crimes in London. Special Branch, by contrast, reached out well beyond the capital and into distant territories. Their international scope gave some of its officers inflated ideas about their operational significance. Donald Breen was one of them.

He was a big, beetle-browed, stooping man in his forties with a face that was defiantly motionless. When he gazed in turn at the visitors, Marmion and Keedy felt as if they were being expertly frisked by his eyes. They were in a small, rather stuffy office. Nothing had been left on the desk to give them any idea of what Breen had been working on. In response to a nod, they sat down. Though they had no idea of his rank, he was behaving as if he was superior to both of them.

'You sent for us,' said Marmion.

'It's good to meet you both at last,' said Breen, offering no handshake. 'I've followed your careers with interest.'

'What about *your* career, sir?'

'What about it?'

'Well, it would be helpful to know something about you so that we can make some sort of judgement on our own account. All we know about you is your name.'

'That's more than adequate, Inspector.'

'Why are you being so evasive?' asked Keedy.

'I don't have time for pointless digressions.'

'They wouldn't be pointless to us.'

'I'm trying to help you,' said Breen with mild irritation. 'Who I am and what I do is irrelevant. You're obviously in need of assistance. Why not accept it?'

'The sergeant was making a reasonable point,' said Marmion.

'And I've given him a reasonable answer.'

'It was more of a rebuff than an answer.'

'Not in my opinion.'

His eyes glinted from beneath the beetle brows. The visitors were forced to accept the fact that the conversation had to be on his terms, relegating them, for the most part, to the position of passive listeners.

'I want to tell you something about David Ackley,' said Breen.

'We already know a little,' said Marmion.

'*Really?*'

'His father came to see us.'

'That's news to me.'

'Whoever compiled the dossier on us needs a rap on the knuckles,' suggested Keedy. 'I took Mr Ackley to the morgue to identify the body. That's how we finally discovered the name of the murder victim.'

'What else did you discover, Sergeant?'

'We learnt that Ackley was a Communist sympathiser.'

'He was rather more than that.'

'And that his parents had to throw him out.'

'Yes,' said Breen, wearily, 'we have details of his domestic life. David Ackley aroused our interest several years ago. That's why we've been keeping him under the microscope.'

'Then why didn't you come forward when he was killed?' asked Marmion. 'It would have saved us a huge amount of time and effort. We could have had this conversation days ago.'

'No, we couldn't.'

'Why not?'

'We were unaware of Ackley's hiding place.'

'I thought you had him under the microscope.'

'We did,' said Breen, flatly, 'but he . . . found a way to elude us.'

Opening a drawer, he took out a packet of cigarettes, slipped one of them between his lips then lit it with the lighter on his desk. Without offering the packet to the others, he put it back in the drawer. He drew on the cigarette then exhaled smoke.

'David Ackley,' he began, 'was enticed into the Communist ranks for a number of reasons, one of them purely personal. He was revolted by everything that his father did and stood for – the phrase he once used of him was that he was "irredeemably bourgeois". That might sound like a compliment to some people. In Ackley's eyes, it was a supreme insult. He saw his father as a willing part of a ruthless capitalist system exploiting the working class.'

'That's not how we saw him,' said Marmion. 'He struck us as a decent man in an awkward situation. And why should the son start siding with the working class when he wasn't – and never could be – part of it?'

'He overlooked that problem, Inspector.'

'When did he come to your notice?' asked Keedy.

'It was when he started writing articles for a magazine produced by a group that had various names. An umbrella title would be Friends of a Free Russia but that disguises the fact that they didn't extend friendship to their own country. Some of their propaganda advocated violence to achieve their ends.'

'And what were those ends?'

'Revolution in Russia itself was the first step, to be followed in time by some sort of insurrection here in Britain. It may sound ludicrous to us, but people like Ackley believed this nonsense and wrote in praise of it.'

'Why didn't you close the magazine down?'

'We did just that. It was revived under a different name.'

'How many members did this organisation have?'

'At the start,' replied Breen, 'it was only a handful, but it steadily grew in strength. After a couple of years, Ackley was the editor of the magazine. All of a sudden, he had some influence.'

'Excuse me,' said Marmion, 'but this doesn't sound like the man who finished up in my brother's hostel. According to Raymond, he was desperately shy. Yet he was surrounded by men from the very depths of society. You'd have thought he'd leap up onto a chair and start giving fiery speeches about poverty in the midst of plenty.'

'He needed to keep out of sight, Inspector.'

'What was he afraid of?'

'Us, for a start – and of the man who was sent to kill him.'

'*Sent* to kill him?' echoed Marmion.

'We believe that it was a targeted assassination.'

'Who was behind it?'

'There are a number of possibilities.'

'Then perhaps you'd be good enough to tell us who they are,' said Keedy, impatiently. 'You might also tell us how he managed to shake off your surveillance. It doesn't say much for the reputation of Special Branch that you managed to lose track of a lone man with a battered briefcase.'

'Don't pass judgement till you know all the facts, Sergeant,' said Breen, stung by the criticism. 'We have limited resources. It's impossible to watch all of the people on our list of subversives. That being the case, we put Ackley where he didn't need to be monitored every hour of the day.'

'And where was that?'

'Knockaloe Camp on the Isle of Man.'

'But that's reserved for civilian internees like Germans.'

'We make use of it for our own purposes.'

'How long was David Ackley there?'

'It was almost three months. We hoped that we'd put him and his vile propaganda to sleep indefinitely but it was . . . not the case.'

'How on earth did he escape?' asked Marmion. 'Knockaloe is on an island of barbed wire. Security is very tight, by all accounts.'

'Ackley got out,' said Breen, crisply. 'That's all I'm prepared to say. I just wanted you to know something about the man whose murder you're investigating. He was a dangerous man. It was deemed sensible to lock him up.'

'That's not all,' said Keedy.

'What do you mean?'

'Well, if he was that much of a danger, it could have been deemed sensible to have him killed. Is that what happened at the hostel, sir? Did someone from Special Branch finally catch up with him?'

Snatching the cigarette from his lips, Breen stubbed it out in an ashtray. He was seething with fury at Keedy's question. The interview was over. They'd learnt all they were going to learn. Marmion thanked him for speaking to them and led the way out. Keedy was unrepentant.

'I'm sorry about that, Harv. I had to speak out.'

'You were right to do so, Joe,' said Marmion, smiling. 'I just don't think you should ever apply for a transfer to Special Branch.'

* * *

Ellen had no difficulty in finding the vicarage in Gillingham. Delighted to catch Mavis Tandy at home, she was pleased when she was invited in. It was an improvement on the treatment she'd received from Barbara Fryatt. On the other hand, Mavis was palpably uneasy about meeting Paul Marmion's mother and her manner was guarded. She was a tall, plain, rather gawky girl with red hair and freckles. There was a faint resemblance to Sally Redwood. Sitting on the edge of her chair, she kept her hands entwined together.

'Did Paul send you?' she asked, nervously.

'No, that's not why I'm here.'

'We're not friends any more, Mrs Marmion.'

'I gathered that.'

'Has he . . . said anything about me?'

'Paul said very little, I'm afraid. It's the reason I know so little about you. For instance, I had no idea how to get in touch with you. I had to ask Colin's mother how I could find you.'

'I didn't get on with Mrs Fryatt,' said Mavis, sadly. 'Since Colin and I had been so close, I thought she'd like to meet me from time to time but she didn't. She said that we had nothing to say to each other.'

'Mrs Fryatt is finding it hard to cope with what happened.'

'It's the same for me. Colin's death was like a thunderbolt. I was in a daze for weeks. I kept praying that the news was a terrible mistake.'

Mavis went on to talk about her former boyfriend for minutes on end, omitting the fact that their relationship had been an extremely short one. Ellen didn't interrupt her. The girl had obviously been deeply in love for the first and only time in her life. It was because she was so eager to know every last detail about Fryatt's death that she'd got in touch with Paul. When she reached that point in the narrative, Mavis hesitated.

'That's when I . . . wrote to Paul.'

'I understand.'

'I had to talk to someone who knew Colin, you see. The obvious person was Mrs Fryatt but she was so unfriendly. I don't know why.'

Ellen could hold back her news no longer. 'Paul has run away.'

'Oh, I'm . . . sorry to hear that.'

'He left no explanation. He just went.'

Mavis was worried. 'You didn't think that he'd come here, did you?'

'No, I was certain that he hadn't.'

'That's a relief.'

'The thing is, Mavis . . . May I call you that?' The girl nodded. 'The thing is, Mavis, that you are the only person Paul showed the slightest interest in since he came out of hospital. You sort of . . . brought him back to life somehow.'

'It wasn't what I intended. I just wanted to talk about Colin.'

'But you did meet up with Paul two or three times. Did he ever talk to you about wanting to leave home?'

'No, he didn't.'

'Did he say that he was unhappy or restless?'

'I could see that he was both, Mrs Marmion. He couldn't seem to make up his mind. One minute, he was talking about rejoining his regiment so that he could get revenge for what happened to Colin. The next minute, he was complaining

293

about what the war had done to him and how he hated being in the army.'

'We had the same problem with him.'

'Where could he have gone?'

'We don't know, Mavis. I'm just trying to find out why he went. Since you got close to Paul for a short while, I was hoping you might know something that we don't. It's horrible being so completely in the dark.'

Ellen could feel the tension in the air. Now hunched up protectively, Mavis looked as if she didn't wish to continue a conversation making her increasingly uncomfortable. Ellen asked the crucial question.

'Why did you and Paul stop seeing each other?'

Mavis recoiled as if from a blow. 'I'd rather not say.'

'But you were the one who contacted *him*.'

'I did, Mrs Marmion, and I take the blame.'

'*Blame?*'

'It would never have happened if I hadn't written that letter.'

'What wouldn't have happened?' Seeing the girl's distress, she nevertheless pressed on. 'I must know, Mavis, don't you see that? It might give me a clue about my son's behaviour. I know he's not an angel – to be honest, living with him has been a trial at times – but we love him as a son and we're anxious to know where he is. Any scrap of information would be useful to us.'

Mavis took a long time to gather up enough strength to speak again. Because of the way it ended, she'd tried to put her fleeting friendship with Paul Marmion out of her mind. Brooding on it was too painful.

'The last time we met,' she said at length, 'Paul did something to me.'

'What was it? He didn't hurt you, surely?'

'He tried to, Mrs Marmion. He grabbed me and . . . tried to molest me.'

'That doesn't sound like Paul.'

'You asked for the truth and that's it. I liked him until that point. The worst thing was that it happened in the church. I had to fight him off and run to safety. To tell you the truth, I never want to see your son again.'

Mavis began to sob but Ellen felt unable to reach out to her. She was too stunned by what she'd just been told. Paul had done something of which she'd never have thought him capable. It was a sobering reminder of how little she actually knew her own son. Eventually, she got up and enfolded Mavis in her arms for a couple of minutes. When the girl finally calmed down, Ellen left the room without another word and let herself out of the vicarage.

During the bus ride back to London, her mind was ablaze.

Maisie Rogers soon tired of being followed. The detective no longer came into the pub where she worked but she was nevertheless aware of his presence every time she stepped into the street. She missed Wally Hubbard and she knew just how much he would be missing her. It was not difficult to shake off the pursuit. Having got permission from the landlord to take time off, she changed out of the clothes she'd worn to work and into something very different. A wide-brimmed hat hid much of her face. There was a group of women in the bar, enjoying a drink together before going home. They were loud but good-humoured. When they surged out into the street, Maisie Rogers was tucked away in the middle of the women, using them as shields. It was five minutes or more before she broke away from the group. After she'd looked in every direction, she was able to relax. Nobody had spotted her.

'It was easy,' she later boasted to Hubbard. 'Someone is still waiting outside the pub for me to put in an appearance.'

'Well done!'

'They'll watch me more carefully in future, Wally.'

'Don't take any chances.'

'I *had* to see you. We're partners now.'

'We are,' he confirmed, hugging her.

'How are you getting on?'

'It's a very cold bed when you're not here.'

'Well, there'll be plenty of time to warm it up.'

They laughed. Over a drink, they each described what they'd been doing since they last met. Maisie was astonished to hear how far he'd travelled in the interim. On the table was a pile of newspapers.

'Why did you buy all those?' she asked.

'I wanted to see if I was still on the front page,' he said, 'but I got hardly a mention in most of them. One of them cut me down to six lines.'

'You should be glad, Wally. You're no longer the main news.'

'No, that comes from France. We've had another setback on the battlefield. The Krauts have seized more territory from our lads. On top of that, of course, the papers are still buzzing about the murder at that hostel. That's why I had to have them.'

'I don't understand.'

'They've got vital information for me, Maisie. I've learnt something new from each and every one of them. I'm letting the police help me in my search. It will soon start to pay off.'

'The papers don't tell you where Ben Croft is hiding, do they?'

'Maybe not,' he replied, 'but they've given me an important clue.'

'Have they?'

'Yes, Maisie. When I opened the *Daily Mail* this morning, I couldn't believe my luck.'

'Why? What did it say?'

'I'll tell you later. Let's go and see how warm that bed is, shall we?'

Having discussed it beforehand, Marmion and Keedy, of one accord, delivered their report to Claude Chatfield. They believed that Breen had been holding back more than he actually told them. When they'd left his office, they were still toying with the possibility that Special Branch had been directly responsible for the death of David Ackley. The superintendent scotched that idea at once.

'It's inconceivable,' he said. 'Had they wanted to kill him, they'd simply have arrested him and spirited him away somewhere. They certainly wouldn't have gone to the trouble of ordering one of their agents to knock out a bandsman, steal his uniform and slip into the hostel. Besides, Ackley was not that important. He was just a minor figure trying to stir up trouble.'

'He was important enough to be locked away,' Marmion pointed out.

'They just wanted to shut him up.'

'But why send him to Knockaloe and not to a mainland prison?'

'Special Branch needed him far away and out of sight. They probably arrested him on a charge of sedition and shipped him off.'

'But all he did was to write some articles in a magazine,' said Keedy. 'Is that enough to justify incarceration on the Isle of Man?'

'No, Sergeant,' said Marmion, 'it isn't. At face value, all that he was doing was to let off steam and wave his fist at the government. A lot of people do that. Ackley would have been in good company in Knockaloe. Like him, most of the internees have committed no crimes at all. They're harmless people with the misfortune of being immigrants.'

'Yet they had to be locked up,' insisted Chatfield. 'Many of them are blameless, I agree, but there's a hard core of dissidents among them. They really belong behind barbed wire.'

'How difficult would it be to get into the camp, sir?'

'Why do you ask?'

'Well, we might find that someone else is hidden away there.'

'Ben Croft?'

'It's a possibility, Superintendent. Ackley could have met him there and stolen his papers. How else could he have got hold of them?'

'That's what I was thinking,' said Keedy. 'One murder could help to prevent another. David Ackley's death is pointing us in the direction of Knockaloe. If we can get to Croft first, we can save his life.'

'I remain unconvinced that he's on the island,' said Chatfield.

'Will you at least find out, sir?'

'Yes,' added Marmion. 'There must be some way of checking the list of internees at the camp.' Chatfield pursed his lips. 'He *could* have been interned because of his German heritage, sir. It's worth investigating.'

'What if he *is* in Knockaloe?'

'There's an easy answer to that, Sergeant.'

'What is it?'

'One of us will have to go to the Isle of Man to warn him.' Marmion patted him on the shoulder. 'That's a job for which you're ideally suited.'

When she got back to the house, Ellen wept for a long time. Her search had been futile. She'd not only had a very unpleasant meeting with Barbara Fryatt, she'd learnt something appalling about her son. Mavis Tandy was young, unworldly and patently virginal. The news that Paul had assaulted her – in a church, of all places – made Ellen feel sick. What had the army done to him? How had it changed him from an essentially good person into one who was a danger to women? Hearing what Mavis had to say was a searing experience. When she confided in her husband and daughter, Ellen would have to go through it all again. They would be as disgusted as she felt. Throwing darts at a sketch of Sally Redwood had been bad enough. What Paul had inflicted on Mavis was far worse.

There was one consolation. Outraged as she must have been, the girl had not run straight to her parents and described what had happened. Mavis chose instead to bottle up the experience and to suffer in silence. Had she confided in her father, he would surely have come knocking at the door of the Marmion house and demanded to see Paul. There might even have been a threat of legal action. That thought brought fresh tears from Ellen. How would it have looked if the son of a Scotland Yard detective had been arrested and charged by the police? Did Paul have no consideration at all for his family?

Ellen was torn between two extremes. As a mother, she had to love, nurture and protect her son; as an independent observer of the situation, however, she felt that Paul was unworthy of belonging to a family that set high standards when it came to behaviour. Two innocent young women had been abused. In the company of such women, Paul could simply not be trusted. He was becoming a positive menace. It was a giddying realisation on Ellen's part. Still determined to find her son at all costs, she heard a voice whispering a seductive question in her ear.

Wouldn't it be better for all of them if he *never* came back?

It had been a dreadful day for Reuben Ackley and his wife. Now that the murder victim had been identified as their son, every newspaper has broadcast the information. They'd also dispatched reporters to Oxford to besiege the parents at their home and demand to know details of David's involvement in political activism. Neither Ackley nor his wife was equal to the intense and invasive pressure. It left them confused and alarmed. Ackley was at ease in the groves of academe where the biggest demand on him was to deliver a lecture on the operation of the British legal system to a room full of attentive students. Facing a mob of reporters, he could only gibber. Questions were fired at him indiscriminately like so many bullets and the photographers made him blink with their flashbulbs.

The parents could never mourn for their son in the normal way. The rift between them and David was too wide and of too long a duration. In their perception, he'd died years ago. That was when they'd felt real anguish. All that his actual death did was to arouse a distant sympathy and a deep hatred of the political beliefs that had led him astray. Shocked by the murder, they somehow managed to feel that it had happened to a stranger.

In return for giving them a long interview, Ackley had gained a promise from the press that they would not pester him the next day. Incredibly, they kept their word. When he opened the bedroom curtains the following morning, there were no serried ranks of reporters with their notepads at the ready and no photographers lying in wait. The worst, it seemed, was at last over. Ackley even dared to think that he could cycle into college and work in his study. Over an early breakfast with his wife, there was no mention of the horror that had descended upon them or of the funeral arrangements that would have to be made. They pretended that their son simply didn't exist.

Ackley was about to mount his bicycle when the man appeared at the gate. He was a solid individual in a raincoat and a trilby.

'Good morning, sir,' he said, cheerily.

Ackley waved a hand. 'I'm not giving any more interviews to the press.'

'Oh, I'm not from a newspaper, sir. I'm Detective Constable

301

Rogers. I've been sent to make sure that you're not troubled by reporters.'

'Then you're a blessing in disguise.'

'Have they made your life a misery?'

'It was torture.'

'Well, you'll have me to keep them at bay now.'

'Thank you. What was the name again?'

'Rogers, sir – Detective Constable Rogers.'

Wally Hubbard had no qualms about borrowing Maisie's name. Nor did he mind lowering his rank to that of a detective constable in the local constabulary. He simply wanted to get close to the father of David Ackley. The man might well have information that Hubbard could use.

'It's a bad business, sir,' he said, soulfully. 'You have my condolences.'

'Thank you.'

'The worst of it is that you don't know who killed your son.'

'We don't know who and we don't know why.'

'Inspector Marmion will get him in the end.'

Ackley was surprised. 'You know the inspector?'

'Yes, I've had the good fortune to meet him once or twice. He's something of an icon at Scotland Yard. The investigation is in the best possible hands, sir.'

'I sensed that. The inspector is so kind and understanding.'

'He knows how to comfort grieving parents.'

'It's not comfort that we seek,' said Ackley, cocking a leg over his bicycle. 'It's an explanation of how it happened. That's all we want. Inspector Marmion has promised to keep us informed at every stage.'

'That must be very reassuring for you, sir.'

'It is, I can tell you.'

'And has he been able to tell you anything *new* about the case?' asked Hubbard, casually.

'Oh, yes. In fact, he rang us first thing this morning.'

'What did he say?'

'He's discovered something about our son that he felt we should know.'

'That was considerate of the inspector.'

'It turns out that, before he ended up at that Salvation Army hostel, David had been held at Knockaloe Camp. That's on the Isle of Man.'

Hubbard grinned. 'I know where it is, sir. Good day to you.'

Raising his hat in gratitude, he went skipping off down the road.

CHAPTER EIGHTEEN

Before they reported to the superintendent, Harvey Marmion wanted a private word with Keedy. He invited the sergeant into his office and closed the door before speaking. When he'd got home late the previous evening, he explained, he'd been given some disturbing news. Keedy was stunned by what he heard.

'When did this happen?' he asked.

'It was several weeks ago, Joe. The girl got in touch with him by letter and Paul agreed to see her. Ellen was glad that he'd finally found someone with whom he actually wanted to spend time but the friendship was short-lived.' Marmion frowned. 'Now we know why.'

'Did he really jump on her in a church?'

'That's what Mavis said and there's no reason to disbelieve her.'

'What a stupid thing to do!'

'It's more than stupid. It's verging on something much nastier. Ellen was overwhelmed with shame. Thank heaven that Alice was there to comfort her. She spent the night with us again, by the way.'

'What was *her* reaction?'

'She was as horrified as I was.'

'It seems so unlike Paul,' said Keedy. 'He was such a relaxed, easy-going sort of person. The last thing I'd expect of him was assaulting a girl like that. And didn't you say she was a vicar's daughter? What on earth made Paul think that she was likely to welcome his advances? From what she told Ellen, it's clear that Mavis gave him no encouragement at all.'

'The girl simply wanted to talk about Colin Fryatt.'

'Paul should have read the signs.'

'His eyesight wasn't so good when this happened, Joe.'

'It's not a question of eyesight,' said Keedy, airily. 'Women give you little hints. There's a sort of Morse code you have to learn. Master that and you know exactly when to make your move.'

Seeing the look in Marmion's eye, he fell silent. Having talked familiarly as if he was in a pub with a male friend, he remembered that he was with his future father-in-law. Keedy's comments – and the tone he used to make them – were not well received. For his part, Marmion was once again obliged to speculate on what sort of sexual relationship the sergeant had with Alice. He had to force himself to concentrate on the plight of his son.

'Where the blazes can Paul *be*?' he asked, banging a fist on the desk.

'Don't ask me.'

'And why hasn't he got in touch just to put our minds at rest?'

'He's not thinking about you and the family, Harv.'

'Then what *is* he thinking about?'

'Himself – he's on some kind of journey.'

'And where is it taking him?'

'I can't answer that one,' said Keedy with a shrug. 'Does he have any money?'

'He has his savings.'

'Did he take them with him?'

'Yes, it's one of the first things that Ellen checked. He's always been careful with money, so he must have quite a bit.'

'There you are, then. That should give you some reassurance.'

'What do you mean?'

'He's not going to be starving and sleeping rough. If he has money, he can always buy himself a bed and a meal. You can live very cheaply that way.'

'I'm not so sure, Joe.'

'There's no shortage of accommodation, especially in holiday resorts. The war has robbed them of business. Prices have gone right down.'

'Somehow, I don't think Paul would take advantage of that.'

'How do you know?'

'It was that message Ellen found in the dustbin.'

'Ah, yes . . .'

'Paul knew he'd done wrong. He was telling us that he felt worthless. He didn't want to cause us any more trouble.'

'But that's precisely what he's doing by running away. He must know the heartache it would cause the rest of you. He's not doing you a favour,' said Keedy. 'He's putting you through hell.'

'No,' said Marmion, thoughtfully, 'he's putting *himself* through hell.'

'That doesn't make sense.'

'It does to me, Joe. I feel that Paul has looked back on all the trouble he's given us and, perhaps, on what he did to Sally Redwood and to Mavis Tandy. He's accepted that he created untold damage. That's why he's taken himself off.'

'I don't follow you,' said Keedy.

'He's *punishing* himself.'

There was a cracked mirror in the public lavatory. When he stared at himself, Paul saw that he had a two-day growth of beard. Though he'd brought shaving equipment with him, he wasn't tempted to use it. From now on, he wanted to look different.

The visit to Oxford had been made on impulse and paid him a handsome dividend. Wally Hubbard had been quick to make a logical deduction. David Ackley had been held at Knockaloe. When he'd been at the hostel, he had papers to show that his name was Benjamin David Croft. It had said so in the newspaper reports. The only place he could have got them was from Croft himself. It followed that the person Hubbard was after must also be on the Isle of Man. Without realising it, Marmion's telephone call to Oxford had put Hubbard in possession of some priceless information. On the train journey back to London, the escaped prisoner had not stopped smiling to himself.

For most of the way, his compartment was quite full. Only when most of the other passengers got out at various stations did he have the room to take out the map of Britain he'd bought in Oxford. When he opened it, his eyes went straight to the Isle of Man. That was where he'd find the man he'd sworn to kill. It wouldn't be easy to get to the island and it would be even more difficult to get access to the camp once he was there. But he was undaunted. Hubbard had got the breakthrough for which he'd been waiting and it was all down to a telephone call from Scotland Yard.

When it was all over – and he'd achieved his aim – he'd make sure that he sent a message of thanks to Inspector Marmion. The signature at the end of the letter would be that of a very grateful Detective Constable Rogers.

Iris Goodliffe let her set the pace and the mood. If Alice wanted to walk along in silence, her partner was happy to humour her. The moment she saw her, Iris could tell that something had happened. Alice was grim and preoccupied. Though she was on duty, she was not thinking about police work. She was simply following a daily pattern, matching Iris stride for stride on their beat. It was the scream that finally jerked her out of her reverie. They were walking past an alleyway when they heard a loud wail of protest from nearby. It was followed by the sound of a slap that only intensified the scream. A man's voice ordered the woman to shut up, then there was a noisy scuffle.

Alice and Iris responded at once, running swiftly down the alleyway. As they rounded a bend, they saw a pathetic sight. A woman of roughly their own age was trying but failing to fight off a much older man. Both wore tattered clothing and swayed drunkenly. Having dropped his trousers, the man was trying to lift her skirt. When he saw the two policewomen, he gave them a mouthful of abuse before tugging his trousers back up again and staggering off. Huddled against the wall, the woman began to cry. Iris stepped in quickly to console her.

The incident had a deep effect on Alice. It made her think of her brother, grabbing Mavis Tandy against her will. Neither of them had been drunk at the time and Paul was much younger than the ragamuffin they'd chased away, yet the image of abuse remained in Alice's mind. Was that Paul's future? Unable to relate properly to women, would he take by force what he couldn't get by agreement? Absorbed in her thoughts, she didn't notice that the victim had just collapsed in a heap.

'Snap out of it, Alice!' yelled her companion. 'Why are you just standing there? Can't you see I need help?'

Claude Chatfield had been as good as his word. Having promised to make enquiries about the men interned at Knockaloe Camp, he did some exhaustive research. It involved a number of phone calls and a long interlude when he went through a bewildering list of names. When he summoned the detectives to his office, he had disappointing news for them.

'He's not there,' he announced.

'Are you sure?' asked Keedy.

'I'm absolutely sure, Sergeant. I spent hours going through the record of admissions and Ben Croft's name is not among them. Do you realise how many people are locked away in that camp?'

'I expect it's a lot, sir.'

'Give me a number.'

'Would it be around . . . 5,000?'

Chatfield laughed derisively. 'No, it wouldn't.'

'I fancy that it's much more than that,' said Marmion, stepping in. 'Knockaloe is near Peel on the Isle of Man. It was ready-made, so to speak, because it's on the site of what used to be Cunningham's Holiday Camp. When a friend of mine went there before the war, he was one of almost 3,000 men.'

'Men?' repeated Keedy. 'Were there no women?'

'No, Sergeant – just men. They slept in bell tents.'

'It's still a male enclave,' said Chatfield. 'There are no females interned there. Much to my disgust, I'm told that women of a certain sort do somehow manage to sneak in there from time to time in search of . . . customers. I've no idea how they get in and out of the camp.'

'I daresay they bribe the guards with favours, sir,' said Marmion.

'Well, it shouldn't be allowed. As for numbers, my research yielded the fact that between the outbreak of the war and the present time, well over 20,000 men have entered the camp and around a third of them have left. That still leaves a substantial total.'

'I had no idea it was that many,' said Keedy.

'Neither did I until I had to plough my way through the lists.'

'They're mostly Germans, aren't they?'

'No, Sergeant, they're persons of German extraction with British passports. Some have been here for most of their lives but it makes no difference. They had to be rounded up and interned in civilian camps like Knockaloe or incarcerated in prisons. Since we left nothing to chance, people from countries allied to Germany were also rooted out and arrested.'

Marmion leapt in to stave off the lecture that seemed to be in the offing.

'Did you find any record of David Ackley in the camp?'

Chatfield was nonplussed. 'No, I didn't.'

'Yet we know he was there. Breen confirmed it.'

'The truth is that I wasn't *looking* for Ackley's name.'

'That was very remiss of you, sir,' Keedy interjected.

'Keep out of this, Sergeant.'

'Yes, sir.'

'Even if you weren't specifically searching for it,' said Marmion, 'my guess is that you'd have spotted it. A man with your eagle eye doesn't miss much.'

'That's true,' said Chatfield.

'So if you saw no mention of David Ackley, then the name was deliberately omitted from the list. Special Branch must have had their own reasons for keeping his whereabouts to themselves. Do you agree, sir?'

'I do, indeed.'

'Then the same may be true of Ben Croft. His presence on the island could deliberately have been left unrecorded.'

'They're not parallel cases, Inspector.'

'They might be.'

'Ackley was sent to Knockaloe for questionable political activities. As far as we know, Croft was never involved in politics. He was an insurance agent. There was no reason to send him to the Isle of Man.'

'Yes, there was, sir. You're forgetting that his mother was German.'

'Then why was he walking freely around this country over a month ago? If there's been a good reason to arrest him, he'd have been whisked off to a civilian internment camp long before now. Your reasoning is unsound, Inspector,' said Chatfield. 'Croft is not and has never been at Knockaloe.'

'Then how did Ackley manage to steal those papers from him?'

'I agree with the inspector,' said Keedy. 'Croft is there and I should be sent to find him. He told one of his women friends that he was going to sail somewhere. It was to the Isle of Man.'

Chatfield glared at him. '*I'll* make the decisions.'

'Then I hope you'll grant our request, sir.'

'What do we have to lose?' asked Marmion.

'We stand to lose the services of Sergeant Keedy at a time when he's most needed here. Both of you seem to have forgotten that we have other priorities. We have to solve the murder of David Ackley and recapture that infuriating wretch, Hubbard. When we've dealt with those problems, we can turn our attention to Croft.'

'But he's linked to Wally Hubbard, sir. The one way to keep Croft alive is to find him first and offer him shelter.'

'You've just defeated your own argument, Inspector.'

'Have I?'

'Let's assume – for the sake of argument – that Croft *is* in Knockaloe.'

'I'm convinced of it, sir.'

'And so am I,' said Keedy.

'Then we can stop worrying about him,' declared Chatfield.

'We certainly don't need to get in touch with him and arrange sanctuary. He already *has* it. If he's marooned on the Isle of Man, he's in the safest place possible. Hubbard would never dream of looking for him there.'

Back in the house he'd borrowed from Felix Browne, he spread the map on the table and pored over it. Situated off the west coast of Britain, the Isle of Man was a blob in the middle of the Irish Sea. Hubbard knew that there were internment camps there, though he had no idea of their exact location or of their size. Getting there was the initial problem and there were two potential solutions. He could either bamboozle his way somehow on to a ferry or he could hire a small boat along with someone to sail it. There were immediate objections to the second mode of transport. A small vessel would take much longer to reach its destination and would cost a lot of money to hire. Something else worried him. In any expanse of water around the British coast, German submarines were always a threat. If he was travelling in a trawler or a similar craft, Hubbard didn't wish to be torpedoed because that would end in his death.

If, however, the submarine attacked a large ferry, the chances of survival were much higher. The vessel would have an adequate supply of lifeboats and a well-drilled crew to get all the passengers into them. Before it sank, it might even be possible to send out an SOS. Hubbard would be rescued along with everyone else. For that reason, he elected to travel in some style. His one regret was that he was unable to take Maisie Rogers with him. She deserved a treat.

* * *

The two detectives keeping the barmaid under surveillance were still not sure if she'd deliberately tricked them or if they'd not been as alert as they should have been. It made them address themselves to their task with more care that morning. Maisie Rogers left the house at the same time and caught the same bus to work. When they'd seen her enter the Dun Cow, one of them watched from the opposite side of the road while the other walked around to the rear of the property. There was no way, they believed, that she could slip past them unseen again.

The man outside the front of the pub had not forgotten Wally Hubbard. Since Maisie was prevented by them from going to him, they felt that Hubbard would come to her sooner or later. When he saw a figure tapping his way along the pavement opposite with a white stick, the detective felt the thrill of recognition. It was the disguise that Hubbard had used before. If he was foolish enough to use it again, he deserved to be caught. The detective bided his time until the man was only a dozen yards from the pub, then he ambled across the road as if about to enter the building. Instead of doing so, he suddenly turned around and blocked the way for the blind man. There was an immediate collision and the latter backed off apologetically.

'I'm so sorry,' he said. 'It was my fault.'

'You can see as well as I can, Hubbard.'

'My name is Andrews,' corrected the other. 'I'm Clem Andrews.'

'I know exactly who you are and you're under arrest.'

Moving swiftly, he pulled out a set of handcuffs and snapped them on to the man's wrists before he could move. The detective grinned triumphantly and snatched off the man's dark glasses.

His grin froze. It was not Wally Hubbard, after all. He was looking into the tiny, pale, sightless eyes of a stranger. The man needed no disguise.

He was genuinely blind.

To add to his dismay, the detective saw that someone was watching him from the front window of the pub. Maisie Rogers had seen everything.

'It really shocked me,' said Iris Goodliffe.

'Why?'

'Well, you expect that sort of thing at night when people have been drinking and they look for a bit of excitement.'

'It was more than a bit of excitement,' said Alice. 'He was going to rape her.'

'At least we saved her from that fate. The woman stank of drink and wasn't really able to defend herself. What disgusted me was how much older than her he was. He was repulsive. What gets into men like that?'

Alice was jolted. The question made her think of her brother once again. She had no chance to brood afresh, however, because they were near the end of their beat. Ahead of her was the reassuring sight of Keedy hurrying in her direction. After an exchange of greetings with him, Iris left them on their own. Alice stepped gratefully into his arms.

'I was hoping to catch you,' said Keedy, hugging her before moving back. 'Your father told me about Paul.'

'It's been on my mind ever since.'

'It may not be as bad as it sounds, Alice.'

'That girl had no reason to lie. Can my brother really be . . . ?'

316

Sensing that he was in a rush, she let the words tail off. 'Has something happened?'

'Yes, I'm leaving the country.'

'Where are you going?' she asked, worriedly.

'Don't be afraid. I'm not going into a combat zone. I'm off to the Isle of Man.'

'Why?'

'I have to find someone.'

'Then you must be sailing there. I'm right to be afraid, Joe. There may be submarines on the lookout.'

'Oh, I don't think that ferries are their main targets. They're more interested in sinking our destroyers and torpedoing our merchant fleet so they can starve us out. I'll be as safe as houses, Alice.'

She gave a hollow laugh. 'Iris and I have just walked past some houses that were demolished by German incendiary bombs.'

'You're determined to have me killed, aren't you?' he teased.

'No, of course I'm not.'

'Then stop fearing the worst.'

'I'll try.'

'There's a good girl.'

He gave her a brief explanation of why he was going and what he hoped to achieve when he got there. Alice was puzzled.

'You say that the superintendent tried to stop you going?'

'Yes, he did. Chat was dead against the idea.'

'How did you persuade him to change his mind?'

'We didn't. Nobody could do that.'

'So what happened?'

'We went over his head and appealed to the commissioner. Luckily, he saw the wisdom of our argument and granted me permission to go ahead.'

'Superintendent Chatfield must have been very upset at that.'

'He was,' said Keedy, chuckling. 'That's why I got out of there on the double. I left your father to face the music.'

Marmion was accustomed to withstanding the wrath of Claude Chatfield. As a rule, the superintendent strutted up and down his office, delivering his tirade with blistering force and demanding apologies. It was different this time. Seated behind his desk, he was icily calm. Marmion was kept standing in front of him for minutes. When he finally spoke, Chatfield's voice was quiet and measured.

'I suppose you think that you've got the better of me,' he said.

'I don't think any such thing, sir.'

'Isn't that why you ran off to the commissioner?'

'With respect, I didn't run anywhere. Sir Edward popped his head into my office and asked how everything was going. I simply told him the truth.'

'You sought to undermine my authority.'

'I gave an honest answer to a straight question,' argued Marmion. 'When the commissioner asked why the sergeant and I felt the need to make contact with Ben Croft, the both of us stated our case.'

'In short, you stabbed me in the back.'

'We have the greatest respect for your opinion on operational matters, sir. This is a rare occasion when we disagree with you.

As it happens, the commissioner chose to accept our advice instead of yours.'

'Why didn't you have the courtesy to ask me to join in the discussion?'

'There was no time. It was over and done with in minutes.'

Chatfield's eyelids narrowed and his facial muscles tightened.

'The structure of command is essential to the running of this force,' he said, coldly. 'Those of us in authority – and I include you, Inspector – are entitled to expect obedience from those beneath us. Do you agree?'

'Yes, I do.'

'You've had to discipline officers before and I know that Sergeant Keedy is inclined to kick over the traces.'

'Not if he's kept firmly in check, sir.'

'How would you feel if, having given an order to a detective constable, you found it countermanded by someone of superior rank – if, in other words, you realised that he'd betrayed you?'

'I'd be disappointed,' conceded Marmion.

'Is that all?'

'It would depend on the circumstances, sir. I repeat that we did not go in search of the commissioner. He came into my office of his own accord.' He kept a straight face. 'Sir Edward often does.'

It was an unpalatable truth and it made Chatfield wince. He hated the favouritism shown towards Marmion by the commissioner and resented the faith put in the inspector's judgement. It was demeaning to him.

'Sending the sergeant to Knockaloe is madness,' he said, astringently.

'I disagree, Superintendent.'

'Croft is already in a place of safety.'

'Yes,' said Marmion, 'but what is he doing there? That's one of the questions Sergeant Keedy will be asking. He'll also want to find out how David Ackley managed to escape and who his associates were on the island. I'm counting on the sergeant to come back with a fund of information.'

'Don't bank on it.'

Chatfield lapsed into silence and simply stared at him. It was minutes before Marmion realised that the interview was over. He murmured a farewell and left the room. Though he'd escaped a stern reprimand, he knew that Chatfield would get his revenge in due course. He was still wondering in what form it would come when he saw two figures at the far end of the corridor. A uniformed constable was escorting Reuben Ackley. The old man rushed towards Marmion.

'I had to come, Inspector,' he said. 'I did something very stupid.'

Ellen read the newspaper with dismay. War reports were on almost every page. The list of British casualties was lengthening dramatically. Paul Marmion was only one tiny statistic in the conflict but he was the most important to her. He was not simply a victim of war. He was a symbol of the malign effects it could have on the mind. As she looked back over the time he'd spent in uniform, she saw the slow erosion of his personality and the loss of the values she and her husband had instilled in him. His injuries had accelerated the changes. Clinging on to the hope that he would get better, she had to admit that he'd got steadily worse. Her meeting with Mavis Tandy had shown her the extent of his deterioration. His behaviour had been unforgivable.

Mavis had been quite unlike any of the girlfriends Paul had known in the past. They'd always been short, attractive, lively girls who'd aroused his protective instinct. Mavis, by contrast was a tall, stringy, excessively plain young woman with none of the vitality that Paul found so appealing. Still mourning the loss of Colin Fryatt, she'd given Paul no reason to think that there could be any romance between them though that, as it turned out, was not what he was after. The simple fact that he was alone with her was enough for him. Even in a church, he couldn't resist the urge to force himself upon her. Tossing the newspaper aside, Ellen gave a shudder.

Who would be his next victim?

When he realised why Ackley had come to see him, Marmion marched him straight to the superintendent's office and knocked on the door. He got a frosty reception as he went in but Chatfield's hostility weakened when he was introduced to the visitor.

'I was so naïve,' confessed Ackley. 'I'm supposed to be an expert on criminal law yet I can't recognise a criminal when I'm staring him in the face.'

'What happened?' asked Chatfield.

'I was fooled.'

Ackley went on to describe the visit to his house that morning of the fake detective constable. Having been grateful to him at first, his suspicion had been aroused by the way the man reacted to the information that Ben Croft was in an internment camp on the Isle of Man.

'He grinned broadly as if I'd just given him a present,' said Ackley, 'and he disappeared at once. On my way to the college, I began to wonder if he really was who he claimed to be so I made a detour and cycled to the police station.'

'They have no record of a Detective Constable Rogers,' guessed Marmion.

'None at all, Inspector.'

'So who the devil was he?' asked Chatfield.

'I've no idea.'

'I do,' said Marmion, 'the name gives him away. It was Wally Hubbard. He's making a habit of impersonating policemen and, since his closest friend is Maisie Rogers, he changed her from a barmaid into a detective.'

'I had a horrible feeling he might be that escaped prisoner,' said Ackley, 'and the police in Oxford agreed with me. Hubbard has sworn to kill Mr Croft and I was duped into telling him where he could be found.'

'Don't take it to heart, sir.'

'I might unwittingly have signed Croft's death warrant.'

'That's overstating the situation, sir,' said Marmion. 'As it happens, someone has just been dispatched to the Isle of Man to warn Croft that it would be dangerous for him to return to the mainland until Hubbard is caught. Not that he needs to be told, I'm sure,' he added. 'They have newspapers there. Croft will have been aware of Hubbard's escape. What it does mean, however,' he went on with a glance at Chatfield, 'is that Sergeant Keedy's visit to Knockaloe is more important than we

322

imagined. In the event of an attack from Hubbard, he'll act as Croft's bodyguard.'

'The commissioner's decision was a wise one, after all,' said Chatfield, grudgingly. 'It looks as if the sergeant is in the right place.'

'It's good of you to acknowledge that, sir.' Marmion turned to their visitor. 'There was no need to come all the way to Scotland Yard, sir. You could have spoken to me on the telephone.'

'I had another reason to see you,' said Ackley.

'What was it?'

'I've been thinking about our son, because that's exactly what he is. It's no use pretending otherwise. In spite of all the pain and humiliation he caused us, David is still our own flesh and blood. Instead of retreating to my ivory tower in Oxford, I should be trying to help you solve his murder.'

'How can you do that?' asked Chatfield.

'I can explain in greater detail why we had to ask him to leave. It wasn't just his political stance, you see. It was the company he kept. We had this gang of ill-dressed, unkempt, sneering, disrespectful people dropping in and using our house for their meetings. One man was particularly objectionable – Peter Tillman.'

'Who was he?'

'Tillman was the leader of the group. He was Russian by birth but anglicised his name. My wife found him rather creepy. Oh, he was an educated man, there was no disputing that. He was a brilliant speaker. I blame him for casting some sort of spell over our son. David couldn't do enough for him.'

He went on to describe the activities of what had been

a small but very active sect in the Communist Party. Ackley gave other names but it was Tillman who'd clearly dominated the group.

'What happened to this man?' asked Marmion.

'I don't know, Inspector.'

'Have you heard from him since your son left?'

'We didn't have a single word from either of them.'

'I have a feeling that that suited you, sir.'

Ackley lowered his head. 'To my eternal shame, it did.'

Marmion felt an upsurge of sympathy and fellow feeling. He knew how agonising it was to lose a son and have no idea where he was or what he was doing.

'We should at least have kept in touch with David,' said the father. 'I know it's too late to realise that. This whole business has been so humbling for us.'

'Thank you for coming, sir,' said Chatfield. 'What you've told us is very helpful. Hubbard may go to Knockaloe but we'll be one step ahead of him because we can warn Sergeant Keedy to look out for him. But for you, both the sergeant and Croft would have been in danger.'

'I'd hate there to be another murder.'

'We'll do our best to prevent it.'

'But the other information you've given us is also valuable,' said Marmion. 'You've filled in a lot of blanks about his political beliefs and activities. This man, Peter Tillman, will be worth tracking down. We've been wondering why your son ended up on the streets in the first place. When we discovered that he'd been locked up on the Isle of Man, we realised that he was hiding from the people who sent him there.'

'Your son's arrest raises an interesting question, sir,' said Chatfield. 'He was only the editor of a subversive magazine. Why wasn't the leader of the group arrested as well?'

'I can add a rider to that, sir,' volunteered Marmion.

'Go on.'

'If he needed a place to hide when he got back here, why didn't David Ackley go to the man you've just mentioned? Since they were such close friends, Tillman would surely have taken him in. He was the obvious person to offer a refuge.'

CHAPTER NINETEEN

Iris Goodliffe longed to discuss the brief appearance of Joe Keedy but knew that she had to wait. Alice would only take her into her confidence when she was ready. Evidently, she was upset about something. Iris could see that. On the occasions when Keedy had intercepted them in the past, her friend was usually happy and buoyant afterwards. This time she was troubled. They were on their second walk around their beat when Alice eventually turned to her.

'I had some bad news from Joe.'

'What's happened?'

'He's being sent to the Isle of Man.'

'Why?'

'He's heard that the man they've been after – Ben Croft – is in Knockaloe. That's the internment camp.'

'It sounds like *good* news to me, Alice. Their search is over at last. They must be pleased. What's the problem?'

'It's getting there and back safely, Iris. That's what worries me. Anyone who sails in the Irish Sea is in danger. Submarines have been sighted.'

'But there have been no reports of ferries being destroyed.'

'Joe could be in jeopardy.'

'He faces danger almost every day,' Iris reminded her. 'Look at the fight he had when he arrested that man, Hubbard. You told me how many bruises he had. And there have been lots of times when he's risked his life to tackle some villain.'

'That's different. A submarine is an unseen enemy.'

Iris laughed. 'It's usually unseen because it's not actually there.'

'This is no joke. You've seen the warnings.'

'I think they're just German propaganda. They keep telling us they'll cut us off entirely so that they can spread fear but they can't have *that* many subs. And the navy does manage to destroy some of them.'

'That's true,' said Alice, cheering slightly.

'You should be proud that Joe's been given a dangerous assignment.'

'I am, Iris.'

'Would you be just as worried if they'd sent your father instead?'

'Yes, I would.'

'What would your mother say?'

'She'd be just as concerned as me. Mummy was on tenterhooks when Daddy went off to France to arrest two

British soldiers. So was I – Joe was with him at the time. I feared for both of them.'

'How many subs attacked them?'

'There were none at all.'

'And did they have to go close to the battlefield?'

'They did, as a matter of fact.'

'Yet the pair of them came back without a scratch, I daresay. That's because they're good at what they do, Alice. Have some trust in Joe. He's more or less invincible.'

'Not if his ferry is hit by a torpedo.'

'Oh, well,' said Iris, giving up. 'If you're determined to think the worst, I'll let you wallow in misery for the rest of the day. You can enjoy being afraid that Joe's ferry will be sunk, that your father will be killed in a car accident and that your brother will end up committing suicide. While you're at it, you might as well dream up some gruesome death for your mother as well. You've lost the whole family then.'

'Stop it!' said Alice, laughing.

'Then you stop being so gloomy.'

'I will, I promise.'

'Try telling yourself that Joe Keedy loves you, misses you and can't wait to see you again. He's not going off to a watery grave. He's simply on his way to a very pleasant voyage.'

As the train steamed north, Keedy whiled away the time by reading a newspaper. It was filled with more grim tidings about the war. He looked out at the fields scudding past then reflected on his assignment. It would be an adventure to visit the Isle of Man and to see what a civilian internment camp was. He was very much looking forward to it. Convinced that Ben Croft was there, he was keen to discover why someone whose life was governed by his passion for women would go to a camp exclusively reserved for men. It never occurred to him that he was not the only person going there in search of Croft. Four carriages behind him, Wally Hubbard was also having high expectations of his trip.

When the telephone rang, Ellen was upstairs in her son's room. Hoping to hear good news at last, she raced along the landing and scurried down the steps. By the time she snatched up the receiver, her heart was pumping audibly.

'Yes?' she said.

'Hello, Ellen, it's Lily.'

Ellen sagged. 'Oh . . . hello.'

'We've been wondering if anything has happened.'

'There's been no word from Paul, if that's what you mean, and no reported sightings of him. It's terrible. I'm torturing myself with guilt, Lily. I've just been standing in Paul's room, wondering what I did wrong.'

'This is not your fault,' said Lily, firmly. 'It was Paul's decision. You didn't drive him away. He went because he decided that it was the only thing to do.'

'But we're his *family*.'

'Perhaps he felt the need for a bit of freedom.'

'Then why didn't he tell us? If he was so eager to go, we could have helped him with money and so on. He wasn't being held here against his will. I kept telling him to get out more and see friends. It wasn't natural for him to be cooped up in his room all day.'

330

'Raymond's spread the word around all our other hostels.'

'That's very kind of him but I'm afraid it's unlikely that Paul would ever turn to the Salvation Army. For some reason, he's taken against it.'

'If he starts to struggle, he may change his mind. We've got a good record of finding missing persons.'

'He's not missing, Lily, he's running away. It's deliberate. I think he'll endure any kind of hardship to keep clear of us. Oh,' said Ellen, 'it's so annoying. At a time when I most need Harvey here, he's working around the clock.'

'Raymond wanted me to ask if there's been any development in the case.'

'Harvey rang to tell me that they believe they know where Ben Croft is. He's on the Isle of Man, apparently.'

'What's he doing there?'

'He's being held at Knockaloe, the internment camp.'

'Why?'

'They don't really know. Joe Keedy has been sent to find out.'

'Wait a moment,' said Lily, remembering the papers found on the murder victim, 'that could explain a lot. David Ackley must have been there at some point as well. It's the only way he could have met Croft.'

'That's what Harvey thinks.'

'It solves one problem, I suppose, but there are still plenty of others. Raymond is obsessed by one of them.'

'Is he?'

'Yes, Ellen. After all, he was there when we picked up Ackley off the street. We brought him back here and did our best to look after him. Nobody else had the slightest inkling of where he was.'

'That's right.'

'So *how* did the killer know where to find him?'

Marmion's second meeting with Donald Breen was very different to the first one. Instead of being summoned by the latter, he demanded to speak to him. The Special Branch officer listened to what he had to say but made no comment.

'Well?' said Marmion at length.

'I'm not quite sure why you came here, Inspector,' said Breen, drily.

'I came to tell you what David Ackley's father told us.'

'It's duly noted.'

'Is that all you have to say?'

'What are you expecting me to say?'

'You might start with an apology for failing to give us information that would have given us a greater understanding of Ackley. After all, we are on the same side. We regularly pass on things to Special Branch but we get only limited help in response. You seem to have a code of secrecy that's an end in itself.'

'We guard all the data we gather,' said Breen. 'It's a vital precaution.'

'I agree.'

'So you're wasting your time by charging in here and making demands.'

'In that case,' said Marmion, 'we'll have this conversation in the presence of Sir Edward. It was the commissioner who told me to come here. In short, I have *his* authority. Do you understand what that means?'

Breen was unruffled. 'What is it that you wish to know exactly?'

'The main question is this: when you told us about David Ackley's political activities, why didn't you mention Peter Tillman?'

'There was no point.'

'But he was the leader of the group.'

'He was for a time, I grant you.'

'According to his father, he exerted a lot of influence over Ackley.'

'It's true.'

'By rights, therefore, he should be locked up in Knockaloe as well.'

'We think otherwise, Inspector.'

'Why?'

'Tillman is no longer a threat. Reuben Ackley's information was out of date. He hadn't seen his son for some time so he didn't realise that he'd replaced Peter Tillman as the key figure. To disable their activities, we had to arrest David Ackley. There was a good reason why Tillman lost interest in the group.'

'What was it?'

'He got married. When you have the responsibility of a wife, you tend to think differently. Even firebrands like Tillman are inclined to calm down and weigh the consequences of their actions.'

'Tell me about him.'

'If you wish,' said Breen, looking him in the eye. 'Peter Tillman was born and brought up in Russia. His parents moved here at the start of the century and set up as furriers. Judging by the fact that they have premises in Regent Street, they must be successful. Peter worked in the family business until there were stirrings of unrest back in Russia. We have a record of him going to Moscow in 1910 and again in 1913. On the second occasion, he took David Ackley with him.'

'Then they were obviously close.'

'Tillman had a gift for standing on his soapbox and rousing his audience. One of my agents heard him on a number of occasions. He was mesmeric, apparently, and dangerously so. Ackley didn't have the presence or the talent to do that. His expertise was with the written word. If he hadn't contracted that deadly virus known as Marxism, he'd have made a first-rate journalist. As it was, he pumped out article after article for a small but dedicated readership of converts. Ackley was their arsenal. His magazine provided the group's ammunition.'

'At what point did you arrest him?'

'It was when he began to attract more numbers to the cause. They were mostly the young and the disaffected in society but there were also a few significant scalps, older men with established links to Russia and with deep pockets. Tillman could thrill an audience but Ackley was the one who charmed money out of their pockets. That,' Breen went on, 'meant that they had funds to cause mischief. When they started to set off explosions, we pounced on Ackley and took him out of the game.'

'What was Peter Tillman doing all this time?'

'Are you married?'

'Yes, I am.'

334

'Try to remember what *you* were doing immediately after the event.'

'You're being facetious.'

'I'm only stating the obvious.'

'If you really want to know,' said Marmion, 'I was working in the civil service and enjoying a quiet life.'

'War demolished that luxury. Nobody leads a quiet life now.'

Marmion was unconvinced. 'I find it hard to believe that Tillman could simply discard his beliefs because he found himself a wife.'

'You wouldn't say that if you saw a photograph of her. She's a beautiful young woman – and she comes from a moneyed family.'

'He's supposed to be a Communist, despising private wealth.'

'Every man has his price, Inspector.'

Breen talked for a few more minutes about David Ackley's role as the leader of an increasingly active cell then he rose to his feet and opened the door.

'It was good of you to come,' he said with unfeigned sarcasm.

Marmion remained in his chair. 'I haven't finished yet.'

'I thought I'd answered all of your questions.'

'You mean that you fended them off with great skill.'

'What else do you wish to know, Inspector?'

'There are lots of things.'

'Such as?'

'Where do I find Peter Tillman?'

When the telephone rang at the Dun Cow, the landlord picked up the receiver. He was not pleased when a voice asked to speak to one of his barmaids. He summoned Maisie Rogers with a yell. She entered the back room to be met by a wagging finger.

'I've told you before, Maisie,' warned the landlord, 'this is not for private use.' He handed her the receiver. 'Tell him not to call again and be quick about it.'

'I'm sorry, Eric,' she said. 'It won't happen again.'

'Make sure it doesn't.'

He walked out of the room, leaving her to wonder who was at the other end of the line. Since Wally Hubbard had no access to a telephone, it couldn't be him. She spoke tentatively.

'Hello . . . it's Maisie here.'

'I've been asked to pass on a message,' said Felix Browne.

'Well, please don't ring me again on this number. It's the thing my boss hates most.' She lowered her voice. 'Is the message from Wally?'

'Yes, I found a note waiting for me at the office.'

'What did it say?'

'Tell Maisie that I'll be going away for a while.'

'Where to?'

'He's off to the Isle of Man,' said Browne. 'He reckons Ben Croft is there.'

Chief among Wally Hubbard's many virtues was his perseverance. Once he set his mind on something, he never deviated from it until he'd achieved his objective. Having failed to kill Ben Croft at the first attempt, he escaped from prison in order to try again and, even though he had no idea where the man was, he was certain that he'd catch him one day. His perseverance had finally paid off. As he made his way towards the ferry at Liverpool

Docks, he was congratulating himself on his skill in deceiving Reuben Ackley into giving him unwitting assistance. Nothing could stop him now, Hubbard told himself. All that remained was for him to locate and deal with Croft before returning to the mainland.

His confidence was then unexpectedly dented. When he joined the long queue boarding the vessel, he saw a uniformed policeman standing near the gangway and talking to someone. Hubbard recognised him at once as Joe Keedy. In response to what he was being told, the sergeant was looking along the line of bodies in the queue. Hubbard ducked out of sight immediately. If Keedy was aboard, he had to be avoided. A chance meeting between the two would be disastrous. He'd have to take a later ferry. The delay was tiresome but necessary. He'd get to his destination in due course and he'd be forewarned of Keedy's presence on the island. There was no need for concern. He had everything well in hand.

Marmion was taken aback. When he got to the address given to him by Special Branch, he was told that Peter Tillman was at work in the family business. He did get to meet Tillman's wife, a striking young woman who spoke about her husband with deep affection and who wondered why the police were interested in him.

'Peter has put that life behind him,' she insisted.

'So I understand.'

'He has nothing to do with those dreadful people any more.'

Marmion took his leave and asked the driver to take him to Regent Street. The premises owned by A. D. Tillman and Son,

Furriers, were impressive. The Russian immigrants had clearly prospered. As he entered the shop, Marmion was met by Peter Tillman himself, now occupying a managerial role and dressed accordingly. Ten or more years older than his wife, he was a handsome man of slender build with prominent cheekbones and dark, wavy hair. His voice had no trace of an accent and he exuded charm.

'May I help you, sir?' he asked, solicitously.

'I'm Inspector Marmion from Scotland Yard,' said the other, producing his warrant card. 'Might I have a private word with you, please?'

'Yes, of course.'

Tillman seemed neither surprised nor upset by his arrival. He conducted the inspector into a well-appointed office at the rear of the building. They sat down opposite each other.

'I couldn't help noticing your wedding ring, sir,' said Tillman. 'While you're here, you might like to think about a fur coat for your wife.'

'Oh, I think about it a lot, sir, and my wife thinks about it even more but fur coats are beyond the reach of my income, I'm afraid.'

'That's a pity.'

'Besides, warmer weather will soon be here.'

'There'll be another winter in due course. That's what drove my parents to leave Russia in the first place – the fear of another winter in Moscow. Do you know how *cold* it can get there? People can freeze to death. I know that happens here as well but not to the same extent. Moscow can have Arctic temperatures.'

'Then surely it's a better place to sell fur coats.'

'The English are more amenable customers,' said Tillman with an enigmatic smile. 'But let's not waste each other's time, Inspector. You came to ask about David Ackley, didn't you?'

'Yes, I did.'

'Then let me tell you that I haven't seen him for months.'

'Yet you were close friends at one time, I believe.'

'We were friends and political colleagues.'

'Did you invite him to your wedding?'

'I did, as a matter of fact,' said Tillman, 'but I never got a reply. I had the impression that David thought I'd betrayed the cause, so to speak. The truth is that I grew out of it when I fell in love with a remarkable woman.'

'Yes, I had the pleasure of meeting Mrs Tillman when I called at that very nice house of yours in Belgravia.'

'After years of sleeping on floors and speaking at poorly attended meetings in draughty halls, it's a joy to have basic home comforts again.'

Marmion studied him. During his second visit to Donald Breen, he'd heard a fair amount about Tillman and formed the impression that he'd be a bearded rabble-rouser with manic eyes. In reality, he was cultured, well spoken and fastidious about his appearance. There was no sign of the Communist agitator now.

'David and I grew apart,' he explained. 'For the sake of old times, I wanted him there at the wedding but I'd lost track of him completely. So I sent the invitation to his parents in Oxford in the hope that they'd forward it to him. It may well be that they didn't. Mr and Mrs Ackley rather disapproved of me,' he added with a roll of his eyes. 'They seemed to think that I had horns and a forked tail.'

'It must have been a big change for you,' observed Marmion. 'After years on the margins of society, you're suddenly leading what seems to be a conventional life. What prompted that change?'

'You've met my wife.'

'Mrs Tillman would have an effect on any man but there must be more to it than that. Did you see a light on the road to Damascus?'

'No, Inspector, but I saw my father rushed into hospital after a heart attack. He put years of unremitting commitment into this business. I couldn't let that go to waste. In spite of what people thought, I was not immune to family values. The call came and I answered it.'

'That's very loyal of you, sir.'

'Do you have children?'

'Yes, I do. I have a son and a daughter.'

'Then I'm certain they'd respond to a family emergency as I did.'

'My situation is irrelevant,' said Marmion, wincing at the memory of Paul's disappearance. 'I'm just interested to know how you were, in effect, reborn.'

Tillman sat back reflectively. 'I suppose that I got fed up with giving the same speeches and chanting the same slogans year after year. Besides, much of what we advocated was achieved by the revolution in February. Russia has a new provisional government. But,' he went on, 'if you want the full truth, officers from Special Branch were breathing down my neck. No disrespect to your colleagues, Inspector, but some of them are ill-bred, bad-mannered thugs. They were just waiting for the opportunity to arrest me.'

'That's what they did to Ackley.'

'Yes, I heard the rumours. I'd have finished up in the same prison.'

'He was sent to Knockaloe.'

'Was he? That's even worse. Why did they release him?'

'They didn't, sir. He escaped.'

Tillman smiled nostalgically. 'David always did have a lot of pluck.'

'Can you think of anyone who might have wanted to kill him?'

'I can, Inspector, but I don't think you'd like my answer.'

'Try me.'

'Special Branch.'

'Not guilty,' said Marmion.

'How can you be certain of that?'

'There are two reasons. The first is the manner of his death. The second is the fact that Special Branch had absolutely no idea where he was.'

'But you do admit that they carry out assassinations.'

Marmion met his gaze. 'I have no knowledge of that happening.'

'Does that mean you're trained to look the other way?'

'I find that remark insulting, Mr Tillman.'

'Then I withdraw it at once,' said the other, obligingly. 'But you might care to know that I was given a verbal warning of what would happen to me if I sailed too close to the wind. It was another reason for . . . becoming respectable again.'

'Will you be attending David Ackley's funeral?'

'I think not.'

'Why is that?'

'It's out of consideration for his parents. They're bound to blame me for what happened. It's understandable. I had some fairly lively arguments with David's father. He'll never forgive me for some of the things I said. If I turn up at the service, it will only intensify his grief.'

'That's very considerate of you.'

'I don't want to create scenes any more.'

'What *do* you want to do, Mr Tillman?'

'I already have the perfect wife,' said the other. 'We'll have to start thinking about children soon. That's my ambition now. I want the perfect family.'

Keedy was grateful for the warning. The message passed on to him by the police at Liverpool Docks had been sent by Claude Chatfield. He'd telephoned the information that Hubbard was aware of Ben Croft's whereabouts. Keedy's ears had pricked up. He had another task now. As well as finding Croft, he had to shield him from the man who wanted to murder him. There was no doubting the fact that Hubbard would make for the Isle of Man. He might already be on the ferry that Keedy boarded. As soon as the vessel set sail, therefore, the sergeant conducted a thorough search, even lifting the tarpaulin that covered the lifeboats. Hubbard was nowhere to be seen. Keedy was fearful that the man might have caught an earlier ferry and was already hunting his prey. A chat with another passenger gave him a little reassurance.

'It will be like finding a needle in a haystack,' he cautioned.

'I was told it was a big camp,' said Keedy.

'It's enormous. It just grows and grows. When the *Lusitania* was sunk, we arrested a huge batch of foreigners. Knockaloe had the best part of 25,000 there.'

'How do you cope with numbers like that?'

'We let a lot of internees regulate themselves.'

Short, bald, bull-necked and broad-shouldered, the man was a guard at Knockaloe. When he heard who Keedy was and why he was going to the island, the man couldn't be more helpful.

'It can only function properly,' he said, 'because it's broken down into small units. We actually have four camps. Each one has a number and is subdivided into compounds. At the moment, we have twenty-three compounds, shared among the four camps. Every compound can take up to a thousand men and they operate separately.'

'Slow down,' said Joe. 'The numbers are confusing me already.'

'Each camp has its own kitchens and its own recreation facilities. On top of that,' said the man, 'it has its individual hospital with eight doctors and a few dozen German attendants. There's even an isolation hospital, set apart from the camps so that it can handle contagious diseases and so on.'

'You make it sound as if these camps are small towns.'

'That's exactly what they are, Sergeant. Like a town, they have a wide range of people. Some of them have enough money to buy themselves privileges and even bring in cooks and barbers. We try to respect their religions. Jewish internees, for instance, are allowed to obey their own dietary laws.'

'What about accommodation?'

'They sleep in wooden huts. Each one holds thirty men. We place six huts together so you can work out how many that makes. Inside those huts, they can work, play, eat, sleep or just chat to pass the time. There's a problem with damp,' admitted the man, 'but they're not here on holiday.'

'How many escapes do you have?'

'Very few, considering. We've had tunnels dug and some poor sods have tried to climb over the fence and cut themselves to pieces. Most of the internees simply don't have the strength or the courage to break out. In fact, that's one of the main problems at Knockaloe.'

'Boredom?'

'Depression. When you spend all your time looking at the world through an endless expanse of barbed wire, you begin to lose heart. I never worry about escapes, Sergeant. What upsets me are the suicide attempts. There are more of them.'

The moment she came off duty, Alice headed for home. On her arrival, she was hugged by her mother for minutes. When both had dried their eyes, they sat down in the kitchen.

'I don't know what else we can do,' complained Ellen. 'We've got the police and the Salvation Army looking for Paul but he hasn't been spotted anywhere. I'm afraid that his body will be found on some waste ground or fished out of a river.'

'That's highly unlikely.'

'He must be in despair, Alice.'

'If he was thinking about taking his own life, he'd have done it here and not packed all the things that he valued and walked off with them. That means he wants to start afresh elsewhere.'

'Where – and *why*?'

'We may never know.'

'He must be found eventually.'

'I doubt that, Mummy. He's clever enough to keep out of sight and perhaps even lead a new life in a different part of the country. When he sees how difficult that is, Paul may come to realise just how much you did for him.'

'I do hope so.'

'We just have to be patient.'

'That's easier said than done.'

Ellen got up to put the kettle on the gas cooker. Alice told her about Keedy's trip to the Isle of Man to make contact with Ben Croft. Her mother sighed.

'Oh, I do wish these investigations wouldn't drag on,' she sighed. 'They've come at the worst possible time. I want Joe and your father to catch that escaped prisoner and to solve the murder at the hostel. Then they can concentrate on finding Paul for me. Until someone does that, I'm being eaten away by anxiety.'

Claude Chatfield was pensive. Interested to hear about Marmion's second visit to Donald Breen, he was even more pleased to be told about Peter Tillman. Sitting back in his chair, he stroked his chin thoughtfully.

'Do you know what I believe?' he asked.

'I fancy that I do, sir.'

'Peter Tillman sounds as if he's hiding something.'

'That was my estimation of him,' said Marmion. 'He was too smooth and too plausible. I don't think he's turned his back on political opinions he's held for many years. He's just keeping them well hidden.'

'We may be doing him a disservice, of course. The love of a beautiful woman *has* been known to transform certain men. Look at how many criminals have started to lead more law-abiding lives when they get married or live in sin with a woman.'

'Tillman is not a criminal, sir. He's a fanatic with strongly held beliefs about the way that Russia should be run. For all his protestations about being a new man, I think he's still a committed Bolshevik. The revolution in February wasn't enough to satisfy someone like him. Tillman wants blood running down the streets. In his heart, he still longs for a *real* revolution in Russia.'

'Then why isn't he there to take part in it?'

'He has fur coats to sell,' said Marmion with a grin. 'As a matter of fact, he tried to sell one to me. I saw the prices on some of the coats in the shop window. They made my eyes pop.'

'Let's put Tillman aside and turn our minds to Hubbard. I want that man caught and locked away more securely in Pentonville. The governor keeps ringing me up to demand an arrest.'

'Strictly speaking, it's a rearrest.'

'Do you think he'll head for Knockaloe?'

'I'm certain of it, sir.'

'Sergeant Keedy will have got my message. He can look out for him.'

'The sergeant will enjoy meeting him again,' said Marmion. 'There's unfinished business between the two of them. He won't come home until he can drag Hubbard back with him.'

* * *

346

It was dark when the ferry docked at the Isle of Man. Wally Hubbard looked at the contours of Douglas, silhouetted against the night sky. Somewhere on the island, he reflected, Ben Croft would be sleeping soundly. Hubbard intended to make the slumber permanent. He'd travelled with false papers and in disguise. Though they'd have been warned about the possibility of his arrival, the port officials and the Manx police would never recognise him. The broad Irish accent that he'd perfected would get him past any figures of authority.

As the passengers began to leave the vessel, Hubbard joined the queue and he soon found his feet on dry land again. He took a deep breath.

'Right, you bastard,' he said to himself. 'Where are you?'

CHAPTER TWENTY

Knockaloe was vast. When he took a good look at it in the morning light, Keedy was amazed at its size and regimentation. As he'd been told, it was divided into four camps. They were quite separate and the internees were permitted no contact between them. Douglas, the Manx capital, had its own camp but Knockaloe, near Peel, was the main place of detention on the island. Its individual units were daunting fortresses. Keedy went from one to the other in search of Ben Croft. At the first three, he had no success, luring him into the belief that the man he wanted simply had to be in Camp IV. But there was no Croft listed among the internees. Maurice Hemp was in charge of the camp. A former army major in his fifties, he went through the list of names three times.

'I'm sorry, Sergeant,' he said. 'Your journey was in vain.'

'He must be here,' insisted Keedy.

'Then he's using a false name.'

'How can we find out if that's the case?'

'It will be difficult. We'd have to look individually at thousands of men. And if we couldn't unmask him here, you'd have to go back to Camps I, II and III.'

'That would take me ages.'

'Croft is not going anywhere – if he's here, that is.'

'Let me try another name,' said Keedy. 'What about David Ackley?'

'Now, he definitely *was* here,' Hemp told him, 'and I don't need to look up his name. Ackley was one of our rare escapees.'

Keedy snapped his fingers. 'That proves it. Croft *is* in Camp IV somewhere.'

'What gives you that idea?'

'As you must know, Ackley was murdered on the mainland. He was carrying papers that identified him as Ben Croft. Where else could he have got them from but the man himself?'

'Are you saying that he was party to the escape?'

'No, I don't think that for a moment.'

'Then how did Ackley get hold of the papers?'

'He must have stolen them.'

'Or paid for them,' suggested Hemp. 'If you have money in here, you can buy almost anything – except the means of getting out, that is.'

'What sort of man would sell his identity?'

'A desperate one – we've no shortage of those in here.'

'Croft had no reason to be desperate.'

'Then your first guess may be right. The papers were stolen.'

'How did Ackley manage to escape?'

'He disappeared one night, Sergeant. Somehow he got hold of some wire cutters and created a private exit for himself. The patrol found it too late. We had a team at the quayside, making sure that he didn't catch the ferry. Since there was no sighting of him,' concluded Hemp, 'we can only assume he bribed a fisherman to take him across to the mainland. He was obviously a resourceful man.'

'Not that resourceful,' Keedy observed. 'He got himself murdered. We're still on the trail of his killer.'

'Have you any idea who it might be?'

'We have theories,' replied Keedy. 'That's all I can say.'

With Hemp's permission, he looked through the lists of internees for himself. They were grouped into nationalities. Germans far outnumbered all the other foreigners in the camp. As he went through an interminable list of German names, Keedy suddenly had an idea.

'Supposing that Croft changed his name legally, so to speak?'

'I don't understand.'

'Well, he was christened Benjamin Dieter Croft but altered his middle name to David. What if he changed it back to Dieter and translated his surname into German? That would be enough to get him in here, wouldn't it?'

'Nobody would actually *seek* to come to Knockaloe, surely?'

'Croft might have done. Unfortunately, I don't know a word of the language or I might be able to find his alternative name in one of your lists.'

'It's an interesting idea,' said Hemp, 'but I don't think it holds water.'

'Do you *speak* German, by any chance?'

'I have a smattering, that's all.'

'What about your staff?'

'Oh, we have lots of German-speakers amongst them so that we know what the internees are saying to each other. Give me a moment and I'll put your idea to the test.'

Hemp went out of the room, leaving Keedy to peruse the lists again and to wonder why Ben Croft might choose to belong to them. Even on his brief acquaintance with it, he could see that Knockaloe was a bleak and joyless place in which to be penned. It would not take long for anyone's spirits to be dampened there. After a couple of minutes, Hemp reappeared.

'His middle name was Dieter, you say?'

'That's right – what's German for "Croft"?'

'*Bauernkate*,' said Hemp. 'It's the word for a small farm, like those in Scotland. Search once again, Sergeant. And look for Dieter Bauernkate this time.'

Keedy snatched up the lists with excitement.

The binoculars had been a good investment. They gave Wally Hubbard excellent long-distance vision and they bolstered his claim that he'd come to the island to do some birdwatching. The elderly couple who allowed him to rent a room in their cottage didn't question him. They found him pleasant and undemanding. The old lady was captivated by his Irish brogue. The cottage was outside Peel but it was relatively easy to get into the town. On his way there, Hubbard had his first view of the sprawling internment camps and realised the scale of his task. Finding his target among so many men would be almost impossible. Fortunately, he had an ally to do the work for him. Keedy would, he hoped, bring Ben Croft within range of the binoculars.

Marmion took instant action. Troubled by his meeting with Peter Tillman, he made a point of checking certain details. It did not take him long to establish that Tillman's father had indeed been taken to hospital after a heart attack and was, in fact, still there. His son had promptly stepped into the breach to take charge of the business. Marmion asked one of his detective constables to find out more about his domestic life. The man came back with the information of where and when Tillman had been married and who his lovely bride had been. All the dates seemed to fit. Everything that Marmion had been told at the furrier's shop was confirmed. There had been a decisive break with David Ackley and the group in which they'd both flourished, then Tillman's life was monopolised by courtship and marriage. Having sifted through every word exchanged at the furrier's on the previous day, Marmion recalled something that Mrs Tillman had told him. It was only a phrase, used with unashamed contempt, yet it somehow haunted the inspector. When he called on his brother at the hostel, he was still thinking about it.

'It's good to see you, Harvey,' said Raymond, shaking his hand.

'I'd like to say that we've solved the murder and that Paul

has come home like the prodigal son but neither of those things is true.'

'So why are you here?'

'I'd like to talk something through with you, Raymond. Being here at the scene of the crime might somehow help.'

'Talk away.'

'The reason that the killer was able to walk in here, commit murder and walk right out again is that he caught you all completely off guard. You had no cause to fear an attack on what you saw as a lonely man who'd fallen on hard times.'

'I didn't. For a start, nobody knew that Ackley was here.'

'Someone must have done.'

'How do you know?'

'He came here by invitation,' said Marmion. 'I believe that Ackley wrote to a friend for money or shelter or both. He told him the precise time when he'd be alone in the dormitory because he knew that the others would all charge off to breakfast.'

'I can see what you mean,' said his brother, smiling at the revelation. 'He had to get to Ackley when nobody else was around. It seemed a fluke to me that he struck at the ideal time. You've just explained how he did it.'

'Let me finish. I'm working through it in my mind.'

'And you're doing so very well.'

'What did the killer take?'

'It was something in the briefcase.'

'We know that there was a notebook in there. One of the other men saw Ackley writing in it when he surprised him in the bathroom. What was in that notebook? It must have contained very sensitive information.'

'Then again, it might just have been a diary.'

'The two are not mutually exclusive, Raymond. Ackley might have been keeping a day-to-day record of his meetings with the Communist cell he'd been leading. It would have had names, dates, addresses and policy objectives. It might also have revealed how the group was funded.'

'Wouldn't it have been confiscated when he was interned?'

'Special Branch would have loved to have got their hands on it,' said Marmion, 'but Ackley was a canny customer. He wouldn't walk around with anything as important as his diary on his person. It would have been hidden away somewhere – with that briefcase, probably. When he escaped from Knockaloe, I believe that he retrieved the items then held on to them as if he'd just stolen the Crown Jewels.'

'That's right,' agreed the other. 'He slept with that briefcase beside him.'

'What was he most in need of when you found him, Raymond?'

'Decent food, I'd say. He gobbled it down when he got here.'

'Ackley was on the run. He couldn't dodge Special Branch indefinitely unless he had a safe place to hide. This hostel was a useful temporary refuge but he needed somewhere more permanent.'

'So he wrote to a friend – and the friend betrayed him.'

'Yes,' said Marmion, 'that's one version of what happened. It may be hopelessly wrong, of course. But it does explain why someone knew when and where to strike.'

'Ackley was expecting help and he got a rope around his neck instead.'

'The killer couldn't just walk in here because he'd have been seen by all of you. He used the bandsman's uniform as his cloak of invisibility. It had the double advantage of fooling you and deceiving Ackley himself. He was waiting for a friend, not for a cornet player bent on murder.'

'Why was Ackley betrayed?'

'The answer might lie in that diary of his.'

'You've worked it all out, Harvey.'

'Let's call it a hopeful shot at the truth.'

'What's the next step?'

'I wish I knew,' said Marmion with a mirthless laugh. 'It might turn out to be a resort to prayer. Can you give me any pointers?'

Wally Hubbard had excellent hearing. By drinking at a pub not far from Knockaloe, he overheard off-duty guards talking about their work there. Having picked up a large amount of useful information, he wormed his way cleverly into the conversation and harvested much more.

'What sorts of hours do you good fellows work?' he asked.

'The shifts are long and tiring,' replied one of the men.

'Is it easy to get a job in Knockaloe?'

'Who's asking?'

'My name is Seamus O'Neill. I was a prison officer in Dublin before the Easter Rising. I was appalled by it, so I was. There'll be worse to come one day, so I'm looking for work outside Ireland.'

'What sort of an education have you had?'

'I can read and write,' said Hubbard, holding up both hands, 'and I can count up to ten as well as any man. Will that do?'

The others laughed. He was engaging company. They gave him the advice he was after, inadvertently acting as cheerful accessories in an attempted murder.

Even though he knew that Croft was there, it took Keedy a long time to find him as he toured Camp IV. He eventually ran him to ground, talking in German to a group of fellow internees. The sergeant detached him from the group and took him aside. Croft was astounded to see Keedy again.

'How did you know where to find me?'

'I didn't. I was acting largely on instinct.'

'Nobody told you I was here?'

'No, Mr Croft. Some people have been annoyingly uncooperative.'

'I know why you came,' said Croft. 'You want to tell me that Hubbard is lurking back on the mainland, waiting to slit my throat.'

'Oh, I think he has a more elaborate death in mind than that. What I bring is bad news. Owing to an unfortunate mistake, Hubbard is aware that you're here.'

Croft was panic-stricken. 'He *knows*?'

'He's probably on the island already.'

'Why didn't you warn me?'

'That's exactly what I'm doing now, sir. I'm here to protect you.'

'Hubbard is a madman. He burnt down my house.'

'My job is to catch him before he can reach you,' said Keedy, 'but, if I'm going to save your life, I expect some honesty on your part.'

'What do you mean?' asked Croft, indignantly.

He was a good-looking man in his thirties with a natural arrogance that Keedy had disliked the first time they'd met. The sergeant could see why Croft had been successful as a philanderer. He was tall, slim, sleek, had a seedy charm about him and looked years younger than he really was. Keedy gazed around.

'This must be the worst place in the world for someone like you,' he said.

'Why do you say that?'

'You prefer the company of women, don't you?'

Croft sniggered. 'I'm like any other man, Sergeant.'

'You flatter yourself. But when I demanded honesty, I was warning you not to try to palm me off with lies. There's more than the threat of an angry father like Wally Hubbard involved here. We have a murder to solve. The victim was someone you knew – David Ackley. What can you tell me about him?'

'I can tell you very little.'

Keedy sniffed. 'I think I can smell the first lie.'

'I only spoke to him once or twice.'

'Tell the truth. He ingratiated himself with you so that he could become your friend. You might call yourself by a German name but he discovered that you were really Ben Croft. That means you liked him enough to confide in him.'

'I did,' confessed the other, 'and what did he do in return for my friendship?'

'He stole your papers and fled from the camp.'

'I didn't shed any tears when I read that he'd been killed.'

'Did he tell you if he had any enemies?'

'According to him, the whole British system of government was his enemy. He railed against it. When he talked politics, I never took him seriously.'

'I want names, Mr Croft. Someone killed him. I wondered if he'd mentioned people who hated him enough to want him dead.'

'Well, he didn't. We were never that close.'

'Did you have any idea that he was planning an escape?'

'No,' said Croft, angrily, 'he was a two-faced little bugger.'

Keedy changed tack. 'Do you have any regrets about what happened to Hubbard's daughter?'

'Of course, I do. What sort of man do you take me for?'

'Oh, I've worked that bit out. You were sorry that she died, I'm sure, because it meant that you suddenly had her father baying at your heels. Did it never strike you that, if you hadn't seduced the girl, she might still be alive?'

'That's none of your business,' snarled Croft.

'You're making my job very difficult, you know.'

'Why?'

'It's much easier to protect someone if you actually like them.' Croft turned away sulkily. 'Look at me,' said Keedy, taking him by the shoulder and turning him back. 'And give me a straight answer to the next question. What are you doing here?'

'Can't you see, man? I was interned.'

'Oh, no, you weren't. Had the authorities had any worries about you, they'd have sent you here, or to one of the other civilian camps, years ago. But they didn't, did they? It was because of your father's work, I suspect.'

'My father was a civil servant and proud to serve this country.'

'He worked as a spy during the Boer War,' said Keedy. 'It's the only way he could have earned a medal. *He* was the reason you were immune from arrest. So let me ask you again. Why are you here under a different name?' He shook Croft. 'Come on – who's paying you?'

'It doesn't matter.'

'But you admit you were brought here for a reason?'

'I might have been . . .'

'You're following in your father's footsteps, aren't you, Herr Bauernkate or whatever you call yourself? Hidden away in this mass of German manhood, there may well be the odd enemy agent. Your job is to dig him out.'

'If you know so much,' said Croft, churlishly, 'why bother to ask?'

'I wanted to be sure, that's all. Now, then,' said Keedy, 'we have to decide the best way to keep you alive, don't we?'

'That's easy. I stay right here while you go hunting for Hubbard.'

'What if he gets inside the camp?'

'That's impossible,' asserted Croft.

Keedy was dubious. 'Is it . . . ?'

* * *

Grace Tillman was surprised to find Marmion on the doorstep again and she told him that her husband was at work in Regent Street. He explained that he'd come to see her on this occasion. With some misgivings, she invited him in. They went into a high-ceilinged drawing room with tasteful furniture. Offering him a seat, she perched on the sofa opposite.

'I'm not sure what *I* can tell you,' she said.

'How did you meet your husband?'

'Oh, we've known each other for some time and belonged to the same tennis club. Peter has a passion for the game because it helps keep him fit. I was lucky enough to have him as my partner in a mixed-doubles tournament.' She indicated the silver cup on the mantelpiece. 'We won it, actually. There's the proof.'

'Were you aware of his political opinions?'

'Oh, we never talked about things like that, Inspector.'

'So he won't have mentioned a David Ackley to you.'

'No – who is he?'

'He was once a close friend of your husband's. The last time I came here, you talked about "those dreadful people" in Mr Tillman's past. Ackley was one of them. You obviously did discuss politics at some point.'

'It was only *student* politics,' she said with disdain. 'They don't count. You expect students to be a bit rebellious. It's a rite of passage. Peter is not a natural rebel and he never liked the people he had to associate with at those dreary meetings. He told me how blinkered and unpleasant they were. That's why I called them dreadful.'

Grace Tillman was sublimely unaware of her husband's

involvement in a subversive Communist group. Ackley's name meant nothing to her and she had no idea that he was a murder victim. She was a dutiful wife, still in the early months of her marriage and enjoying the pampered life that it brought her. Peter Tillman had chosen someone who was the epitome of the patronising British bourgeoisie against whom he'd once railed in his speeches. Miraculously, she had tamed him.

'Did you speak to Peter yesterday?' she asked.

'Yes, I did.'

'Then you must have realised he is an exceptionally honest man.'

'You know him better than I do, Mrs Tillman.'

'I just wondered why you felt the need to check up on him.'

'That's not what I'm doing,' said Marmion, politely. 'I was just struck by that phrase about "those dreadful people" and by the way you said it. I wondered if you were referring to people you'd actually met or were just repeating your husband's views.'

'We've all made mistakes,' she said, dismissively. 'When you're lucky enough to find true happiness, as we have, it's best to leave those mistakes buried in the past. That's what Peter and I have done. We have everything we could wish for now.'

'Then I'm very pleased for you, Mrs Tillman.'

Marmion stood up to leave and she showed him to the front door. As she opened it, she remembered something.

'Now I think of it, I have a vague recollection of hearing that name you mentioned. What was it?'

'David Ackley.'

'Who is he?'

'I'm afraid that you'll soon find out,' he said, quietly.

* * *

Deciding that Croft was more likely to be at the main internment camp, Hubbard had gleaned a large amount of useful information about Knockaloe and one overriding fact was clear. Security measures were extensive. He wouldn't be able to get inside any of the four units easily, still less find Croft once he was there. On the other hand, he knew someone who did have authorised access. Keedy had come to the island specifically to make contact with Croft. It might well be that he intended to take him back to the mainland. If that were the case, Hubbard reasoned, he might get his chance, after all. What he had to do was to mount a vigil on Knockaloe. If he saw Keedy emerging from one of the sites, he'd at least know where Croft was located. He began to patrol the perimeter of the camps and study the local bird life while he was at it. Though he couldn't reach his target yet, he could at least cause him alarm. Keedy would surely have warned Croft that Hubbard was heading for the island. That would make Croft sweat. It was the first part of his punishment.

For her own sake, Ellen had to get out of the house. It was pointless to wait for a telephone call that would never come or a letter that would never be delivered. In the manner of his departure, Paul had indicated that he was making a complete break from family life. All links had been severed. He would not be in touch. Ellen forced herself to do some shopping and get some fresh air at the same time. Her footsteps took her insensibly towards the high street and it was only when she was passing a jewellery shop that she remembered that Sally Redwood worked there. She paused to look through the window and saw the girl serving a customer.

Without understanding why, she watched for some minutes. Her concentration was only broken when someone spoke sharply to her.

'You're doing it as well, are you?' said Patricia Redwood, truculently. 'It's not enough to have your son peering at Sally. *You* have to do it as well.'

'I meant no harm.'

'Well, Paul certainly did.'

'You can forget about him. He won't trouble your daughter again.'

'He'd better not.'

'He's run away, Patricia. We don't know where he is.'

'You mean that he's . . . left home?'

'Yes, he just packed some things and sneaked out. It's very worrying. We're afraid that he might not come back.'

'Good riddance,' said the other woman. 'I hope that he never does.'

Claude Chatfield had gone to the commissioner's office to give him the latest news about the two investigations. He was unable to report progress on either of them.

'Sergeant Keedy has gone to Knockaloe to interview Ben Croft,' said the superintendent, 'but there's an unexpected snag.'

'What is it?'

'Hubbard has found out that Croft is there.'

'How the devil did he do that?' asked Sir Edward.

'He's very guileful. The sergeant had left before we discovered what Hubbard was up to. I sent a message immediately. Sergeant

364

Keedy will have received it before boarding at Liverpool. He'll be on the lookout for Hubbard.'

'What about the inspector?'

'He's pursuing a line of enquiry that he forgot to tell me about. I haven't seen him all morning. I can only hope he knows what he's doing.'

'Marmion usually does.'

'These two linked investigations have tested him to the limit, Sir Edward. The cracks are starting to show, alas. Part of the problem is that he's under great stress on the domestic front. It pains me to say this,' continued Chatfield, 'but the inspector seems to be losing his grip. He's getting nowhere.'

The car dropped Marmion outside the furrier's shop in Regent Street. Before going in, he looked through the window and saw Peter Tillman talking to a young male assistant in a smart suit. The latter nodded obediently then went off to the rear of the premises. Tillman crossed to a large mirror, using it to adjust his shirt cuffs and to flick back a few stray hairs from his forehead. He then straightened his coat. When Marmion entered, he beamed hospitably as if he was delighted to see him.

'So you've changed your mind, have you?' he asked, genially. 'You're going to buy your wife that new fur coat, aren't you?'

'I'm afraid not, sir. It's not my wife I've come to talk about, you see, it's your own. I've just been chatting to Mrs Tillman.'

Tillman frowned. 'What reason did you have for bothering her?'

'It was idle curiosity. You've been leading a double life, haven't you?'

'I wouldn't say that.'

'While you were dabbling in revolutionary politics, you kept one foot in the solid, reactionary, middle-class world into which you were born. You were both a Marxist hothead and a leading light at the local tennis club. Mrs Tillman told me what store you set on physical fitness.'

Tillman tensed slightly. 'What are you insinuating?'

'You wanted the freedom of raging against the evils of British life and the comfort of belonging to it. In the end – aided by the lady who became your wife – you opted for comfort and cut your ties with the past.'

'Are you intending to write my biography, Inspector?'

'It's already reached the last chapter, sir. We both know why.'

'*You* may do so. I don't. Enlighten me, I pray.'

'It concerns the contents of a battered briefcase,' said Marmion. 'They were stolen by the man who murdered David Ackley. I believe that man to be you.'

Tillman laughed. 'That's absurd. Why should I want to kill David?'

'It was because he belonged to a world you wanted to wipe out of your existence. This is nothing to do with politics. It's something much more personal. Ackley's father told me that you had far too much influence over his son. I don't think he fully understood why. Academics can be unworldly at times. All that Mr Ackley and his wife saw was something they didn't like.'

'What, in God's name, are you talking about?'

'I'm talking about a man who suddenly gets married in order to obliterate his past, a man who finds an old friend so embarrassing that he has to murder him. David Ackley wrote to you, didn't he?' asked Marmion. 'You were the only person to whom he could turn in a crisis. He told you where he was and when you could pick him up but you decided to kill him instead. You wanted what was in that briefcase, didn't you? I thought at first it might be a diary but I fancy that it was something even more intimate. Am I right?'

'No, Inspector,' said Tillman, coolly, 'you are insultingly wrong.'

'I disagree.'

'Where's your evidence?'

'Some of it was gathered moments before I came into the shop. I saw the way you and that handsome young assistant of yours looked at each other. You were not discussing the way to run this business. Then I watched you preening in the mirror. It's something you do a great deal, I fancy. In addition to that, I've met the beautiful wife you acquired as a convenient screen to hide behind. You're not the first man to do that, by a long chalk.' He lifted an enquiring eyebrow. 'Need I put it into words, sir?'

Tillman tried to brazen it out by threatening to sue him but Marmion stuck to his guns. He stared accusingly at the other man until his confidence slowly began to falter. In the end, Tillman could hold out no longer. He resorted to cold anger.

'You're a poor biographer, Inspector,' he said, bitterly. 'You should double-check your facts before stating them so boldly. Yes, I admit, David did write to me from the hostel but it was not to ask for a place of refuge. What he needed was money and plenty of it. There was only one way he could think of getting it.'

'So that was it. He blackmailed you.'

'That's what he *tried* to do, anyway.'

'He threatened to tell your wife.'

'It was worse than that,' confessed Tillman, lowering his head. 'There *was* a diary in that briefcase but there was also a sheaf of letters. They were . . . foolishly explicit.'

'So in order to get hold of them, you killed a man you'd once loved.'

'What would *you* have done in my position?'

Marmion ignored the question. 'I'm afraid that I must ask you to accompany me to Scotland Yard, sir,' he said. 'Your days of selling fur coats are over.'

There was a long, considered pause. 'Very well,' said Tillman at length. 'May I speak to my staff first? Someone will have to take charge.'

'I've no objection to that.'

'I'll also need to get some things from my office.'

'Yes, of course. I'll come with you.'

'There's no need, Inspector.'

'I insist.'

'You're making this very awkward for me.'

'That's my intention.'

Tillman gave a defeatist shrug. 'So be it.'

As he moved towards the door at the rear of the shop, he passed a rack of fur coats. Without warning, he suddenly grabbed one and threw it in Marmion's face. Before he could be stopped, Tillman darted off at speed. Casting the fur coat aside, Marmion went after him. By the time he reached the office, however, the door had been slammed shut and locked from the inside.

Pounding on the timber, the inspector ordered him to come out.

The sound of the gunshot reverberated throughout the whole building.

When he finally spotted his quarry, Hubbard was almost fifty yards away. He saw Keedy emerging through the main gate of Camp IV and smiled in triumph. Thanks to Keedy, he at last knew where Ben Croft was being kept. Hubbard had survived recapture for so long because of his ability to think on his feet and change his plans at the drop of a hat. Having thought the camp too well fortified, he now saw that there might, after all, be a way of getting inside it. He needed to get possession of Keedy's warrant card and return to the camp much later when the guards who'd admitted the sergeant that morning had gone off duty and been replaced by a new team. They'd have no idea what the real Joe Keedy looked like.

Hubbard followed him from a safe distance but his pursuit was short-lived. A police car arrived to pick up Keedy. He got in and was driven away, yet Hubbard was not deterred. Knowing that the sergeant would be back, he was prepared to wait. Every day he spent in prison, he'd been thinking obsessively about catching and killing Ben Croft. That obsession remained. As a result, he was prepared to wait indefinitely for his chance to get inside the camp. He laughed as he thought about the absurdity of his situation. Having broken out of a prison, he was now determined to get into one.

'You deserve heartiest congratulations,' said the commissioner, shaking his hand. 'Well done, Inspector.'

'Thank you, Sir Edward,' said Marmion.

'I was beginning to think that the murder would never be solved.'

'Frankly, so was I.'

'It's a tribute to your tenacity,' said Chatfield. 'I was right to let you take on the investigation. However, I'd have preferred it if you'd made an arrest so that Tillman could face justice.'

'I'm not sure that I agree,' said the commissioner. 'Tillman not only saved the cost of a trial, his suicide means that there won't be the same chance for the press to print unsavoury details about his private life. We'll be able to suppress far more than we'd otherwise have been able to do.'

'The details are not merely unsavoury, they are truly scandalous.'

They were in Chatfield's office. Pleased that the hunt for the killer was finally over, the superintendent was appalled by the revelation about the relationship between David Ackley and Peter Tillman. It was beyond his comprehension how such an unnatural relationship, as he saw it, could ever have taken place.

'Your brother will be especially grateful to you, Inspector,' he said.

'Raymond deserves a share in our success,' explained Marmion. 'It was only because I went back to the scene of the crime and went over the problem with him that I began to see the way forward.'

'One case over,' said the commissioner, 'and one case left.'

'There won't be a suicide next time, Sir Edward. That's for certain. Hubbard would never take his own life. He'd see that as cowardly.'

'I feel sorry for Tillman's young wife. It will come as a shattering blow.'

'My sympathy goes out to his father,' said Marmion. 'He's already struggling to stay alive in hospital. This could well finish him off. Then, of course, we must remember David Ackley's parents. They'll be shocked by what happened but – thank God – they'll be spared endless lurid stories in the newspapers about their son. I'm not sure that they could have weathered that.'

'Sergeant Keedy needs to be apprised of what we achieved,' said Chatfield, staking a claim to some of the glory. 'I'll send a telegram to the Isle of Man.'

'I can save you the trouble, sir.'

'Can you?'

'I'll deliver the message in person. With your permission,' said Marmion. 'I'd like to be on the next train to Liverpool.'

Alice Marmion didn't need to rush home again. When her shift came to an end, she found her mother waiting for her outside. After a warm embrace, they adjourned to a tea room two blocks away and found a table.

'Has anything happened, Mummy?' asked Alice.

'Yes, it has, I'm afraid.'

'Is it bad news about Paul?'

'No, I've still heard nothing.'

'So what brought you all the way here?'

'I just felt the need for some support, Alice. Being stuck in the house was driving me mad so I made myself go out. When I got to the high street, I happened to pass that jeweller's where Sally Redwood works. For some reason – I still don't know why – I stopped to look at her. It made me so envious,' said Ellen. 'There she was, a young woman of Paul's age, doing an important job, loving every second of it and making her parents proud of her into the bargain.'

'I rather hope that that's what I do for you and Daddy.'

'Oh, it is, Alice.'

'Did Sally Redwood see you?'

'Thankfully, no – but she'll find out eventually.'

'How can she do that?'

'Her mother caught me. I felt so humiliated. She said that I was doing exactly what Paul had done. When I told her that he'd run away, I expected at least a grain of sympathy but it never came. Patricia Redwood was glad. In fact, she was delighted.'

'That's horrible of her!'

'No, it isn't. Put yourself in her position and you might think differently. Remember what Paul did to her daughter, and I don't just mean the time he leered at her through the window. There were those drawings of her that he threw darts at. Imagine how the girl would have felt if she'd known about that.'

'I'm beginning to see what you mean, Mummy.'

'Patricia wasn't the only person glad that he was gone. There've been moments – and I'm so ashamed of them – when *I've* been glad as well, Alice.' Despair came into her voice. 'Isn't that a terrible thing for any mother to feel?'

Hubbard was thwarted. Though he caught sight of Keedy a few times, the sergeant was never alone. He was always in the company of a uniformed policeman. In fact, the island's police force was very much in evidence. They were on duty everywhere.

Hubbard decided that he was responsible. Word had gone out that he was in Douglas and officers had been brought in from other towns to swell the ranks in the capital. Knowing that he himself might be in danger, Keedy had found himself a bodyguard. It was frustrating for Hubbard but he was prepared to wait, confident that his opportunity would eventually come.

Having taken such care with his disguise, he had no qualms about being caught. He walked around the town as if he were one of its inhabitants. To pass the time, he sat on a bench on the promenade and used the binoculars to watch the ferries coming and going. From time to time, he wandered back to the entrance to Camp IV and walked idly past the main entrance. On one such foray, he saw Keedy being escorted by the policeman. They parted at the main gate and the sergeant went in. It was too dangerous to lurk there for any length of time. Hubbard moved discreetly away but strolled past every half an hour in case Keedy came out.

It was well into the evening before his surveillance was rewarded. The camp itself was brightly lit and so were its immediate environs but there were dark shadows beyond. Hubbard found a place where he could hide with safety while keeping an eye on the main gate. He'd come prepared. He'd bought rope from a ship's chandler and cut it into the right sizes. The heavy binoculars could now be used as a weapon with which to knock Keedy unconscious. Hubbard planned to drag him away to a disused ammunition dump he'd found nearby, relieve him of his warrant card, then leave him bound and gagged like the hapless Pentonville warder he'd overpowered. Early next morning, he resolved, he'd enter the camp while the guards on the night shift were still on duty. His claim to be Keedy would go unchallenged. Somehow – no matter how difficult a task – he'd find Ben Croft and wreak his revenge.

Hubbard was too single-minded to consider the possible pitfalls. He felt that everything was now in his favour. He just needed to dispose of Keedy and take his place. Having gone over the details of his plan, he'd worked up a fever of excitement. When Keedy actually came out of the main gate, Hubbard was all but slavering. The sergeant was alone. There was no police car this time. He walked away from the camp with an air of nonchalance until he reached the point where he was plunged into half darkness. Taking the binoculars from around his neck, Hubbard lifted them in readiness. Two or three blows would be enough to knock Keedy out. The same plan worked with the prison officer. After hitting him with a cosh and tying him up, Hubbard had taken his place and escaped. He'd have similar success this time.

As the footsteps got louder, he came out to intercept his victim. But Keedy was no prison officer foolishly turning his back on Hubbard. He was a man who'd spent years on the beat working night shifts. The experience had given him a sixth sense when it came to danger. Though he walked on as if unaware of the figure creeping towards him, he was already on the alert. When Hubbard raised his arm to strike, Keedy moved nimbly out of the way then swung a vicious kick at his assailant. It sent Hubbard reeling.

'Come here, you bastard!' he cried.

Keedy recognised the voice. 'So it's you, is it, Wally? I knew you'd pop up sometime.'

'I want something from you, Sergeant.'

'Then you'd better come and get it.'

Hubbard lunged at him again and swung the weapon at his head. Ducking beneath it, Keedy dived hard at his midriff, knocking the breath out of him and forcing him to drop the binoculars. Hubbard went berserk, flailing away with both fists until the punches began to have an effect. Keedy fought back, opening a gash over the man's eye then connecting with his nose and producing a spurt of blood.

Enraged by the pain, Hubbard grappled with ferocity, using his hands, knees, head and teeth. He was not simply trying to knock Keedy unconscious any more. It was a fight to the death and he intended to win.

With a sudden grab, Hubbard got him in a bear hug and exerted immense pressure. Keedy was being slowly crushed. Managing to get a leg behind Hubbard, he twisted sharply and threw him off balance. As they fell to the ground, Hubbard released his grip and Keedy's hands were free to pummel him. While he was getting in some solid punches, however, he was having to take his share of them and was gradually weakening. Hubbard had the manic strength of a man who feared that his mission might fail. He rolled over so that he was on top of Keedy and held him down with one hand while punching away with the other. It was impossible to dislodge him. Hubbard was winning the fight.

It was only for a few moments. The two men were then caught in the glare of a torch as two people came running up to see what was happening. Marmion didn't hesitate. Though he had no idea who was involved in the brawl, he grabbed the man on top by the collar and hurled him off. Hubbard tried to fight back but his energy had been badly sapped by the fight. Strong and fresh, Marmion had the assistance of a uniformed policeman. Between them, they soon subdued and handcuffed him. His roaring voice had given Hubbard away.

'I was hoping to meet up with you again, Wally,' said Marmion.

Keedy was amazed. 'What are *you* doing here, Inspector?' he asked, dragging himself to his feet. 'Who cares?' he added, shaking his hand warmly. 'I've never been so pleased to see you.'

'I was told that you'd be in Camp IV, interviewing someone. I thought I'd like to meet the elusive Mr Croft again.'

'So would I,' said Hubbard, ruefully.

'This constable was very kindly taking me there. I also came to deliver a message,' explained Marmion. 'The murder is solved. You can have all the details later. Meanwhile,' he went on, turning to Hubbard who was now dripping with blood, 'I have a message for you as well. It's from the Governor of Pentonville. He's looking forward to welcoming you back home.'

'Don't talk to me about that turd!' growled Hubbard.

'Speak more kindly of him,' warned Keedy. 'He's going to look after you for the rest of your life. In addition to the crime you've already committed, you'll be charged with grievous bodily violence during your escape, impersonating prison and police officers, and attempted murder.' He dusted off his coat and picked up his hat from the ground. 'You and the governor will have a long, long time to get to know each other, Wally.'

'You wait – I'll be back one day.'

'I'm afraid not. Your days of freedom are over for good.'

'I'll kill that bastard, Croft, somehow.'

'You're talking about someone who's performing a valuable service for his country. He'll be delighted to hear that we're taking you back where you belong.'

'Let's get him to the police station,' said Marmion. 'They can clean him up and put him behind bars for the night.' He used the torch to examine Keedy. '*You* could do with cleaning up as well, Joe.'

'I could also do with a drink.'

'Don't worry. The constable has been telling me about an excellent little restaurant that stays open late. I'll buy you as many drinks as you like and tell you how I tracked down Ackley's killer.'

The policeman took Hubbard by the arm and marched him away. Marmion and Keedy walked behind them, thrilled that their investigations, albeit problematical, had been a resounding success. One murder had been solved and a second one had been prevented. It was all over.

'I'm starving,' said Marmion. 'I can't wait to find that restaurant.'

Keedy felt his jaw gingerly, 'I'm not sure that Wally has left me enough teeth to eat anything.'

'You'll manage somehow.'

'I may need to drink my beer through a straw.'

'It will still taste as nice, Joe.'

'Isn't it wonderful to have something to celebrate at last? And while we've been chasing criminals, Ben Croft – to his credit – has been trying to ferret out the enemies within. Talking of which . . .'

'No,' said Marmion, understanding what he meant, 'there's no news about Paul. That's why I'm glad we've cleared the decks, so to speak. These investigations are closed. When I get back home, I can at last start looking for my son.'

EDWARD MARSTON has written well over a hundred books, including some non-fiction. He is best known for his hugely successful Railway Detective series and he also writes the Bow Street Rivals series featuring twin detectives set during the Regency, as well as the Home Front Detective series, of which *Under Attack* is the seventh book.

edwardmarston.com

Under Attack

June, 1917. While German Gotha bombers raid London from above, a man's body is fished from the Thames below. The man had been garrotted and his tongue cut out before he was left to his watery grave, and as the killer has taken care to remove identifying items and even labels, Detective Inspector Marmion and Sergeant Keedy struggle to name the victim before they can begin properly with their investigation.

As family and business associates are found, the list of suspects grows ever longer, and as Marmion wrangles with the case, he and his family must also contend with their anxieties for his now-missing son Paul. The interminable presence of war and, closer to home, pitched battles in the East End between rival adolescent gangs, suggest the Home Front is more insecure than ever before. With great care, Marmion must pick his way along a twisting path that will lead him towards the killer.